and politically and culturally savvy. They are true heroines; she-ros, if you will. And Olivia Norley is definitely a she-ro."
—*Bookpage* on *Who Wants to Marry a Duke*

"Best-selling Jeffries brilliantly launches her new Duke Dynasty series with another exemplary Regency-set historical brilliantly sourced from her seemingly endless authorial supply of fascinating characters and compelling storylines."
—*Booklist* on *Project Duchess*

HAZARDOUS ~to a~ DUKE'S HEART

SABRINA JEFFRIES

KENSINGTON
PUBLISHING CORP.

kensingtonbooks.com

For Kimberly Rozzell, my wonderful publicist, thanks for always looking out for my interests (and giving me good advice).

And for my sweet Nick, who will always be my baby, no matter how big he grows. You have a good and open heart, son, and that's all that matters in this world.

Imagine going on vacation to a foreign land, only to be held captive for eleven years . . .

During the Napoleonic Wars, France, Spain, and the United Kingdom signed the Treaty of Amiens in 1802, promising to cease all hostilities. Thousands of upper-class British civilians flocked to France, eager to see the wonders of Paris for the first time since the war began in 1792. But the uneasy peace didn't last. On May 18, 1803, shortly after capturing several French and Dutch ships sailing near the British Isles, Great Britain declared war on France once more. Napoleon retaliated by capturing all British civilian males between the ages of eighteen and sixty who were still in France, sometimes with their wives and families. These thousands of civilian prisoners were called détenus. Except for those who successfully escaped or negotiated their way out, Napoleon kept them prisoners until the end of that phase of the war in 1814.

This fictional series is about three such détenus.

Prologue

April 1814

Lord Jonathan Leighton's mentor was at death's door.

Jon didn't need the naval surgeon attending Dr. Isaac Morris to tell him so. Even by dimmest candlelight, Jon could see Morris's swollen, discolored leg and the feverish flush of his skin, could hear his tortured moans as he lay on the thin straw mattress.

Guilt stabbed Jon through the heart. How he ached to flee this dungeon and take his tutor with him. But attempting to escape their civilian detainee camp had been what had consigned him and his friends to Bitche Prison in the first place. And Morris wasn't well enough to manage it, anyway.

The surgeon approached Jon. "I fear it won't be long now."

A shudder swept Jon. "Can't you amputate?"

The doctor, a fellow prisoner, shook his head. "The gangrene has progressed too far for that, and in his weak state, the surgery would probably kill him. Perhaps if they had let me see him a month ago, but even then—"

Even then, the flesh surrounding the untreated bone fracture had begun to fester because Morris kept trying to walk on it.

"I gave him water with a bit of wine mixed in," the surgeon said, "but that's all I can do."

"At least make him more comfortable. Give him something to help his pain, for God's sake." Perhaps then Morris could hold on long enough to make it home if they were finally freed.

Rumor had it that the war might be ending. But those rumors had surfaced before, only to come to nothing. After eleven years of captivity, three of those in Bitche, the now thirty-year-old Jon had seen his hopes battered so often that they could no longer rally.

"Dr. Morris has refused even the small amount of laudanum I have," the surgeon said.

Schooling his features to calmness, Jon approached the man he'd spent years with, awaiting the war's end. "Won't you take a swallow for your pain, sir?"

Morris shook his head. "It will . . . make me sleep. I have things . . . to tell you before . . . I die."

A chill ran through Jon that had nothing to do with the dank air in the cell hewn from rock. "You're not dying," he lied.

"Let us . . . be as honest with . . . one another as we . . . as we've always been," Morris rasped.

Not always. Morris had secrets, but Jon couldn't ask the man about them on his death bed. It didn't seem right to press him, given his present condition.

Jon dropped onto the stool beside Morris's farce of a bed. "Tell me whatever you wish—I'll always keep your confidences." *I owe you that much and more.*

Morris managed a smile. "It's nothing . . . like that. First, I want you . . . to know . . . I consider you . . . the son . . . I never had."

Then fight, damn you! Jon dismissed the words as soon as they came to his lips. Morris *had* fought the entire time they'd been in Bitche, but the wounded thigh he'd suffered in their escape attempt had pained him from the moment of his injury. Morris had a right to seek an end to his agony.

"And you," Jon said instead, "have been a father to me when I had none."

When they'd come to France as part of his grand tour, Jon had been a reckless youth, third son to the twelfth Duke of Falconridge and the only son by the duke's second wife. But once Jon and Morris had become captives, it hadn't taken Jon long to figure out that recklessness and youth led to being taken advantage of, not only by their French captors, but by their fellow detainees, or détenus as the French called them. He'd learned to be more careful and not trust anyone but his two friends and Morris, his bellwether and guide.

Jon stiffened. He had to be as strong for Morris as Morris had been for him. "I couldn't have survived captivity without you. I only wish I hadn't been so rash as to—"

"Don't . . . blame yourself . . ." Morris paused as a spasm of pain apparently seized him, making his face contort. Then he nodded to Jon's scarred hands. "You suffered, too."

Morris's kind words even in the midst of his agony sliced through Jon's reserve. "Ah, but if I hadn't pushed you to attempt escaping with us—"

"I couldn't abandon you. Besides, your plan . . . might have worked . . . if we hadn't . . . been betrayed. Not. Your. Fault."

It was, though. Jon had been the one to misjudge the distance they would have to drop and the length of rope they would need, which had caused Morris to fracture his femur. And if Jon hadn't insisted, Morris would never have joined him and his friends, never been recaptured with them, and never been punished by being sent to what everyone called the "Mansion of Tears."

Jon and his friends had been young and hardy enough to survive their own injuries from their failed escape, not to mention the damp cold, the sparse food, the ever-present threat of disease, and the cruelties of men trapped together at Bitche and left largely to their own devices. At nearly sixty, Morris had not.

That was without considering that if not for Jon, he and Morris would never have ended up as captives in France in the first place.

Seeing the flask of water nearby, Jon held it to Morris's lips and watched as the man swallowed, the fragile muscles of his throat trembling with every motion. "I know my father convinced you to be my tutor, sir, when you didn't wish—"

"Doesn't matter," Morris said impatiently. "Must remind you . . . in my belongings . . . is the codicil to my will . . . making you executor . . . of my estate."

"I remember," Jon said hoarsely, although Morris hadn't let him read it yet.

Morris raised his head. "Promise me . . . you'll make sure . . . Ida is safe."

Ida was Morris's wife. "I vow that I will. I'll handle it myself." *If we get to return.*

"Ida has family . . . in Yorkshire," Morris continued. "And there's a small . . . bequest for her . . . in my will."

Guilt overtook Jon anew. She would bear the brunt of Jon's mistakes. And he'd have much to conceal from her if his suspicions about the "friend" Morris had left behind in their detainee camp, Mademoiselle Bernard, were correct. Even worse, what if Morris had left money to the woman? How would Jon explain that to Mrs. Morris?

Although, he should be glad Morris even *had* a will. His wife would need it, given that Jon and Morris had used up their ready cash on bribes, food, and medicines.

"What about your daughter?" If Jon remembered right, she'd be in her twenties. He'd never met her, but he thought he had the age straight. It was hard to be sure. One easily lost track of time in Bitche.

"Victoria is . . . a different matter." Morris groaned. "Promise me you will . . . help her to find a . . . good husband."

"I'll do what I can, I swear," Jon said. That was all he could promise without knowing how things were at home.

Before Napoleon had halted all communication between France and England eight years ago, Jon had learned of his own beloved father's death, but no news since. His eldest half brother, Alban, must be duke now, and his second eldest half brother, Aubrey, must be the heir. Jon supposed that made *him* the spare, assuming Alban hadn't borne an heir already. Anything was possible in eleven years.

Morris tried to raise himself off the mattress but fell back moments later. "The lease on . . . our cottage ends . . . soon. Once that happens . . ."

Victoria and her mother would be without a home, unless they went to those relatives in the north, who could have died or changed circumstances by now. Victoria could already be betrothed—or even married—to someone. Hell, Morris's wife and daughter could both be dead themselves.

Jon shoved that thought into the dungeon of his heart where he dumped nearly everything lately. Otherwise, he'd have to consider the possibility that his own mother might be dead. Or his two half brothers might be mistreating her and his sister without him or their late father around to stop it.

Best not to dwell on that or he wouldn't be of any help to Morris.

Jon heard the clank of a key in the iron lock, and before he could prepare himself, the prison door opened to admit his two closest friends.

First came the youngest of their group at twenty-eight—black-haired, green-eyed Rupert Oakden, the ninth Earl of Heathbrook ever since his father, the eighth earl and a fellow détenu, died at the detainee camp.

Right on Heathbrook's heels was the next youngest at twenty-nine—Captain Quentin Scovell, third son of the Marquess of Glencraig. A naval officer and commander of the *HMS Willoughby*, captured near Egypt, the Scottish Scovell was a true prisoner of war and thus technically not a détenu.

"How did you get permission to come here in the middle of the night?" Jon asked. The separate cells for détenus and officers were generally locked from 8 PM to dawn.

The two men exchanged glances before Heathbrook answered in the quiet tone one used around sickbeds. "Napoleon has abdicated the throne. The guards and commandant are waiting to hear what will happen to all of us, and no one is paying much attention to what we do or where we go. Indeed, it was a guard who let us in, and he left the door unlocked."

Jon's blood stampeded through his veins. "So the rumors are true. The war is over."

Scovell's scowl matched the skepticism in his dark eyes. "I won't believe it until I see proof. They've given us false hope too many times."

Jon nodded, fighting the ever-present despair that was their daily burden.

"How is Morris?" Heathbrook asked.

With a glance at his mentor, whose moans grew apace, Jon pulled them aside. "The surgeon says he's dying."

Scovell didn't bother to hide his pity. "What will you do about him if they do set us free?"

"Surely that will take time, like everything else in this cursed place."

"If it doesn't?" Scovell persisted.

"Then I'm not leaving him here to die alone. Besides, when he passes, I want to arrange his burial and speak a few words over his grave. So, if we are indeed freed, you should both go on without me."

When the two men protested, Jon added, "I insist. Someone must tell his family and mine what has happened to us." Jon drew out a letter he'd written once Morris had taken a turn for the worst. "If one of you would give this to my mother when you reach England, she'll make sure Morris's wife and daughter know what the situation is here with him. Tell everyone I'll return as soon as possible."

The earl took the letter. "Since Scovell may have to rejoin his ship, I'll carry your correspondence with me as long as you promise we'll meet again in London."

Jon nodded. "I'll send a message as soon as I arrive in that fair city."

Another détenu burst into the prison cell, his face alight. "Talleyrand has signed the order freeing the prisoners of war!"

"What?" Jon's heart took a leap. "Are you sure?"

"It's in all the papers!"

"Does that include freedom for the détenus, too?" Heathbrook asked.

The other man broke into a smile. "Everyone. We're leaving this damned place for good. Despite confusion concerning how and where we are to depart France, we could walk out of Bitche right now, and no one could stop us."

At last, some good news. Jon hurried over to Morris and grabbed his arm, hoping to encourage him to rally. "Did you hear that, sir? We're free! We're going home at last!"

Morris gave no answer. His skin was cold and gray, and his eyes stared up at nothing.

Heart thundering in his chest, Jon clung to hope as the surgeon felt for a pulse and placed a mirror over Morris's parted lips.

Then the doctor lifted a saddened gaze to them. "I'm sorry, gentlemen. There's no breath and no pulse. He's gone."

Gone. The word sucked Jon's bones dry, leaving an ache so deep he didn't know how to assuage it. Until this moment, he hadn't realized how closely his life had been tethered to his mentor's. Now that the tether was severed, casting him adrift with the other casualties of war, he found himself left to his own devices in wildly uncertain circumstances.

And he had only himself to blame.

Chapter 1

Falcon House, London

June 1814

When the hackney carriage from the coaching inn drew up before the London residence of the Duke of Falconridge near dusk, what Jon saw took him aback. Between the scaffolding and scurrying workmen, he couldn't tell if the house was being torn down, renovated, or repaired. And the funerary hatchment over the front door plus the black ribbon tied to the door handle struck terror to his heart.

It couldn't be for his father, who'd died years ago. His half brothers and sister were surely too young, but Mother . . .

A chill skittered down his spine, making him stiffen. She couldn't be dead. He wouldn't believe it. Why, the ribbon and hatchment could be for anyone—an uncle, a cousin, a great-aunt. The place might even belong to someone other than his family by now.

No, the house couldn't be sold—it was entailed upon his eldest half brother. But it wouldn't be the same household to him, regardless. Once upon a time, he'd been the apple of his mother's eye and the indulged youngest son of his aging father. As a child, he'd lolled about on the worn old sofa in his mother's dressing room. He'd spent hours in Father's library, poring over gilt volumes that spoke of adventures in foreign lands with unusual names like Zanzibar and Malaya. That boy was gone. All that was left was the man with an ever-burdensome guilt and no place he belonged anymore.

So, even the fresh yellow drapes in the windows couldn't cheer him. The iron door knocker of a fierce lion had been replaced with a gleaming brass one of a Greek goddess, and the door itself had been painted a bright turquoise, but that was all just appearances—it didn't change the fact that here in this part of London, nothing was quite as it had once been.

His father was dead, his half brothers, Alban and Aubrey, were in charge and probably still bullying Jon's mother—their step-mother—and he would have to figure out if he could find a place in this odd England with its gleaming new buildings, freshly laid roads, fancy equipages, and unfamiliar sounds.

He only had two promises to fulfill: the one he'd made to Morris concerning the man's family and the one he'd made to himself the day they'd been recaptured and sent to Bitche—that he would find out who'd betrayed them and would make sure the villain or villainess paid for it. After that, he would do his best to get on with his life, such as it was.

Stifling a sigh, he stepped down and paid the hackney coach-man from his small store of coin. Like most détenus, he'd had to go into debt in France just to find a way home. Unlike many of them, however, he intended to pay his debts once he gained access to his allowance. Surely, he still had some sort of allowance.

A footboy in Falconridge livery went running by with what looked like wrapped sandwiches for the workmen, and Jon hailed him with a word.

Jon asked the most pressing question first, "Who is being mourned here?"

The boy gaped at him. "Do ye not know, sir? It was in all the papers at the time. The duke hisself and his brother died near six months past."

The duke himself? "You're speaking of the Duke of Falconridge and his brother, Aubrey?"

"Aye. Who else?"

Both of his half brothers dead. Jon could hardly fathom it. "How did they die?"

"Drowned in the Thames when the ice broke at the Frost Fair."

This sounded more fantastical by the moment. "Frost Fair! What the bloody hell is a Frost Fair?"

The footboy blinked at his profanity. "When the Thames froze."

Ah. Jon had forgotten it did that sometimes. He'd been five the last time the great river had frozen, but it had been considered too unsafe for him to be out on the ice, so only his half brothers had been allowed to venture there.

Good God, Alban and Aubrey. What a horrible way for them to die. Even they hadn't deserved that. He tried to drum up some grief over their untimely end, but considering how they'd tormented him his entire childhood, and how long it had been since he'd seen them, he couldn't feel much of anything.

The footboy waved his hand at the house. "The last duke started this renovation before he died. Now the duchess is trying to finish it for when the new duke arrives. They say he's on his way from France."

Oh, damn, the new duke. That must be *him*. He was now Duke of Falconridge? Father's heir?

God help them all if he had to be duke. He could barely fathom the changes to England, much less the changes to a dukedom.

His dukedom.

His hands grew clammy inside his pathetically worn gloves. No. How did that make any sense? He'd been in a prison for years— how could he now be a man of such lofty rank?

Jon stood there lost. No one had ever expected him to be duke, and he'd never been trained to be duke. It was madness.

His stomach churned at the thought.

A voice cried from above him, "Your Grace!" and startled him. *Get hold of yourself, man. You're duke now whether you accept it or not.*

"Good afternoon, Kershaw," he said as formally as he could manage.

Their butler marched down the front steps with distress and

concern on his weathered face. Kershaw had aged a decade since Jon's departure, and it showed in his gray hair and wrinkled brow. "We did not expect you until tomorrow," the man said in a choked voice. "Forgive me for not watching for you—"

"No, no, nothing to forgive. I hadn't expected the roads from Dover to have improved so much in eleven years. We arrived faster than even I thought we would."

"It's so good to see you . . . Your Grace." Kershaw gestured to a footman in the doorway, who came running.

"It's wonderful to be here at last, Kershaw." What an understatement.

The footboy Jon had hailed earlier was gaping at him as if at a god. "You don't look like a duke," he said, with a hint of suspicion.

Jon managed a smile. "Don't feel like one, either."

Kershaw waved the lad off. "Where is the rest of your luggage, sir?" he asked as the footman hauled Jon's battered trunk from the back of the carriage.

"That's all of it, I'm afraid." Jon was wearing his only good suit of clothing. Through the years, most of his belongings had been sold or stolen. What remained was in no shape for wearing, especially after the weeks-long trek he and a few other détenus had endured from Bitche to Paris in less than decent weather.

"Well, you're home now, Your Grace," Kershaw said softly. "I can recommend an excellent tailor, bootmaker, glover, hosier—"

"Thank you. I'll need all of those, I'm afraid."

"You're most welcome, sir." Kershaw flashed him a kind smile. "I will have your valet, Mr. Gibbons, examine your belongings and make a list of everything you require, sir."

"No need. Assume that I require everything, and just burn the clothes in my trunk. None are wearable in polite society. Wait until tomorrow, and you can burn these, too. All I want this evening is to see my family, eat a good English meal, and have a glass of—" He paused. "I assume the cellar and study are as well-stocked with ale and whisky as ever?"

"Whisky, sir?"

"I haven't had any good Scotch in a decade, so yes, whisky." His voice hardened. "I've drunk enough bad wine to last me a lifetime, and I shall never drink French brandy again."

"I see. Then I can assure you that the cellar and study are more than adequately stocked, Your Grace. As you may recall, your brothers were wont to imbibe a great deal of spirits. Shall we go in so that you might choose a Scotch?"

Jon still hesitated. It felt odd being able to "choose" a Scotch when there'd been none available to him for over a decade. And Father had never allowed him any at seventeen. Certainly, Alban wouldn't have offered any.

If the man were alive. Which he wasn't. Neither he nor Father nor Aubrey were. That left only Jon as head of the family. Duke.

Kershaw went on, with a catch in his voice. "The duchess will be ecstatic to see you, sir. When your friend delivered your letter, your mother could hardly believe it. Until then, she thought you dead. We all did, after so many years without hearing from you. Your last missive from France was eight years ago, and we heard so many stories . . ."

"No doubt," Jon managed to say. "So did we, at Bitche." Stories of escapees being murdered, of gendarme cruelties . . . of why the war was dragging on. He thrust the memory from his mind. "But nothing much of England. I certainly never got word about my brothers."

"Yes, well, you see before you a house still in mourning," Kershaw said solemnly. "May they rest in peace."

As the footman started up the steps with Jon's trunk, a flurry of blue-garbed female flashed past the servant and down the steps.

"You're here! You're finally here!" cried a voice he vaguely recognized as his sister's. She halted in front of him, her green eyes sparkling. "We feared your impending arrival was a lie," she said in a voice choked with emotion, "and you'd turn out to be dead, after all!"

She hugged him rather awkwardly, and he hugged her back, fighting to swallow the lump in his throat. "No chance of that, Chloe. I fought to avoid the grave just so I could see you and Mother again."

Clearly, his sister was a woman now. Illogically, he'd expected to encounter the impetuous 8-year-old he'd remembered, as if she'd been frozen in time. It disconcerted him to see her otherwise.

He drew back to look her over. Even wearing a demure debutante's gown with her black curls swept up into a sophisticated coiffure, she couldn't hide how she'd filled out everywhere. And she was only a few inches shorter than his six feet—tall for a woman, like their mother.

"You grew up," he said inanely.

"So did you." She reached up to smooth a streak of gray at his temple. "You look like Papa."

"You mean, old and grizzled?"

"Of course not! But your brown hair hasn't darkened to black the way mine has and Papa's never did. Plus, you're . . . a lot thinner than I remember."

He couldn't resist the urge to chuck her under the chin. "You're more ladylike than *I* remember. No more pinafores and pigtails, I see."

"I grew out of the pinafores, I'm afraid," she said with a light laugh. "And I cut my pigtails off years ago so you couldn't pull them again when you returned." She frowned. "I had *no* idea you meant to take your time about the latter."

"Trust me, Mopsy, it wasn't planned."

Sadness flashed over her features before she managed to smile. "Don't call me Mopsy—you'll scare away my suitors. I'm in the midst of my second Season." She lifted her nose in a mocking approximation of someone high in the instep. "My father was a duke, you know, so I am quite the catch."

"Then why are you in your second Season?"

She lifted an eyebrow. "Because there are no good men to be had in London, silly. But the war is bringing them slowly back, so perhaps I will have offers I can actually consider taking."

That sounded worrisome. "How many offers of marriage have you turned down?"

"Several," she said with a shrug. "I'm rather particular, as every sensible woman should be. But I do mean to marry if I can *ever* find a decent fellow."

Apparently, he would have to add finding Chloe a husband to his list of responsibilities.

She bumped his shoulder with hers. "Which is why you simply cannot call me Mopsy anymore."

"Very well. Would you prefer the more elegant Cockleshell Chloe or Denice of the Fairies?"

Clearly struggling not to laugh, she shook her head. "I'd rather you use my proper name. Or Sis, if you simply *must* be informal. You gave me those other nicknames eons ago—they're hardly appropriate now. I give them back to you to stow away forever." Her sly expression reminded him of her at eight, full of wild plans and silly pranks. "Otherwise, I shall call you Bonny Jonny as Mama did when *you* were young."

"Ah." The familiar nickname saddened him. That lad was a lifetime away from who he was these days. "*Now* I remember why I stayed away so long," he managed to tease.

Lightly swatting his arm, she said, "Come, let's go find Mama." She tugged him toward the steps. "She's upstairs overseeing the men putting in the new marble. Tory went to tell her of your arrival."

He hesitated, caught off guard. "Tory?"

"My governess, Victoria Morris. You know, Dr. Morris's daughter." When he stared at her disbelievingly, she said, "Did you receive *none* of the letters we sent?"

"None after Napoleon's edict in '06. The commandant was ordered to confiscate whichever ones got through. I bribed a gendarme to get me one, but he lost his position over that, so that was the last I read, sometime early in '07, I believe?" And once he'd been sent to Bitche, letters from home had been a distant memory, anyway.

"Well, that was nearly a year before Tory became my governess. It also explains why neither you nor her father ever wrote us back." She took his arm and headed for the steps again. "We were most distressed."

"As was I, not hearing from home." He squeezed her arm. "Before we encounter Miss Morris, can you please explain how you ended up with her as your governess? She can't be much older than you."

"Seven years older, actually. Mama hired her after Mrs. Morris died when Tory was twenty."

"Mrs. Morris died?" His mind reeled.

"Tory says she died of a broken heart. After a year of no letters, Mrs. Morris was convinced he was dead. She went into a decline after that. The doctors said she had consumption, but . . ."

He'd seen that happen to too many of his fellow détenus. Not having their families with them had sometimes made them waste away. It was why he believed people could actually die of broken hearts. And why he never intended to give his heart to anyone. Best to safeguard it.

She sighed. "Anyway, having allowed Papa to send you on that grand tour in the first place, Mama felt responsible for Tory's lack of parents. Or rather, lack of any who could help. So she asked Tory to be my governess. And Tory readily accepted."

Jon stiffened. Of course, she had. Practically orphaned at twenty? What choice had she? He was glad Mother had swooped in to help the poor girl.

When they reached the top of the steps, he paused as he realized his father was truly gone. How strange that this house belonged to him now. But he would have given it up—given the entire dukedom up—to be able to see Father alive again.

The blow to his chest was swift and painful. Still, he masked it long enough to walk through the entrance with his sister. They were just in time to see their mother hurrying down the hall, her face wreathed in smiles.

He spotted the tears glimmering in her green eyes a second before she threw herself in his arms, and whispered, "Oh, my precious son, is it really you? You're finally home!"

In the face of her tears, Jon felt helpless. His family had heard as little of what was happening to him as he'd heard of their affairs. Now he hardly knew how much to tell them. Should he be truthful about what he'd endured? Surely that would be cruel and accomplish nothing. On the other hand, he didn't know if he could merely pick up where they'd left off as a family.

He settled for clutching Mother tightly while she sobbed.

At last, she drew back to wipe her eyes with her handkerchief. "I'm just so happy to see you." She gazed at him with such love that it warmed him to the depths of his battered soul. "And look at you! Why, you're a grown man now!"

He laughed. "I was a man when I left, Mother."

"Barely," she said with a sniff. "More like a boy setting off on his first adventure."

Meanwhile, she looked more like a matron than the youthful mother he'd remembered, especially in her black and gray mourning attire. Her hair was salt-and-pepper instead of its original inky color, and fine lines etched her face like the brush strokes of an artist. They told him only too well how much she'd suffered. It made him want to weep. He'd lost so many years with her.

"In any case," he said, trying to hide his reaction, "it's good to be home. I'm sorry you had to face Father's death without me."

"He tried everything to get you released from France before he died, you know, as did I." She swallowed hard. "It was so horribly unfair and cruel you ended up in such an unpleasant situation there for so long."

"Jon was in a *prison*, Mama," Chloe chided her. "A bit more than 'an unpleasant situation.'"

"It doesn't matter what we call it, Sis," Jon said, and patted her arm. "It's over now."

"It had better be," Mother said, tears welling in her eyes again. "We're not giving you back. With your brothers gone, we need you here more than ever." She gazed at him and sighed. "I know that they weren't always . . . kind to you, but Alban and Aubrey tried to be a help to me after your father died."

"I'm glad to hear that." *And surprised.* No, that was petty of him. He did have the occasional good memory of them when they hadn't been resenting him for being indulged by Father. No doubt losing them both at the same time had been a great shock to Mother and Chloe.

If Aubrey and Alban had been here, might he have been able to mend fences with them after all his time away? He'd never know, and the thought choked him up a bit.

Determined to lighten the mood, he looked around at the signs of obvious construction. "I can see why you feel you need me. Someone must finish this project before it runs away from you."

Flashing him a grateful smile as she wiped away her tears, his mother swept her hand to indicate the foyer. "What do you think? I know it's only half-done, but surely you, of all people, can see the potential. You always did have an artistic eye."

"Did I? It's all so long ago." He swept his gaze around, taking in the figured silk wallpaper in a pale lemon hue, the mahogany chairs with their Egyptian prints and black tassels, and the matching set of draperies, which he'd spotted from outside. "It's perfect. You've always been more stylish than Father gave you credit for."

"I'm glad you haven't forgotten your mother's talents." She pointed to one end of the spacious area. "Later, I mean to have that wall taken out so we can turn our plain staircase into a grand double-curved one. Then, in the drawing room..." Catching herself, she added, "But I can show you that another time. I'm sure you'd like to rest after your travels."

He flashed her a rueful smile. "I wish I could say otherwise, but the trip has been long and arduous, and what I want most right now is a warm fire and soft bed."

"And some food, too, I would imagine," she said. "I'll make sure Cook sends up something warm for you to eat."

"But Mama, I want to know—" Chloe began to protest.

"Hush, dear. Can't you see that your brother is exhausted?"

Jon reached out to press Chloe's hand. "You can quiz me all you like tomorrow, Sis, and I promise to answer."

"Oh, all right," she said petulantly. "But I will hold you to your promise."

"I'd expect nothing less." Jon touched his mother's arm. "I also need bed clothes for tonight and something to wear tomorrow. Is there anything in the house that would fit me?"

She assessed him with a gaze that misted over again. He knew what she was seeing: a too-thin frame for a man of his height, a gaunt face, and that pesky gray at his temples.

"Actually," she said shakily, "y-your own clothing from before you left might fit, even though you were younger." Her voice steadied a bit. "It will be out of fashion, of course, but it should be fine until you can arrange for new attire."

"What about Aubrey's or Alban's clothes?" Chloe suggested.

His mother shook her head. "No, those would be too big in some parts and too short in others, as would your father's, I'm afraid."

"My old clothes will do for now, I'm sure," Jon said.

Mother nodded, then forced a smile as she turned to the butler, who'd been standing nearby, obviously trying hard not to listen to the conversation. "Kershaw, could you arrange a tray to be brought up, along with some clothing for Jon?"

"Of course, Duchess."

As Kershaw headed off, Jon's mother took him by the arm. "I'll show you to the master bedchamber."

"The master bed—" Jon caught himself. "Right." That was where the head of the house slept. And *he* was now head of the house. How would he ever get used to it?

He wanted to tell his mother he still knew his way around the house well enough to find his new bedchamber, but he suspected she merely wanted to spend a few more minutes in his company, and he couldn't deny her that. Knowing how many détenus hadn't made it home, he was grateful just to be one.

She brought him into the room and glanced around. "I hope it won't bother you that this was previously your brother's bedroom."

"It was also Father's, which is what I remember."

"Well, then." She hugged him. "Kershaw will have you settled in shortly, and I'll see you in the morning. We have much to discuss about the—" She caught herself. "But it will keep until tomorrow." Gazing up into his eyes, she smiled tremulously. "It's so good to have you home, son."

He bent to kiss her forehead. "I'm glad to *be* home. Now go on. I'm sure you must dress for dinner. Things can't have changed that much."

"Not as long as I am mistress of this household," she said with a smile. Then she left.

Looking around the room, he tried to discern what had changed, but too many years had passed for him to even remember what Father's bedchamber used to look like. No matter, he would make it his own eventually. Or he would try, anyway.

If he could ever become accustomed to being duke.

Chapter 2

When Jon first awakened the next morning, he couldn't remember where he was. His bed felt softer than anything he'd slept in for a decade, and the heavy curtains kept the room so dim, he wasn't even sure what time it was. But since he'd had his first dreamless sleep in years, he wasn't complaining.

He sat up and looked about. Only then did he remember he was home. In Father's bedchamber. Because he was now duke.

Right.

Running a hand through his hair, he left the bed and opened the curtains, shocked to see how high the sun was.

A scratching at a nearby door was all the warning he got before a man entered. Father's valet, Gibbons, who was apparently Jon's valet now.

Gibbons set down a tray holding a full coffee and tea service and a newspaper. "I wasn't sure which you preferred to drink in the morning, Your Grace, so I brought both."

"Coffee. Please."

Gibbons set the tray on a little table by the window and poured a cup of coffee. "If *The Times* is not your first choice for reading material in the morning, I can offer you a selection of other papers.

And do tell me if the coffee is to your liking. I wasn't sure how strong to make it."

Jon sipped some. "This is perfect, thank you, and *The Times* will be fine." When Gibbons visibly relaxed, Jon realized the man was as out of sorts as he. The staff must be nervous about serving a duke whom they hadn't seen in over a decade. "Did Kershaw tell you I'll need new clothes? I can't wear the ones from my youth forever."

Gibbons nodded. "The tailor comes this afternoon at three to take your measurements. In the meantime, I have put a selection of your most suitable older attire in the closet. If you wish to try them on now, I can take them in as needed."

"Excellent." He rose from the bed and went to examine his old clothes. "Have I slept too long for breakfast?"

"Hardly. We're still in the midst of the Season, so the ladies often don't come down for breakfast until the afternoon."

"Ah." He'd forgotten how late everything was during the Season.

"Although, actually, your mother is waiting for you in the breakfast room."

He chuckled. "That is hardly a surprise."

After being shaved by Gibbons and getting dressed, he headed downstairs to find his mother drinking tea in the breakfast room. She rose to greet him with a kiss on the cheek. "I trust you slept well, son."

"Any man would sleep well after a hot bath and the meal I had last night. Thank you for arranging those."

"It's the least a doting mother can do," she said fondly.

"Of course. I'm just . . . not used to it is all."

"How could you be?"

Waving him toward the breakfast sideboard, she returned to her seat and waited while he filled a plate and sat down across from her. As he began to eat—British sausages, how delicious!—his mother cleared her throat.

"What do you have planned for today?" she asked.

He bit into a flawless peach and wondered what Mother would think if she knew how many times he'd eaten around the spoiled parts of an apple in Bitche. "Apparently, a visit from the tailor."

"Certainly. That is important. But do you think . . . that is, do you believe you might be rested enough to . . . er . . . look at some things in the study with me?"

He tried to imagine what that might be and failed. "Such as . . ."

"Oh, this and that. Matters having to do with the estate."

After polishing off a slice of toast, he asked, "Urgent matters, I take it?"

"Somewhat urgent, yes."

Just like that, he lost his appetite. "I see." He set his plate aside. "We can do it now. Just have someone bring a pot of coffee to the study." He would undoubtedly need it for this.

"Forgive me, Jon," his mother said. "I know you would probably like to rest some more, but—"

"It's fine, Mother, I swear." He rose and offered her his arm.

"Thank you, son," she murmured as she took it.

As they left the breakfast room, Chloe came running up to him. "Oh, good, you're awake! I was so hoping I'd see you before Tory and I left."

Tory? For "Victoria"? "Where are you going?" he asked.

"To the park," said a voice from farther down the hall. "It's such a lovely day for a walk."

That could only be Miss Morris.

When Jon looked beyond Chloe, he saw a woman in black coming down the hall, and his breath halted. Petite and blue-eyed, with honeyed hair coiled into a simple coiffure, she had the perfect figure of a Helen of Troy, but the serene and otherworldly face of a saint. He felt a perverse desire to kneel on one knee and pledge his allegiance to her like a knight of old.

How absurd. He was in no condition to be anyone's knight. And he doubted he ever would be.

Still, he couldn't stop staring. She was not what he'd expected.

"Jon," Chloe said before his mother could perform the introductions, "may I present my governess and friend, Miss Victoria Morris? Tory, this is my brother, Jonathan Leighton, the Duke of Falconridge."

The pride in his sister's voice shook him. He didn't feel like a duke at all.

Miss Morris didn't seem to notice, for she curtsied with admirable poise. "Your Grace."

"Please," he said, offering his hand to her, "don't stand on ceremony with me. Your father was my closest companion for years. I feel as if I know you already."

When pain glinted in her eyes, he regretted the mention of her father, for whom she was clearly in mourning. He was about to question why Chloe wasn't in mourning for their half brothers when he remembered that sisters didn't have to mourn as long as parents and children.

Miss Morris let him press her ungloved hand, which was firm, with nails that appeared oddly ragged for such a lovely woman. "Then we're even," she said tranquilly, "since your sister has sung your praises for years."

"And do I come up to snuff in the flesh?" he asked.

The frank question seemed to startle her. Then a smile crept over her face that banished the serenity of her countenance in a flash. "It's a bit early to tell, isn't it? Appearances are deceiving. You might take snuff, for example, and that would be a great disappointment."

Ah, she wasn't a saint after all, but an impish fairy hiding her wings. "I do not take snuff, but I have other annoying habits. Like preferring coffee to tea. The French make very good coffee, but good tea was hard to come by."

"Preferring coffee to tea is indeed an annoying habit," she answered, "but I'm sure we can break you of it."

"You can try," he said. "That does seem like an office suitable to a governess."

"Depends on the governess," she quipped.

"Depends on the office, too," Chloe said petulantly. "You cannot steal my governess to teach *you* to like tea again."

"I can if I'm paying her salary," he countered in a teasing tone. When his mother and sister looked horrified by the implication of his paying Miss Morris to do anything for him personally, he groaned. "I meant . . . I did not mean . . . Forgive me, ladies, it's been some years since I was in polite company."

"Apparently, you *do* need a governess to teach you," Miss Morris shot back with a faint smile. "But I'm afraid I already have a paying post, Your Grace, and I'm sure you wouldn't want me to abandon your mother and sister in the midst of Chloe's second Season."

Instantly, that smoothed over everything. And now he understood why Mother had hired her for Chloe. Like Morris, she was adept at maneuvering in delicate situations. "Of course not," he said. "I spoke out of turn."

"You most certainly did," his mother said, then turned to the two young ladies. "Victoria, why don't you and Chloe go on your walk? That will give me time to catch up with my son."

"I'll see you both at dinner," Jon added to soften his mother's dismissal of the pair.

"You'd better," Chloe said stoutly, and headed down the hall as Miss Morris followed on her heels. He couldn't help watching them go. It turned out Miss Morris was just as interesting from the back as from the front. Her shawl kept slipping off her shoulders to reveal a swanlike neck he wouldn't mind exploring.

With a scowl, he shook off that unwise thought. A gentleman did not lust after a woman in his employ, especially the beloved daughter of the one man whose life he had already ruined.

"Come, son," Mother murmured, "let's go into the study where we can be private. There are things we should discuss."

God help him. "I honestly did not mean to imply earlier that Miss Morris—"

"I know." She slid her hand in the crook of his elbow. "Unless you've changed dramatically, you're nothing like your brothers."

He stiffened. "Speaking of my brothers, they weren't too cruel to you and Chloe, were they? After I learned of Father's death, I worried they might be."

"It wasn't anything we couldn't handle. I might not have held the purse strings, but your father made sure in his will that my position in the household was unassailable. Mostly, your brothers went about their business, and Chloe and I went about ours."

"And . . . er . . . Alban and Aubrey didn't try to take advantage of Miss Morris, did they?"

"Try? Yes. Fortunately, the young woman is very good with hatpins, and after a couple got 'accidentally' stuck in their derrieres, they stopped."

That roused every protective instinct in him. "She shouldn't have had to stoop to such tactics. Their behavior is . . . *was* abominable."

"I quite agree. Thankfully, since I pay her salary out of my widow's portion, there was naught they could do to punish her for her reaction."

"Ah, but now that I'm duke, you needn't use your widow's portion."

"I can afford it," she said blandly as they entered the study, and she closed the door behind him. "Besides, then no one could question that her loyalties lie firmly with Chloe if anyone ever found out who paid whom."

"Right." But it bothered him that he might not be allowed to do anything to help Miss Morris. Her father had given him a very specific mission, and he meant to follow it to the letter. He must find her a husband somehow.

While taking on an entire dukedom. That sobered him. How ironic that he'd be doing what his own father would surely have thought him incapable of.

Only too well did Jon remember overhearing the discussion between his parents about his proposed banishment from England.

"How can you send him on a grand tour?" his mother had asked his father. "It's not safe. Napoleon is still causing trouble on the Continent, isn't he? I don't want Jon hurt."

"My sources tell me the war is over. Besides, what else can I do? Would you rather I buy him a commission?"

"And risk him getting killed in battle in India somewhere? Indeed not."

"Then this is my only choice, my dear. I caught him in bed with an actress last week, for God's sake! Then there was that woman whose husband found them together and tried to shoot him. Not to mention, the prank he played on the mayor's son that nearly got him thrown in gaol. I had to pay the irate fellow off to get him to back down. Bad enough Jon got into trouble at Eton for smuggling spirits into his dormitory—I won't have him running wild in London, too."

"But sending him away—"

*"He'll be fine. You indulge him too much. Going on a
grand tour will civilize the boy, show him the world, teach
him a gentleman's discipline and reserve. When he returns,
he'll be ready to settle down to a useful profession, the way a
duke's third son should."*

*"What if he runs wild abroad, too, my love, and we're not
there to protect him?"*

*"I've taken care of that. With much difficulty, I persuaded
my friend, Dr. Morris, to go with him as tutor. Morris is a
good man, who led many a grand tour before his marriage.
He'll be a proper bear leader to our son, make sure he
doesn't get into trouble. And it's only for two years, after all."*

Their conversation had always caused Jon pain whenever he
thought of it. It meant Morris hadn't wanted to be his tutor, hadn't
wanted to leave his family—he'd had to be talked into it. His father
had been so worried about Jon's scapegrace ways that he'd preferred to send him off on what Jon could now see had been a fool-
hardy journey than keep him at home.

And what had Jon done? Behaved as recklessly as always. Only
he'd dragged Morris into trouble, too. That was precisely why Jon
shouldn't be lusting after the man's daughter.

His mother walked over to the brandy decanter that had sat on
that one console table for as long as Jon could remember. She opened
the decanter. "Would you like some?"

"No."

That seemed to startle her. "Why not?"

"It's French, isn't it?" He gave her a thin smile as he settled into
his old spot on the sofa in front of the desk, out of force of habit. "I
know it's a small and petty revenge against my captors to refuse to
drink their liquor, but I do need my little enjoyments."

"Yet you drink coffee now, a habit you learned in France."

"The French don't *produce* coffee. Well, they do in Martinique,
but I hardly need worry that Englishmen are importing coffee from
Martinique."

"My, my, you do know your French beverages." She poured a
glass of brandy and took a rather large sip.

That caught him off guard. "When did you start drinking spirits?"

"After your brothers died." Staring down into the glass, she added, "I figured someone should drink it up. Your brothers bought a great deal from a smuggler, and I didn't want to just . . . throw it away."

"Right. Because you can afford to pay for a governess for Chloe out of your widow's portion, but you can't afford to throw away illegal brandy you wouldn't drink normally."

"Oh, all right, I like it, do you hear?" She took another sip with a defiant look in her green eyes. "It's very warming at the end of the day. And you weren't here, and your father was gone and so were your brothers and . . ."

When it was clear she was about to dissolve into tears again, he jumped up to put his arm about her. "It's fine, Mother. Drink whatever you please. I am in no position to dictate what you do, believe me."

"Good." Setting the glass down, she took a long breath, apparently to calm herself, then walked over to the desk. "Because that's not what I wished to discuss." She pulled out a stack of papers and plopped them on top of the desk with an air of belligerence. "I haven't tackled any of this since Aubrey and Alban—"

She caught her breath. "There are things that must be handled by 'the duke,' and since you were gone, there was no one to handle them. So, I think it best that we take care of some of the most urgent as soon as possible."

"Of course."

That seemed to mollify her somewhat. "And you have to go through the official process for gaining your title."

"Certainly."

"You needn't do any of it right away, you understand," she said as it seemed to register that he wasn't resisting her. "I know you need time to rest and adjust to the household and—"

"Mother," he said sharply. "I'm ready and willing to do these things. I'm beyond happy to be here with you and Chloe. Nor am I the same reckless youth I was. I promise I won't run wild or get into trouble."

If she remembered saying she feared he'd "run wild" abroad, she didn't show it.

He fought to soften his accusatory tone. "Nor will I spend my evenings in fleshpots or gamble the family fortune away. I intend to live a quiet life managing the dukedom and enjoying my family." And fulfilling his obligation to Morris and figuring out who'd betrayed him and his friends. Those took precedence as far as he was concerned.

Mother released a long breath. "Hearing you say that cheers me considerably. I was worried that after everything you probably endured . . . Well, it doesn't matter. We shall take things slowly."

"Slowly, yes." Except for his other two priorities. "Although I would like to know how well you think Alban managed the properties."

She sighed. "I can't be sure. He never let me near the books, and to be honest, I wouldn't have known what to do with them if he had. After he died, your father's land steward tried to talk to me about the rents, but I was afraid to delve into it too much, not wanting to mess things up."

"So you did nothing," he said blandly.

Her gaze shot to him. "Our solicitor said not to worry about it, that they had already put someone in charge of all that."

Jon stifled a curse. Now he had to make sure their solicitor was trustworthy. "I'll take care of it, Mother."

She nodded, still appearing nervous. "We should discuss one more matter: Victoria. Chloe doesn't need a governess anymore, of course. But I fear if I ask Victoria to be Chloe's companion, which is what Chloe wants, the young ladies will spend all their time in public making sly remarks about the gentlemen, instead of ensuring that Chloe dances with some of them. Then Chloe will never find a husband, even though she's got suitors fighting each other to court her."

"If that's true, why would she prefer to chat with Miss Morris instead?"

She sighed. "Growing up around Alban and Aubrey has made your sister cynical about gentlemen. Victoria's determination never to marry doesn't help."

Another shock. "Why on earth would a woman as beautiful as Miss Morris decide never to marry?"

When the word "beautiful" made his mother shoot him a sharp look, he stifled a groan. He must start watching his words. This wasn't Bitche, after all, where the only words that would get you into trouble were "Napoleon is an arse" and "I demand to be released immediately." His friend Heathbrook had tried them both. It had gained the earl nothing but harsh punishments for the former and laughter for the latter.

"You will have to ask *her* that question," Mother said. "Lord knows I have no idea. She's rather reticent about her reasons."

As well she should be. For a woman of her station to choose not to marry was foolish. Her father had family connections that would enable her to move, if not in the very center of Society, then on the outskirts. Morris had been the cousin of a viscount, for pity's sake. His daughter ought to be able to find, at the very least, a gentleman for a husband.

Jon had no idea how small was the bequest Morris had left to his late wife, but surely that would pass on to his daughter and be enough to provide her with—

He broke into a smile as he realized how to help Miss Morris while also aiding his sister in her debut. "Don't worry, Mother," he said, one of his burdens lifting. "I'll handle Miss Morris. I have the perfect solution to your dilemma."

Chapter 3

That evening, after Chloe dismissed her maid, Tory sat on Chloe's bed and watched her friend choose her jewelry for dinner. "You must be so happy to have your brother home."

"Thrilled, to be honest," Chloe said, "although I feel like I barely know him. What did you think of him?"

Tory pasted a smile to her lips. "He wasn't what I expected."

"What did you expect?"

Either a stiff and formal fellow who looked down on her as any duke would. Or the youth, Lord Jonathan, whom her father had described as "a reckless fellow who takes advantage of his position to live like a rogue."

She couldn't say that. "I don't know. Someone like your half brothers, I suppose."

"He was never like them, even before he left. That much I remember."

"Well, from the little I saw, he seems nice enough."

"Nice enough!" Chloe put on her favorite bracelet. "That's certainly damning with faint praise."

Yes, it was. But Victoria dared not tell the duke's sister that she found the duke witty and engaging and quite attractive. Too attractive, to be honest. Not handsome, exactly, for that implied the sort of polished good looks typical of a famous actor or an excellent artist's model. But he was definitely striking, with his strong jaw-line, sharp blade of a nose, and full lips. Even those two wings of silver hair at his temples enhanced his appeal.

"Your brother seems to be making the best of the awful hand he was dealt, which is impressive," Tory ventured. "How's that for a description?"

"A mealy-mouthed governess answer, if ever I heard one," Chloe said archly, and plopped down onto the bed beside Tory. "Don't you at least think he has gorgeous eyes?"

"Yes." And the hooded shape of them, so beautifully deep-set, made her fingers itch to sculpt him. "Hazel is a very *nice* color for eyes."

Chloe looked as if she would protest, then caught Tory smirking at her and rolled her own "gorgeous" eyes. "How amusing. You're teasing me."

"Why do you care what I think of your brother, anyway?"

Her charge suddenly became inordinately interested in arrang-ing her bracelet on her wrist. "I just want your opinion of him, that's all. It's been so long since I've seen him that I don't even know what *I* think about him."

Tory patted her hand. "Of course. How could you, after all this time? For part of it, you thought he might even be dead. Why, I've been mourning my father for years, fearing the same, only to learn from your brother's letter that he nearly made it home. It's . . . it's . . ."

"Awful, I'm sure." With a horrified expression, Chloe threw her arms around Tory. "I am so sorry—I hadn't even thought of your dear papa, and how you must be feeling to see Jon here with-out him."

Fighting back tears, Tory let Chloe hold her. She could use some comfort from her charge right now. "To be honest, I thought I'd made my peace with it. But seeing your brother so thin made me realize Papa must not have been eating well either, for months, possibly years." The tears were flowing now, and she brushed them away. "What they must have suffered, the two of them."

"I know," Chloe said. "It sounds dreadful. But I'm sure they were glad to have each other, instead of being there all alone."

"True." It was Tory's one solace—that her father, whom she remembered as a solemn, studious sort of fellow, seemed to have found a friend in Lord Jonathan . . . the duke, that is.

Heavens, she'd best remember he wasn't Lord Jonathan anymore before she slipped up and called him that. She should practice saying, "Your Grace" or "Duke" or "Falconridge," although those last two were probably presumptuous. The family might treat her as one of them, and he might say she shouldn't stand on ceremony, but Tory was still, for all intents and purposes, little better than a servant.

Taking out her handkerchief, she blotted her eyes. "Are you ready to go down to dinner? You know how your mother prefers us to be prompt."

Chloe rose. "Yes, but I think tonight she'll be more focused on Jon. She's been so anxious to see him that now she's liable to spend the whole dinner ignoring the two of us."

"That's to be expected," Tory pointed out as she rose and fluffed out her skirt of black bombazine. "He is her long-lost son, after all."

"I know, but I have concerns, too, which I need him to address," Chloe said. "Remember, we should emphasize in conversation how useful it would be for me to have you as my companion, so that you may guide me at balls and help me choose what to wear and things like that. Since Jon is back, he'll be the one to make the decision."

"I am in no position to emphasize anything, my dear. You will need to do that on your own."

With a sigh, Chloe headed for the door. "I suppose that's true. But regardless, I need *someone* who will stand up for me, in case Jon proves to be like Alban—determined to see me married at all costs. I won't marry for anything less than true love."

"As well you shouldn't." Meanwhile, Tory wouldn't marry at all. *Couldn't* marry at all. Though she yearned to find a husband who would share her interests and take her as more of a partner than a mere piece of chattel, she doubted the likelihood of that. Especially given her other circumstances.

They strolled down the hall toward the stairs and nearly ran into the duke as he left the master bedchamber.

"Oh!" Chloe exclaimed, "Don't you look handsome, Jon. He looks handsome, doesn't he, Tory?"

Uh-oh. Chloe clearly had got it into her head to match Tory with the duke. "Very attractive, yes."

Definitely damning with faint praise. His old clothes fit him to perfection except in the waist, where the trousers were clearly too big. But the heavy cravat and the tailcoat, with its old-fashioned cut and wide velvet collar, thickened his neck so he didn't look quite as thin.

"The two of you look very pretty, too," he said, although his intent gaze scanned only her attire.

"Even though I'm wearing mourning for Papa?" she said, half-jokingly.

"I daresay you'd look pretty wearing a burlap sack, Miss Morris." As if realizing what he'd said, he added hastily, "Although I wouldn't recommend that sort of attire. It would probably be hard on one's skin."

"Very scratchy," she quipped.

"Indeed." He seemed to catch Chloe's knowing expression, for he changed the subject. "I'm not sure whether to be alarmed or pleased that my old clothes are too big. I never considered myself plump, but perhaps I was, after all."

"Or perhaps you were merely well-fed," Tory replied. "Which we hope you will be again."

"I do need to start exercising at Gentleman Jackson's or riding or taking long walks or something." The duke gestured for them to walk ahead of him. "Get some strength into me. It was hard to do much of that at Bitche."

"Could you not exercise within the prison?" Chloe asked as they headed for the stairs together.

"We got two hours a day in a yard about the size of our back garden," he said, "but we mostly spent it plotting how to get better victuals, which proved virtually impossible at Bitche. And even if we could have exercised enough, a man needs plenty of meat in his diet to improve his muscles."

"What *did* they feed you?" Tory ventured.

"Oh, the usual fare," he said, obviously reluctant to speak of it.

"Just not much meat. And we certainly didn't dine as well as I hope I'll dine here at home." He glanced at his sister. "Is Monsieur Dubois still our cook?"

"Oh, no," Chloe said. "Mama pensioned him off, at his request. He was getting old and crotchety, anyway, and losing his sight besides. You'll like our new chef. His goose pies are spectacular."

"Then we must certainly have one soon. I can't remember the last time I ate goose."

They were just passing Aubrey's room when a servant came out and, catching sight of the duke, bowed. The duke nodded and continued past him, then paused midstep to stare into the room behind the servant.

"What is it?" Chloe asked.

"Why is Aubrey's room papered in my costly collection of prints?" he asked, an edge to his voice.

"Oh! Oh, dear," Chloe said. "That's rather embarrassing. We meant to have them all taken down before . . . well . . ."

"You see, your brother . . . your half brother, that is," Tory said quickly, "decided to . . . er . . ."

"Take my prints to adorn his room? How brotherly of Aubrey." The sarcasm in his voice was understandable, unfortunately.

"We did think you were dead," Chloe said matter-of-factly. "Although *I* always held out hope you weren't. Mother even protested Aubrey's actions, but—"

"He ignored her," Falconridge cut in. "What a shock. I'm sure he and Alban were hoping I never returned."

"Hoping?" Tory said. "No. Taking advantage of your absence? Definitely."

"Some things never change, I suppose." His eyes narrowed on her. "But I'm surprised you're making excuses for them. I gather they were rather ungentlemanly to you at times."

When Tory blinked, then scowled to hide her mortification at his knowing about that, probably from his mother, Chloe appeared confused. "What are you talking about?"

That seemed to startle him. He must not have heard that Chloe didn't know of those incidents. "Nothing." He smiled at his sister. "I just wanted both of you to be aware that I mean to run things differently than Alban." His gaze shifted to Tory. "Better, I hope."

Tory hoped so, too. Already he seemed cut of a different cloth than his half brothers, but she didn't always trust her impressions. They'd steered her wrong before. And judging from her father's early letters, Papa had seemed very unsure of Lord Jonathan's character in their first few months abroad. "We'll be late for dinner if we don't go on," she murmured.

He nodded, and they all descended the stairs. They entered the drawing room to find the duchess waiting for them. She was dressed even more finely than usual but twisted the end of her scarf fichu nervously until she spotted her son.

Breaking into a smile, she picked up her usual glass of pre-dinner sherry. "Would you like some, Jon? I promise it's not French."

"No, thank you, Mother. I'm not much of a sherry drinker. But I'd enjoy a glass of port, if you have it."

"Before dinner?" She handed glasses of sherry to Chloe and Tory.

"Port is for after dinner," Chloe said archly. "And only for the men. Women don't drink it at all, but instead are sent out of the room."

The duke frowned. "Right. I forgot."

"Never mind," his mother said quickly. "It will all come back to you soon enough. It's good that you'll be dipping your toe in with us instead of leaping right into the grand events."

His frown deepened. "Are there many grand events coming up? Isn't the Season drawing to a close?"

"Oh, no," the duchess said. "Parliament is in session until the end of July, and we have a rather full calendar up to then. Sadly, we missed several events surrounding the visits of the Allied Sovereigns to England, since we were in mourning, but there are more to come, and now that I'm nearly out of mourning and Chloe is done with it, we can accept the invitations. We've been invited to attend the King's fete for the Duke of Wellington, who hasn't yet arrived in England. It's expected to be a grand occasion."

"Forgive me, Mother," Jon said wearily, "but I would rather not be part of any celebrations involved with the war, under the circumstances. I'd just as soon put it behind me."

"Oh!" There was sadness in her eyes as she reached out to put her hand on his arm. After a moment, she continued hesitantly,

"Well, why don't we see how you feel in a week or two? There are many other things we can do. I'd already planned to go to the theater this week, assuming you arrived here on time. I mean to make use of the Falconridge box at the Theatre-Royal in Haymarket. They're performing *The Beggar's Opera.* You always did like the theater."

"Ah. I forgot Father kept a box there."

"I've invited the Duke and Duchess of Grenwood to join us," his mother added.

When her son looked at her blankly, Chloe explained, "He's a newly minted duke, too, so you'll have much in common. And she's quite clever. They're a very nice couple."

"Then Lady Sinclair's ball is fast approaching," his mother added, "and we wouldn't want to miss that. It shall be most enjoyable."

"I see."

But clearly, he didn't. A fact not lost on his mother, who looked uncertain again.

Tory tried to imagine a world where the social whirl of the Season didn't exist—which, of course, it wouldn't in a French prison!—but it was simply beyond her ken. What he must have endured!

Kershaw came in to announce that dinner was served, and they all trooped into the dining room, with the duke leading his mother.

Tory marveled at how gentle he was with his mother compared to his late half brothers, who'd been so condescending to her most of the time. The duke's behavior impressed her, although once he found his bearings in London—and got some strength in him, as he put it—perhaps he would change back into the arrogant, autocratic fellow he apparently used to be.

But for now, Tory enjoyed watching mother and son together. The duchess needed someone to lean on these days. Her stepsons had rarely provided her with that, and she'd taken on far too much with this renovation. Perhaps helping her would also help the duke become accustomed again to the life he once knew.

As soon as they took their seats at the dining room table and the soup was served round, Jon removed his gloves, and Chloe gasped.

"What happened to your hands?" she asked, which drew both his mother's and Tory's attention to them. They gasped, too.

There were marks etched deep in both of his palms. Tory could only imagine the pain he'd gone through to have them wounded like that.

"It's a rope burn." He paused as if to consider what he should say. "Some of us were playing French and English." When they looked blank, he added, "It's that schoolboy's game where two teams pull a rope in an attempt to force the other side to cross a line. Life in a detainee camp can be very boring."

Tory didn't believe him. Those marks were too deep to be from a schoolboy's game. But it wasn't her place to challenge his tale.

His mother took his hands and rubbed them gently. "Poor baby. It looks so awful."

"I haven't been a baby in some years, Mother," he teased.

"You'll always be my baby," she said, and kissed his hands in turn.

As they began eating, Chloe asked, "Why did it take you longer to get home than your friend who brought us your letter over a month ago?"

With a furtive glance at Tory, he said, "I had to bury Dr. Morris near the prison and have a stone carved to mark the grave. Forgive me, Miss Morris, but there was no other choice."

Tory smiled sadly at him. "I am so grateful to you for taking care of that."

"By the time I could leave Bitche, every available carriage, cart, wagon, and horse for rent or sale had been taken by the first prisoners who'd decamped, so walking to Paris was the only possibility."

"How far did you have to walk?" Chloe asked.

"Two hundred miles or so."

The table went quiet, all expressions filled with shock.

"No wonder it took you so long," Tory said, the first to speak.

"I didn't mind it all that much. It was wonderful to be outdoors after three years in a cell carved out of rock. Fortunately, we were able to find transportation after our small group reached Paris. Even then, the roads were choked with people either fleeing France or rushing to Paris now that the war was over, not to mention the various troops marching everywhere. I was relieved to get on the ship from Calais to Dover, and then I nearly kissed the ground once we reached England. Even up to the last, my fellow détenus and I feared we might be recaptured and taken back."

"If I may ask, what exactly are détenus?" Chloe asked.

"That's what the French called us. We took to calling ourselves that." His voice turned bitter. "When we weren't calling ourselves hostages, which is what we really were."

His mother blinked back tears. "From the time you were taken, we started asking the Foreign Office to have you and Dr. Morris released. They said it was impossible. Yet I know the French let certain English officers return, and I should think a duke's son would be more important than some captain."

"A few high-ranking English officers *were* allowed to leave," he answered, "but only in exchange for equally high-ranking French officers. Dr. Morris and I were civilians. Why would our government release French combatants in exchange for civilians?"

"Because it was the right thing to do!" Tory said angrily, thinking of her father being denied a chance to return simply because he wasn't a soldier.

He turned to her. "Ah, but you can see their point, can't you? England's argument was that Napoleon shouldn't have imprisoned civilians in the first place, so England wasn't about to reward such behavior by offering military people for, in this case, a scholar or a duke's third son on his grand tour. A soldier for a soldier is fair, but a soldier for a civilian is a bad trade."

Chloe gazed at him wide-eyed. "But . . . But I heard that they let the Duke of Newcastle return."

"Only after he'd spent three years in captivity. And it was because his mother—also a détenu—convinced Napoleon to free her son who had been only seventeen at the time of his capture. Napoleon's own decree stipulated that only men between the ages of eighteen and sixty be taken. I was the right age and wasn't the heir or even the spare at the time, so definitely, no one was letting *me* go," he said, a tinge of anger in his tone. "Hell, there was a marquess and his wife who died of cholera in our detainee camp. No one let them come home, either."

When silence fell on the table, he apparently realized he'd said too much, painted too graphic a picture.

Then his mother murmured, "Language, son. You simply cannot say 'hell' in polite company no matter how much you wish to." The duke sighed. "Forgive me, Mother. It appears Bitche has beaten the gentleman out of me. I'll try to do better." After the footmen removed the soup bowls, he glanced at Tory. "Your father *taught* me better. He was a fine man whom I greatly respected. He could speak of nothing but getting home to you and your mother. I'm glad he didn't know of your mother's death when he was alive."

The kind words made her throat tighten. "And now they're together at last. I take comfort in that thought."

For a moment, he looked inexplicably uncomfortable. "Indeed. In time, I'll relate to all of you everything about my years there, but for this evening, I simply want to enjoy being home." He paused as the footmen brought in the fish course. "So, ladies, tell me the latest gossip, the most interesting scandal, whatever frivolous bit of news you can think of as a diversion from my more morbid thoughts."

"What makes you think we're gossips?" Chloe asked archly.

"Everyone who is anyone in Society is a gossip, Sis." He cut a piece of spiced salmon. "I know things can't have changed *that* much since I left."

So Tory searched her memory, then said matter-of-factly, "Lady Manchester ran away with her footman." She ate some salmon. "I can't say I blame her. Her husband was always gone—first as a soldier, then as governor of Jamaica. What good is a man if he doesn't stay around?"

The duke appeared to be choking back a laugh.

"For pity's sake, Tory, don't encourage Jon," Chloe said. "We don't want him to think he can just order up gossip at his whim."

Ignoring Chloe, the duke asked Tory, "And the Manchesters have children?"

"Eight, actually," Tory said.

"Do the children favor the footman, then?" Falconridge asked, with a knowing wink.

Tory resisted the impulse to wink back. "Well, they could hardly favor the father, could they?"

The duke laughed heartily at that.

"Must we be so vulgar?" his mother asked, thin-lipped.

He reached over to take her hand and press it to his lips. "So tell me something not vulgar."

His mother mused a moment. "Lady Foxstead's soiree included a gorgeous harp-lute."

"What the devil is a harp-lute?"

"A harp and a lute combined," Tory said dryly.

"You have to see one to understand," Chloe added. "Or rather, you have to hear one. It's the most beautiful instrument I've ever heard played."

"That was likely due to the woman playing it," Tory said. "Lady Foxstead is quite accomplished musically."

"I should think it wouldn't be that hard to learn," Chloe said.

Tory smiled. Chloe's passions had included the playing of several different musical instruments, quilling, cross-stitching, and some others Tory didn't even remember. Although her latest passion for painting looked as if it might stick.

The duchess shot her son a sly glance. "*We* should acquire a harp-lute for my next soiree."

Dread crossed his face. "You're having a soiree? When?"

"When we're officially out of mourning. In a couple of weeks, I suppose." She patted his hand. "We need to celebrate your return. *And*, of course, showcase Chloe's many talents."

Chloe rolled her eyes. "Mother keeps expecting me to take Society by storm. But that isn't my wish. In my experience, Society men aren't interested in tall or clever or even talented women. They prefer short and stupid ones who giggle at their every overture."

"I somehow doubt that, Sis," the duke said with a smile. "I certainly don't prefer it. Neither do my friends."

Chloe sat up straight. "When are we going to see them? We met the earl, you know, but what about the marquess's son? Is he handsome? Witty? Worth knowing?"

He chuckled. "He's all of the above, but I don't know when you'll see either. We'll be busy catching up with our properties and figuring out what needs doing." He paused as the fish was removed and a plate of roast beef and potatoes placed before him. "Although, I'm sure you can lure them here by serving meals like this.

Do you know how long it's been since I've had English beef and potatoes?"

"Eleven years, I would imagine," his mother said. "And I'll have none of this talk about being too busy for Society affairs. It will be good for you to make time for a soiree, and we will invite all of your friends. When it happens, I demand that there be a harp-lute played beautifully. We too could be the talk of Society."

Falconridge seemed to be struggling not to laugh. "You're a duchess, Mother. You're always the talk of Society, whether you wish to be or not." He turned to Chloe. "What about you, Sis? Aside from wanting to learn the harp-lute, have you no frivolous news of your own? Perhaps a suitor who should concern me?"

Chloe sniffed. "I wouldn't tell you if I did. How could you possibly know anything about such a man when you haven't been here for years?"

"That's what Bow Street runners are for, dear girl," he quipped. "They find things out and report them to their employers."

"Jon!" Chloe cried. "You would *never*—"

"I would." He arched an eyebrow. "Now that I'm home, I mean to make sure you're well taken care of, and that means no fortune hunters or rakehells or scoundrels sniffing round your door."

Chloe tipped up her nose. "Then I shall go out immediately and engage a rakehell to court me. It would serve you right."

"And serve *you* wrong," Tory pointed out. "Haven't you heard the saying, 'Never cut off your nose to spite your face'?"

"I always found that saying absurd, myself," the duchess put in. "What does it mean to 'cut off your nose despite your face'?"

Chloe sighed. "It's '*to* spite your face,' not 'despite your face,' Mama."

Her mother frowned. "I'm not sure that makes any more sense. Why would anyone want to cut off one's nose? Of course, it would spite one's face!"

"Forgive me, Duchess," Tory said, stifling a laugh, "but I think that is exactly the point." She caught Jon staring at her as if intrigued, and she colored. She wasn't used to being stared at, except by his brothers, who'd leered. It wasn't the same. Or perhaps it *was*, and he was merely more subtle.

He sat back in his chair. "So, Miss Morris, *does* my sister have any secret and inappropriate admirers?"

She felt Chloe's eyes boring into her but had to think of an answer that would suit everyone. "Not that I know of, Your Grace." Which was true. "But even if I did know, I would hope you would depend on me to handle the matter sufficiently on my own without having to resort to betraying Chloe's trust. Your sister is, after all, an intelligent young woman who responds readily to reason."

That was probably doing it up rather brown, but Tory wasn't about to risk damaging Chloe's faith in her just to satisfy her new employer.

His beautiful eyes gleamed in the candlelight as he lifted his glass of wine to her. "Nicely done, Miss Morris."

She nodded coolly. But her heart was racing, and her hands clammy. She'd always found ways to get around his half brothers, but *this* duke might prove someone to reckon with. And while that might be good for the family, it might prove ill for her.

So, she'd best stay on her toes around him.

Chapter 4

Jon thought the rest of dinner went well. He'd managed to keep his cursing to himself, and he hadn't even blinked when Mother announced what the cost of the renovations had come to so far. He was reserving opinions about expenses for when he had a chance to go over the estates' books with their accountant.

Accountants, plural, actually. There were three at the company his father had used. Kershaw had told him that much. Father had also kept a land steward for all the estates and more than one estate manager. This would definitely take some getting used to.

Chloe had shown herself to be both clever and too young to appreciate what she had. Miss Morris, however, had been astonishing. His mother had chosen Chloe's governess well. Or perhaps Miss Morris had risen to the occasion out of necessity, although he somehow suspected that any daughter of Morris's would be like the man himself—circumspect, intelligent, and thoughtful.

It was her whimsical side that caught him off guard. He had *not* expected her to relate such a "vulgar" piece of gossip. That was something Morris couldn't have taught her.

"Jon," his mother said as the servants were clearing away the last of dessert, "would you like to join us in the drawing room? You can bring your port in there. We won't mind."

"Actually, Mother, I need to speak to Miss Morris alone for a bit." When all the women stiffened, he wanted to shout, "I am not my brothers!" But he couldn't blame the ladies for being uncertain of him, given the circumstances. It would take them time to adjust to him as he was now.

So he went on hastily, "Since there aren't any gentlemen present, I thought Miss Morris might join me here for port, as there are matters I must discuss with her in private regarding her father's estate." When the women relaxed, he added, "But if you think it better that we retire to my study—"

"The dining room is fine," Miss Morris cut in, then ventured a smile.

God, but she had a lovely smile—as bright and engaging as a siren enticing a sailor. That made her dangerous to a man who'd been without a woman for a good long while.

"May I have some port, too?" Chloe asked, probably just to provoke him.

"As long as you take it into the drawing room," he said, obviously surprising her. And his mother.

"Jon!" Mother cried. "Chloe may not have port! Don't be absurd."

"You're drinking brandy these days, Mother," he pointed out. "I don't see why Chloe can't have port, which isn't nearly as potent."

His mother rose and tossed down her napkin. "Fine. But if I catch her dipping into the brandy, I will box *your* ears."

Jon stood, trying not to laugh at the image of his mother doing such an asinine thing. "She won't actually like port, you know. It's something of an acquired taste."

Chloe rose, too, casting her mother a furtive look as she followed her out. "It's all right, Mama. I don't really want to try the port. I was just bamming Jon. But about the brandy . . ."

He could hear his mother's remonstrations even after they'd left the room, especially since his mother was careful to leave the door open. But he dismissed the servants. This conversation had to be between him and Morris's daughter only.

When he looked over at Miss Morris, she was staring at him with interest.

"What?" he asked.

"I can't quite make you out, Your Grace," she said, the candle-light shimmering over her features. "Are you *trying* to annoy your mother? And if so, why? Because we all know the duchess enjoys a nip of brandy now and then, but we would never dare mention it to *her*. I think she assumes she's fooling us all."

He shrugged as he walked over to look for the port in the cabinet where it used to be. He wasn't surprised to find it still there. Many things could change in the life of an English gentleman, but where they kept their port never seemed to.

As he poured himself a glass, he considered his answer. "All these polite niceties are difficult for me now—the willful blindness and delicate ways of saying things and the circumscribed rules for men versus women."

He turned and lifted the bottle in the universal gesture for "Want some?" and to his surprise, she nodded. After pouring her a glass, he brought it over, then took the seat closest to hers at the end of the table.

She sipped the port, then made a face and set the glass aside. "Definitely an acquired taste."

"Mother would probably like it. Port is a mix of wine and brandy."

"French brandy?" she asked.

"I don't know. I'll have to find that out." He sipped his and couldn't suppress a sigh of pure pleasure. "But I hope not. Apparently, I still like port."

"May I ask you something now that your mother isn't here protesting the inappropriate nature of our conversation?"

He tensed, readying himself for anything. "Of course," he said, attempting nonchalance.

"How exactly did my father die? You didn't say in your letter."

Damn. He'd hoped not to have this conversation so soon, but she had the right to know. "I should have explained. But when I wrote the letter, I was still hoping he'd survive. Once he died, right as we were being freed, I had to scribble a few additional words hastily so I could send the missive off with Heathbrook."

When she just stared at him expectantly, he added, "The surgeon said your father died of gangrene from a fractured thigh bone.

A piece of the bone broke free and poked through the skin, setting off infection and . . . well . . ."

She began to cry, and guilt surged through him again.

"Oh, God," he muttered under his breath, and whipped out his handkerchief and pressed it into her hand. He patted her shoulder. "There, there," he said, then winced as he heard the inane words. "I'm sorry."

"Please, don't be," she said, clearly struggling to stop her tears. She wiped her eyes and blew her nose into his handkerchief. "I don't know why I'm being so weepy. Long before your letter came, I'd reconciled myself to the possibility he was dead. Before your friends arrived, your mother made inquiries and was told there was no record of you and Papa after 1811."

"When we went to Bitche. No, I don't imagine they'd tell you of that."

She eyed him closely. "I know from earlier letters you were sent to Verdun initially."

"Right. Our first eight years were spent in the detainee camp there." He shot her a glance. "You know what parole is, don't you?"

She blinked. "Just that it involves prisoners of war."

"Only officers. When soldiers are taken prisoner in most countries, the officers are considered men of honor. They're asked to sign a pledge giving them the freedom to live in the town where they're held—to rent housing, eat food from the markets . . . essentially to live as any gentleman would—as long as they don't attempt to escape."

He returned to his spot across the table from her. He needed some distance. "There are rules, of course. Officers must check in once a week, for example. If they break the rules, they're put into actual prisons with the regular soldiers. The system is called parole."

"It sounds civilized," she ventured. "But you and Papa weren't in the military."

He leaned forward. "That's because Napoleon, in a fit of pique, decreed that all Englishmen of a certain age—any civilian who *could* become a soldier—had to be seized along with the prisoners of war and kept in one of those prison towns."

"Verdun was one, I assume." When he nodded, she asked, with eyes wide, "But are civilians generally kept prisoners in wartime?"

"No. That's what made it unfair. Civilian travelers are usually allowed to return home when war breaks out." He stiffened, remembering receiving the awful news that they would not be going home. "To add insult to injury, those of us who fell under Napoleon's decree were ordered to sign the same pledge officers were. If we didn't, we were imprisoned in the actual dungeons contained in such towns. As you might imagine, most of us chose to sign and check in, even when our commandant moved it to every day rather than every week unless we paid a bribe. Make no mistake, we were still prisoners in our gilded cages."

He ran a finger around the rim of his glass. "In Verdun, as long as we kept our heads down and didn't anger the gendarmes or commandant—and had enough money—we could live decently and have a sort of 'good' society. There were wives and families there, since many women didn't want to leave their husbands. While some détenus were people of rank, there were also tradesmen and professional sorts with families. A little spot of England in France, if you will."

"How many civilian prisoners?"

He shrugged. "Across the ten prison camps? Napoleon claimed it was ten thousand, but I've heard numbers quite a bit lower. At Verdun, there were as many as fifteen hundred of us at one point."

"Good heavens. That's the size of a town."

He nodded. "We did our best to look after each other. The true prisoners of war—almost all Royal Navy sailors—were kept in the Citadel, a real prison, but the rest of us could live in town, eat decent food, read books from the détenus' library, join clubs, even race horses . . . as long as we could afford it. We just couldn't go home or leave Verdun."

"It doesn't sound *too* awful."

"Except that we couldn't see our families and were subject to our commandant's whims, which often included marching people off on foot to another camp for some infraction."

He dragged in a heavy breath, debating whether to tell her about the attempted escape, but decided against *that* almost at once. She would undoubtedly blame him and rightfully so. He wasn't ready to . . . to deal with that. "Something happened to change our situation, however, and your father and I and our two friends were sent to Bitche Prison."

"One of those whims of your commandant, I assume?"

"Something like that." He drank deeply of the port. "Like the Citadel, Bitche was a real prison but worse." When her eyes went wide, he continued hastily, "Anyway, when you're locked up in a prison with every sort of fellow you can imagine—not only merchantmen but sharpers and thieves and . . ." He gazed into his glass. "Bitche was a different kind of place from Verdun. That's all I'm saying."

"Different for both you *and* my father, I assume?" she asked softly, her face paler than before.

"Yes. And for our two friends. We four looked out for each other. But we began to fear we might die there if the war didn't end soon." He suppressed a shudder of remembrance. "All of that to say that with the lack of mail and other . . . difficulties, your father decided to write a codicil to his will. He made me executor. And he included a substantial amount of money for you and your mother."

She gaped at him. "Derived from *where*, for pity's sake? When Mama died, she didn't even leave a will because she owned nothing. I can hardly believe Papa would have had anything to speak of, either."

Now came the tricky part—persuading Miss Morris to believe his lie. "Not here in England perhaps, but he earned a great deal at Verdun by teaching other détenus. Plenty of families of good reputation and fortune were eager to have their children taught by a man of such educational prowess."

When she eyed him askance, he embellished the tale. "He taught the children of titled gentlemen, and they paid him handsomely. At Bitche, he taught German to the commandant who hoped to take over some post in Prussia, and the commandant paid him well, too. In short, your father managed to accumulate five thousand pounds, all of which goes to you."

Miss Morris gaped at him. "From *teaching*? That much money? That hardly seems possible."

Damn. She really was too intelligent for her own good. "You must remember—we didn't get to continue on my grand tour, so he also had the monies Father provided for our trip. Your father insisted that I take half, of course, but his half was substantial, which added to his saved fortune." And God would probably strike him dead for laying lie upon lie like this. But surely, he could be forgiven the falsehood for such a good cause.

Miss Morris picked up her glass of port and downed half of it in one long gulp. Looking a bit wobbly, she rose to pace beside the table. "I-I can hardly believe it! Mama always thought Papa capable of achieving more, but this . . . How utterly wonderful!"

Then she seemed to catch herself. She leveled a hard gaze on Jon. "Are you *sure* it was that much? Perhaps you misread the amount."

"No, it's five thousand pounds, give or take a few." Although God help him if he couldn't find that much in the Falconridge accounts to "bequeath" to her. Still, if his mother was talking about buying harp-lutes and doing more renovations, Jon ought to be able to give Morris's daughter a small fortune.

After draining the rest of her port, she roamed the room as she seemed to ponder what this meant for her. He didn't mind that. She had an excellent figure, and though her gown was demure by dinnertime standards, there was enough of her bosom showing that he couldn't stop staring.

What was more, every time she turned to walk the other direction and her skirts swept around her, briefly outlining her bottom, he couldn't stop watching, utterly mesmerized.

Because she had a very *fine* bottom. It made him wonder what it would be like to smooth his hands over the soft globes. Especially if she were naked and in his . . . God, he would burn in hell for thinking of her like this. Morris was probably scowling at him from heaven.

She halted in front of him. "Once the duchess received your letter informing us of Papa's death, I consulted his solicitor, but the attorney was reluctant to tell me what was in the will until he was sure of the circumstances. He said he preferred to wait until your return to see if you have a certificate of death. Frankly, until just now, I had *no* idea Papa had amassed so much."

She'd consulted with Morris's solicitor? *Already?*

Damn.

Jon had been hoping to speak to the man first. He'd assumed—stupidly, as it turned out, given that the woman had already proved quite clever—that she'd be one of those helpless females who would let him guide her to her fortune, and would thank her stars for having such luck in fathers.

"You realize," he pointed out, "the bequest wouldn't be in his present will, anyway. I have a codicil to that one, so the codicil would supersede what is in his solicitor's copy."

"Of course!" she said, beaming at him. She sat down once more, smoothing out her skirts. "I hadn't thought of that."

Thank God. How in hell he would alter the codicil was anyone's guess, but he had the original and knew a fellow who could probably forge changes to it, assuming the man had survived Verdun and made his way to England.

"The thing is," he said, determined to press on with his plan, "there's a bit of a catch."

Instantly, her face fell, and her lovely azure eyes flashed him a look of utter hopelessness. "Of course. Isn't there always?"

"It's not a bad one, I assure you," he said hastily. "Your father merely required that the money be used for your dowry." That had been the easiest way Jon could think of to accomplish what he'd promised Morris—to help her to a good husband.

While dressing for dinner, Jon had chosen the amount—not so large that fortune hunters would be sniffing around her, but large enough that a decent gentleman could see the advantages to marrying a woman who'd been a governess.

Still, she said nothing, just sat there blinking at him like the baby squirrel he'd fed outside his window when he was a boy.

He eyed her closely. "Did you hear what I—"

"I heard you." She fingered the locket he'd noticed her wearing all day. "I just... Well, it's not surprising Papa wanted me to marry—he was always traditional in his beliefs about women—but for a moment, I thought perhaps..."

His stomach knotted. "Perhaps what?"

"I...I was having other dreams of how to use that money is all." A wan smile crossed her face. "But that's silly, since I didn't even know it existed until moments ago."

Guilt assailed him again. He tamped it down. He was doing

what her father had asked. Mostly. "Your father said the lease would almost be up on your cottage. Were you hoping to renew it with those funds? Surely you wouldn't wish to live there alone."

"No, I wouldn't pay for another lease." She worried her lip with her teeth. "The cottage is much too expensive for me to keep it up."

"Then you wish to put the funds into an annuity and live on it." Her father would *not* have approved of that, Jon was certain, if it meant that she lived alone her whole life.

"It doesn't matter," she said, although her expression said otherwise. "I never intend to marry, so I'll never have a chance to do anything with it, anyway."

He wouldn't let that sway him from his plan, not without knowing her reasons. "Why on earth would a woman as intelligent and attractive as you make such a choice?"

She cocked her head. "Do *you* intend to marry, Your Grace?"

The question startled him. "Eventually, since I'm expected to produce an heir. But not anytime soon."

"So, 'Why on earth would a gentleman as intelligent and attractive as you make such a choice?'" she said in a vague approximation of his voice.

She was mocking him now, but he didn't care. "Because I have my hands full learning to run a dukedom I never expected to inherit."

"The right wife could help you with that."

"I suppose, although my mother never did anything to that end with Father. Besides, I fear I am no great catch, Miss Morris." Certainly not for Morris's daughter.

A bitter laugh escaped her. "Right. You're merely a young, wealthy duke with extensive properties. Why would any sensible woman wish to marry *you*?"

He ignored her sarcasm. "Appearances can be deceiving, as you so adroitly pointed out earlier today." And that was all he would say about that, because when he got married, it would not be to *her*. He would always fear she might learn the truth concerning her father's death, then blame him for it.

"In any case," he went on, "you're not answering my question. A woman of your talents, with a five-thousand-pound fortune to her name, could pick any man she liked for a husband and then not be alone in the world. I thought every woman wanted to be a wife and mother."

"Not every woman," she said tightly.

"Very well. Then purely for argument's sake, why don't you tell me what *you* would want to do with the money?"

"You really want to know?"

"Of course."

She gazed at him steadily, her chest rising and falling in soft, captivating swells. "I should like to start a school for female artists."

Chapter 5

Tory would have enjoyed the duke's shocked look if she hadn't been so annoyed. How could he offer her the world with one hand and snatch it away with the other? She ought to blame Papa, but honestly, Papa had behaved as always.

Falconridge, however, had fooled her into thinking he was different, with his enlightened approach to his mother's brandy-drinking and his handling of Chloe. Now Tory was so disillusioned that she wasn't at all surprised when he said, in an incredulous voice, "You want to do *what?*"

"Open a school for female artists."

The man rose to pour himself another glass of port, and although she considered asking him to pour her another, too, she must keep her wits about her. She already felt fuzzy-brained.

It had to be the port. It couldn't possibly have anything to do with the attractive figure he cut in his fine clothes, now that they didn't accentuate his thinness. Or how his gorgeous hazel eyes gleamed golden in certain lights. Or how nicely rumpled his medium brown hair was, with its glints of blond. Certainly not.

What did his good looks matter? He was, apparently, just as much an arse as her father had deemed him to be at eighteen.

I thought every woman wanted to be a wife and mother.

Of course he did. Every *man* thought that. And every man wanted every woman to be a wife and mother. Because God forbid a woman should have her own interests and purpose in life.

She sighed. Not that she wouldn't *want* to be a wife and mother, mind you, but since that wasn't feasible . . .

The duke took a healthy sip of port. "Did your father know of this . . . er . . . desire of yours to run an art school?"

As if that mattered. "No. I hardly knew it myself until I began sculpting."

He stared at her. "Sculpting?"

"You keep questioning what I'm saying, Your Grace," she said in the sweetest tone she could muster. "Are you perhaps hard of hearing?"

The minute she said it, she wanted to take it back. He quite possibly *was* hard of hearing, given all that had happened to him in that French prison.

Especially considering how he was glowering at her now. "Very amusing, Miss Morris," he grumbled, and returned to the chair with his glass. "No, I hear perfectly well, I assure you. I simply wish I didn't. Because I'm having trouble comprehending the fact that you want to open an art school."

Ah, apparently the *arrogant* version of the duke was already making his appearance.

She pasted a smile to her lips. "Plenty of women run schools."

"Not for artists. It's a preposterous idea." He swallowed some port. "What do you know about opening a school for artists, female or otherwise?"

"I know how to teach—I've been teaching your sister for six years now. I know how to sketch, paint in oils and watercolors, and sculpt. I will need some help with the business part of running a school, I'll grant you, but if I could have that five thousand pounds free of conditions, I'm sure I could find someone to teach me that part, too."

"I'm sure you could," he muttered, and set down his glass hard enough to make port slosh over the rim.

She tipped up her chin. "What's that supposed to mean?"

"It means, madam, that any number of men would happily do

whatever you ask if it gave them the chance to swindle you out of either your money or your virtue."

Her temper rose, which wasn't a good thing. She'd worked hard at learning to keep it in check. "I'm not as easily gulled as you seem to think, Your Grace."

As if he'd begun to realize how annoyed she was, he gave her a considering look. "Why a school for *women* artists?"

Well, perhaps he wasn't entirely an arse. He was offering her a chance to make her case.

Eagerly, she took it. "Because there isn't one. Even though two of the founders of the Royal Academy of Arts are women, the place doesn't teach art to females. They allow women to exhibit, however, which gives those artists a chance to demonstrate their work *and* their abilities. As a result, a number of ladies have found financial success in the arts: Catherine Andras, Anne Damer, Maria Bell . . ."

"I see." He rubbed his chin consideringly. "Where did they learn their skills if there was no school?"

"From private tutors or brothers and friends who are artists. The problem is some women don't have those connections."

"I can understand how that would be the case." He stared at her. "Just out of curiosity, who taught *you*? As far as I could tell, your father couldn't even draw a simple map."

She uttered a wry laugh. "Perhaps if he could have, he wouldn't have got lost every time he left the house. Although that might have happened because he was too absorbed with the ideas in his brain to pay attention to something as mundane as his surroundings. So, no, Papa never taught me how to be an artist. That was left to my mother, when she had the time."

Tory had also possessed an artist friend down the street from her family's cottage who'd been amazingly helpful . . . until Tory had realized Mr. Dixon was more interested in her as a woman than an artist. Despite his obviously pregnant wife. Tory had avoided him ever since the day he'd forced a kiss on her in his workroom.

"And this is truly what you wish to do with your newfound fortune?" Falconridge asked.

His continued questions confused her. "What does it matter?

You said Papa made it a condition that the money be used as my dowry."

Rising again, he strolled over to look out the window. "True. But he did . . . er . . . leave me some discretion in the matter."

Hope sprouted in her heart.

"I'll need to consult with your attorney to confirm the terms," he went on, "but I can do that tomorrow. I still maintain it's a foolish way to use the money, which won't do you nearly as much good as a plump dowry. And your father wouldn't have approved, I daresay."

She stood to press her point. "We'll never know, will we? Perhaps if he'd lived, he would have. He supported Mama's artistic endeavors, after all." Because Mama had been the daughter of an engraver who'd made a bit of money with her talent. "He might even have chosen to run the school with me. But he never got that chance, did he?"

The duke's back went rigid. "No. He never did."

"So we can't dismiss outright the idea that he *might* have approved."

Falconridge faced her, his expression oddly conflicted. "I suppose not. I'll discuss it with his solicitor. But in the meantime—"

"In the meantime, let me show you my abilities as an art teacher. Why don't I teach you to sculpt? If I'm successful at impressing you with my teaching skill, perhaps you'll consider letting me use the money for the school instead. Assuming that Papa's solicitor approves."

"I was about to say, that in the meantime you could let my mother give you a Season."

That was odd. She eyed him skeptically. "The Season is almost over."

He shrugged. "All right. Half a Season. From what Mother said at dinner, there are still many events to come."

She stared down at her gown. "I'm in mourning."

That seemed to give him pause. Then he waved the protest away. "You don't have to be." When she stared at him, outraged, he added, "I daresay no one knows when you started wearing mourning. Because from what I understand, until now, you haven't been in Society much. So you could probably leave off mourning attire, and no one would realize you were ending it too soon."

"*I* would realize it," she said, a bit wounded he would think her so callous.

"Miss Morris," he said gently, "earlier you told me that you'd reconciled yourself to his death before you even read my letter."

"All right, that's true ... but not mourning him properly just seems to show a lack of respect ..."

"We all know you respected your father. Does it matter if anyone else knows?"

"I ... I suppose not." Besides, as part of the Falconridge household staff, she'd been expected to mourn for Alban and Aubrey, too. So she'd been wearing black ever since their deaths. Indeed, she had mixed so seldom in real Society that no one had probably even realized she'd been absent from it for nearly six months.

"So, if you come out of mourning, there would still be plenty of opportunities for you to meet gentlemen and decide if you really want to give up any hope of marriage for a harebrained scheme like starting an art school."

Harebrained scheme? The audacity of the man!

"I think the real harebrained scheme is putting the money toward a dowry that may or may not gain me a husband." She shook her head. "I'm not of any rank or consequence, after all."

"As I recall, your father was cousin to Viscount Winslow, making you the viscount's first cousin once removed. That is of *some* rank or consequence, surely."

"Do be serious. That viscount has three brothers, so Papa would never have inherited. One of his other cousins is a gardener, for pity's sake. Besides, at twenty-six, I'm teetering on the edge of the shelf. So, honestly, why would I garner any particular attention among all the glittering lights of society?"

He scanned her from head to toe, his gaze heating up in a look that inexplicably sent delicious shivers over her skin. "Believe me, Miss Morris. You'd garner attention wherever you go, twenty-six or otherwise."

She fought the reaction that his rumble of a voice provoked in all sorts of interesting places. "Me and my five thousand pounds, you mean."

He blinked. "Right. Of course. Though you can't blame a younger son for seeking out a rich wife. He has few other recourses."

She would argue that, but it seemed unwise to antagonize the man who might help her achieve her dream of running an art school. "I suppose not."

"My point is, you're a lovely, well educated woman—any man would consider himself fortunate to have you."

Even you?

The moment the thought entered her head, she squelched it. The last thing she needed was a romantic entanglement with the duke, who would never marry a woman of her station. "In my experience, Your Grace, men don't generally consider education an asset in a woman."

"Then they're fools." His eyes gleamed bright in the waning sunlight. "Education is an asset in everyone. Why do you think your father did so much teaching? Because he believed in education. As do I."

"But not art education." When he didn't answer, she added, "How about this? During the day, I'll give you lessons in sculpting, and at night, your mother can bring me to whatever event you deem worthy or whichever one your sister is attending that doesn't require an actual invitation. At the end of the Season, we can reexamine how you think I should use my five thousand pounds."

For a long moment, he seemed to be considering that. Then he nodded. "But we must establish some rules."

She suppressed a smile. "Oh, by all means, establish rules. Society *and* schools seem to run best with rules."

That barely raised his eyebrows. "At social occasions, you will not hide in a corner or sit with the chaperones. Or merely chat with my sister. You must at least attempt to be part of Society."

"You do realize a woman doesn't simply get to choose to be 'part of Society.'" She folded her arms over her waist in the primmest pose she could manage. "I can't ask a man to dance, nor can I approach anyone without an introduction. For that matter, I can't even invite myself to the sort of events you seem to think I should attend."

"Of course not. But Mother can make sure you're invited. Then we'll all go together and manage the introductions."

"We? You'll attend as well?" she said, unable to hide her skepticism.

He chuckled. "Someone must ensure you keep to your word. I doubt my sister or mother will enforce it."

True, although Tory wouldn't admit it to *him* for the world. Besides, if he attended, he would rapidly see she wasn't the diamond of the first water he seemed to think. "As long as you understand the 'rules' of society. You seem to have forgotten a few while in France."

"I'll catch up eventually." He shot her a boyish grin as devastating to her insides as his rumbling voice had been. "And you can steer me in the right direction from time to time, if it makes you feel any better."

"If you wish. I shall try not to steer you into the weeds, Your Grace."

His grin faded. "You should also stop calling me 'Your Grace.' If you're to attend Society events as a participant, you should stop speaking like a servant."

"I *am* a servant."

"Not really." He arched one finely shaped eyebrow. "And not for long, no matter which choice you make for using that money. After all, my sister is getting a tad old to need a governess, don't you think?"

"On that, we agree . . . Duke."

"Better." He frowned. "I'd tell you to call me 'Jon,' but that would attract the wrong kind of attention in public."

"It most certainly would."

"Though you can surely call me 'Jon' in private," he drawled. "From what I can tell, you're practically a member of the family."

His voice had gone all soft and husky, sending strange sensations along her skin, as if someone were stroking it with feathers.

Good Lord. What a thought.

"I think it best we preserve the proprieties, even in private." *Especially* in private. She cocked her head. "And may I point out you're very dictatorial for a man who just found out he's a duke? Where did you learn such a skill?"

"In France." He shrugged. "Reminding people I was still a duke's son occasionally enabled me to get out of, shall we say, dicey situations."

She eyed him closely. "I would very much enjoy hearing more about those."

"I would very much enjoy hearing more about what has put your back up regarding marriage," he said, "but I somehow suspect you don't yet trust me enough to tell me."

"I don't share my thoughts with just any old duke, you know," she said lightly. "I must have a royal one at the very least."

"Perhaps we'll find you a royal duke to marry," he countered.

That was so ludicrous as to require a flip answer. "In such a case, I'd consider marrying him, too, although if he marries me for a mere five thousand pounds, I won't respect him."

A smile tugged at the corners of his rather full lips. "Neither would I." Abruptly, his smile faded. "But we have traveled far afield. Do you agree to my conditions?"

"You still haven't explained how I'm supposed to participate in the dancing if no one asks me."

"You'll be asked," he said, looking oddly serious again, "if only by me and my two fellow détenus, Commander Scovell and Lord Heathbrook."

Having never met his friends, she didn't know how to respond. She tried not to imagine what dancing with the duke would be like, but she knew it would be either magical or mortifying. Hard to tell which. "How old are your friends?"

"Younger than I," he said, with a raised eyebrow.

"That's fine then. Besides, I'm quite good at pity dances."

He snorted. "Trust me, Heathbrook and Scovell will end up standing in line to get to you. I'm sure of that much."

"That statement alone shows how long you've been out of Society, Your—" When he lifted an eyebrow, she caught herself. "Sir. Men of rank don't readily take to governesses who've suddenly been transformed into heiresses. Or at least not until they're sure that the governesses are indeed heiresses."

"Should I announce it in the press?" he asked dryly.

She colored. "No, indeed."

He leaned close. "Keep blushing prettily like that, sweetheart, and you'll have men dropping at your feet."

"Keep calling me 'sweetheart,'" she shot back, fighting to ignore how her pulse reacted to the surprising endearment, "and the press will be speculating about why you're championing me."

He looked truly chagrined. "Forgive me. That . . . er . . . just slipped out."

"Fine." Despite her pounding heart, she managed a nonchalant smile. "I will watch my use of 'Your Grace' if you will refrain from calling me 'sweetheart.'"

"I can do that. Although I assume this means you've agreed to my conditions."

She strolled past him to the port and shakily poured herself a second glass. She would need it. "You haven't yet let me establish *my* rules for our lessons."

That seemed to bring him up short. "By all means, establish your rules. Just keep in mind that I need to spend a good portion of every day examining the dukedom's books, speaking with my accountants and land steward and estate managers, familiarizing myself with—"

"In other words, you're already trying to wriggle out of your part of our agreement."

He opened his mouth, then closed it. Finally, he said, "Of course not. Do continue with your rules."

She sipped the port as she realized she had no rules. She was an artist—rules were anathema to her.

Then again, she liked making rules for *other* people. How else could she have been Chloe's governess? So, of course, she could create rules for him.

"First," she said silkily, "you must give me at least three hours a day to teach you."

"Three *hours*—"

"Yes. You must take these art lessons seriously, especially if you mean to be parading me about town like some trained poodle with a golden collar. Or rather, a silver collar, since five thousand pounds isn't all that much as grand dowries go."

Though it was a fortune when it came to starting a school.

He snorted. "I somehow doubt you could ever be trained like a poodle. You seem too recalcitrant for that."

"True." When the word brought a smile to his lips, she went on. "The thing is, I realize you have a great many important ducal things to do, but when you are in a lesson with me, I expect you to pay attention."

He smirked at her, the beast. "I always pay attention."

"Good. Because I expect you to treat it as you treat your other activities—with focus and the intention to learn. When you're having a lesson, there shall be no interruptions of any kind—from your land steward or your valet or even your détenu friends, for that matter. I never allowed interruptions for Chloe, and I shan't allow them for you."

That wiped the smirk right off his face. "If Chloe could follow that rule, I damned well can."

"Language, sir," she couldn't resist saying.

Eyes glittering, he strode toward her. "Don't assume that because you're giving both me and Chloe lessons of a sort, you may treat me as your charge, Miss Morris. You are not *my* governess. And I'll curse as much as I damned well please."

And here the officious duke reared his ugly head again. "Did my father put up with your cursing?" she had to ask.

He halted inches from her, a look of consternation crossing his face before he smoothed it away. "Not at the beginning, no. But only because he was trying to teach me to be a proper gentleman, with a wide knowledge of history, the arts, philosophy, and the classics."

His voice grew bitter. "He gave up on that when Napoleon decided to teach us and our fellow détenus that there were no rules in war, gentlemanly or otherwise. Your father even began doing some cursing himself. Hard not to when you're in a French prison."

The prickly duke was back, the one who couldn't seem to escape the scars of his exile. That made her rather sad. "Then we shall dispense with the non-cursing rule. I could hardly expect you to follow one that my own father could not."

"Very well," he snapped. "Have you any others?"

It began to dawn on her she might be going about this the wrong way. The duke needed a place where he didn't have to feel bowed down by responsibility . . . or bad memories. More than anything, he needed a friend.

Besides, she would get nowhere by antagonizing him. "Yes. One more rule."

He crossed his arms over his chest. "Go ahead."

"The only important one: that you enjoy our lessons."

That obviously took him completely off guard. "I beg your pardon?"

"Our lessons . . . and the subsequent work." She softened her tone. "Creating art is a glorious thing, Duke. It's also painful and freeing and provocative and sacrificial, a rewarding experience when all those disparate emotions come together. Creating art can make your very soul sing. But only if you give in to it. Only if you coax that side of yourself out to play. So, have fun with it. That's my last rule—that you have fun with our lessons."

He looked positively flummoxed by the idea. "I'll . . . er . . . try." Then smoothing his features into an inscrutable expression, he held out his hand. "*Now*, have we agreed to the terms of our bargain?"

She shook his hand. "I believe so, yes."

But when she started to withdraw hers, he held it a few moments longer, staring down at her fingers, where the nails were ragged and short. She'd been struggling to carve a piece of marble when he'd arrived, hadn't had time since to pretty up her nails, and had removed her gloves to eat dinner without remembering how bad they looked. She'd have to be more attentive to that in the future.

Still, they were an artist's nails, nothing to be ashamed of. But under his scrutiny, she grew embarrassed. Especially when he traced them with his thumb, as if bemused by their very existence.

"You really do sculpt, don't you?" he said softly as he lifted his gaze to hers.

"I really do." She glanced at *his* hand, wincing to see his scars close up. "And you really were a prisoner."

Stiffening, he dropped her hand. "I really was. Not that it has anything to do with this."

She suspected it had a great deal to do with this. The whole situation seemed odd—the dowry, the way he always spoke of Papa with a trace of guilt in his tone, and even his reluctance to talk about his time abroad.

Turning his back to her, he walked over to draw his gloves on and murmured, "I shall see you tomorrow."

The vague way he said it made her determined to nail things down, so he couldn't avoid the commitment. "Tomorrow morning, to be exact. Because we begin our lessons in the art room at nine AM."

Then before he could protest, she fled.

But as she hurried down the hall, half-afraid he would come after her to chide her for her insolence, she realized she might not mind that so much. The duke was proving to be quite the fascinating fellow.

And fascinating fellows had always been her downfall.

Chapter 6

Have fun with our lessons? We begin our lessons in the art room at nine AM?

Jon stood confounded after the woman he'd just crossed swords with swept from the room with infinite grace and a hint of . . . arrogance? Yes, that would be the word for challenging a duke with supreme confidence that she would win, then giving him no chance to retort.

They were certainly making English women different these days, something else that would take getting used to.

And where was the bloody art room? They'd never had one before. More importantly, how was he supposed to start "lessons" *tomorrow*, for God's sake? He had far more important things to deal with than indulging Miss Morris's fancy that she could run an art school.

"Well?" asked his mother's voice from the doorway. "What in creation were you two discussing for so long?"

Devil take it, he'd have to tell his mother some of the truth or she'd ask Miss Morris about it herself.

"I was informing Chloe's governess that I'm executor of her father's estate. And he left her a tidy inheritance." But he wasn't about to reveal where the money was coming from. He doubted his mother would approve.

She entered the dining room, her brow wrinkling in a frown. "How much is 'tidy'?"

"Five thousand pounds."

It was her turn to stand there slack-jawed. "Dr. Morris had that much money? Why didn't his wife know about it? I suspect she could have used those funds. Especially since she was too proud to take any from me."

"He acquired it at Verdun, so there was no way of sending it to her safely. Until I returned, of course." Now he was lying to his mother, too, but it couldn't be helped.

His mother snapped open her fan. "He *earned* more money abroad than your father paid him to take you on the grand tour?"

"Some of it came from what Father paid him. Since Dr. Morris was only in Verdun because of my grand tour, I told him he could keep whatever was left of what we spent." Which had petered out sometime in early 1809. "Wait, you know how much Father paid Dr. Morris initially?"

"Well . . . I mean, your father didn't say *exactly*, but I know how much such things cost. My friend Angela told me what her son's bear leader . . . forgive me, his *tutor*, was paid. It was only half that sum."

"Father was more generous to Morris. Who, by the way, hated the term *bear leader*. He had more respect for those he tutored than that." Although in Jon's case, the term had been close to the truth.

"I'm glad to hear it," his mother said. "And equally happy your father was generous. Although given how much difficulty Dr. Morris left his wife in, I'm rather surprised. One would think the man would have been generous with his wife as a result."

Jon winced. Another crime lay on his shoulders now, of portraying Morris as less than honorable. Although the truth was somewhere in the middle.

Flicking her fan back and forth, Mother circled the dining table. "What does Victoria intend to do with five thousand pounds? Lord knows, with that amount of money she needn't stay in any position here."

"It's complicated." He told her about the "requirement" that Miss Morris use it for a dowry.

"Well, her father was right to limit it so. A dowry would be the best use for her inheritance. She *is* gently bred, after all."

He had no idea how gently she was bred, but she was certainly beautifully bred, with her dancing blue eyes and their silver flecks, her golden hair with tendrils escaping her coiffure, and her curvy figure that he ached to explore. She would certainly have no trouble finding a husband . . . and then getting around the man with one blown kiss from those perfect pink lips.

Yet she hadn't tried using her attractions to get around *him*. How surprising. More than one woman in France had attempted it, though they'd mostly failed.

Miss Morris might have succeeded. Her subtle smile, somehow both coy and innocent, raised his pulse to a fever pitch every time she offered it. That was decidedly annoying. Immune to women's usual blatant manipulations, he'd found her slipping under his guard with her unwitting ones.

Why else would he have agreed to that cursed bargain with her, instead of merely telling her how things were going to be?

That bargain would surely blow back into his face no matter how hard he tried to escape her potent attractions. For one thing, how was he to be with her in such close quarters without being tempted to kiss her . . . caress her . . . seduce her? None of which was acceptable, of course, especially given how he'd ruined her father's life and thus hers.

Damn it all. He'd been too long without a woman if he was salivating over his sister's governess.

His sister's fetching, clever, and completely forbidden-to-him governess.

He forced himself to return to the matter at hand. "I'm pleased, Mother, that you see the advantages to Miss Morris of using the money as a dowry. She wasn't quite as happy about her father's requirement, I'm afraid."

"Oh, pish, I will make her see the wisdom of it. Just leave that to me."

"Actually, I was hoping you'd do more than that."

His mother raised one gray eyebrow.

"I'd like you to present her in Society."

Mother looked bewildered. "Present her as what?"

"An eligible female on the marriage mart, of course."

She blinked at him. "At the same time I'm showing off your sister?"

"Ah, but that's the beauty of my plan. If they are *both* being championed by you, then both will be asked to dance, and given Miss Morris's current situation, she'd be a fool not to take the opportunity to find a husband. That means Chloe will have no choice but to accept dances herself."

"Oh! I take your meaning now." Mother wandered over to the fireplace, stared into it a moment, then whirled to face him. "Did Miss Morris agree to be presented?"

"She did." With certain conditions attached. He definitely shouldn't mention *those* to Mother.

His mother eyed him suspiciously. "Even though she didn't like the idea of using the money for a dowry."

"As I said, her father didn't give her a choice. It's in a codicil to his will." The slightly forged version of it that Jon meant to produce somehow. "I'm executor of his estate, you know." Such as it really was.

"Well then. It's all settled, isn't it?"

To his relief, Mother didn't seem to balk at the idea of Miss Morris joining Chloe in the Season.

Then she started pacing. "Of course, there's not much time left in the social calendar."

"I believe you told me earlier there was plenty of time left in the social calendar," he said with a hard stare.

She colored. "For *you*, my dear, not for Chloe and especially not for Victoria, given her age. She will have trouble finding a husband even with her dowry."

He somehow doubted that, unless all the men in Society had been struck blind and deaf while he'd been away. Anyone could see that Miss Morris was quality, no matter how remote her connection to nobility.

"So, we must ensure her success by putting her forth properly." His mother halted to place her hands on her hips. "Will you be able to use some of her inheritance for gowns and shoes and such? Because she will need those things."

Damn, he hadn't thought of that. "I will have to speak with her father's solicitor. I plan to do that right away." He would have to pay for them himself, in secret, of course. "But I'm sure there are funds for that, too."

"Are you? Because such things aren't cheap. And we'll have to include her in my soiree, which means adjusting the focus a bit."

His plan grew more complicated by the moment.

His mother started pacing again. "We could begin by consulting the Duchess of Grenwood when we're at the theater. She's always been kind enough to invite Victoria to her own affairs. The duchess likes to solicit advice from Victoria about her sketches."

"Does she?"

Mother waved a dismissive hand. "Oh, you know how young women are. They fancy themselves artists and such. I can't imagine why. But Victoria does have good sense when it comes to color and line. I have solicited her advice myself about the renovations from time to time." She stopped. "Have you told Chloe about this idea of presenting Victoria?"

"For God's sake, Mother, I just now told *you*. How the devil could I have told Chloe?"

She sniffed. "No need to be so grouchy. I was merely asking." She paused. "Although, come to think of it, she's probably told Chloe herself by now anyway, so that's done. Those two are quick as thieves."

"I believe you mean '*thick* as thieves,' Mother."

"I do not." She eyed him askance. "I mean that they're quick to tell each other everything. You know, like thieves when they plan their crimes. How would thieves be thick? That makes no sense."

"All right." His mother had butchered popular sayings for as long as he could remember. Father had ignored it, so the rest of them had. Perhaps it was a sign of Jon's cantankerous mood tonight that he no longer tolerated it easily. She quite clearly meant that Chloe and Miss Morris were "thick" as thieves.

He groaned. Which meant his sister probably already knew he was having "lessons" with her governess. He didn't even want to consider what Chloe would make of that.

"Anyway, we can't give Victoria a real debut," Mother said, "because the queen has already hosted her only drawing room for this year. Her Majesty says she's getting too old for them. In truth, these days she looks rather ill."

"I'll leave to you the business of figuring out how best to present Miss Morris. Just let me know what services I can provide, either accompanying you three to events or wrangling invitations, though I daresay people are more likely to listen to you in that regard than to me."

His mother shook her head. "You're the duke now, son. Everyone will listen to you." She approached to take him by the arm. "But at present, you appear to be exhausted, and it's been a long day, I'm sure, so perhaps we'd both best retire."

Gently, he extricated himself from her arm. "I will, I promise. But first I have a few things to do in Father's . . . in *my* study, after I finish one more glass of port. I'll see you at breakfast."

"As you wish." She kissed him on the cheek. "Sleep well, my darling. I am *so* happy to have you back."

He watched until she left and gave himself ten more minutes for good measure. Then he was out the door and down the hall, asking the drowsy footman for his greatcoat. "I assume that Kershaw made arrangements for my carriage to be brought round."

The footman nodded. "It's waiting outside, Your Grace."

"Thank you."

Within moments, Jon was on his way to the Traveler's Inn and Tavern, which he'd earlier determined was still in existence in Eastcheap. He pulled out his father's old pocket watch, now his, and noted the time. He should be there with time to spare. Heathbrook and Scovell were meeting him there—they'd both sent notes agreeing to the assignation.

To his surprise, when he arrived, he was shown into a private room, where his friends were already waiting, obviously well into their first tankards of ale.

Scovell rose to shake his hand. "It took you long enough."

"According to my watch," Jon said, "I'm right on time."

Heathbrook remained sprawled in his armchair. "I believe Scovell means that it took you long enough to arrive *home*."

"Oh. I suppose it did." Jon ordered a tankard of ale from the servant standing just outside the door. "You two seem to have fallen right into step with the new London."

"To the extent that I could," Scovell said. "I've been promoted to captain. There's talk of shipping me off to Portsmouth to train new recruits. Although why we need them when the war is over is anyone's guess."

"The war in America is still going on, isn't it?" Jon pointed out.

"True. But I'm damned well not going to accompany a lot of raw recruits to America if I can help it. I just now got my new uniform back from the tailor, and I have no desire to put any holes in it."

Jon could tell from his tone he was only half-joking.

"We both purchased fresh clothing," Heathbrook quipped. "Meanwhile, you look like you stepped right out of 1802."

"And you look as if you've been stuffing yourself with too many pork pies."

Which was stretching things, to be honest. Heathbrook might appear more hale and hearty than he had in years, but there still wasn't an ounce of fat on him. While Jon had spent his captivity soaking up knowledge, Heathbrook had spent *his* taking advantage of his enforced close contact with British military men to learn every method of fighting there was. The earl had said he was determined not to be caught unawares again.

"At least *my* old clothes fit me now." Heathbrook rose with studied nonchalance to shake Jon's hand. "You're a skeleton in a coat . . . *Your Grace.*"

"Enough of that," Jon said with one eyebrow raised. "People have been lobbing 'Your Grace' at me every five minutes since my arrival."

"What do you expect?" Scovell chuckled. "You're the duke now."

"Good God, we'll have to start calling him Falconridge, won't we?" Heathbrook said with a smirk.

"I don't care what you call me," Jon said, "as long as it's not 'Your Grace.'"

"Better get used to it," Scovell said. "That will be happening all over London for the rest of your life."

"Or the next few days, anyway," Heathbrook put in, "since it looks as if you'll soon perish of hunger." Gesturing to Jon to take a seat, Heathbrook dropped back into his own comfy chair.

"There's a reason for that." Jon sat down and told them of his complicated and tortuous route back to England.

Scovell crossed his arms over his chest. "At least that explains why it took you so long to get here."

"Also," Jon added, "I stopped in Verdun to pick up whatever items I'd been forced to leave behind when we were sent to Bitche and to ask questions."

"About?" Scovell prompted.

"Mademoiselle Bernard, of course. I also took a few days in Paris to look for her."

"Oh, for God's sake," Heathbrook muttered as he straightened in his chair. "She is not the one who—"

"Wait," Scovell broke in, pausing to scan outside the room with that vigilant awareness of his surroundings only military men seemed to possess. When the servant appeared with Jon's tankard, Scovell waited until the man left. Then Scovell closed the door and leaned against it to stare at Heathbrook. "Go on."

With a roll of his eyes, Heathbrook scowled at Jon. "Mademoiselle Bernard didn't reveal our escape plans to Commandant Courcelles at Verdun. I don't know why you persist in thinking she did."

Jon snorted. "You do agree she was probably Morris's mistress."

"Hard to be sure, honestly," Scovell put in. "Just because they spent time together doesn't mean they were lovers. She did have a post, after all, working for our landlady. But I'll admit Morris was quite secretive about her, and whenever they were together, they seemed very cozy."

"*Seemed* being the operative word," Heathbrook muttered. "Did you find her in Paris, Jon?"

"I didn't find her anywhere. I was told she left Verdun at the same time we were hauled off to Bitche, but I couldn't locate her in Paris. That alone is suspicious."

"Perhaps, but Paris is a big city," Scovell pointed out. "And in the turmoil of the war's end, it would be damned hard to find anyone."

"I found some neighbors of her mother, who told me both ladies left France as soon as the abdication happened, which was all the neighbor would say. That spoke volumes."

Heathbrook snorted. "Perhaps one volume, if that."

Jon stared at the earl. "Why do you always defend her?"

"Why do you always blame her?" Heathbrook shot back.

"Because someone bloody well betrayed us," Jon bit out, "and she's the most likely suspect."

Heathbrook cocked one black brow. "You merely dislike her for ruining your hero worship of Morris."

"And you merely can't believe a woman that beautiful could be a villainess."

Scovell stepped forward. "This gets us nowhere, gentlemen. We have other suspects, some of whom we can't even investigate without returning to France."

"I don't know about you," Heathbrook said, "but I'm not returning to France until Napoleon dies on Elba."

Jon eyed Scovell consideringly. "I thought you said you could find out more information from your cousin, the major, once we were in England."

"He hasn't come back from the war yet. I'll continue to keep my ear to the ground, though."

"Why would he even know anything about our villain?" Heathbrook asked.

When Scovell remained silent, Jon said, "Because he was involved in intelligence during the war, so he might have heard things concerning Napoleon's spies."

"I'm more concerned about *Courcelles's* spies," Scovell said, "since one of those told him our plans. If not for that person, male *or* female, we would never have ended up in Bitche."

"We don't know for sure that Mademoiselle Bernard was one of Courcelles' regular spies," Jon said uneasily. "She might just have reported on us because she overheard talk of the escape, either from us or from Morris himself."

"Yes, but why would she report on us, if she was Morris's lover?" Heathbrook snapped.

"Because Courcelles trained his spies to get close to their subjects any way they could," Scovell said.

"Now see here," Heathbrook said. "You told us you overheard that gendarme saying that a fellow Englishman was the one who informed on us to the commandant."

Scovell's French was fluent, though he'd hidden the fact from their jailors from his first day of captivity. He'd said it allowed him to hear things they thought he couldn't understand—another way in which he was a military man to the core.

"I didn't say that exactly," Scovell retorted. "I said that the gendarme joked about how one of our own people had it in for us. He didn't say an 'Englishman.' He didn't even say it was a man."

"Still," Heathbrook countered, " 'one of our own people' could include the owners of the house we were renting, the owners of the shops we frequented—"

"Or Mademoiselle Bernard, who would have been considered part of our circle," Jon said, crossing his arms over his chest.

"Or another détenu," Scovell pointed out. "That's not off the table as far as I'm concerned. The commandant excelled at playing on our fellow captives' weaknesses, as you both well know."

That theory had always made Jon uneasy. "If it *was* another détenu, then that person is probably back in England now. That would really be a betrayal, wouldn't it? I can't bear to think one of our own kind turned us in for money or special privileges or anything else."

"It happened to others before us, so it's not inconceivable." Heathbrook's voice hardened. "Though if I do find out it's a détenu, I'll take great pleasure in putting my hands around the bastard's neck and squeezing the life out of—"

"Stop with the bloodthirsty threats, Heathbrook," Scovell said. "We agreed we would turn the person in to the authorities if we discovered he's British."

"For myself," Jon said, "as long as justice is meted out to him or *her*, I am content."

"But to be honest," Scovell said, "we still don't know enough right now to move forward."

He was right. Scovell was invariably right when it came to strategy.

"Then we must find things out, mustn't we?" Jon said. "Here's what I suggest. Scovell, you should continue to explore your connections in the Navy, and in the Army, too, if you have them. Especially among the intelligence chaps. Despite what the government says about its lack of spies, we all know it has them."

Jon turned to Heathbrook. "You and I should root out the other détenus in London who spent at least eight years at Verdun.

Between us, we might be able to learn more about who could have betrayed us and why. The others might know something we couldn't possibly know, given that we never returned to Verdun after we were caught escaping."

"There are a number of books written by détenus and published here in London," Heathbrook said. "We should read those as well. You never know when a random comment might point toward something else the author isn't aware of."

"Good idea. And we should meet whenever you both are in town to compare notes." Jon rose. "One other thing. Do any of you know if that engraver, Beasley, who forged our French passports for our attempted escape, made it back to England? I'd like to ask him about something."

"He's living in Cheapside with his family at this address." Scovell jotted it on a piece of notepaper and handed it to Jon. "Heathbrook and I encountered him in a tavern not long ago and spent a pleasant two hours learning everything that happened in Verdun after we were sent off to Bitche. He said Sir Percy Tindale was rumored to have died in Arras, more's the pity."

"Damn," Jon said. "I hope rumor has it wrong." The baronet had been planning to escape with them until he'd been caught in an infraction by Courcelles two weeks beforehand and packed off to Arras as his punishment. "He might have overheard something from the gendarmes along his way."

"Beasley says they got rid of Courcelles not long after we left," Heathbrook added, "and the new fellow proved quite honorable."

"Yes, I heard that when I stopped there on my way to Paris." Jon tried not to show his chagrin. "We should have listened to Morris and just stayed where we were instead of attempting an escape."

"We didn't know that the war would end in three years," Heathbrook said. "No one did."

Heathbrook had a point, but it didn't assuage Jon's guilt. If they hadn't been sent to Bitche . . .

No point crying over spilled milk. "Well, gentlemen," he said, tucking the address in his pocket, "I must return to the house before I'm missed."

"You should," Heathbrook said. "You're starting to look peaked, old man."

"I'm starting to *feel* a bit peaked, to be honest." Jon paused to gaze at the two men. "But once I'm more myself and have had time to get some decent attire, I'd like to introduce you both to my family. You could come for dinner. I'm sure my mother would be delighted to meet you."

Heathbrook grinned. "I already met your charming mother when I delivered your letter. I also met your lovely and equally charming sister."

"Great!" Jon said, hiding his consternation at the idea of Heathbrook attracted to Chloe. The man had already been a budding rakehell when they'd arrived at Verdun. "She could use a decent suitor."

"Suitor!" Heathbrook said, clearly alarmed. "Bite your tongue. I've got some living to do before I get leg-shackled." When both Jon and Scovell laughed, Heathbrook scowled. "Well, I do."

"Don't worry," Jon said, not bothering to hide his relief. "She's dragging her feet a bit herself, so you're probably safe from Chloe."

He ought to tell them about Miss Morris, too, and his bargain with her. But something held him back. It seemed . . . private somehow.

Private? No, indeed. That sort of thinking would get him into trouble. He should just tell them. Be nonchalant. Explain the situation emotionlessly.

Yet, a while later when he and his friends parted, he had somehow not found a way to mention her after all.

Chapter 7

On his second night at home, Jon slept badly. The house was too quiet after all those years in Bitche, and despite his exhaustion, he kept thinking of more tasks he'd need to handle. Pursue the official naming of him as duke. Make courtesy visits to his late brother's employees to assess their circumstances. Go over the books with the accountants, Father's banker, and the land steward to determine the financial situation. Tour the dukedom's properties and consult with the estate managers to see what needed doing. And on and on.

He groaned. No one had ever prepared him for any of it, because no one had ever expected him to become duke.

Nor had he wanted to. Father's purpose in sending him on a grand tour was to knock the recklessness out of him, to make him a gentleman. But once Jon had ended up at Verdun, he'd chosen to learn skills that would make him useful to his father once they were released. He'd hoped to become an expert in legal issues or architecture or tenant management. He had read every book he could get his hands on in France. He'd learned a great deal.

Except what it would be like to run *everything*. It would be daunting—that much he was quickly discovering.

Somewhere near dawn, he fell asleep, only to be awakened a few hours later by one of his usual nightmares about Bitche. He lay there looking about his room, reminding himself he was home. By then, it was seven. Might as well begin his day. He rang for a servant, hoping for coffee. A short while later, Gibbons hurried in with a tray containing *The Times* and a coffee service.

"Forgive me for my lateness, Your Grace," the older man said, a hint of worry in his tone, "but yesterday you said to wake you at—"

"I know. I couldn't sleep."

"I'm very sorry to hear that. If you wish, I could make you a libation at bedtime that might help."

"It's worth a try," he said, though he doubted it would make a difference unless it could take over running the dukedom for him.

Sometime later, Jon entered the breakfast room, half-expecting to see Miss Morris there. But only Chloe was at the table, eating a slice of toast liberally spread with raspberry jam as she read one of the many gossip rags that had apparently bloomed in the city in his absence.

"I see you still have a fondness for sickeningly sweet preserves," he said as he filled his plate at the sideboard before taking a seat across from her.

"Doesn't everyone?"

"I prefer butter myself." He poured himself some tea, just to see if he liked it better now that he was home. "Where is Miss Morris?"

Chloe set her paper down to eye him closely. "Why do you ask?"

Because I have a lesson with her soon that I will have to cut short. "Merely curious."

"She's probably in the art room." Chloe shrugged as she returned to her paper.

"So we actually have an art room."

"Of course." With her eyes still fixed on her reading, she pointed vaguely up at the ceiling. "It's what used to be the schoolroom."

He ate quickly in silence, then rose to leave.

"She'll like you better if you bring her a piece of that plum cake," Chloe said.

"Who?" he asked, playing dumb. "Mother?"

Chloe rolled her eyes at him. "Tory."

"What makes you think I'm going to see *her* and not Mother?"

His sister chuckled. "I noticed how thunderstruck you were when you first saw my governess."

Damn. "You're imagining things."

"If you say so." Chloe continued to smile. "But if it helps, she has that effect on most men who meet her."

It didn't help one whit. He hated the idea of men leering at her. She deserved better. He would make sure she found someone better to marry, too, even if he had to go to every blasted Society event Mother drummed up between now and the end of the Season.

God, how the thought of that tired him.

"Any other words of wisdom for me?" he drawled.

Chloe suddenly grew serious. "Be careful with Tory. She's lost so much. If you don't intend to stay around, don't get close to her."

"Why would I not stay around?" he asked, taken aback.

"I don't know." She stared up at him. "I get the feeling you have plans you're not telling us about."

Chloe had grown perceptive in the years since he'd seen her. Now she waited as if to see if he'd share. Little did she know, he was not the sharing kind. He'd learned not to be in Verdun. When he merely stared back, she sighed. "I don't wish to see her hurt."

"Miss Morris is the last person in the world I would hurt," he clipped out. "I owe her father more than you can imagine, and I'm not about to repay his kindness by injuring his daughter."

"Good. She's going with us to the theater tomorrow night, you know."

"Is she?" He'd rather hoped she would be.

"Do *try* not to curse and say vulgar things." Chloe eyed him over the top of her newspaper. "I'd like you to make a good impression. On the duke and duchess, I mean."

"I'll do my best. Tell me, is it Miss Morris that has had this apparently sudden effect on your manners or are you up to something?"

"Don't be ridiculous. Of course, I'd like you to impress the Grenwoods. You could use some friends."

"I *have* friends."

"Who are probably just as ill-mannered as you." She returned to her gossip rag.

With a shake of his head, he started to leave, then paused at the sideboard. He placed a slice of plum cake on a plate and poured a cup of tea, adding sugar to it in the off chance that Miss Morris liked her tea sweet, as his mother did. He might need to bribe the young woman with breakfast just to soften her temper when he told her he couldn't stay long.

He turned to find Chloe watching him with raised eyebrows. "For Mother," he said.

"Uh-huh." His sister's musical laugh followed him down the hall.

It took him some time to reach the art room while juggling dishes, but he was pleased he'd taken the trouble when he looked inside to find Miss Morris standing in the center of the room, still dressed in mourning black. The light pouring from a large window at the other end of the room showed her in profile, and he was struck once again by her elegant but shapely figure.

Then he groaned, remembering his sister's words about Miss Morris's effect on men. And the woman was worried about finding a husband? They'd find *her*, and probably in droves.

Miss Morris frowned as her teeth worried her lower lip, and he had the perverse urge to go soothe the poor abraded flesh with his mouth, then kiss away her displeasure.

He shook off that unsettling thought. *Remember, you're trying to help her, not upset her life . . . or your own.* The last thing she needed was a physical wreck of a man for a husband. And the last thing *he* needed was to court a woman when the weight of a dukedom had just been dropped onto his shoulders. He had enough to do right now.

At that moment, she looked over and spotted him. "There you are!" Her frown vanished. "I thought for sure you'd forgotten. Or overslept. Which would be perfectly understandable under the circumstances but . . ."

"I brought you breakfast in case you hadn't had any," he put in, not wanting her to speculate further on what might be *understandable under the circumstances.*

"Oh! How kind." She took the cup and saucer and the plate he offered and set them down on a little table. "I . . . um . . . had breakfast earlier."

"Ah." Now he felt foolish. A pox on Chloe for her ill-considered matchmaking.

Then he caught Miss Morris's furtive look at the plate. "Although I do love plum cake." Removing one black glove, she broke off a piece of the cake and ate it, bliss spreading over her features. "And your cook makes a very good one."

"I agree. The tea isn't bad, either."

She lifted an eyebrow. "Coming from someone who doesn't like tea, that's high praise." Dutifully, she took a sip. "But I'm afraid we can't linger." Picking up a nearby leather satchel, she looped the strap over her shoulder. "The British Museum opens soon, and we'll need every bit of our available time to tour it."

Uh-oh. "Why are we touring a museum?"

"Because this particular museum contains a wealth of sculpture, which enables me to point out techniques and you to gain inspiration for your own piece."

He stifled a groan. "I saw plenty of sculptures in France before we were taken prisoner."

"I doubt Father knew enough about technique to speak of it intelligently." When he hesitated, she added, "See here, I'm doing *my* part by going to the theater with the duke and duchess tomorrow night, so you must do yours."

"Ah, but that won't expose you to eligible men."

"Of course it will. Chloe *always* draws eligible men to her, wherever she goes. Your mother makes sure of it." After pausing to eat another bite of cake, she pulled on her glove. "So, we're off to the museum."

Damn. The woman had clearly seized the bit between her teeth.

She headed for the door. "And we should probably go down the servants' stairs and through the garden to the mews. It wouldn't do for anyone, like our neighbors, to see us leave the house together unchaperoned."

"Or my mother, for that matter, who doesn't know of this arrangement." He eyed her closely. "Unless you happened to tell her? Or Chloe?"

Two spots of color appeared on her cheeks. "Did *you?*"

He opted for the truth. "And give the scheming little matchmakers grist for the mill? I think not."

"Because you know what they'd make of it," she said, looking a bit too relieved for his pride. "Us having such a bargain, I mean."

"I do know." He shrugged. "If they happen to find out, so be it, but best not to encourage them."

She brightened. "Exactly. Or anyone else."

"Right." As they walked toward the back stairs, he asked, "What's in the satchel?"

"Sketchbooks."

That explained why the blasted thing was nearly half her size. "At least let me carry the bag."

"Certainly." She handed it to him. "Thank you."

"Good God," he said as he hoisted it over his shoulder. How could such a petite woman haul around anything so heavy? "How many sketchbooks do you have in here, anyway?"

"Only two, although they're rather large. But I also have pencils and a book on drawing figures, and a few other things. It's always good to be prepared."

"For what?"

She flashed him a knowing look. "You'll see."

Damn. What had he let himself in for?

Tory rarely encountered anyone she knew in the museum, especially this early when most people in good society were still abed. So she was fervently hoping no one would be here to wonder who her companion was.

Nonetheless, she'd chosen her attire carefully. Combined with the mourning ring on her left ring finger, her black gown gave the impression she was lamenting a late husband. Which meant that her accompanying a man without a chaperone wouldn't raise an eyebrow.

For all people knew, Falconridge could be her brother. He hadn't appeared in Society yet since his return, and she sincerely doubted that anyone who'd known him eleven years ago would recognize him. Besides, most art lovers were probably at the Royal Academy of Arts exhibition, since it had recently opened for the summer.

Sure enough, the halls were bereft of people. She and the duke made their way with ease to the place where the Greek and Roman marbles were exhibited. But when they entered the sculpture gallery, he muttered a curse and pivoted to step in front of her and block her way.

"What on earth are you doing?" she snapped, attempting to get past him.

He grabbed her arm to halt her. "I'm trying to protect your innocent eyes. The statue behind me is of a man with no clothes."

The outrage in his voice made her laugh. "I know. It's the Discobolus. I've viewed the discus thrower at least fifty times and sketched it more than once. How else am I to learn male anatomy?" Pulling free of him, she rounded him to approach the six-foot-high sculpture.

"Good God," the duke muttered as he whirled to follow her. "Does my mother know of your interest in such salacious subjects?"

"Probably not." She smirked at him. "If it makes you feel any better, I don't bring Chloe to this part of the museum when we come here."

"I should hope not." He viewed the statue closely. "Although I'm not sure you should use this as an example of male anatomy. Few gentlemen have muscles as pronounced as this fellow. Besides, he's missing a . . . er . . . key portion of his anatomy. It appears to have been lopped off."

"I realize that."

Now he looked shocked. "You've seen that portion of a man's anatomy?"

She could feel the heat rise in her cheeks. "Not in real life, of course. But this isn't the only naked male statue in the British Museum. The Greeks and Romans were quite fond of those. If you'd like to see the others to compare their private parts to this one . . ." She gave him a cheeky grin.

"Very funny," he said in that dry tone of his.

"But I wasn't coming in here to show you the Discobolus, anyway. I had another sculpture in mind." She continued on until she came to one of the collection's most famous pieces—the Bust of Clytie.

Before she could launch into her description of its merits, the duke said, "I know this sculpture." He glanced at her, frowning. "I saw it at Charles Townley's house once. Did he donate it to the museum?"

"Actually, his family sold his entire collection of sculptures to the museum for twenty thousand pounds after he died."

"Charles Townley is dead?" He stared at the sculpture. "When? How?"

"I don't know the how, but it happened a few years after you left for France."

A ragged breath escaped him. "I wonder how many people of my acquaintance died while I was gone."

His wistful tone broke her heart. "I imagine there were quite a few. You were away for many years."

He nodded absently, but she noticed he still looked pensive.

She wished she dared take his hand to comfort him, but settled for saying, "To be fair, Charles Townley was nearly seventy when he passed away, so he did live long enough to travel some of the world and collect many antiquities."

For some reason, that made him smile at her. "You probably consider that the epitome of a life well-lived."

She avoided his too-perceptive gaze. "It's the epitome of *one* life well-lived. For me, a well-lived life would include being known for carving a highly regarded bust or inspiring women artists or teaching the next great Anne Seymour Damer. She has a bronze portrait bust of Sir Joseph Banks here in the museum, you know."

"I did not know."

The wry amusement in his voice stung. "Please do not laugh at me."

"Forgive me. I'm not laughing, I swear." When he sounded genuinely apologetic, she looked over to find him regarding her with a serious gaze. "I'm merely marveling at how sculpting can mean so much to you. I walked through Townley's house of sculptures years ago without paying them any mind."

"Stab me through the heart, why don't you?" she said lightly. "How could you not notice them? Sculpture is...is..." She turned to the Bust of Clytie, realizing it was probably better to illustrate her feelings than try to describe them. "Do you know the story of Clytie?"

He eyed her askance. "Your father taught me classical literature for years. What do *you* think?" When she just kept staring at him, he drew himself up to recite in the pedantic tone of a lecturer, "Clytie was a water nymph who fell in love with the sun god Helios. He didn't love her, and when she couldn't gain his affections by ridding him of the woman he did love, Clytie just stared at him from the ground every day until she turned into a heliotrope."

"It's a bit more complicated than that, but that description will do. Now, what do you see when you look at this bust of her?"

"A woman's head and scantily clad bosom emerging from a bunch of petals."

Scantily clad bosom? Good Lord, he was such a *man*. But if he was expecting to make her blush again, he didn't know her at all. "Her head, neck, shoulders, and draped bosom, yes. Rising from a flower."

"A heliotrope."

"Some experts question whether the flower is actually a heliotrope."

"Huh," he said, glancing at the petals. "Aren't heliotropes those purple blooms with all the tiny petals? Because if so, this doesn't look like one."

"No, it does not. And Townley variously called it a lotus blossom and a sunflower. Which is odd, since they didn't have sunflowers in ancient Greece. But that's neither here nor there. How would you describe Clytie's expression?"

This time he examined the sculpture more closely. "Doleful?"

"I would call it 'yearning' but that's fine. How does the artist, whoever he was, demonstrate her dolefulness?"

"No idea."

She sighed. The duke was going to make her pull this out of him, wasn't he? "Fine. How would you describe her chin?"

That brought him up short. "Her chin? I don't know. Pugnacious?"

"What makes you say so?"

The duke thrust out his own chin. "It looks like Chloe's as a girl when she was preparing to dig in her heels."

"Good." Time to put him out of his misery, since he clearly disliked the Socratic method of teaching. "Clytie won't give Helios up, even though she knows he has no interest in her, yet her down-turned lips show she despairs of him. Her head is tilted, as she follows his path through the sky each day and—"

"—her eyes have the vacant look of someone doing the same thing over and over even though the act no longer has any real meaning," he said thoughtfully. "She truly has become the flower, whichever one it is."

"Yes!" She beamed at him. "Very good."

He gave an elaborate bow. "Happy to please, madam. Does this mean I shall earn high marks in your class?"

She met his sarcasm with sarcasm. "Only if you bring an apple for the teacher tomorrow."

"I brought you plum cake. That should count."

"I suppose it'll do . . . for now."

"It'll have to do," he said, clearly fighting a smile. "It's not apple season."

"You're a duke," she said dryly. "Surely you can find an apple out of season." Then she groaned. "Not that I'm suggesting you should. I can wait until apple season. That is . . . I didn't mean you ever have to give me—"

"Don't worry. I understood you were making a joke." He stared at the bust, and mused aloud, "I wonder why Townley used to call the sculpture his 'wife.' She's missing over half a body. Or was he just wanting a woman who would do no more than bask in his shining glory?"

The remark startled her. "Townley really called her his wife?"

"He did. Or so I was told by the scores of art students who visited his house. I never heard him do so myself, but I only went there once, to see his Venus."

"That's here in the museum, too."

"Is it?" Suddenly alert, he looked around. "Where?"

She frowned. "You just want to view it because she's half-naked."

"What?" he said in mock outrage. "I am deeply interested in the art of sculpture. Can't you tell?"

"Oh, yes, it's been quite apparent."

"You got to see a naked man," he pointed out, "so I should get to view a half-naked woman, at the very least."

"You're already viewing a partially naked woman," she said, reproaching him. "And you're missing the point I'm making about sculpture. It presents more than just people who are pretty to look at. It captures the nuances of how people *feel*—what makes them yearn, what turns them petty, who inspires them. It illuminates the human condition."

"Ah," he said, although she could see he still didn't quite understand why that mattered.

That made sense. He might not have become duke until now, but he'd always had the cushion of his father's dukedom to break his fall.

Well, except in France. But surely the memories of that would fade as he became comfortable with the privileges of being duke. Before that happened, she should try her best to instill in him the importance of allowing for people's feelings, especially those of the people beneath him.

If he would even listen. He was doing this only to fulfill the obligation of getting her a husband.

She sighed. "Let's move on."

They continued around the gallery as she pointed out various sculptures that provoked thought. They were about to leave the room when a certain booming voice assaulted her ears.

She froze. Of all the people to show up here...Mr. Dixon. Why, she barely saw him in her neighborhood, much less out in town. "This way," she hissed, and tried to tug the duke through some curtains covering a doorway that led to an upcoming exhibit.

He resisted. "What are you doing?" he asked, at least having the good sense to whisper.

"I can't encounter that fellow entering the gallery. Please..."

Letting her pull him through the curtains, he slipped with her into a small, unlit room where sculptures lay under drop cloths.

They could hear Mr. Dixon's voice even in there. "This is the famous Bust of Clytie," Mr. Dixon announced in his pompous voice. "Note her petulant expression, typical of a woman who couldn't get her way and chose to pout about it."

While his companions laughed, Tory bristled at the man's flippant characterization, even though there was some truth to it.

Falconridge bent to whisper in her ear, "Who is this arse?"

"A neighbor who once taught me about sculpture," she

breathed, drawing him deeper into the little room. Did she imagine that he stiffened a bit?

"A friend?" he asked.

"Until he forced a kiss on me," she muttered.

Even in the dimness, she could see his outraged expression. "Forced a—"

She covered his mouth with her hand. *"He must not discover us in here."*

When he nodded, she removed her hand, but not before the warmth of his breath on her palm sent a strange excitement down her spine. Heavens.

Meanwhile, Mr. Dixon droned on. "I used to know a sculptress in my neighborhood who fancied me in much the same fashion as Clytie did Helios."

What? The audacity of the man!

She lunged forward, ready to throttle him for lying, but Falconridge drew her back against him and held her still.

To her mortification, Mr. Dixon went on. "I had to be firm with her, explain that my wife needed me."

The duke's arm tightened about her waist. "He was *married,* for God's sake?" he hissed in her ear.

"Shh!" she said, a bit too loudly.

Mr. Dixon quieted. "Did you hear something?"

The chorus of voices that answered him in the negative made her groan inwardly. He was telling this fairy tale to all of them!

Fortunately, the group moved on down the gallery as Mr. Dixon continued spouting his ridiculous opinions about art and sculpture and women. She and Falconridge stood motionless until the voices faded enough to convince her that they'd passed into the next gallery.

She slipped from the duke's arms. "How I loathe that man," she grumbled.

"I couldn't tell."

Her gaze flew to him. "You didn't believe him, did you? About me having a fancy for him?"

"I expect you have better taste in gentlemen. Besides, the men who brag the most about their conquests are generally the ones with the least to brag about." He eyed her closely. "But I must ask—is he the reason you don't wish to marry?"

"Of course not!"

He arched an eyebrow.

"All right. Partly."

"Because he 'forced' a kiss on you," the duke said.

"He didn't do it right off, mind you. To be honest, when I met him initially, I was a bit starstruck. After all, he has exhibited at the Royal Academy more than once. So, I thought him very kind because he deigned to explain aspects of sculpting to me."

"Did you know then that he was married?"

"Certainly. As I said, he—and his wife—lived in the neighborhood. I had already met her—she was expecting, I should point out. My previous encounters with him had been perfectly innocent. So when he . . . er . . . insisted on kissing me in his workroom, he utterly shocked me."

Falconridge's intent gaze was fixed on her face. "What did you do?"

"I resisted, of course, but he was very strong. Fortunately, nearby sat a bucket of soapy water he was using to wash the marble dust from his latest work." She tipped up her chin. "I . . . um . . . grabbed it and poured it over his head, then shoved him off me."

The duke laughed. "Of course, you did."

His laughter provoked her own. At the time, she hadn't been amused one whit, especially since the soapy water splashed on her, too, but now that she remembered it without her haze of anger, Mr. Dixon had looked rather comical with marble dust all over him.

After a moment, the duke asked, "Was it his lack of fidelity to his wife that put you off of marriage or was it the kiss itself?"

Strangely enough, in this dim and secretive little room full of covered sculptures, it seemed somehow natural to be honest. "Both, I suppose. Still, I've been kissed a few times since, and I don't understand the appeal."

He looked astounded. "You're basing your opinion on a handful of kisses? Perhaps you haven't been kissed by the right man. Or at least not by one who knew what he was doing. You might be swearing off marriage for no good reason."

Since her lack of enthusiasm for kissing wasn't her main reason for not marrying—which she also couldn't tell him—she could hardly argue his point. "What do you suggest, Your Grace?" she snapped. "That I kiss every man I meet until I have sufficient experience to confirm my opinion?"

"Why not? I'd be happy to offer my services." Then he grimaced. "God, I can't believe I said that aloud."

She chuckled. "I can. It's the sort of thing you seem to say. Fortunately for you, I know you didn't mean it, and—"

His sudden kiss took her by surprise. But not the way Mr. Dixon's had. The duke's felt non-threatening, as if he were giving her a chance to protest at any moment.

Yet he kissed her unlike any man had done before. His kiss was soft but direct, gentle but surprisingly thrilling, too. None of the other men's kisses had been thrilling. Then again, she hadn't liked the men very well, either. She rather liked Falconridge. When he wasn't being officious and overbearing, that is.

Once he drew back, far too quickly, she touched her fingers to her lips where they tingled. Like other places in her body just now. That made no sense. Why him? Why did it have to be *him*—a man so far beyond her station—who did this to her?

"Well?" he asked in a rumbling voice that resonated throughout her body. She instantly forgot he could be officious and overbearing.

"That was hardly long enough for me to form an opinion," she said truthfully.

He narrowed his gaze on her. "I can remedy that, if you wish."

Without thinking, she said, "Can you, indeed?"

Apparently, he took that for a sort of challenge, because to her surprise—and secret delight—he caught her to him with one hand, while his other cupped her chin so he could kiss her again.

This kiss wasn't quick. Or direct. It was more . . . sensual. He was tender and rough by turns, his lips playing with hers, then seizing hers, then doing both all over again.

She couldn't breathe, yet the scent of his spicy cologne engulfed her. Couldn't catch her bearings, yet his arm around her made her feel safe.

What a heady sensation. She slipped her arms about his waist and leaned up against his solid chest. Apparently taking that as encouragement, he angled his mouth over hers and delved between her lips lightly with his tongue.

Oh, dear Lord, how that made her blood roar in her ears. No one had ever kissed her that way. It both shocked and emboldened her. She touched her tongue with his, and with a groan, he caught her head between his large hands and began to kiss her in the most erotic fashion she'd ever encountered.

So, with her heart doing flips in her chest, she gave herself up to it.

Chapter 8

Jon told himself he was merely giving her more experience with men, tempting her into considering marriage as her father had desired. But he was lying to himself. He'd wanted to do this from the first moment he'd seen her.

He only hoped his skills weren't too rusty. Because her innocent responses entranced him even more than he'd expected. He couldn't seem to stop himself. He just kept kissing her soft, yielding lips, anchoring her luscious body to his, and reveling in the pleasures of her. He wanted to explore her, to peel off her dull black gown and worship every inch of her body with his mouth. She tasted like plums, sweet and succulent and ripe for the taking.

No taking allowed, he reminded himself.

But with her supple body pressed to his, her breasts practically imprinting themselves on his chest, he wanted desperately to fill his hands with that plump flesh and show her—

He forced his mouth from hers. "We must stop this," he breathed. It was downright dangerous, especially given how long he'd been without a woman. Besides, he was supposed to be helping her, not thinking of ways to seduce her.

A sigh escaped her. "Yes." Leaving his arms, she drew back to smooth her gown. "Forgive me, for . . . for—"

"Letting me kiss you so thoroughly? I won't forgive you for that. Not when I enjoyed it so very much." He wondered if she was blushing. He couldn't tell in the dim light, but he could imagine it—the swift pinkening of her cheeks as warmth climbed through her.

Or perhaps that was just wishful thinking.

Her eyes gleamed up at him. "I enjoyed it, too, I must confess. Thank you for the . . . er . . . lesson, Duke."

"Come now, given what we've been doing, surely you can call me Jon, at least in private."

She averted her gaze. "We shouldn't be in private again."

"It's unavoidable. Our lessons will be private. And surely, we'll encounter each other in the house from time to time."

"Very well . . . Jon," she said softly. "Under such circumstances, you may call me Tory." Then she released a shuddery breath that made him want to kiss her once more. "But not around Chloe or your mother. They'll read too much into it."

Oh, they definitely would, damn their eyes. "Still, *Tory*, it was nothing more than a kiss between friends. A lesson, as you say, in kissing." One he wished he could repeat over and over.

God save him.

"Of course," she said with an overbright smile. "A very good lesson, so there's no reason to have another."

Wasn't there?

No. He was doomed if he kissed her again. Another kiss and he could never go back to thinking of her as Morris's daughter, a woman he was supposed to be helping to a better husband.

In any case, he dared not start a dalliance with his sister's governess. And a dalliance was all it could be until he had his life more settled. Perhaps not even then. Because how could he be sure that once she knew everything about what had happened in France, she wouldn't hate him for taking her father from her, in more ways than one?

"So, we're agreed," he said. "We mustn't let this happen again."

"We mustn't," she echoed, still not looking at him. "Besides, as pleasurable as your kisses were, they haven't changed my mind about marriage. I still would rather have my school for artists."

Pleasurable, she called them. Not *irresistible*. Not even *exciting*.

He groaned. So much for tempting her. Although that was how it should be. Better that she be tempted by the man who *would* convince her to marry. It couldn't be him, mustn't be him.

"In any case, my encounters with Mr. Dixon make me fear that many men are incapable of fidelity." Tory glanced at the curtain. "Thankfully, I think he is long gone now."

"And if he isn't," Jon said in a hard voice, "I might take the opportunity to knock him down a peg." If only for making her doubt men's fidelity.

"My word, don't do anything like that," she said, wide-eyed in alarm. "It would merely rouse his suspicions about what's going on between you and me."

Of course. "Then I will restrain myself. But only because you ask it."

"Thank you," she said, looking bemused.

He walked toward the curtain and glanced out, disappointed that no one was around. Right now, he wanted nothing more than to take out his frustrations on Dixon. "It appears the coast is clear." He offered her his arm. "Shall we go?"

Hesitantly, she took his arm. "Of course."

After that, there was no more discussion about kisses and Dixon and why she didn't want to marry.

He fought the urge to pull out his pocket watch and check the time. He ought to make an excuse for why they should leave early. He had to visit the détenu forger, so he could, with any luck, get the codicil work accomplished before meeting with her solicitor.

But he was loath to end their morning. She'd seemed so delighted to be teaching him about sculpting that he hated to spoil her fun, especially after that arse Dixon had said such asinine things about her.

Especially after Jon himself had kissed her so audaciously, knowing he had no right to do so.

Instead, he let her take him through the Townley gallery. She said little at first, obviously still uncertain of her footing with him. But he asked questions, and she soon warmed to her topic.

She pointed out different mediums of sculpting—bronze, marble, and terra-cotta—then expounded on how they would be approached by the artist, and which was most effective for which subject. She talked about themes and techniques and tools.

To his surprise, she proved quite knowledgeable about her craft. From the way his mother had spoken of her interests, Jon had assumed she was more of a dilettante. Clearly, that wasn't the case.

"Do you have a preferred medium for sculpting?" he asked. "Or a preferred subject?"

"I like bronzes, but they're expensive to create, so I generally have to settle for marble. As for subjects, rather than sculpting the usual busts of famous people, I prefer sculpting ordinary people in motion: a mother cooking, a child with a ball, men boxing . . . things like that."

Until she'd said *men boxing*, he'd assumed her subjects were all domestic. Apparently not.

"What about you?" she asked. "What subjects do you think would interest you?"

"I haven't considered that. Something simple, probably, like an object. A pitcher or a bench. Or perhaps an animal, like a horse."

She smiled. "I know just the thing. But before we start on a piece, you must first try your hand at sketching."

He eyed her warily. "Why?"

"So you can sketch your object in preparation for sculpting it. It will give you a sort of blueprint for the piece, an idea of how you wish to proceed. That's what the sketchbooks are for. Have you ever done any sketching?"

He gave her a hard look. "Once again, remember who served as my tutor. Sketching existing works of art or landscapes is part of what every chap does on the grand tour. Especially in places like the Louvre." He paused to say acidly, "Or, as the emperor renamed it, '*Musée Napoléon.*'"

She blinked at him. "You've been to the Louvre? How fortunate! I would love to visit it."

"Not now, you wouldn't. France is still in too much of an uproar for that. Don't make the mistake I did, of thinking that the war was over when it was merely in a lull."

"I couldn't make that mistake even if I wanted to." She flashed him a thin smile. "I could never afford to visit France. Besides, no respectable woman travels alone, so I would have to find someone to travel with me."

An enticing image of him and her on a ship headed to Italy or Egypt or Greece, assailed him before he squelched it. He was never leaving England again. France had destroyed his desire to travel after it cut him off from his family.

Unaware of the ridiculous wanderings of his thoughts, Tory halted in front of a fairly simple sphinx figure, then took the satchel from him with a grin. "This is both an animal of sorts *and* an object, since Townley claimed it was originally used as a support for a candelabrum." She pulled out a sketchbook. "You could draw it in preparation for making a copy."

"I could never create a sculpture that elaborate," he said truthfully. "I don't have the skill." For one thing, the sphinx bore the head of a woman, and he feared he wasn't ready for sculpting a face. He could barely envision sculpting a table.

Tory looked as if she was about to answer when a shaft of sunlight came through the window and shone right in her face. She stopped and stared, then turned to him with a panicked look. "What time is it?"

He pulled out his pocket watch. "About ten minutes till eleven. Why?"

"Eleven!" Tory said to him, her eyes wide. "We have to go. We have to go *now*."

"Again, why?"

Stuffing the sketchbook into the satchel, she looped the strap over her shoulder and headed for the door. "I'm so sorry, but I promised your mother and Chloe that I would join them to go to the dressmaker's at 11 AM. Apparently, I need gowns for this . . . introduction into society that you're insisting on."

Taking the satchel from her, he strode beside her, annoyed that *she* was the one putting an end to their lesson and not him after he'd chosen to stay. "I seem to recall your saying something about not allowing interruptions and the like. I suppose you mean to follow that rule only when *I* wish to interrupt our lessons."

She must have heard the irritation in his voice, for she shot him an arch look. "Absolutely, at least in cases involving my 'Season.'

After all, it wasn't *my* idea to be presented in polite society. And gowns do not make themselves overnight, you know."

She had a point, which made him even more disgruntled. "Neither do sculptures," he grumbled.

Lifting her gaze heavenward, she said, "Oh, for pity's sake, do not pretend you wanted to be here. Now you can hurry off to do your more important duke business."

Had he wanted to be here? No. Was he glad he'd come? Yes. Because talking to her was nothing like talking to anyone else. He could be himself around her.

And kissing her . . .

No, kissing her had been a mistake. Not one he regretted, but a mistake, nonetheless.

Why was he even arguing with her about cutting their time short, anyway? He did have a great deal to do, after all. "Very well," he said evenly, "I shall accompany you home and then head off to do my 'duke' business." My mountains of "duke" business.

The very thought of it made him tired.

"You needn't accompany me," she said. "I walk to and from the museum by myself all the—"

"That is not negotiable," he said firmly. "Your father would turn over in his grave if he thought I'd even consider it."

They headed for the entrance to the museum in silence. After they got out into the sunshine, however, she said, "You and Papa were close, I take it."

A sudden thickness clogged Jon's throat. "At the end, he said he considered me as the son he never had."

She shot him a sharp glance, the color draining from her face. "What is it?" he asked.

Jerking her gaze from him, she hastened her steps. "Nothing. He always wanted a son. He never was quite sure what to do with a daughter."

"Oh, but you and your mother were all he spoke of at the end," he said gently. "He didn't know she was dead, of course. I'm sure if he had, he would have been even more insistent that I help you to a good husband."

A sigh escaped her. "Probably. And of course, he chose you to oversee that endeavor precisely because he saw you as a son, a sort of brother for me, the kind who looks after his sister."

God, he didn't feel remotely like Tory's brother and doubted he ever could. Not when the very nearness of her made him wish he didn't have to spend his time elsewhere this afternoon. "Then he would be disappointed, since I cannot see you as a sister."

That apparently startled her into laughing. "I should hope not, given how you kissed me. If you ever kissed Chloe like that—"

"Don't even think it," Jon said with a shudder. "Seriously, though, I promise to be more circumspect in the future."

"Now, *I'm* disappointed. I like when you're less than circumspect." When he shot her a glance, she groaned. "I-I didn't mean . . ."

"Why, Tory Morris," he said, "are you flirting with me?"

She gave him a considering look. "Of course. I need the practice if I am to make my grand debut in society and snag a spouse as you and Papa want," she said bitterly. She swished ahead of him, looking for all the world like a snooty lady of rank. "And who else can I practice upon?"

God help him. If she started honing her feminine wiles on *him*, she'd have him kneeling at her feet in a matter of days and throwing caution to the winds.

"*Although* . . . Given how you three ladies keep protesting my ill manners and my language, I suppose I could use the practice, too." He flashed her a dark glance. "Not in flirtation, mind you. But in polite society discourse."

"Excellent idea. I'm a governess, after all. If I can't help you mend your ways, who can?" She lifted her chin. "We shall start at the first ball we attend. That will give me something to do while I'm waiting around for gentlemen to ask me to dance."

He seriously doubted she'd be waiting around for dance partners, but she'd find that out for herself soon enough.

She halted two blocks from the house. "And here, Jon, we must part ways, so we don't enter together." With a smile, she held out her hand for her satchel, which he gave her grudgingly. "Besides, you have things to do, I'm sure. And if you need a horse or carriage, you can dart back to the mews from here to get one from the sta—From *your* stables."

"Very well." He bowed. "Then I'll see you at dinner tonight."
Consternation filled her face. "You won't, actually. Friday is my night off. I spend that evening at the cottage."

"By yourself?" That seemed odd, but he wasn't quite sure why it bothered him. Perhaps it was the way she was acting. Bitche had taught him to notice when something was off in a person. Or perhaps he just couldn't trust anyone after what had happened in France.

"I . . . er . . . have a servant who comes in." She smiled. "I create my sculptures in my workroom."

"You don't have to do your sculptures there," he said to see how she reacted. "You can bring them to the art room. I'll make sure you have everything you need to do your work. Just give me a list—"

"Jon," she said firmly, "I like to work there. I can be alone and uninterrupted. Mrs. Gully gives me dinner, cleans up, and stays with me, while I get a night to myself." She turned toward the house. "I'll see you in the morning."

"All right." He was probably imagining that her night off was odd. Still, after spending so many years alone in a cell with Morris, he couldn't imagine wanting to be alone in a cottage with a servant. He might feel the weight of the dukedom on his shoulders, but he was still glad to be with his family.

Then again, she wasn't *with* her family. She had no family anymore, partly thanks to him.

As she walked away, he called after her, "I'll watch to make sure you get inside safely."

"If you insist," she said with a shake of her head. "But I promise I am perfectly safe in Mayfair, especially dressed like this."

Then she marched down the street. He watched her go with an unfamiliar tightness in his chest. It wasn't just that she was beautiful, or that he was even looking forward to tomorrow night when he'd finally get to see her in something other than black.

No. When she was around, she made him feel alive again, which he hadn't felt in a long time.

All those years at Bitche, he'd had invisible burdens weighing him down. Always having to watch one's back. Constant worry about Morris's health. His own fear over what was happening to his family back in England. There'd also been the anger over his and his friends' unfair situation, the fear that they'd never make it out alive, and the sheer drudgery of days spent trying to keep themselves rested and fed, a nearly impossible task.

Being back in England had lifted that particular weight, but his new situation had given him other burdens. Yet today, when he'd talked to her and witnessed her enthusiasm for her art, when they'd kissed and flirted . . . he'd felt free, if only for a short while.

It made him wish he *could* marry her. But once he told her about her father, *everything* about her father, including the fact that Morris had probably been unfaithful to her mother with some young Frenchwoman—she would surely resent him for taking her father away from her and for showing her Morris's true colors.

No, he mustn't ever tell her those particular suspicions. That would hurt her deeply, he suspected.

He watched her enter Falcon House. Then he headed for the mews. Time to go see his man Beasley. The sooner he could get that codicil matter worked out for her father's solicitor, the sooner he could get her married off to someone she liked.

Too bad it wouldn't be him.

Chapter 9

It was nearly eight when Tory hurried from the Falconridge mansion, heading for the cottage where she spent as much time as possible. She still could hardly believe she was to have a full wardrobe of lovely gowns, with shoes, reticules, bonnets, and jewelry to match.

Well, *some* of the latter would be hers. Some would be borrowed from Chloe. But not the shoes. Tory's feet were far too small for that.

Still, the idea of having Jon see her in one of those new, gorgeous gowns sent a dart of excitement through her. She was woman enough to want to impress him. Especially after their kisses.

No, she wouldn't think of *those* right now, or Mrs. Gully would surely read her feelings from her face.

It wasn't long before she was approaching her dear home. The cottage might not be in the finest part of town, although Falcon House was a mere mile away, but the area was respectable, full of tradesmen and merchants and their families. Besides, everyone was aware of her position with the Duchess of Falconridge and her daughter, so they treated her with respect.

And if a ruffian did happen to accost her, one of the men at the nearby coffeehouse invariably sent him packing. It rarely happened, thankfully, but she was grateful to the fellows who treated her like one of their own and looked out for her during her comings and goings.

She opened the cottage door and raced inside, grateful to see Mrs. Gully waiting patiently. It was Mrs. Gully's night off, too, after all.

"I'm sorry I'm late." Tory took off her coat and hung it on the coat rack. Reluctant to reveal she was having a partial Season, with a full new wardrobe and everything, Tory decided not to mention it at all. Mrs. Gully would find it highly suspicious. "The duchess talked my ear off. I thought I would never be allowed to leave."

"Do tell," Mrs. Gully said with a smile as she kneaded bread. "What's Her Grace doing this week?"

"Well," Tory said, "with the duke home, she's beside herself."

Mrs. Gully paused in her kneading. "I heard His Nibs finally arrived. What's he like? Is he as full of hisself as his half brothers was?"

"I'm not sure yet. Sometimes he is. But sometimes he can be quite friendly." When he was kissing her especially. "Unless he's talking about his imprisonment in France. Then he appears more sad than anything, I suppose you'd say. He doesn't seem to have had a good time of it there. Also, he could use some of that excellent bread you're planning to bake in the morning."

"A thin one, is he?" Mrs. Gully said.

"Not by choice, I don't think. But I'll tell you all about it tomorrow before I leave. I know you're chafing to get home to your new husband tonight, so you can go see the reenactment of the Battle of Trafalgar in Hyde Park."

"Pish, George can wait. We still have time."

George Gully was Mrs. Gully's third husband. She'd buried two before. And she'd been with the Morris family through all three marriages. Tory didn't know what she'd do without her.

"Do y'know what my daft husband said to me the other day?" Mrs. Gully went on. "He thinks we should get ourselves a cow. And who does he think would milk it? I ain't touchin' any cow teats, that's for sure. I'll buy milk like everybody else. A cow, for pity's sake." She shook her head as she placed the ball of dough into a pan and put it in a cool spot to rise slowly overnight. "Where would we even keep it? And who's goin' to clean up after it?"

"It doesn't sound terribly practical," Tory ventured.

"No, indeed."

"I want a cow," a voice came from the doorway. "To ride."

"There's my dear boy!" Tory said, as her brother, Cyril, barreled toward her and threw one arm about her waist while clutching the remnant of his favorite old blanket in the other. He was already tall enough that his forehead touched her chin.

"The lad was so restless today," Mrs. Gully murmured. "I could hardly get him to take his bath."

The eleven-year-old had the mind of a boy of five, which sometimes made rearing him difficult. Mrs. Gully always said he was too big for his brain, but she was still clearly as fond of him as Tory was.

"I was waiting for you, Sissy!" Cyril looked up at her, his blue eyes alight with his usual exuberance. "I caught a butterfly. Want to see?"

She ruffled his blond curls. "Of course."

Cyril ran into his bedroom—he never walked anywhere—and came back without the blanket and with a glass jar in both hands. He pointed to the piece of cheesecloth tied over the top with a string. "To help it breathe. Like me!"

The irony didn't escape her. Cyril's umbilical cord had been wrapped around his neck at birth, and the midwife had had a devil of a time undoing it. Since he caught his first breath almost at once afterward, they'd thought—hoped—all was well. But as he'd grown, it had become clear all wasn't. By then, Mama had died, leaving Tory with Cyril and no father.

None of them had written to Papa about Cyril, wanting to wait until his return. Now she wished she had informed her father. Perhaps he could have held on longer if he'd known he had a son at last.

Then again, with mail not getting to its destination, he wouldn't have received the letter anyway. Besides, if he'd known about Cyril's difficulties . . .

"Can I keep the butterfly?" Cyril asked, his expression hopeful.

"He won't live for long in a jar, sweetie. Tomorrow, you must let him go, so he can eat nectar from the flowers."

"I want to take him to school," he said plaintively.

She sighed. "You know you can't go to school."

"Because I'm stupid," he muttered.

Her heart twisted in her chest. "Don't say that!" She took his head in hers and looked deep into his soulful eyes. "You are *not* stupid. Didn't you figure out how to catch the butterfly? And keep him alive?"

He thrust out his bottom lip. "Mrs. Gully helped me."

"As well she should, since she and I are your teachers. You probably would have figured it out on your own."

He brightened a little. "Prob'ly." His eyes filled with tears. "Then why can't I go to school? With the other boys?"

She swallowed hard. "Oh, sweetie. Perhaps one day, when you're older."

But she knew she could never send him. Children were cruel to those they didn't understand. And an eleven-year-old who acted like a five-year-old would be treated badly indeed.

Here in her neighborhood, comprised of older folks whose children were grown, people were generally kind to Cyril. And if their grandchildren who visited sometimes eyed him askance, they had the good manners not to say anything.

But the one time she'd brought him to the market closer to town, the children had made fun of him, mocking him for the bedraggled baby blanket he carried everywhere and for his wide-eyed wonder at the animals. Worse yet, they'd called him "stupid," which clearly had made quite an impression on him.

Even that hadn't changed Cyril's mind about wanting friends and going to school. It pained her that she couldn't give him that.

"Now," she said, forcing a smile to her lips, "it's getting dark, so let's go put you into bed. That way you'll be well rested to play with your butterfly in the garden tomorrow." She tickled him under his chin, and he giggled, then took her hand.

She soon had him situated in the trundle bed in her mother's old bedchamber. Sleepily, he clutched his blanket remnant tight while she gave him a goodnight kiss. Then she returned to the kitchen.

Mrs. Gully still stood in there, her hands on her hips.

"You didn't need to wait for me," Tory said.

"Them folks at your solicitor's sent you another letter about the lease." Mrs. Gully's forehead wrinkled with worry as she handed it to Tory. "Have you thought any more on what you'll do when it runs out?"

Tory still held out hope for her school, but it couldn't be located here—the cottage wasn't large enough and was much too dear for the amount of space. Besides, she had her eye on a set of rooms near the Royal Academy. It had once been the lodgings of a society of artists—all men, of course—that had foundered for lack of funds.

The place had loads of light, several rooms big enough for classes, and even a small apartment where she and Cyril could live. It was rather dear, too, but if she could convince the duke to give her the money Papa had left to her . . .

"I shall go over to the solicitor's later this week and see if I can't buy us a bit more time until the will is settled," she said as she walked into their small parlor. "According to His Grace, Papa left me an inheritance."

"He did, did he?" Mrs. Gully asked as she followed Tory, clearly suspicious. "Then how come we ain't never heard of it?"

Tory explained about the duke's and her father's odd imprisonment, but even as she did, she had more questions. There were so many gaps in the duke's story, so many matters she still didn't understand. During their lessons, she should see if she couldn't get some of those questions answered.

With a shake of her head, Mrs. Gully wiped her hands on her apron. "I still say you're better off finding a husband. Now, the gentleman my George works for has a son a few years older than you. He's handsome and well-off, and he ain't married. You could do worse."

She could do better, too. Mrs. Gully was as bad as the duke, thinking that a husband would solve everything. "And what would I do with Cyril, mind you?"

That brought a pained look to her servant's face. "You can't keep him with you forever, luv. What will you do when he's taller than us? How will you keep feeding him? He already eats more than you and me put together."

Tory thrust out her chin. "I have plans in the works."

"That school you want to start." Glancing heavenward, Mrs. Gully held her hands together in a gesture of prayer. "Lord only knows how *that* would go. Won't pay as much as you think. You have to start thinkin' where to put the lad."

"I am *not* sending him to one of those awful places where they chain people to the beds and half the inhabitants are mad!"

"I ain't saying to do *that,* dearie," Mrs. Gully protested. "But there's people as might take him in if he can earn his keep. Nice people in the country. I'd take him myself if not for George's mother." Mrs. Gully made a face. "That woman could strip the hide off a horse with her tongue. But my George loves her and won't hear of sending her away, so there ain't much I can do about it."

"I wouldn't expect you to take Cyril, anyway. You have enough to deal with." Suppressing a sigh, Tory sat down on the nearby sofa. "I don't want anyone to take him."

"But ain't too many men who'll marry a woman with a half-wit . . . a *boy* like Cyril in tow."

"How well I know," Tory said bitterly. It was why she would never marry. She couldn't bear to think of Cyril without her. She had this irrational fear that if she weren't around to oversee his care, he'd wither away and die.

As it was, she hated she couldn't spend more time with him. She and Mama had been his constant companions until her mother's death the year after the duchess's husband had died.

Back then, there'd been little communication between the two families. After Mama's death, however, Tory had found herself stuck firmly between a rock and a hard place. So she'd accepted the duchess's kind offer to make her Chloe's governess and had kept Cyril secret from the Falconridge family ever since.

Partly, it was just easier to keep their worlds apart. Cyril wouldn't be wounded if the family proved hateful to him—as the previous duke and his brother would surely have been—and she wouldn't be wounded if they professed pity for her. But things were messy now, with the new duke's arrival and the deaths of his half brothers and the lease coming due . . . and so many other complications.

She rubbed her temples. She had to find a way out for her brother. Because if children were already cruel to him, she could only imagine how any man who courted her would treat him.

In her experience, men weren't tolerant of people like Cyril. They weren't even tolerant of fully grown females who asserted themselves or made demands—which was evidenced by how the duke had regarded her desire to start a school. So, Lord only knew how a husband would treat a boy who didn't fit into his stringent rules about how the world should work. He'd have Cyril packed off somewhere before she could blink. Worse yet, a husband would have the right to do so.

She refused to risk exposing Cyril to that. Better to keep him safe here where he could be happy. Even if it meant she stayed a maiden the rest of her life.

Chapter 10

The next morning, Jon was surprised when Tory, still wearing mourning attire, met him at the door of the art room.

"I'm exactly on time," he pointed out.

"So you are." Her smile warmed him through. "I just wasn't certain you understood we would still have our lesson today."

He stared at her, perplexed, as he walked into the room. "I did agree to the rules you established."

"Well, I didn't know how you perceived our bargain. Is it one lesson for every social event I attend? Because I didn't attend any social events yesterday."

He chuckled. "I'm not that rigid, I swear. But if you prefer, should we find ourselves with two social events in one day, I'll make sure you attend both. To keep us even."

She cocked her head. "And just how exactly do you mean to 'make sure' I attend?"

"I think you know I can be very persuasive," he said in a low voice.

When she colored, he had a moment of pleasure at seeing her react as strongly to him as he did to her. Then he chided himself. He wasn't courting her, nor was he trying to seduce her into his bed. Since neither was acceptable, he must keep their encounters professional.

Even if he *had* spent the night dreaming of her naked. Indeed, that had been the reason for his sleeping late and barely making it to the art room on time.

Turning on her heel, Tory removed her black shawl and hung it on a nearby hook, then headed toward a long table set directly below the largest window. "Perhaps we should draw up a contract so there's no confusion about the specifics of our bargain."

He laughed. "Shall I add that to the many things I mean to discuss with your father's solicitor this afternoon?"

She halted to glare at him. "You can't see my solicitor without me."

"I can. I'm executor of your father's estate. I must consult with the man."

"Oh. I suppose that's true." She crossed her arms over her bosom. "Then I wish to go with you, at least the first time." Her stance screamed *irate female here*.

He considered her demand. Yesterday afternoon, Beasley had doctored the codicil to Jon's satisfaction, and the extra page had matched the others quite well. But well enough to fool a solicitor? That, he did not know. Still, this was the only way to continue in his scheme, so he might as well let her be there. Because if it all went to hell in a handbasket, he'd rather it be sooner than later.

He'd also arranged with the family banker to have five thousand pounds put aside for Morris's family. If anyone questioned why the dowry was coming from the Falconridge account, Jon would merely point out that Morris had entrusted his money to Jon on his deathbed, and Jon had dutifully put it into an account for Morris's daughter.

"We'll ride to my solicitor's in Alban's phaeton," he said. "That way you won't need a chaperone."

Only then did she relax.

He joined her at the table, noticing a small, marble sphinx sculpture, along with a real pear, a horse figure, and a lumpy clay reproduction of the Discobolus.

When he picked up the last one to examine it, she said, "I made that one. I wanted to show you that you couldn't do any worse than my awful first sculpture. And that effort was despite all the time I spent studying the original."

"So, you chose a naked man for one of your early attempts?" He tried not to smile, but his lips weren't listening, for they curved up in spite of him. "Clearly, you're as enamored of nude figures as I am."

With a frown, she snapped, "I wanted to portray a nude in motion. None of the Venuses are in motion."

"That certainly explains your choice," he drawled.

She narrowed her gaze on him. "How about if we don't focus on *my* choice and instead focus on yours?"

That brought him up short. "Good God, you sounded so much like your father just then. He liked to turn things back on me, too."

"It's a good teaching technique, you must admit," she countered, arching one eyebrow.

"It is, indeed."

"So, have you thought any more about what you'd wish to sculpt?"

He hadn't, though he knew better than to admit it. Besides, he really wanted to sculpt *her*, for when she finally found a husband and disappeared into married life. Sadly, he lacked the ability. "Why don't we start with the pear? That seems simplest. And I wouldn't need a sketch for it, do you think?"

"You can probably get by without one." She pulled a bucket from beneath the table. "You can recreate it in clay. If it's good enough, we'll make a mold of it, and do a casting in bronze." She flashed him an impish smile. "Assuming you can afford such an expensive metal, Your Grace."

"I have no idea what I can afford, to be honest." The banker could only tell him what was in the various accounts, not what his financial obligations were. "I stayed up late last night looking through the account books and papers Mother gave me, but I can't clarify anything until I speak with the accountants and the land agent. Which I hope to do today after I meet with your solicitor."

She nodded. "Then we'd better get started. You can work right here by the window. I'll sit beside you and give you instructions where needed."

When they were seated, she was so close to him that her skirts brushed against his trousers—so close he could easily pull her onto his lap.

Stop that! You won't be pulling her onto your lap, for God's sake. You're a gentleman now, and not the wild young fellow you were when you left London.

More's the pity.

"Don't you think?" she asked.

Damn. He had no idea what she'd just said. "I . . . er . . . sure. I agree."

"Wonderful! I was worried you wouldn't. But you won't regret it. Chloe has been dying to see your friend Heathbrook again, and she'll be ecstatic when she hears you'll invite him to your box at the theater tonight. She was hesitant to ask you herself to invite him. I think your comments about Bow Street runners gave her pause the other night."

Oh, bloody hell, he'd just agreed to put Chloe and Heathbrook in a box together? *His* box, which he'd only two days ago remembered that the family had? His mind raced, but he couldn't think of a way to get out of inviting his friend.

A sigh escaped him. He'd better invite Scovell, too. And make sure Mother was fine with it. Because he didn't trust Heathbrook one whit when it came to women, and certainly not when it came to his sister.

This was what he got for lusting after Tory—he lost his wits when he was around her. He had to stop doing that.

Reaching under the table to the bucket of clay, Miss Oblivious-to-His-Lusting Morris dug out a lump much bigger than the pear. "This shape is very easy to create. Essentially, you start with two balls—one half the size of the other."

An inappropriate joke came into his head that he squelched with some difficulty. The old Jon would have spoken it just to see the reaction of the woman he was with.

The old Jon had been an arse.

Meanwhile, she divided the clay into two unequal parts and offered him the larger part.

He reached for it with his gloved hand, and she said, "You

won't want to wear your gloves for this. You'll get them too grimy to keep."

"Right," he said, though he still hesitated, hating that she would see his marred flesh again.

As if reading his mind, she said kindly, "Your hands aren't as bad as all that, you know. Nor am I the squeamish sort."

"I didn't think you were," he said coolly, and yanked his gloves off.

She placed the lump of clay in his ravaged palm. "Now, roll that into a ball."

"I believe I can manage that. I might never have done any sculpting, but I certainly played in mud as a boy." As he rolled his, she rolled hers, and his mind wandered again . . . to what it would be like to have her hand fondling a certain part of his anatomy—rolling and squeezing lightly and . . .

"Very good!" she said. "What a perfectly round ball."

"Er . . . thank you."

"Now I suppose you can figure out what to do next."

Lay you down on the table, and have my wicked way with you?

God, he was damned well going to hell. "Not really."

She tsked at him. No one had ever tsked at him before.

"Surely you can see it." She placed her ball on top of his. "This forms the basic shape of a pear." She moved the snowman-looking thing to sit before him. "Now you press down on the small ball to make it meld better with the larger ball."

He did as she said, but now the two just looked like one disk set on top of another. "It doesn't resemble a pear in the least."

She was clearly fighting a smile. "That's because you smashed them together. You needn't use so much force." Swiftly, she took each disk and rolled it back into a ball, then put the small one on top of the other again. "Now," she said, and took his hand in hers, "press lightly."

This time she guided his hand to apply far less pressure than he'd done. Her palm was soft against the top of his hand, but her fingers felt strong and capable as they bent atop his. Thank God it wasn't his palm she was touching. He had very little feeling there, and he wanted to feel every delicate touch of her hand.

She leaned so close that he could smell the scent that seemed uniquely hers—orange flowers and honey. Only this time it was mixed with something more earthy. Clay, probably. All he'd have to do is shift his head a quarter turn, and he could easily lean forward to cover her mouth with his. But before he could follow that insane impulse, she released his hand and sat back, leaving him feeling bereft.

"That's much better," she said. "Now, you should smooth the two together into the actual shape of a pear."

"Ah. Right." Feeling rather awkward, he curved his hand around the place where the two balls were joined.

"For this part," Tory said, "you needn't be so careful. Clay requires some work at times, so feel free to really get in there with your fingers and work it hard until you achieve that pear shape."

He stifled a groan. This was not what he wished to be working "hard" just at this moment. And since when had he started hearing double entendres in whatever a woman said?

Probably since he'd met *her*. At Verdun, eligible young Englishwomen had been few and far between, and he'd been warned against the other sort since it was hard to know whom to trust. At Bitche, there had been no women at all.

That explained why he desired her so badly. What he felt was mere lust, pure and simple. Surely, he could keep his lust in check no matter how many double entendres entered his fevered brain. So, he forced himself to concentrate on his "sculpture," such as it was.

"Good," she said. "That's better." She watched a moment, then added, "Did you and your fellow prisoners have pears and the like?" When that odd question made him blink at her, she said, "I-I'm just wondering if your diet included fruit. In the prison, I mean."

"No," he said tersely. "Fruit was rarely on the menu at Bitche."

"What *was* on the menu?"

"A pound of bread. Half a pound of beef. Water."

"For every meal?"

"For every *day*. If we were lucky. That was the amount allotted to each prisoner, but we didn't always get it." When she gasped, he shrugged. "We could supplement that as we wished with our own funds, but by the time your father and I were at Bitche, we had little money left and no way to establish credit."

He didn't realize he'd blundered until she asked, "But what about the money Papa got from teaching? The money he designated for my dowry? Why didn't you just use that? I'm sure my father wouldn't have begrudged you that."

Damn it all. Clearly, his attempt at sculpting had so absorbed him that he'd just blathered the truth. Nor did it help he wasn't used to lying so blatantly. "Oh, those funds were with a banker in Verdun." He met her suspicious gaze with the most innocent look he could muster. "We had no way to access it. I had to stop in Verdun on my way out of France just to withdraw the money he'd banked there."

He patted himself on the back for coming up with a believable lie.

"But . . . but you said he was paid for teaching the commandant at Bitche, too," she said, looking truly perplexed. "That some of the funds came from that."

He suppressed a groan. This time he'd put his foot in his mouth so deep he was choking on it. "Some of the funds did, but not all of it. Since that was the only money we had at Bitche, I used it for the doctor and medicines and other things for your father's care at the end."

Her cheeks pinkened. "I'm sorry. I don't mean to sound ungrateful for what you did for my father. I was just trying to understand what you both went through."

"Of course. That's not surprising."

He was beginning to regret ever coming up with a scheme to give her a dowry. He should have just told her that her father had died in service to him, and so he was gifting her with five thousand pounds.

Then again, if he had, he couldn't have done the only thing Morris had asked of him—make sure she married well. "I'm happy to answer whatever questions you have." He was probably going to rue the day he told her that, but if he didn't appear open to that, she would get suspicious.

"Thank you," she said, her voice soft as silk as she laid her hand on his arm. "You have no idea how much that means to me. After thinking on everything you said the first night you were home, I have so much I'm curious about. You said Bitche was like a real prison. How exactly? I mean, I've read about prisons, but have never seen one. Were your cells in a dungeon or a building or . . . what?"

"Prisoners of our class lived two to a cell, but the common sailors and soldiers—and criminals—were thrown into the dungeons below us. Those fellows caroused and fought and made trouble for their guards day and night. That made it hard for us to sleep sometimes, what with the wild sounds that rose from below, but we weren't allowed to venture into those areas, so we could endure it."

When he noticed her worried look, he added, "You don't want to hear all the details of our imprisonment, trust me. Suffice it to say, it was unpleasant."

Her eyebrows lifted. "What's unpleasant for a duke might not be all that unpleasant for a professor."

The rebuke stung a little. "You forget I wasn't a duke then. And believe me, it was 'unpleasant' for all of us, if one can even use such a tame word to describe it. Your father and I shared a cell. Our experience was mostly the same."

"I should think it was worse for him once he was ill."

"It was indeed." She had no idea how much.

"How did he fracture his thigh bone, anyway?"

He tensed. "In a fall." But he couldn't talk about this, or he would tell her things he'd regret. "Perhaps we should get on with this lesson. Otherwise, I'll never finish before it's time to go to your solicitor's office."

"I suppose you're right." She eyed him closely. "But I have more questions."

He stifled a groan. "And I will answer them in due time, I promise."

That seemed to satisfy her, but probably not for long. One day he would have to give her a full reckoning of what had happened in France. And he was certainly dreading *that*.

Chapter 11

Tory couldn't tell if the duke was just avoiding her questions or was genuinely keeping track of the time. But he'd agreed to take her with him to the solicitor, which was more than she'd expected, so she could hardly complain.

Besides, she enjoyed watching him attempt to sculpt. He seemed to have no qualms about getting his hands dirty, which was a surprise, considering his station. Then again, he *had* spent quite a bit of time in a dank prison.

Now, his hands moved more fluidly as he got comfortable with the clay, reminding her of how his fingers had felt beneath hers—all warm and firm to the touch. She'd dreamed of those masterful hands last night—having them touch her in the most intimate places while he kissed her even more passionately than he had at the museum.

She'd awakened wanting more, then had chided herself for such a foolish yearning, one he could never fulfill. Even if he desired her, he would never marry her, and she wouldn't want him to, anyway. A duke was highly unlikely to let her bring Cyril with her when she married.

The thought depressed her, forcing her to turn her attention back to the matter at hand—his lesson in sculpting. With his brow furrowed, he seemed to be earnestly working on his pear now, although it still looked lopsided. She couldn't yet tell if he would one day get better at this, but if he didn't, it wouldn't be for lack of trying. While she went to the washbasin to wash her hands, he smoothed and shaped the clay for quite a while. At last, he pushed back from the table to eye his creation from several vantage points before turning to her. "What do you think?"

"I think it's . . . er . . . interesting," she said, wiping her hand with a towel.

"Yes, but is it any good?"

What a difficult question to answer. "That is entirely subjective. Do *you* like it?"

"It's the best I can do, I fear."

"Then it's fine," she said.

"Hmm." He crossed his arms. "So, what do we do now? I mean, to turn my clay masterpiece into bronze."

His dry tone as he said *masterpiece* made her chuckle. "It's not like spinning straw into gold, you know."

"Of course not, or everyone would be turning their clay into bronze, and then where would all the bricklayers be? I daresay bronze houses wouldn't be the least bit practical."

With great difficulty, she stifled a grin. "Has anyone ever told you that you're quite mad, Your Grace?"

"No one would dare," he said loftily, then grinned. "After all, dukes are allowed to be a bit daft, aren't they?" He waggled his eyebrows, making her laugh. He was certainly not like any duke *she'd* ever met.

"People do tend to look the other way when a duke is involved, I'll admit." She flashed him a mock frown. "Now, do you wish to learn how to turn your clay into bronze or no?"

"By all means." He gave a regal swipe of his hand. "Carry on."

Fighting another laugh, she returned to her seat and described the rather complicated process of lost wax casting, surprised that he not only followed her explanation but asked pertinent questions.

Once she was satisfied that he understood the process, she said,

"Before we can proceed with any of that, you must first be sure you've done all you wish to your creation. Is this the version you prefer to use as a model for your bronze?"

He lifted an eyebrow. "Should I want it to be?"

"It's up to you. Does it resemble the pear in your imagination?"

"I hate to tell you this, Tory, but my imagination has better things to do with itself than conjuring up pears."

"Oh? What does it conjure up?"

His eyes turned a molten gold as he stared intently at her. "You don't want to know," he said in a husky voice that found an echo in her very blood, like the spell of a general issuing a call to arms. Then he smiled, breaking the spell. "The most I can promise is that my masterpiece vaguely resembles the real pear you have there on the table."

Only Falconridge could put it like that. "What I'm asking is if you're happy with the way you've sculpted it. Because if you go on to cast it, you can't make many changes."

"It's a pear," he drawled. "How many more changes could I make?"

She bit back a smile. "I give up. You are never going to take this seriously, are you?"

"Probably not. Or at least not until I'm sculpting something more interesting than a pear."

"That's fair."

"Appropriate, since my rendition of a pear is merely fair. It's a fair pear." He cocked his head. "A pity you aren't interested in poetry. I'm much better at rhyming than sculpting."

"That's not saying much."

He thumped his chest with his fist. "You wound me to the heart."

"I do try." She softened the remark with a smile. "Do you even want to turn your pear into a bronze? You might prefer to see it as a practice piece and work on something 'more interesting,' as you put it."

"That's an excellent idea." He glanced at the clock on the mantelpiece. "But I fear we've run out of time. I told your solicitor I'd be there at one PM, and it's past noon already. Besides, I haven't eaten yet today, so before we set off, I must have something to keep me going until dinner."

"You didn't even eat breakfast?" she asked, surprised he hadn't said anything.

"After poring over the account books until the wee hours of the morning, I slept late, I'm afraid. I only had time to down a cup of coffee in my room. Then I rushed up here before you could accuse me of ignoring my part of our bargain."

"You should have said something! I could have gone down to fetch you breakfast while you worked on your sculpting. You must be starved by now, you poor man."

Something glinted in his eyes. "Starved, indeed," he said in a husky murmur, his gaze dropping to her mouth.

A shiver danced along her skin as she realized he was no longer speaking of food. In an attempt to dispel the charged air in the room, she picked up the real pear and thrust it at him. "You could eat this."

Instead of taking it from her, he caught her by the wrist. Keeping his gaze locked with hers, he bit off a piece of pear. "Mmm," he said as he chewed, his eyes gleaming.

Her breath seemed to thicken the longer he held her by the wrist. But when juice ran down her thumb and he licked it off, her breath got stuck in her lungs.

Heaven help her. What was he doing to her? Had he read her dreams somehow?

Because his rough tongue lapping at the juice made her ache to have it other places—the spot on her wrist where her pulse now beat wildly . . . the tender inner skin of her elbow . . . between her lips.

Then, as if he at least read her thoughts, he bent forward to take her mouth with his. Her heart hammered in her chest as he began to feed on her lips the same way he'd fed on the pear. Oh, he was very good at the kissing, curse him. She couldn't help but respond.

He tasted of fruit and smelled of shaving soap as his mouth plundered hers. Dropping the pear to the floor, she slid her hands up into his hair, marveling at how thick and silky-soft it was as she speared her fingers through it.

That only made him kiss her more ravenously until her knees felt like jelly and her blood ran hot.

"Tory," he whispered against her lips.

She uttered a long sigh. "Didn't we say we mustn't do this?"

"I don't remember that," he rasped.

Next thing she knew, he had hauled her over and onto his lap.

"Stop that!" she hissed. "Someone might see." Yet she couldn't bring herself to leave his lap.

"No one knows we're up here, do they?" He settled his hands on her waist and started kissing along her cheek to her jaw, then down the side of her neck, where another pulse beat madly.

When he pressed a kiss right against that pulse, she let out a ragged breath. "I-I hope not," she murmured. Still, she looped her arms about his neck to hold him there.

"I've wanted you on my lap from the moment I came up here," he whispered in her ear, then tugged her earlobe with his teeth. "If I had any artistic ability at all, I'd sculpt *you.*"

"Clothed, I hope," she whispered, and nuzzled his jaw with its wonderful masculine lines.

He chuckled. "I thought you liked nudes in motion."

The thought of posing for him naked made her breath quicken. "Other nudes than I," she said in his ear.

"That's a pity. I could sculpt you sculpting."

She drew back to eye him askance. "I hardly think you're ready for that."

He smirked at her. "After a few more lessons, I might be. You're an excellent teacher."

"Flatterer," she said.

With a chuckle, he kissed her mouth again—softly at first and then hard and hungrily, with a kind of urgency that made her want to swoon, if she were ever inclined to do such a ninny thing.

Then she felt a hard bulge against her bottom, and her cheeks heated, along with certain hidden parts of her own body, as she realized what that substantial bulge must be. Her mother hadn't raised a fool, after all. Once Tory had turned eighteen, her mother had told her everything about how babies were made. But when Mama had said the man put his stiff penis inside the woman, Tory hadn't realized . . .

Good Lord, that felt like a rather ... *fierce* piece of male flesh he was sporting.

Before she could react, he kissed a path down her jaw to her throat, then murmured, "I would love to sculpt your elegant neck..." He kissed along her collarbone. "And your bare shoulders..." Then his hand covered her breast through the fabric of her gown, corset cup, and chemise. "And this, too, along with its mate."

"Jon ..." she murmured, "you really ... shouldn't." But even she could hear the breathy excitement in her voice as he molded her breast with his hand. How could such a wicked thing feel so very good? "Heavens, *Jon* ..."

He uttered a soft groan. "I love the sound of my name on your lips," he said as he fondled her breast shamelessly through the layers of material.

She could feel her nipple tighten and prayed he couldn't feel it, too, through all the fabric, but when he ran his thumb over its point repeatedly, she feared he had somehow managed to do so.

Then just as she was thinking she'd lost her mind, the sound of boot heels on the stairsteps came to them as the voice of doom echoed up the stairwell. "Tory, are you in the art room?"

It was Chloe, of all people.

Stifling a cry, Tory sprang up from his lap, then bent to whisper, "Hide! She cannot find you here alone with me."

For a moment he hesitated, his eyes bearing a glazed look to them, and she nearly despaired of making him understand.

Then he shook off his torpor to rise and look around. "Hide *where*, for God's sake?"

"Quick! Behind the door. But quietly!"

He darted that direction just in time, for a few moments later, Chloe appeared in the doorway. "Did you not hear me calling you?" she asked petulantly. "We're supposed to go to Wood for your shoes this afternoon, remember? Your slippers for tonight are supposed to be ready."

"Oh! Right." Tory moved over to hide the half-eaten pear beneath her skirts. "I completely forgot." So much for going with Jon to the solicitor's. "I was so caught up in my work that my mind was elsewhere."

Chloe looked past Tory to where Jon's clay pear sat on the table.

"What on earth is that ghastly thing? Surely you didn't sculpt *that*, did you?"

"Of course not," Tory said indignantly, and thought quickly. "A lady in my neighborhood asked me to do a casting of it."

"For heaven's sake, why? It's hardly worth putting into bronze."

"Yes, but she can afford it, and I agreed to cast it as a favor. It can wait until later, though. I can't take it to the foundry until tomorrow anyway." She hurried toward the open door before Chloe could advance too far into the room. "Let's go to Wood. I'm eager to see my new slippers."

They headed down the stairs. Halfway down, Tory paused. "I forgot my shawl. You go on. It will only take me a moment to fetch it." And before Chloe could point out that there were any number of shawls downstairs in the coat closet, Tory hurried back up the stairs.

She entered the room to find Jon at the table, staring at his clay pear. "It's not really *so* bad, is it?" he asked.

"Oh, for pity's sake, I wouldn't worry about it," Tory whispered. "Is there any way you could change your appointment with the solicitor to tomorrow, so I can go with you?"

"Sorry, sweetheart," he said in a low voice, "but I have other meetings set for then."

The word *sweetheart* both delighted and exasperated her. "I suppose it can't be helped. But you'll tell me everything he said?"

"Of course. We can talk about it tomorrow morning during our lesson."

She blushed, thinking of everything they'd done during *today's* lesson. "It must not involve any sort of . . . misbehavior, you realize."

He turned to fix her with a remorseful gaze. "No, it must not. I swear I will keep my hands to myself tomorrow. And I should really apologize for getting carried away today. You shouldn't have to endure my . . . attentions."

"Good. I mean, thank you." How could she tell him she could *endure* them quite happily if she knew they meant anything more than a moment's dalliance to him? She didn't dare say such a thing. She refused to be one of those women who wore her heart on her sleeve.

Then she groaned. Not her heart. Never her heart. She couldn't be that foolish, surely. Might as well be a deer longing for a duke. "I have to go," she said, and whirled toward the door.

"Wait," he said softly, and walked to where her shawl hung from the hook. "You'll need this."

"Yes. Right. Good." Lord, but she sounded like a fool.

He brought it to her and settled it over her shoulders. "There you go."

"Thank you," she said, cursing herself for wishing she could just lean back against him for a moment. That they could just return to what they'd been doing before Chloe had interrupted them. "I-I'll see you this evening."

Then she fled.

Jon stood staring at the open door for a long time after she left. Then he collapsed into a chair and cursed a blue streak. He'd clearly lost his mind. Had he really just treated Tory like some dockside whore, yanking her onto his lap and putting his hand on her breast?

Yes. Yes, he had. And that was after telling her a mere two days ago that he would not treat her as his brothers had.

He banged his head on the table. He wouldn't blame her if she wanted nothing more to do with him. Or perhaps came to their next lesson armed with a few hatpins.

Rising from the chair, he fought to compose himself, then waited until he was sure they were gone before heading downstairs. Chloe's unexpected appearance had been far too near a miss for his comfort. The only good part about that was he now got to speak with the Morris family solicitor—a man named Trimnell—without Tory.

Once Jon ate and set off, he had no trouble finding the fellow's office. After determining Jon was indeed the executor of the Morris estate, the aging attorney was surprisingly forthcoming. Trimnell revealed that the family coffers had run dry during Morris's extended absence, and that the lease on the cottage was set to expire in two months. Which, to Jon's mind, made it even more urgent that Tory find a husband and soon.

Trimnell was also delighted to hear that Morris had left his daughter a substantial dowry. He barely looked at the codicil to the will and took at face value Jon's assertion that Morris had entrusted the money to Jon to set aside for Tory's dowry. Clearly, Trimnell wasn't going to prove an obstacle to Jon's scheme.

Meanwhile, Jon made no mention of Tory's desire to use it for a school. He still considered that endeavor doomed to failure but told himself that if she couldn't find anyone she liked well enough to marry in a decent amount of time, he would make sure her school was properly funded. He and the attorney parted ways as amiable business acquaintances.

His meeting with the accountants and land steward was more trying. While they seemed to have done their jobs as well as they could, he didn't entirely trust any of them. That was probably because of his life in France, where everyone seemed to have some hidden reason for their behavior. He was finding it hard just to accept things at face value.

Especially because it quickly became obvious Alban had done the bare minimum in managing the dukedom after Father's death. There were stacks of papers waiting to be reviewed and signed, letters piling up concerning various aspects of the estates, and reports of investments Alban had considered and never acted upon.

Those were only the documents that had piled up *before* Alban's death. The ones afterward filled an entire room. Indeed, it took them a couple of hours just to discuss a plan of attack. Then after Jon looked over the most urgent of the papers, he signed them and left, promising to return the next day.

He considered telling Tory he had to stop the sculpting lessons for a week at least, but if he did, she was liable to refuse to go to any social affairs. The Season was almost over. If she was to find a husband, he had to hold to their bargain. That left him little choice— he could deal with the estates in the afternoons and evenings, as long as he made sure she went out into Society with his mother and sister, even if he didn't go with her.

That was probably just as well. His reckless behavior this morning still weighed on his conscience. She deserved better. Some time apart wouldn't hurt, and he wouldn't mind staying out of Society for a while, anyway. Except, of course, for tonight. He wasn't about to bow out of going to the theater when he'd already promised to invite his friends there.

To that end, after leaving the accountants and land steward, Jon dropped in at both his friends' London homes and left a note inviting them to the theater and apologizing for the short notice.

Then he stopped at Beasley's house, pleased to find him there on what ought to be a business day. Since Beasley had insisted on not being paid until Jon was certain the codicil passed muster, Jon felt it only right that he pay the fellow in due course. Besides, yesterday he'd noticed that Beasley, his wife, and his four children were living in rather hard circumstances, and Jon meant to do what he could to change that.

"Your Grace!" Beasley cried as Jon was shown in by the man's unsmiling wife. "Why are you here?" Beasley's face fell. "Was something wrong with the codicil?"

"Actually, no. The attorney found it utterly convincing. I'm grateful to you, and though Miss Morris will never know of it, I'm sure she would be grateful, too, if she did."

That was an exaggeration. She might not appreciate him going to such lengths to gain her a husband.

"I'm right happy it worked out," Beasley said.

Jon drew out a bag of guineas and handed it to the man. "I know we agreed on ten pounds, but I was so pleased with the outcome, I threw in a few extra."

Beasley frowned as he hefted the bag. "Quite a bit more than a few extra, I daresay. I can't accept this, Your Grace. It's too much. I don't want charity."

"It's not charity, Beasley," he said. "You've done me a great service, and I know you risked much to do it. Forgery is punishable by hanging, after all. But if anyone asks about what I had you do, you must tell them I forced you to do it. They'd never hang *me*." There were privileges to being a duke, to be sure.

"Oh, mum's the word, sir. I would never tell anyone about it. You can count on my discretion." He stared at the bag, then added, "To be honest, Your Grace, I would rather have your help with another matter than take the money."

"Keep the money, please. You earned it. And of course, I'll help you with whatever else I can do."

Beasley rubbed the back of his neck, looking suddenly nervous. "Well . . . you see . . . I haven't been able to get work since my return to England. I was hoping Your Grace would be willing to put in a good word for me with some of your friends or family—"

"Are you looking for engraving work?"

"If I could get it, that would be wonderful, sir. But with so many soldiers returning home and so little work to go around . . ."

"I understand." Jon thought a moment. "Actually, I own a number of engraved prints that require valuation, since I mean to insure them. Might you consider *that* sort of work?"

Beasley brightened. "Anything, Your Grace, would be welcome."

"Excellent! I'll send you a note once I'm available to show you my prints. In the meantime, I'll ask around about printmakers who could use good engravers. Miss Morris is an artist and so was her mother before her death, so she might know of someone requiring your services."

That cheered Beasley even more. "She might indeed. Professor Morris's wife was the daughter of an engraver, or so he told me at Verdun."

Jon hadn't even known that. How many other things did he not know about Tory? That made him wary. "Very well, then I'll speak to Miss Morris about it and let you know what she says."

"Thank you, sir. That's most kind of you."

Jon was about to take his leave, then paused. "Beasley, are there many returned détenus who need work?"

"Quite a few, Your Grace."

"If you'll give me a list of names and occupations when you come to Falcon House, I might be able to find them work at one of my estates or those of Lord Heathbrook. Captain Scovell might be aware of work at his brother's estates, too."

"I'll do that, sir, thank you."

After Jon took his leave, he drove his brother's phaeton back to Falcon House and considered what he'd just offered. He'd said it primarily because it had become painfully clear during his meeting today that he would need more staff. But now he realized it would also accomplish something else—allow him and his friends to reestablish ties to the détenu community in London so they could unmask the person who'd betrayed their escape plans.

All in all, a good afternoon's work.

Chapter 12

That evening, Tory stood before the duchess and Chloe in the drawing room at Falcon House, nervously awaiting their opinion. Both were taking way too long to speak as they looked her over.

The duchess cleared her throat, then dabbed her eyes with her handkerchief. "Oh, my dear, you're gorgeous in that gown. I'm so delighted your father thought of giving you a dowry. I can't wait to show you off to my friends. I daresay you will impress everyone in the theater."

Though the duchess's kind words were gratifying, the only person Tory wished to impress was Jon, and he'd already sent word he would see them at the play, so they weren't even traveling to the theater together.

"If I hadn't seen you try that gown on myself yesterday," Chloe said, "I would scarcely believe you had the same one on! I told you Mrs. Linley would turn it into something amazing once she removed the trim and fussy bits. That fabric is gorgeous, but also simple and elegant. We're lucky she'd already had a dress half-done in your size that her other client hadn't been able to pay for."

"We're lucky she had a color that suited me," Tory countered. "A good dressmaker can fix size but color . . ."

"True. And that soft shade of lilac always looks so good on you.

It would turn me as gray as a goose." Chloe circled Tory slowly. "I do love how low the back is! Perfection. Not to mention the cap sleeves."

Tory sighed. "I wish the skirt weren't so short. When I sit, it shows my ankles."

"That's the fashion these days, my dear," the duchess said. "I wouldn't worry about it."

"And you have nice ankles, anyway," Chloe put in.

"So do you," Tory said.

"Not that it will matter much at the theater," Chloe said. "No one will notice our ankles while we're sitting in rows of chairs in a box."

"True." Tory glanced down at her bodice. "You don't think the gown is cut too low, do you?" Though to be honest, Jon was certain to think it perfect, given his interest in touching her bosom this morning. Which, of course, she must never let him do again.

Never. Even if it had felt like the most daringly sensual moment in her life.

Turning to her mother, Chloe asked, "Mama? What do you think? Is the neckline too low?"

"Oh, pish," the duchess said, with a wave of her hand. "You catch more beaus with honey than with vinegar."

"It's certainly better than catching *flies* with honey," Chloe said, winking at Tory.

"Don't be ridiculous, Chloe," the duchess said. "Why would anyone wish to catch flies? It's beaus you want to catch, and showing a bit of your feminine attributes is sure to help."

"Thank you, Duchess," Tory said, hiding her smile. "You've reassured me admirably."

"And those lilac slippers you and Chloe bought today are perfect with the gown. I had my doubts, but they match better than I imagined they would."

"They really do, don't they?" Chloe said. "I picked those out. It's always nice to buy shoes for Tory—her feet aren't my gigantic ones."

"Your feet aren't gigantic," Tory protested. "They're simply larger than mine."

"Oh, no," Chloe's mother said with a sniff. "Chloe does have her father's feet. Nothing to be done about that. But she also has an elegant nose, and that makes up for it. Gentlemen hardly notice feet, but they always prefer elegant noses."

Did they? In Tory's experience, they seemed to prefer shapely figures more than anything. Besides, what made a nose elegant?

Tory shook her head. This was precisely why she hadn't wanted to go husband-hunting in Society. She had never understood the rules of the courtship game, and she preferred games where she did. She'd much rather sit and sculpt than try to find a husband, thank you very much.

Although if a certain person were to court her in truth . . .

No, that wouldn't work, either. She could only imagine Jon's reaction to Cyril. If anyone understood what was expected of a duke, it was Jon, and he wouldn't wish to risk having an heir who might be . . . not quite right in the head, no matter how much she explained that Cyril's difficulties had begun during birth.

His mother certainly wouldn't want him to risk it. She was always commenting on the stupidity of some of Chloe's suitors, which was precisely why Tory had never introduced the duchess or Chloe to her little brother.

"We should go, ladies," the duchess said. "We'll want time to chat with Diana and her husband beforehand. And you both shall want to flirt with any gentlemen who come to the box before the play begins."

"Most definitely," Chloe said with a knowing look at Tory, who'd already told her that Jon had promised to invite his friends. "Personally, I'm looking forward to the play, too. I've never had the chance to view *The Beggar's Opera*. It should be great fun!"

Privately, Tory agreed. She was as pleased to be seeing the famous satire on Italian opera as to be meeting people she didn't know, gentlemen or otherwise.

Well, except for Jon's friends. She did want to meet *them*, mostly because she was hoping to find out more about their time at Bitche. Jon didn't seem to enjoy talking about it much.

The three of them had just turned for the door when Jon walked in.

"Jon!" the duchess exclaimed. "I thought you weren't coming here before the play."

He didn't answer at first, just stood there gaping at Tory and making her self-conscious.

"You look amazing," he said in a husky voice, his gaze gleaming bright as he skimmed her gown. Then he finally seemed to realize his sister and mother were watching with great interest, for he hastily added, "All of you look stunning."

"Why are you here?" Chloe asked, examining his decidedly casual clothing with a frown. "Please tell me you aren't planning to bow out."

"No, no, I'm going, but I stopped at the tailor's to pick up my new evening attire. Can you wait for me to dress? It won't take long."

His mother sniffed. "I suppose. You can't wear *that*, to be sure."

As he hurried out, Tory sighed. She was dying to know what the solicitor had said. Sadly, she would have to wait to get him alone, since the pertinent part for her of his discussion with Mr. Trimnell was how much leeway there was in Papa's bequest. That couldn't be discussed around the duchess and Chloe.

A short while later, he returned and they were on their way to the Theatre-Royal in Haymarket. Jon sat opposite her by the carriage door, with his mother next to him and Chloe next to Tory. The sun hadn't gone down, and it streamed into the carriage, making them all a bit warm. Tory removed her shawl, then caught Jon staring at her neckline before he jerked his gaze up.

That was rather gratifying.

Meanwhile, he looked delicious in appropriate evening attire. After having felt the muscles in his arms in the art room as he'd held her this morning, she could almost imagine she saw them through his well-fitted black tailcoat. Certainly, his white, figured waistcoat admirably showcased his broad chest.

And those white breeches and stockings! He had the most muscular calves she'd ever seen on a gentleman, probably from all that walking he'd done leaving France. Due to his height and the closeness of the space, his knees were pressed against hers, and she fancied she could feel them even through her gown and petticoat.

The only peculiarity in his attire was a curious-looking flat and round black thing on his lap.

"Oh, Jon," Chloe cried, "you have one of those new opera hats with the springs in them, don't you? I've heard of those. Do let me see."

"Only if you don't destroy it," he said, chuckling as he handed it over. "They're called 'elastic round hats.' Or *chapeau claque*, if you prefer, because of the clicking sound they make when they're opened."

Tory and Chloe spent the next few minutes popping the hat open to top hat size, then flattening it again.

"It's as practical as a *chapeau bras*," Chloe said, "but so much more attractive. Those look as if someone is wearing a boat on his head."

"I'll keep that in mind next time I wish to don a bicorne," Jon drawled. "Although the hatter informed me that the *chapeau bras* is going out of fashion anyway."

"Of course, it is," Chloe said. "They look ridiculous. Besides, these new opera hats have handy little ribbons to keep the hat closed, making it much easier to tuck it under a carriage or theater seat."

To demonstrate, she bent to fit it under their seat.

"Stop that!" her mother cried. "You'll get it dirty."

"Mother has a point," Jon said as he bent to retrieve it. But he took his time straightening again because . . .

Oh, Lord, he was staring at Tory's exposed ankles.

Heat rose in her cheeks. It didn't matter that Chloe's dress was of the same length as hers or that Tory's ankles were covered with white stockings—Tory still felt exposed. Nor did the feeling go away when Jon settled back against the seat to fix his intent gaze on her face.

How unnerving. She couldn't look away. Everything they'd done this morning came flooding back, and as if he remembered it, too, his gaze dipped to her bodice, and desire flared in his features.

Her heart thundered in her ears. What was he doing? Why did he persist in these flirtations?

If one could even call them that. They were more like sensual reminders of their private moments together that he kept bestowing on her like so many rose petals scattered on the grass.

It made her want to do the same to him just to test her own

power over him. Taking out her handkerchief, she blotted the tops of her breasts. "It's very warm in here, considering that we've had quite a cold June until now. I do hope it won't be too warm in the theater."

"I doubt it will," Chloe said. "Although, to be honest, I prefer the warmth to the cold any day."

"On that, we agree," Jon said as his gaze hungrily followed the motion of Tory's hands. "I had enough of the cold in France. Both Verdun and Bitche were in the mountains on the northern border."

Then he caught her watching him watch her. Stiffening, he turned his attention to his sister, who obliged him by asking how they'd dealt with the cold in prison.

He shrugged. "We wore all our clothes at once. And they did let us have coals occasionally to cook our meals in the grate, although there was never enough for us to warm our cells at night, too. Besides, the windows high above us were open to the weather, so trying to warm our cells was useless anyway."

The way he said such things so nonchalantly broke her heart. How had he endured the contrast between his cell at Bitche and the memory of his palatial surroundings at Falcon House? He must have missed his home so much.

Papa must have done so, too. The thought made her tear up, forcing her to dab at her eyes with her handkerchief. But if Jon noticed, he didn't show it, for he was now gazing out the window at London's streets.

"I wonder if I'll ever get used to how much the city has changed," Jon said absently. "I feel like a stranger in my own land."

"Ah, but at least you're among friends," Tory pointed out.

"And family," Chloe put in. "If you wish, I'd be happy to take you on a tour of the city so you can see everything new."

"Thanks, Mopsy."

She lifted an eyebrow at him. "You're welcome, Bonny Jonny."

When he groaned, his mother and sister laughed.

Tory grinned. "Am I allowed to use these pet names, too?"

All she got were glares from the two siblings. Now it was her turn to laugh.

They soon arrived at the theater, and Jon climbed down to help the ladies out. She was the first to step down and painfully aware of her gloved hand in his, especially when he squeezed it before turning to help his mother. But even when he was no longer touching her, she couldn't stop being aware of his every motion—how he snapped the hat open to place it on his head, how he smiled at his sister, how he spoke to the footman in a tone of command, as if he'd been a duke all his life.

While the three women waited for Jon, the footman pointed to something in the carriage, and with a nod Jon reached in to get it. To Tory's embarrassment, it was her lace shawl. Apparently, she'd been so focused on him that she'd left it behind, just as she'd done in the art room earlier with her other one. Lord, he was sure to think her an absolute widgeon if she kept leaving things everywhere.

He approached and, as before, draped her shawl over her shoulders himself instead of handing it to her. She felt every whisper of his hand settling it into place, every light touch as he smoothed the lacy fabric. Her skin came alive wherever he touched her. Thankfully, once he was done, he moved to escort his mother into the theater ahead of her and Chloe.

Chloe moved closer to whisper, "You and Jon are becoming quite chummy."

"I don't know what you mean," Tory answered, hoping her cheeks weren't blazing bright. "He's just being polite."

"I think the word you're looking for is 'attentive,' and it's not the same at all."

No, it wasn't. But until she figured out Jon's game, she didn't know what to think about it, let alone do about it.

They'd just entered the theater lobby when Jon was greeted by two handsome gentlemen.

"Lord Heathbrook!" the duchess said before her son could speak a word. "How good to see you again. I confess I will forever have a special place in my heart for you since you brought Jon's letter to us."

Ah, so these were Jon's friends. Chloe leaned close to whisper, "The Earl of Heathbrook is quite attractive, isn't he?"

He was, indeed, with his black hair and green eyes and roguish smile, the full force of which he now bestowed on the duchess, who fluttered her fan coquettishly.

But it was the other man who interested Tory more. His attractions—a head full of chestnut-brown wavy hair, warm brown eyes, and a military bearing that showed in every inch of his lean frame—were more understated than the earl's but every bit as potent. Most importantly, his gaze was fixed on Chloe and had been from the moment they approached.

How very interesting, especially considering that he and Chloe had never met as far as Tory knew. When Jon introduced his mother to him, Tory learned that the man's name was Captain Scovell.

"Scovell, Scovell . . ." the duchess said, holding out her hand for him to take. "Oh, wait. You're one of the Marquess of Glencraig's sons, aren't you? The one who is a naval officer?"

"I am indeed," the captain said, bowing over her hand. "Did you know my father?"

"I did, back in my day. I was very sad when I heard he'd died. But I understand that your eldest brother inherited the title and the estate. You're, what, your father's third son?"

"Second son now," Captain Scovell said. "My elder brother, William, died not too long ago. Now there are just four of us."

"Still, that's a lot of sons." When the duchess eyed him consideringly, Tory bit back a smile, knowing exactly what the duchess was thinking—that the captain was now next to inherit the title. Assuming that his oldest brother hadn't had any heirs of his own and didn't live to a ripe old age.

"Is your eldest brother . . . married?" the duchess asked.

Captain Scovell smiled. "I daresay Your Grace knows he is. A woman of your obvious stature probably also knows he hasn't sired an heir yet."

The duchess cast him an assessing look, then looked over at Jon. "You didn't tell me that your friends are so clever, my dear."

"We had to be to survive Bitche," the earl put in. "Eh, Falconridge?"

Jon darted a glance at Tory, for no reason she could see. Then he introduced Chloe to Captain Scovell, who gave the man her usual placid smile, clearly saving her genuine ones for the earl. But Captain Scovell didn't seem to mind, since he continued to stare at her with unveiled interest.

Next, Jon introduced Tory to his two friends as his sister's former governess. The second the name Victoria Morris left Jon's lips, Lord Heathbrook gave a start. "You're Morris's daughter? Jon, why didn't you tell us you'd already met Morris's daughter?"

"Didn't I say so?" Jon remarked, avoiding her gaze.

"You know perfectly well you did not," Captain Scovell told Jon, then offered her his hand. "Miss Morris, your father was a man we all respected greatly. We were devastated when he died."

She pressed his hand with a smile. "Thank you for saying so. That means a great deal."

The earl held out his hand, too. "Morris was a fine fellow, and a man we were proud to call a friend."

As she took his hand, tears started in her eyes despite her efforts to restrain them. "I'm just glad he had friends like you three at the end."

"We join you in mourning him," the captain said. "He was a very decent fellow." He shot Jon a veiled look. "But I'm curious, Miss Morris, to hear how you came to be Lady Chloe's governess."

Tory smiled at Jon's mother. "The duchess was kind enough to give me a position after my mother died."

"*Mrs.* Morris is dead?" the earl exclaimed. "Jon, you really are quite the secretive fellow, aren't you? You couldn't even tell us about *that*?"

"I didn't get the chance the last time I saw you, remember?" Jon bit out. "We were discussing other things."

Both men looked at him and got quiet.

"I forgot that," the earl said. "Yes, other things."

"Right," Captain Scovell said.

The three men shared a covert look.

"I see that His Grace is not the only one who's secretive," Tory said.

"Forgive us, Miss Morris," the captain said. "We have a great deal to do now that we're back in England, and that requires much discussion. But tonight, we'd rather enjoy our delightful company." He held out his arm to her. "May I?"

"I'd be honored," Tory said.

Lord Heathbrook offered his arm to Chloe, who smiled back at

Tory as she took it. After hesitating a moment to dart a glance at Tory himself, Jon took his mother's arm. Then the three couples trooped toward the stairs.

"May I ask you something, Miss Morris?" Captain Scovell said as they walked.

"Of course."

He nodded to where Lord Heathbrook and Chloe were talking as if they'd known each other all their lives. "Does Lady Chloe have a suitor?"

Tory figured she should be truthful. "She's had several. At present, I'm not sure who is top of the list."

"Ah."

"Your friend there seems to have gained her attention handily," Tory said. "If you're seeking to court her, you might have to compete with him."

The captain chuckled. "I'm not worried about Heathbrook. He charms every woman he meets, but I've yet to see one capture his heart." He stared down at her. "I hope Lady Chloe's own heart isn't already engaged."

"No," Tory said. "*She* charms every *man* she meets. She and your friend are probably too much alike in that."

"She's not the only woman who charms men," he said, patting her hand.

Tory recognized flattery when she heard it. "Thank you, but I'm under no illusions on that score. Few gentlemen in Society are interested in former governesses."

"You might be surprised," he said.

Tory decided that she liked this friend of Jon's. He had a way of making her feel at ease. She never felt that way with Jon. Excited, yes. Fully engaged, yes. But at ease? Hardly.

They were nearly to the box when it dawned on Tory that her new friend might answer one question Jon had been evading.

"Now I have something to ask *you*," she said. "How, exactly, did you three end up in Bitche prison? Every time I ask the duke about it, he changes the subject."

"That's odd. It's no great secret, I would think. We were sent to Bitche after we tried to escape from Verdun."

Chapter 13

As Jon overheard the last exchange between Scovell and Tory, he groaned. Damn it all to hell. He should have warned his friends about how much he'd told her and prepared them for Tory's inquisitive nature. But they wouldn't have understood his reticence to discuss the escape. They didn't view the events quite as he did.

Unfortunately, he couldn't do anything about it at the moment, for they were entering the box to find Mother's guests, the Grenwoods, already there.

Over the next few minutes, introductions were made all around. The Duke of Grenwood's size rather surprised Jon. The man wasn't only tall but beefy, uncommon for any other duke Jon had met. The Duchess of Grenwood was not much shorter than her husband, with a flaming head of hair and a smile nearly as kind as Tory's. It only took a few moments of pleasantries for Jon to realize they were every bit as amiable as his sister had said.

Grenwood's wife had already become friendly enough in the past with Jon's mother, sister, and Tory that they called her Diana. Within moments, the four women were situated in a corner, discussing a sketch Diana had brought to show them, leaving the gentlemen to their own devices.

Grenwood approached Jon and his friends with a jovial smile.

"My wife tells me you three are some of Napoleon's prisoners lately come from France."

"Civilian prisoners," Jon said. "Well, except for Scovell. As a naval officer, he was a prisoner of war."

"I have two brothers-in-law who fought in the war, both in the army," Grenwood told Scovell. "I should introduce you sometime. You probably have a lot in common."

"If a hatred of Boney counts," Scovell said, "then yes, we do."

Jon nodded. "We all have that in common, I'm afraid."

"I'm sure you're happy to hear he's ensconced on Elba," Grenwood said.

"Delighted beyond words," Heathbrook said. "If I never hear Napoleon's name spoken again, it will be too soon."

They continued chatting about the end of the war until the musicians entered and began tuning their instruments. Even though everyone knew that signaled another fifteen minutes before the play would begin, his mother rose to gather her guests like ducklings whom she expected to follow her lead.

Jon had to admit his mother had become rather domineering since his father's death. He found it amusing, although more times than not he resisted her machinations. But tonight he was content to sit where she'd placed him—in the box's second row between her and Grenwood. Jon had several questions about running a dukedom for the man.

Unfortunately, that meant his mother paired Chloe and Tory with Heathbrook and Scovell. Like turtledoves, the two couples were to sit in the front row of seats. That was as things should be, Jon told himself. Though he heartily wished Chloe wasn't with the earl, he did agree that Tory *ought* to be with other unmarried men, no matter how much he wished it otherwise.

The two duchesses rose and left to find a retiring room before the play started, but Chloe and Tory stayed with the gentlemen, and the sight of Tory seated next to Scovell rubbed Jon raw. Not that Scovell would be a bad choice for a husband—she'd never find a more loyal, caring gentleman than him, but every time he tried to imagine her in Scovell's arms, a fierce desire to snatch her away overtook him.

As if she read his mind, she shot him a furtive look, which he pretended to ignore. Then she turned to Scovell. "So, tell me about this escape you were all punished for. Why were you not successful?"

Jon stiffened at the question. She had a right to know, of course, but it would only provoke more questions, he was sure.

Scovell settled back in his seat. "Someone learned of our plans—we don't know who—and told the commandant of Verdun, whose gendarmes intercepted us in the attempt. He marched us off to Bitche for it."

"But surely they expected you to attempt such escapes," Tory said heatedly.

"They did indeed," Heathbrook said. "There had been so many successful escapes before our attempt that Napoleon had decreed that any British officer trying to escape the camps was to be court-martialed and shot by firing squad."

The two young ladies gasped. "And yet you risked such a thing?" Tory cried, glancing back at Jon again.

"Napoleon later rescinded the proclamation," Jon said, "but at the time we feared he might shoot détenus as well. We just didn't care. We'd been there eight years with no end in sight. From everything we'd heard, Napoleon was winning the war, and we didn't know if we'd be there another eight years or more. We were watching our youth melt away while we did nothing of value except exist."

"Not to mention that my father, who was in Verdun with us, had just died shortly after reading in a smuggled English newspaper about Mother's death in England," Heathbrook added. "So, I had nothing keeping me in France, and I knew he would want me to go back and make sure my younger brothers were doing all right under the rule of my cousin, who'd taken over running the estate in Mother's stead."

"And were they?" Tory asked.

Heathbrook shrugged. "They will be. My cousin packed them off to school, so at least they had limited exposure to the bastard."

"Lord Heathbrook, you may wish to watch your language," Tory chided him, with a glance at Chloe. "There is a young lady present."

"Two of them, to be precise," Jon quipped. When Tory raised an eyebrow at him, he said, "At least now you know I'm not the only one who picked up some bad habits in France."

She merely shook her head.

"I beg your pardon, Miss Morris," Heathbrook said. "The duke is right. We're all having to get used to being proper gentlemen again. Anyway, the main reason we wanted to escape was we wished to go home. We missed our families awfully."

"Of course, you did!" Chloe cried, looking indignant on their behalf. "Who wouldn't?"

Scovell snorted. "Well, some of us were reluctant to try it after a friend who was supposed to accompany us was packed off to another dungeon for a transgression two weeks before our escape, where he quite possibly died. Not to mention, a group attempting to escape Bitche was slashed to pieces by—"

"Enough, Scovell," Jon said. "Such gory tales are not for our fair young ladies, either." And he didn't want Tory learning that her father was the chief one to hesitate, with good reason it turned out.

Tory drew herself up, clearly irate. "On the contrary, sir, hearing these things helps us all understand what our men went through in their efforts to get home."

"No, no," Scovell said, "the duke is right. After so long living among the coarsest of men, we sometimes forget where we are now."

"And we did come to the play to be entertained, Miss Morris, not to talk about our past in France." Jon realized how harsh his rebuke sounded when a shocked silence descended over both Chloe and Tory.

"Forgive me, ladies," he added hastily. "I seem to have lost the knack of polite conversation myself. I'm just sick to death of talking about what happened in Verdun and Bitche. But I realize it is selfish of me to deny you answers to your questions." More selfish than they could possibly know.

"Oh, Jon," Chloe said, instantly softening. "I understand what you mean. Well, I don't understand it *entirely*, because I couldn't possibly without having gone through what you have, but I do want you to enjoy yourself tonight." She met Tory's gaze. "I want *all* of us to enjoy ourselves, and I know Tory feels the same."

Tory stared directly into his eyes. "I do," she said softly. "But I also feel that just as the pain of lancing an infected wound often leads to healing, talking about what is giving us pain can do the same."

He had no reply for that. How could he? His wound was so long and deep that he feared lancing it would cause him to bleed to death. "I'm sure you're right, Miss Morris. But if we could please put off the lancing until such time as I have brought sufficient bandages . . ."

That startled a laugh out of everyone except Tory. She merely flashed him a pitying smile. "Of course."

It was her pity that slayed him. What would she say if she learned he didn't deserve it?

He hoped she never did. Or not yet, anyway. He would rather bask in her soft smiles and gentle sympathies a while longer. How selfish was *that*?

As if by general consent, his companions began talking of other things. Tory and Scovell were speaking more intimately—which made him grit his teeth—but Heathbrook and Chloe made no attempt to hide their conversation.

"How often do you and Miss Morris come to the theater with your mother?" Heathbrook asked Chloe.

"As often as we can. But Tory doesn't usually come. Mama said it wasn't appropriate for my governess to attend the theater with us."

Jon bristled. Tory and Chloe were friends now, more than anything. He couldn't believe his mother would get in the way of that.

Chloe went on, "I think she was worried I wouldn't talk to the right gentlemen if Tory was with me."

Ah, yes, Jon did remember *that* conversation with his mother.

"But Miss Morris is here tonight," Heathbrook said, glancing over to where Tory was talking to Scovell.

"Yes, well, things have changed. Mama is presenting her in Society now. Her father left her a nice dowry, so Mama is making sure she has the right gowns and introductions and everything."

Jon stifled a groan when Heathbrook's questioning gaze shot to him. Damn Chloe's big mouth. Now he would have to deal with his friends' questions. They knew perfectly well that Morris's money had been gone by the time he died.

Fortunately, the play began then, his mother and the Duchess of

Grenwood entered, and things quieted for a while, giving him the chance to think up a plausible story in case they *did* ask him about the dowry. By the time the break between acts came, Heathbrook and Scovell obviously felt comfortable enough with their companions to entertain the ladies with witticisms that brought forth Tory's musical laugh more than once.

Jon couldn't stand it anymore, so he engaged Grenwood in conversation to find out exactly how the duke handled his estates. They didn't have long to talk, however, so Grenwood invited him to go riding in a few days, and Jon agreed.

Then Act Two began. It was fine at first, until Scene Two opened and Jon realized that this act, although still a satire full of humor, took place mostly in a prison, complete with fake bars and fake guards. He glanced over at his mother to find her gazing at him in horror.

"Oh, Jon," she whispered, "I had no idea that this was . . . We can leave if you wish."

"No need for that, Mother."

"But it's about a *prison!*" she hissed.

"Yes, I realize that," he said, a wild laugh bubbling up inside him. Only his mother could choose a play about the one thing he'd been trying to escape for the past decade.

He looked at Heathbrook, only to realize that the same conversation was going on between his friends and the ladies.

The earl rolled his eyes at Jon, but Scovell leaned back to whisper, "Did you know?"

"Not a clue," Jon said with a shrug. "None of us had ever seen it."

"I had," Grenwood said beside him. "In Newcastle. I did think it odd under the circumstances that your mother would choose that play, of all things."

"I didn't know," his mother leaned forward to whisper to Grenwood. "I thought it was a nonsensical farce about beggars writing an opera, not criminals cavorting in a prison. If I'd had any idea—"

"Trust me, it's not a problem, Mother." Jon patted her hand. "This pretend prison bears no resemblance to our real one, anyway. There was no cavorting and certainly little singing, humorous or otherwise."

"He's right," Heathbrook said. "And Bitche had no women, either. Not to mention that the guards were just as often short and ugly as they were tall and handsome like those fellows."

"Actors all have to be tall and handsome," Tory said, her remorseful gaze meeting Jon's, "or no one will come to the plays."

"Did *you* know what it was about?" he bent forward to whisper. When she shook her head no, he smiled. "I guess it was a surprise for all. Except Grenwood here, who's clearly more familiar with popular plays than the rest of us."

"Newcastle does possess some exceptional theaters," Grenwood said in so matter-of-fact a fashion that the rest of them laughed.

After that, the dam broke, and they mocked the play mercilessly. At one point, Jon noticed Heathbrook and Scovell talking privately. He only prayed they were discussing Chloe and not Tory's dowry. Then Scovell went off to talk briefly to Jon's mother, and he relaxed a little, especially after Scovell returned to chatting with Tory while Chloe and Heathbrook did the same.

When the break came between the second and the final act, Jon rose from his seat, eager to escape the flirtations between the four in front of him. "Would you ladies like some refreshments?"

To his surprise, Scovell and Grenwood stood as well, and after taking note of their companions' requests, joined him in heading for the saloon outside the boxes, where there was not only punch and other mild beverages but wine.

As soon as they were out of hearing of the ladies, Scovell took Jon aside. "I now see why you didn't tell us about Miss Morris. You wanted to keep such a jewel for yourself."

"No, indeed," Jon protested. "But Morris's last request was that I help her find a good husband, and I didn't think either of you were looking for wives."

He could feel Scovell's steady gaze on him. "So, you're truly not interested in her for yourself?"

"I have no time for a wife at present, and she needs a husband soon." He struggled to keep his voice even and nonchalant. "Chloe is too old to have a governess, and Tory is, as you say, a jewel. She deserves better than a life watching some other lady's children." Or a life serving as Chloe's companion, where Jon could see her every day, yearn for her every day . . .

Damn. He would get past this. He *would*.

"If your mother is to be believed," Scovell said, searching his face, "she'll find a husband easily enough. Morris left her money for a dowry, I understand."

Bloody hell. Being the strategist he was, Scovell's tone was neutral, but Jon could practically hear the questions in the man's mind.

Much as he hated to lie to Scovell, Jon saw no other way out of this. His friends had never understood his guilt over what had happened to Morris. They would try to talk him out of it, and he couldn't bear it.

"He did, indeed. It was as much a surprise to me as it clearly is to you. But unbeknownst to any of us, Morris had put some money in the funds before he'd left England, and after eleven years, it had grown into quite a nest egg."

"Five thousand pounds, your mother said." Again, Scovell's tone was as even as could be. "That's an excellent return on Morris's investment. I wonder why he couldn't get credit on the basis of that while in France?"

Damn it, the farther Jon continued in his scheme the more he found himself floundering. His mother and sister certainly weren't helping. But he couldn't blame Mother—it was her job to tout Tory's dowry. Jon had *made* it her job.

"Are you looking for a rich wife, Scovell?" Jon countered. "Because my sister has a nice dowry as well, though you may have to fight Heathbrook for it."

Scovell bristled. "No need to get nasty, *Falconridge*. If you didn't want to talk about Miss Morris's supposed 'dowry,' all you had to say was it's none of my affair."

"It's none of your affair," Jon bit out.

"Very well. But I'd be careful, my friend. Miss Morris strikes me as quite a clever woman—"

"You don't know the half of it," Jon muttered.

"And one day," Scovell went on, "she might demand a reckoning of her father's money. If she does, she may not be satisfied with some nursery tale you've drummed up about her father's investments."

"Are you calling me a liar?" Jon asked, meeting Scovell's gaze steadily.

Scovell's look was pitying. "No. But I do suspect you're helping

Morris's daughter in an effort to meet some ill-conceived sense of obligation you feel toward the man. And before you proceed down that path, I'm merely trying to point out it may grow rockier the farther you travel."

Jon opened his mouth to speak, but before he could, Scovell held his hand up. "But as you say, it's none of my concern."

Then the man walked off.

With a long sigh, Jon followed him at a slower pace. Scovell had put his finger right on the problem—the more Jon was forced to embellish his tale, the more insupportable it became. And the more he wished he could offer for Tory himself. But his reasons for not doing so hadn't changed.

Wouldn't he be quite the prize for any woman of quality—a duke who sometimes woke up in a cold sweat imagining he was back at Bitche, who spoke too bluntly for polite society . . . who'd failed the woman's father, ultimately causing his death? She would be better off with anybody else. Because leading a woman's father like a lamb to slaughter was an unpardonable sin for any suitor.

Indeed, after tonight he was thinking he should find a way out of his bargain with Tory. Every time they were alone together for sculpting lessons, he would be tempted to misbehave, and every time he came to his senses, he would regret he had done so.

Besides, he was besieged on all sides by people who needed his attention, and he *had* promised Mother that he'd take over managing the dukedom. He wanted to do so.

Now that he'd established a way to move among his fellow détenus in England without rousing suspicions, he wanted to be free to do that where he could. Since Mother and Chloe had made it clear to several people that Tory was being presented in society, Tory wouldn't dare refuse to do *her* part of their bargain, or his mother would get to the bottom of it.

Jon winced. All right, so he was taking the coward's way out, but he saw no other way to keep from touching her, kissing her, or worst of all, telling her everything she wished to know about what her father had suffered leading up to his death, thus ensuring that she hated him anyway.

He didn't want her hating him. Nor did he want her thinking there was a future for them, and then finding out the full truth about the escape and hating him. If he bowed out of his part of the bargain for a while, she'd be disappointed he wasn't doing as he'd promised, but that wasn't the same as hating him. She could get over that.

He could endure *that*.

Very well, he would tell her tonight, draw her aside once they arrived home, while his mother and sister were still about, keeping an eye on them. He wouldn't be able to misbehave under *those* circumstances.

And if sometimes he lay in bed at night dreaming of her, well, whom did that hurt? At least he wasn't trampling over Morris's memory by seducing his daughter. That was the important thing.

Chapter 14

Tory stared out of the window for most of the ride home. Everything she'd learned this evening had stunned her. Jon and his friends—and her father, presumably, since he'd gone to Bitche, too—had tried to escape from Verdun. She still didn't completely understand why. If life at Verdun had been such a benign existence, why try to escape?

Then again, she couldn't trust Jon to be telling the whole truth about Verdun and what it was like. He seemed reluctant to reveal anything that might make her sad about Papa.

What he didn't seem to realize was not knowing was worse. She imagined awful things, especially after Captain Scovell had let slip that comment about escapees being slashed to pieces. And it wasn't just Papa she was sad about, either. Jon seemed almost desperate to put France behind him, which told her that plenty of awful things had happened there to him, too. Like his scarred hands.

But she still thought it would be better if he talked about it. She would have to press him for more information tomorrow during their lesson when they could be private, and he didn't feel as if he had to spare his mother's and Chloe's feelings. She would press him now, but it had been a difficult evening for all of them, and she didn't wish to make it harder still.

"Jon's friends seemed to be enjoying the company of you ladies," the duchess said, obviously well-pleased with herself. "There were other gentlemen in the theater who asked after both of you, too, although many did know of Chloe already. I made sure to tell everyone who *you* were, Victoria, and that you had a nice dowry. That should get things off to a grand start."

"Thank you, Your Grace," Tory said, not sure what else to say. "I did like Jon's friends. They might be a bit unpolished, given where they've been all this time, but they're both very clever and rational, and I'm sure they'll get used to behaving like gentlemen soon enough."

"I hope not," Chloe said. "They're more interesting when they're speaking frankly."

"My dear, have I taught you nothing?" the duchess said. "Speaking frankly isn't a skill a lady or gentleman should foster. The rules of civility require one to hide ugly truths. How else would we all get along?"

Tory glanced at Jon, only to find him smiling indulgently even as he shook his head. No doubt he was in Chloe's camp. But for herself, Tory was torn between Chloe's opinion and his mother's. Tory always thought honesty best, but she also believed in being kind, and being frank wasn't always kind.

"Well, Lord Heathbrook said Captain Scovell was clearly quite impressed with Tory," Chloe said, nudging Tory with a smile. "And apparently he isn't easily impressed."

"We are all impressed with Miss Morris," Jon drawled, his gaze settling on her with great intensity. "She has weathered her difficult circumstances admirably."

"I actually think the captain was more impressed with *Chloe,*" Tory said. "He couldn't take his eyes off of her all evening."

"Oh, pish," Chloe said. "I didn't notice any such thing. Besides, he's too solemn for me. I much prefer a jovial fellow like the earl."

"And the earl would be of higher consequence as a husband," the duchess said. "Unless the present Marquess of Glencraig dies without siring a son."

"We're probably getting ahead of ourselves, anyway," Tory said. "The gentlemen only arrived in England recently. I doubt they're hunting for wives yet."

More was the pity. The captain would make an amiable husband for Chloe, even if he *was* ten years older than she. Chloe needed someone to adore her, and unless Tory was mistaken, Captain Scovell seemed as if he would.

As for herself, Tory hoped neither gentleman was interested, because she would hate to turn them down after all they'd suffered abroad. But she still was bent on starting her school, so she could take care of herself *and* Cyril.

"You did end up enjoying the play, didn't you, Jon?" Chloe asked. "Despite the prison scenes?"

"It made me laugh, yes." Jon met Tory's gaze. "One might even say it eased my pain."

"What pain?" the duchess asked sharply.

"Your son is just giving me grief over something I said at the play." Tory arched an eyebrow at him. "Pay him no mind."

"On the contrary," Jon said, "I do enjoy a good laugh, and nothing takes me out of myself more than laughing."

"I'm pleased to hear it," Tory retorted.

He was in quite a mood. As usual, she didn't know what to make of it.

"Yes, you must humor Jon if you wish to cheer him up," the duchess said. "He was that way as a boy, too."

They all looked at her in bewilderment. Then it dawned on Tory what the duchess was trying to say. "You mean, you must give him something to laugh at."

"That's what I said," the duchess replied. "Humor him. Give him humor. You know."

"Ohhh, of *course,*" Chloe said, exchanging a look with Tory.

Thank heaven Jon sat next to the duchess because he rolled his eyes so obviously that Tory could see it even in the dim light of the interior carriage lamps. It took all her will not to laugh outright.

"That's why I, for one, loved the play, prison scenes and all," the duchess continued. "It amused me enormously. The songs were very entertaining, too."

"They were, indeed," Tory said. "They humored us all."

That got a laugh out of Jon, which pleased her more than it should.

They arrived at the house moments later. She was relieved to finally be where she could get comfortable away from people. But when Jon helped her out as before, he bent to whisper, "I must have a word with you in the drawing room before you retire."

She nodded. What could he be wishing to discuss?

Oh! He must be planning to tell her what the solicitor said. She definitely wanted to hear *that*, although she was rather surprised he hadn't just waited until tomorrow's lesson to tell her. And why not ask her to come into his study? Wouldn't that be perfectly acceptable?

Ah, but if anyone overheard them in there, it might raise questions. This was between her and Jon, of course. Everyone knew about the dowry, and that was fine, but she and Jon had still managed to keep their bargain secret, which is what she preferred. Thus, when Chloe asked if Tory would come to her room when she was done changing clothes, Tory said she would be along later. That got a raised eyebrow from Chloe, but Tory didn't care.

As the duchess and Chloe climbed the stairs, Tory wandered into the drawing room oh so casually. Jon entered a short while later.

He gestured to two cozy chairs by the fireplace, where no fire had been lit on the excessively warm day. The fireplace was as far away from the door as possible, so that was good. It would give them a bit of privacy.

"Would you like some sherry?" he asked.

"I would, thank you."

He poured her a glass and then poured one for himself. When he handed hers to her, she said, "I thought you weren't much of a sherry drinker."

With a shrug, he took the chair next to hers. "I figured I'd better become one if I want to be part of Society."

She took a fortifying sip, then smiled brightly. "I assume this is about your visit to Father's solicitor."

Jon's eyes went wide, and his expression clearly said he hadn't expected that.

"Is it not?" she asked, her heart pounding. "Weren't you able to go?"

He let out a ragged breath. "Yes, I did go. Everything went smoothly. He was . . . er . . . a bit cautious about the clause involving giving me discretion in the matter of what's to be done with the money, but he said he would consult with a colleague and determine if such a clause was enforceable. Although he did agree with me that you would be better off marrying."

As a bitter disappointment settled in her chest, a sigh escaped her. "Of course he did. He's a man, isn't he?"

"What's that supposed to mean?"

"Men always agree on the subject of women marrying."

Jon swallowed the rest of his sherry in one gulp, then rose to go pour himself another glass. "My mother agreed you should marry. She's not a man."

"She wouldn't gainsay her son, the duke." Then, realizing how ungrateful she must sound, she added, "Forgive me. I appreciate everything that you and your mother are doing for me. Truly, I do. I'm just not sure it will get you what you want."

He faced her with a frown. "And what is that?"

"Me off your hands." She stared down into her glass.

"We are *not* trying to get you off our hands," he said so sharply that her head snapped up. He was staring at her with an unreadable expression. "I'm not, in any case." He sipped some sherry. "And as far as Mother is concerned, you could stay with Chloe forever as long as Chloe finds a husband."

"I should think Chloe's husband would have something to say about that."

He strolled toward her. "It won't come to that. I daresay you'll have an offer by the end of this Season."

"Oh?" She rose to face him. She didn't like him looming over her for such an important discussion. "Are you an expert at divination now?"

He swallowed some sherry. "No, but I'm not blind. I could see how the men in the theater were looking at you. That was enough to realize you will easily attract a husband."

"I don't want a husband!" She planted her hands on her hips. "Why can't you get that through your thick head?"

"Because it's unfathomable," he said in a guttural voice. "You deserve a mate, one who will adore you and take care of you and make sure you never want for anything."

Are you offering? The words were on her lips but died there unsaid. He wasn't offering or he would have done so when he was kissing and caressing her earlier.

The sudden silence between them teemed with the unspoken. His stare was a mixture of desire and pure male pride, and she felt such a palpable need to be in his arms that she was sure he could feel it thrum in the air. He took a step forward, and she thought for certain he would take her in his arms again and kiss her senseless. She wanted him to.

Then he seemed to catch himself. "That is not what I brought you in here to discuss, however."

She dragged in a steadying breath. Of course he had caught himself. She was not a fitting bride for a duke by any means. "What *did* you wish to talk about?"

He ran his fingers through his hair in an uncharacteristic motion of frustration for him. It reminded her he was out of sorts in this new world.

"I have to suspend our sculpting lessons for a while," he said.

Anger smoldered in her stomach. "You're reneging on your part of our bargain."

"No," he said hastily. "I'm merely postponing the lessons, I swear. But my meetings this week have shown me I must take hold of my responsibilities to the dukedom before it all runs away from me." He began to pace. "Apparently, Alban didn't do a damned—a *single* thing during his last year as duke."

She folded her arms over her waist. "I could have told you that. He started out well, especially since your father had left things in perfectly good order, or so I was told. But over time, Alban got bored and left most of the work to various managers. He primarily spent his days at his club, when he wasn't riding to hounds in the country or going with Aubrey to the stews. That pair did nothing useful, even when your mother was at her wit's end."

His expression cleared. "Then you understand why I must do this. There are mountains of papers at the accountants' office, not to mention urgent documents to be gone over with the land agent. Tomorrow, I'm meeting with the estate managers from all the properties. Oh, and next week, I've a fellow détenu coming here to look at my engraved print collection with an eye toward evaluating them for insurance purposes."

"Well, that sounds important," she said frostily.

He shot her a sharp glance before turning to stare at the cold fireplace. "Actually . . . the man needed work. He's an engraver by trade, so that was all I could think of to offer. Also . . . well . . . I hope you don't mind, but when he said Morris mentioned that your mother was an engraver, I thought you might know of some printshops looking to hire engravers. I told him I'd ask."

He was trying to help someone? Now she felt awful for her snide remark.

He faced her with an imploring look. "Beasley has a wife and children. They're not doing well. None of the détenus are unless they had family positions to return to."

That softened her even more. "Oh, dear, of course, I'll help however I can. If you wish, I can take care of discussing the engravings with him."

"That would be wonderful, thank you. He's also bringing me a list of détenus who could use work, and I told him I'd see if I could find places for them at the estates or . . . somewhere."

"That's very kind of you," she said. "I'm sure they will appreciate it."

Scrubbing his face with his hand, he said, "I'll be honest with you, Tory. I'm overwhelmed by all that needs to be done." He must have seen the pity in her expression, for he went rigid. "But I do wish to continue the sculpting lessons eventually, although I'm not sure there's any point. I can already tell that you know your business and you're good at teaching."

"Thank you," she said, wary again. "Yet you still think I should marry rather than pursue a profession I would love."

"Yes, I do." He hesitated as if thinking through some idea. "But if, after you've gone through the end of the Season, you don't have any offers you *wish* to accept . . ." He dragged in a heavy breath. "I will consider giving you the five thousand pounds to fund your school."

She blinked. "Truly?" Then the words fully registered, and she narrowed her gaze on him. "What do you mean, 'consider'?"

"Just what I said. You'll have to convince me that it's a workable proposition, present me with reports on your plans . . ."

"Yes, yes, I can do all of that!" she said eagerly. "I even found a place to lease that's perfect as a location for it."

He frowned. "You did?"

"I chose it before you even arrived home. I keep checking to see if they've leased it out, but no one else seems to have taken it yet."

"Ah."

When that was all he said, she said, "Thank you, Jon."

"I haven't agreed to the scheme," he warned.

"I know. But thank you for keeping an open mind about it."

Jon nodded. "You *will* still keep attending social affairs with Mother and Chloe, won't you?"

She rolled her eyes. "Yes. Although you'll soon see it's pointless."

"I doubt that," he said softly. "Now go on before I'm tempted to change my mind. Chloe's waiting for you."

With a quick grin, she hurried out the door. She was halfway up the stairs before she realized that if they weren't having sculpting lessons anymore, she wouldn't get to question him further about how her father had fractured his thigh.

Oh, well, it wasn't as if he was going anywhere. She could always ask him at dinner or some other social affair. After all, it sounded as if she had plenty more of those to come. But she would endure all of them gladly if in the end, she got to have her school.

Chapter 15

Jon scarcely saw Tory over the next few days. Even on the two nights when he'd accompanied the ladies to a soiree and a dinner, he'd arranged to meet them there, so he could avoid those painful moments in the intimate confines of the carriage. Once there, he'd chosen to speak with his friends—if they were there—or old friends he hadn't seen since before his time in France. Anything to stay away from her.

But that was its own special hell. He had to watch as other men made her laugh or touched her arm or whispered in her ear. Although none made her blush, even Heathbrook with his teasing remarks or Scovell with his quiet, earnest ones; one day someone would. Jon didn't know how he'd bear that.

Tonight he'd promised to squire the ladies to the first ball Tory was to attend—the one at Lady Sinclair's—and he was dreading it. For the first time, he'd have to watch her dance with other gentlemen.

Unless no one asked her to dance. Neither Heathbrook nor Scovell could attend, since the former was at his estate and the latter with his recruits in Portsmouth for the naval review before the Allied Sovereigns. And Tory seemed convinced her background would preclude her gaining any other partners.

As his phaeton hurtled toward Lady Sinclair's, he told himself she was worrying for nothing. Tory was sure to be dressed in a flattering gown if his mother and sister had anything to say about it, and anyway, she'd look lovely wearing sackcloth and ashes, so the gentlemen would surely line up to dance with her for her beauty alone. Within ten minutes of speaking to her, they would find her an interesting conversationalist, and her experience as a governess would ensure she knew all the complicated protocols for a ball.

So he'd be proved right, and she'd be proved wrong about her suitability as a wife. Which meant he must brace himself for an evening of watching her with other men. He ought to just dance with other ladies, if only to take his mind off her, but he had no stomach for it. He told himself it was because he wasn't ready to think about marriage, but that was a lie. He had all the stomach in the world for marriage if it meant having Tory.

He groaned. Unwittingly, Morris had chosen the perfect penance for him—asking him to find a husband for the beauty he couldn't in good conscience bed or marry himself.

Unfortunately, the moment he walked into the Sinclairs' London townhouse, his torture began.

"There you are, Jon!" Chloe tugged Tory along with her as she approached to greet him. "We thought you might try to get out of it, and we were so looking forward to introducing you to more of our friends. Weren't we, Tory?"

"Of course," she said in a neutral tone, her gaze steady and sure on him.

He smiled at them both. "Where's Mother?"

"Oh, she's off talking to Diana somewhere," Chloe said. "We wanted to wait for you and see if your attire came up to snuff."

"And does it?" he asked.

Chloe looked him over. "It will do," Chloe said archly.

"Pay her no mind, Your Grace," Tory said. "You look splendid."

"Thank you, Miss Morris. And both of you ladies outshine the stars."

Chloe lifted an eyebrow. "That's a rather clichéd compliment. Surely you can do better than that. I mean, just look at Tory's gown. I picked it out myself. What do you notice?"

"It's very . . . pink." Like her cheeks and lips and blushes. The sleeves were short, exposing a pair of beautiful arms, and the bodice was low enough to expose the creamy tops of two lovely breasts. How would he look at anyone but her? Especially when the skirt was a clingy silk, settling around her legs so he fancied he could see the shape of them. God help him.

"You are such a *man*," Chloe said. "You don't know how to pay a lady a proper compliment."

He didn't think they'd appreciate him saying what exactly he was appreciating. "And I suppose you think Heathbrook does?" he drawled.

"As a matter of fact, yes." Chloe pulled up her long gloves. "It's just a pity he couldn't be here tonight."

"I'm sure neither of you will have trouble finding partners," Jon said dryly.

"Well, then, let's go see if that's true," Chloe said. "Come, Jon, escort us, please."

Laughing at her impudence, he let each lady take an arm so he could walk into the ballroom looking like some battered old gentleman at the theater with a pair of gorgeous actresses hanging off him.

It became obvious fairly early that Chloe would have a wealth of partners. She was, after all, the daughter of a previous Duke of Falconridge and the sister of the present one. Meanwhile, Tory . . . charming, beautiful Tory . . . had half the *married* gentlemen in the room asking her to dance. She accepted each request—she could hardly do otherwise—and each time shot him an *I told you so* look.

After he'd watched five such men partner her, his mother came up beside him. "I was afraid this would happen."

"What?" he asked, sipping from his third glass of champagne. It was either drink or go mad watching Tory dance with men who couldn't marry her but who ogled her just the same as their wives entertained themselves elsewhere. Meanwhile, Tory's *I told you so* look grew more pointed.

His mother sniffed. "I overheard some gentlemen talking about Victoria in a less than proper way. Someone apparently remembered her as Chloe's governess and has told several of the eligible bachelors. Now they think it beneath them to dance with a 'servant,' and are vowing they won't be fooled by some 'jumped-up adventuress.'" She snorted. "Women aren't the only ones who gossip, by any means—men can be worse than women, I swear."

His temper surged to think of Tory's good name being besmirched by a lot of young arses bloated with their own consequence. They had no idea of the jewel they were tossing aside.

"I have let it slip to some of the mothers that Tory is Chloe's friend, now possessed of a tidy dowry from her father," his mother continued, "but it doesn't seem to have been passed on to the bachelors. And if *none* of the unmarried gentlemen dance with her, they will continue in their opinion of her." He knew precisely whom she was implying should dance with her.

"Which supposed gentlemen were talking about her so rudely?" he bit out.

She leaned close to whisper, "Those fellows milling about the punch bowl."

He set his empty glass on a passing tray. "I'll take care of it, Mother."

"Wait, Jon! What do you mean to do? You can't just walk over and berate them for not dancing with her."

"Watch me," he muttered under his breath before telling his mother, "I will be circumspect, I promise."

But first, he meant to solve the problem of no bachelors dancing with her. Tory was standing with Chloe, who, even as he watched, was invited to dance and went off to the floor. He hastened his stride so he could catch Tory alone.

He halted in front of her to bow formally, pleased to see a couple of unmarried gentlemen standing near her. "Miss Morris, may I have the honor of this dance?"

She stared at him blankly, and for half a second, he thought she might actually turn him down. But she was no fool, of course. She curtseyed, and said, "I would be honored, Your Grace."

He led her to the floor. It was only when he was there that he had an alarming thought. She stood beside him as they waited for the dance to begin, so he moved a bit closer to murmur, "I may have been a bit premature in venturing this."

"Oh?" she asked, her cheeks reddening.

"I forgot I haven't danced in eight years or so. I'm not sure I'll even recognize the music."

When she didn't answer, he ventured a glance at her and found her struggling not to smile.

"You find this amusing, do you?" he grumbled.

"You have to admit it's not the usual situation," she teased.

"Nothing about my life right now is the usual situation."

"Well, fortunately for you, we're about to dance the cotillion," she explained, "and I'm sure they were dancing those when you were last in England."

He breathed a sigh of relief. "They were, indeed." And the cotillion wasn't the intimate sort of dance where he'd be expected to hold her close, thank God. "I can't promise I won't make a hash of it, though. It's been years."

"I'll manage," she said softly. "Is that why you haven't been dancing? Because you're afraid of making a hash of it?"

"Partly. But I knew I'd be safe with you."

That was apparently the wrong thing to say, for she looked away. "I see," she said coolly. "I should have guessed it wouldn't be because you *wanted* to dance with me."

"That's not what I meant. If my lack of skill had been my only reason, I wouldn't have danced at all. I didn't intend to dance this evening. But—" He caught himself before he could reveal he was doing this to help her. That wouldn't go over well, either. She did have a sense of pride.

"But what?" she asked, casting him a searching glance.

"I feared I might never get the chance if I didn't take it now," he said truthfully. "Someone will snatch you up eventually, and next thing I know, you'll be engaged to be wed."

She cast him a hard look. "Perhaps you've noticed that my only partners this evening have been old, married men."

I mean to correct that, he thought, but didn't dare say it. She would take it to mean this was, as she had once put it, a *pity dance.* "That will change eventually. Besides, all those 'old, married men,' whom I'm sure you charmed exceedingly well with your wit and ladylike manners, have sons looking for wives."

"I somehow doubt it was my wit and manners that charmed them into dancing with me." She glanced down briefly, but none too subtly, at her low-cut gown.

He stiffened. "Did any of them insult you? Because if they did, I swear—"

"You will defend my honor?" She gave a brittle laugh. "Oh, do be serious, Your Grace. If you do that, you will ruin me. That would hardly help your plan to marry me off."

She was right, unfortunately. And he was half-tempted to do it anyway. Then he'd have to wed her, and she'd be his.

At least until she learned that his ill-fated escape plan had eventually killed her father.

The music began then, and his heart started pounding as he took her gloved hand. It reminded him of when he'd eaten the pear out of her fingers and licked the juice off them. His gaze shot to her, and he could see she remembered it, too, for she got the same little melting look she'd had then. The one that had made him lose his mind.

He swallowed . . . hard . . . then caught her watching his throat. Damn, this would be the longest dance of his life.

Even though they only touched hands, the long stares, slow turns . . . separations to weave in and out of other couples, only to approach each other again in a sensual completion of the step, were as erotic as any waltz. He couldn't keep his eyes off her. She showed beauty and grace in every motion. And each time he took her hand in the dance, he wanted to tug her into his embrace and kiss her sweet, silky mouth.

She knew it, too. Her cheeks pinkened more and more the longer they danced. Anyone watching them closely would know in an instant that they'd had an intimate connection at some point before the ball. Yet neither could look away. Thank God, none of the dancers was paying them any mind, and all the spectators were too far away to see the desire shimmering in the air between them.

God, how would he ever learn to deal with this longing for her?

All too soon, their set was over, and he had to lead her from the floor. They were silent as they walked. He glanced over to the punch table to see the bachelors still standing there, observing them both. Good.

Then she cleared her throat. "That was lovely, Jon," she murmured. "You may not have danced in a while, but clearly your memories of how the cotillion is performed persevered."

"Thank you," he said. "You were the best dancing partner I've ever had."

She surprised him by laughing. "Considering you previously were probably dancing with either girls fresh out of the schoolroom in England or married ladies at Verdun, that's not saying much."

"Actually, in Verdun, I danced with quite a few French young ladies." He bent close to whisper, just before they reached Chloe, "Yet you're still the best."

She flashed him a shy smile before he released her hand. He wanted to linger with her, but the second half of his mission to gain eligible partners for her wasn't yet done. He bowed to her, then asked both ladies, "Would either of you like punch?"

"I would," Chloe said. "I'm positively parched."

"That would be lovely, thank you," Tory said.

"I'll be right back," he said, then headed for the punch table. He made a great show of pouring punch in a glass, and just as he expected, one of the bachelors edged up next to him. This lot could never resist trying to become chummy with a man of greater consequence than themselves.

"So . . . Falconridge," the beak-nosed chap said. "It's good to see you again."

Jon turned his head to look down his nose at the man. "Again?"

The young man, who appeared to be twenty-five at most, flushed. "We met at my parents' soiree a couple of days ago. I'm Knightdale."

"Ah, right. You're Manderleigh's brat."

The fellow blinked, probably used to being fawned over for bearing the Earl of Manderleigh's subordinate title, Viscount Knightdale. Then he drew himself up haughtily. "I happened to notice Your Grace dancing with Miss Morris, your sister's governess. I confess I was surprised, given that any other, more eligible lady in the room would have been honored to dance with you."

Jon turned back to the punch bowl and ladled out another glass. "Not that it's any of your affair, sir, but it's been some years since I danced at an English ball, so I was concerned about my rather rusty dancing skills. I knew Miss Morris, as a *former* governess, would be happy to guide me through the steps until they came back to me."

Knightdale snorted. "Of course she would. You're a duke, and she's a penniless nobody. You were kind in even deigning to speak to her. Hell, she's damned fortunate to be here dancing among the rest of us."

Bloody obnoxious arse. "As it happens," Jon said smoothly, "my mother, the duchess, is presenting her in Society, as I'm sure you know. Her father was my closest friend in France, and a cousin of Viscount Winslow besides. What's more, Dr. Morris left her a fortune of five thousand pounds."

Jon stared at Knightdale hard enough to make the little weasel squirm. "So, she's quite eligible, probably more so than some ladies here. Thus, I doubt she's too concerned about who among you lot would dance with her."

Then, sparing a moment to use his condescending gaze on the rest of them, he picked up his two glasses of punch and walked away, resisting the urge to look back to see the reaction of Knightdale and his fellow weasels.

He approached the two women only to find that Chloe was on the dance floor with the Baron Something-or-Other awaiting the next set. Handing Tory her glass, he said, "I see my sister won't be around for a while to drink her punch."

"I'll hold on to it for her if you wish," Tory said.

"No need. I'll just drink it myself and fetch her a fresh glass at the end of the set." He turned to gaze out over the floor. "I used to hate these things. All the girls my age used to titter when I walked by, and I didn't know what they were laughing at. But the young ladies do the same thing now, so I guess they weren't laughing at me."

"That's what I would call a nervous laugh. You were a wealthy duke's son even then. Any look you gave them provided them with hope that they might snag you for a husband one day. And now that you have the title? An eligible duke of your age and good looks is the grand prize in the game of husband-hunting."

"But not to you," he said. "No husband is a prize to you."

She met his gaze with twinkling eyes. "At last, you've begun to listen to me."

"Can you really tell me you don't see a single fellow here who would interest you?"

She scanned the room. "Perhaps that gentleman in the puce waistcoat. If we danced together, our attire would match beautifully."

He chuckled. "That's hardly a reason to choose a husband."

"But it's a good reason to dance with him, if he should ask, and I do enjoy the dancing."

When an awkward silence fell between them, he searched for something to say. Miraculously, he thought of something. "I forgot to tell you. I asked my détenu friend, Mr. Beasley, the man who's evaluating the prints, to come day after tomorrow in the morning. I will be otherwise engaged with one of my estate managers, but if you still don't mind meeting with him . . ."

"I'd be happy to," she said. "I've already compiled a list of printshops looking for experienced engravers."

"Thank you. I'm sure he'd appreciate it."

Just at that moment, one of the fellows from the punch group approached and asked to be introduced to Miss Morris. Thank God, Jon remembered his name from a brief conversation they'd had at the soiree. He provided the introductions, trying not to glare at the fellow.

When the arse asked Tory to dance, it was all Jon could do not to ask his intentions. Such a question would, of course, be ludicrous. Jon wasn't her father or brother or anyone with the right to ask such a thing. He was just . . . an interested party providing her with a secret dowry.

Notwithstanding Mother's interference in matters, he needed to keep reminding himself of that.

Tory accepted the man's invitation to dance and went off to the floor without a backward glance. It took only a few moments of watching them whirling about to make him realize he just couldn't watch her dancing with others anymore. Not now that he knew how eloquently she danced, how wonderful it had been to hold her hand . . . how difficult it would be to watch her marry another.

Enough. He had to escape all these courting couples. Remembering that he'd seen a library earlier on his way in, he headed leisurely in that direction. He was stopped quite a few times by people who knew him, but as the last strains of the dance wafted to him, he reached the hall and freedom.

At least for a while.

Chapter 16

Tory couldn't believe it. She'd had perfectly eligible gentlemen partners for the last four dances. Of course, none could hold a candle to Jon, who'd practically melted her into a puddle of toffee sauce with all his meaningful glances and masterful steps, but she wouldn't admit that to him for the world.

No point in continuing a flirtation that couldn't go anywhere.

The duchess approached her, wreathed in smiles. "I don't know if it was Jon's dancing with you or what he said afterward to the young gentlemen, but whatever it was, it worked."

Her heart faltered. "What are you talking about?"

"I complained to Jon about the bachelors not dancing with you, leaving you to stand up with a lot of old husbands, and he said he'd take care of it. And he did!"

A sick feeling settled in her stomach. "That's why he was talking to those men over by the punch bowl? That's why he danced with me?" Never mind that she'd told him repeatedly she wasn't looking for a husband. He hadn't listened.

As if finally realizing the insult behind her words, the duchess said hastily, "No, of course not. You know he's fond of you. He hasn't danced with anyone else here. It's a great compliment to you, my dear. And what a coup you had, dancing with the Viscount Knightdale! He's quite the catch, you know."

"Is he?" Tory said, hardly hearing her.

Of course Jon had stepped in to ensure she had partners. She should have realized it. And it did explain why, on her way to the necessary earlier, she'd seen him slip into the library. Once he'd done his duty by her, he figured he could hide.

Devil take him! Any other woman would have thought what he'd done for her was sweet, but any other woman wouldn't have thought when they'd danced that he'd wanted . . . that he'd needed . . .

Her.

Tears stung her eyes. What a fool she'd been! She should have listened to *him* when he'd said he wasn't ready for a wife.

She drew herself up. Why did she even care? She didn't want him for a husband, no matter how deliciously he kissed. She'd have to choose between him and Cyril, and with both their parents gone, she'd have to choose Cyril.

There could be nothing between them. And she *hated* that.

"Are you all right, Victoria?" the duchess asked. "You look a little faint. Fortunately, supper will be served any minute. A bit of food will hearten you, I'm sure. You're to be taken in by Mr. Pierce Egan. He's quite clever."

Her Grace lowered her voice. "Don't tell anyone, but I read his scandalous book, *The Mistress of Royalty, or the Loves of Florizel and Perdita*, and he's exceedingly humorous. Of course, he wouldn't make you a proper husband—he's Irish, after all—but at least he'll make you laugh at supper tonight."

Suddenly, Tory noticed the Countess of Sinclair hurrying toward them.

"Duchess," Lady Sinclair said, "have you seen your son? He's to take the Duchess of Grenwood in to supper, and I can't find him anywhere!"

Oh, dear. "Did you check the library?" Tory asked.

"Of course, I checked the library. Or someone did, anyway. He wasn't there. But the footmen say he never called for his phaeton, either."

"That doesn't mean he didn't go home," the duchess pointed

out. "He likes to walk. He walked hundreds of miles to get to Paris from where he was kept in France. Walking home would be nothing to him."

"True," Tory said. "But would he really be so rude as to make Diana go in to supper alone? That seems . . . unlike him." And she could hardly see him leaving his phaeton here to walk home.

"I swear, I don't know the man these days," the duchess said, lifting her eyes heavenward. "He has the oddest whims. That French prison did something to him."

Tory could certainly agree with that.

Lady Sinclair was still staring at them. "What shall I do about Diana?"

The duchess sighed, then drew herself up with dignity. "Tell everyone my son went home, and I went home to make sure he was well. That way, since I was supposed to be taken in by the Duke of Grenwood, he can now take in his wife. That will take care of Diana."

"He can't take his own wife in to supper," Lady Sinclair said. "Can he?"

The countess was American, so of course she wasn't sure of such things. Tory wasn't absolutely certain herself. "I don't think there's any rule preventing it if precedence is observed, is there, Your Grace?"

"No one will complain." The duchess waved her hand dismissively. "They'll say you made a good faith effort, Lady Sinclair, and praise you for it. But now I must leave. Would you mind chaperoning Victoria and Chloe? Or perhaps ask Diana to do so? I hate to spoil *their* evening. I'll send the carriage back for them."

"That's fine." Lady Sinclair clasped her hand. "Thank you, Your Grace. This is very kind of you."

"Not a bit," the duchess said. "Just hold supper a bit longer to give me time to gather my things, call for the carriage, and be away. In exchange, I promise to thrash my son when next I see him." Then she marched off.

Tory bit back a laugh at the idea of the duchess thrashing Jon. But she still wasn't convinced he'd left. "If you don't mind, Lady Sinclair, I shall go to the retiring room while there's still time."

It took her a while to get to the hall, since Chloe stopped her to ask what was going on, and she had to tell her *something*. But as soon as she could leave her, she headed for the library. She couldn't believe Jon would so callously insult Diana. Then again . . .

Before entering, she made sure no one was near to see her go in, and once inside, she slid the door silently closed.

She'd been in the Sinclairs' unusual library often and knew it as well as she knew Falcon House. Its large mahogany bookcases connected overhead to form a series of alcoves, each with a table and a Hepplewhite wingback armchair, so one could sit in the back of an alcove and read undisturbed between two bookcases.

"Your Grace," she whispered.

No answer. She walked past each alcove and looked in.

"Are you in here, Your Grace?" she asked again, still whispering.

She heard a heavy sigh from the hidden side of the chair in the last alcove. "Who wants to know?" Jon grumbled.

"You *are* in here! I knew it!"

"Tory?" Shoving the chair back, he rose, book in hand, and spun to face her. "What the devil?"

"What the devil, yourself! Everyone has been looking for you! They said they looked in here but—"

"They did." He shrugged. "When they called for me, I ignored them."

"You were supposed to take Diana in to supper. Now your mother is having to fix things by going home, so that Grenwood can take Diana in instead, and—"

"Wait, what are you talking about? I thought supper wasn't served at these things until at least midnight and it's only—" He drew out his pocket watch and looked at it. "Damn."

"Yes, 'damn,' indeed."

"I was caught up in reading about crops in Shropshire and lost track of the time," he said apologetically. "I meant to be in the ballroom long before supper."

She planted her hands on her hips, still angry with him for manipulating gentlemen into dancing with her. "Well, you ought to be ashamed of yourself! Talk about making a hash of things—"

"I'll go right now," he said, his expression full of remorse as he left the alcove. "It will be fine."

She stepped in front of him. "It will not be fine! You *can't* go in now. Lady Sinclair has probably already told people you walked home—your mother's suggestion, by the way, since the servants said you hadn't taken the phaeton—and your mother is probably already in the carriage. You will not make liars out of either of them. As soon as everyone goes in to supper, you can slip out and take Alban's phaeton home."

"First of all, it's *my* phaeton now. Secondly, if I drive it back, we won't be able to avoid the servant gossip." He narrowed his gaze on her. "And how did you know I was in here, anyway?"

"Lucky guess." When he eyed her suspiciously, heat filled her cheeks. "I . . . er . . . saw you come in here earlier while on my way to the retiring room."

"Were you following me?" he demanded.

She scowled. "Only you would be so arrogant as to assume such a thing."

That seemed to catch him off guard. "You consider me arrogant?"

She threw up her hands. "I hardly know! One minute, you're staring soulfully into my eyes as you say lovely things and whirl me about the floor. The next, you're coldly bribing gentlemen to dance with me so I can gain a husband and get as far away from you as possible. I'd say that 'Jon' isn't arrogant in the least. 'The Duke of Falconridge,' however, is the most arrogant, pigheaded—"

"I did not bribe gentlemen to dance with you," he protested.

"No?" She stared him down. "Did you mention my dowry to them?"

He thrust out his chin. "I might have. But that was the purpose for which it was intended, was it not? To coax gentlemen into considering you as a wife?"

She glared at him. "Gentlemen who otherwise thought me beneath them, I assume?"

He regarded her cautiously. "Only because they don't know you, Tory. Anyone who spends ten minutes getting to know you wants to be with you."

There he went again, saying lovely things he didn't mean. "Anyone except you, apparently, judging from how you disappeared after our dance."

"Anyone *including* me," he said, then muttered something

under his breath that sounded much like *bloody hell*, which was rather vulgar even for him. "But how I feel doesn't matter."

"It matters to me." When his face showed his chagrin, she instantly wished the words unsaid.

"It shouldn't." Then he glanced away. "How were your dances with the bachelors?"

"Oh, for pity's sake." She crossed her arms over her chest. "If you wanted to know that, you should have stayed around to find out."

He winced. "Surely you discovered that one or two suited you. And there will be more, once men hear how kind and clever and accomplished you are."

"I suppose you'll announce *that* at the next ball if I don't have any partners *there*," she snapped.

"Tory, please," he began, his voice thrumming low.

"I am not a charity case, curse you!" To her horror, tears sprang to her eyes. "I told you I don't want a husband, but you won't listen. No, worse than that, you act as if *you* want me! Then you act as if you don't! What am I supposed to think?"

He caught her by her arms, staring down at her with a tortured expression. "Damn it, sweetheart, I do want you. But it's impossible."

That struck a hard blow to her heart. "Of course, it is," she said shakily. "Because you're a duke and I'm a governess—"

"That has naught to do with it, for God's sake! It's just . . ." He lifted a hand to brush her cheek, then shook his head. "Trust me, you don't want me."

"That's the problem. I *do* want you." She knew that now. So, going on sheer instinct, she went up on tiptoe and kissed him square on the lips.

When she drew back, he was watching her with an intensity she'd grown to crave. "God rot it," he muttered, and clasping her head in both his hands, he kissed her as if the world would end if he didn't.

With a happy sigh in her throat, she rose into his kiss, clasping his arms to hold him close. Groaning, he deepened it, turning her knees to butter and her blood to fire as he wrapped his arms about her waist and plastered her to him.

They kissed a long while, eagerly, thoroughly. He dragged the breath from her, then gave it back, his tongue playing with hers and his hands beginning to roam up and down her back, then up and down her sides.

He was breathing heavily now—so was she—and she moaned as he began to kiss his way down her neck.

"We must . . . stop this," he rasped.

"Must we?" She dropped her hands to slide them inside his open black tailcoat to where his white silk waistcoat met his knee breeches. Goodness, he had a lean waist and hips. She was just wicked enough to wish she could see him without his clothes.

She was dying to sculpt his firm muscles, run her hands down his taut chest, get a look at his tight bottom . . .

Suddenly, Jon froze and glanced at the door. That was when she heard it—two men talking on the other side.

"I tell you, I'm almost sure I saw her go into the library."

"Don't be an arse, Knightdale. Why would she go into a library in the middle of a ball?"

"For an assignation, of course."

When Tory groaned, Jon grabbed her hand and tugged her into the alcove he'd been in. Then he turned the Argand lamp off. It sputtered out just as they heard the library door opening.

Lifting Tory soundlessly onto the table, Jon shielded her with his body and pressed a finger to her lips.

"I told you she's not in here," said the other fellow.

Tory's heart pounded so hard, she was sure they must hear it.

"She's probably out there waiting with the rest of the crowd," the man went on sullenly. "Where *we* should be. I'm famished. Why are they waiting so long to serve supper, anyway?"

Tory cut her eyes up at Jon, who rolled his.

Lord Knightdale cursed. "She must have gone back in the ballroom. And I'd been hoping to catch her so I could ask her for the dance after the supper dance."

"Why? You were mocking her earlier."

"That was before I heard she had a fortune. Did you see the titties on her? Any woman who looks like that with a five-thousand-pound dowry is nothing to sneeze at."

"You're such an arse, Knightdale."

Tory quite agreed. Meanwhile, Jon stiffened and looked as if he might vault out of the alcove to take on Lord Knightdale. Hastily, Tory clutched him tightly about the waist, then stretched up to kiss his mouth.

He hesitated only a moment before kissing her back, his tongue making lazy strokes inside her mouth that coaxed all her senses to life. She could feel the faint stubble on his chin, taste the champagne on his tongue, smell the sharp and spicy cologne on his neck.

Not to mention that the fear of discovery gave their kisses an exhilarating edge. He must have felt it, too, for he slid his hand up to cup and knead her breast through her gown, making her wild for more.

So this was what desire felt like, this jumble of sensations turning her to clay in his hands. *More, please,* she thought, then had a moment's panic when she feared she'd said it aloud.

Thankfully, if she had, the other two gentlemen hadn't heard it. "Come on, Cokesbury," Lord Knightdale said. "Might as well look for her in the ballroom."

"She probably went into the retiring room," his companion said, his voice dropping as the two men left.

Tory barely noticed when the door shut with an audible click. But she definitely noticed when Jon's thumb rubbed her nipple through her gown.

"Gave you ideas, did they?" she murmured against his mouth.

"Trust me, sweetheart," he said in a husky voice, "I've had ideas since the day I met you. Which is precisely why you shouldn't be alone with me."

His admission thrilled her. "I probably shouldn't. But I am."

With a low moan, he kissed her throat, all the while moving his hand up to slide her gown off her shoulder.

"Jon!" she said urgently.

"Let me show you how much I want you, so you never doubt it again. I promise I won't ruin you. But . . ."

He left that thought hanging in the air as he kissed his way down to where her breasts were pressed together by her gown and corset. Somehow, he got her gown lowered enough to expose her corset cup and chemise ties. Within moments he'd bared one of her breasts.

She dragged in a shaky breath as he gazed down at it. "Now I wish I hadn't turned off the lamp," he said hoarsely. "I can't imagine anything I'd like to see more than you displayed in all your naked glory. But I'll have to settle for this."

Then he bent his head to cover her breast with his mouth. Oh. Good. Lord! His warm mouth sucked at her breast, and she felt a burst of sensation like . . . like nothing she'd ever known before. Then he tongued her nipple, and she thought she'd go out of her mind. It was exquisite, something she'd never imagined could feel *that* good! Arching up against his lips, she released a long, low moan.

"Like that, do you?" he whispered against her breast.

She had to close her eyes against the satisfaction in his expression.

"God, you taste like heaven." He used his hand to fondle her other breast, two glorious sensations at the same time, and she dug her fingers into his waist. It was divine having him do this to her, better than the best dessert, and she did like her desserts.

Now an ache had started beneath her mons that made her feel wet and hot inside her *fountain of love*, as her mother had called it. Was that normal? If it wasn't, she didn't want to be normal.

"This is madness, sweetheart," he murmured against her breast. "Make me stop."

"Why?" she choked out. "So you can return to treating me coldly? Not on your life. If I only get this moment of you needing me, I shall enjoy it." Especially when he tongued her nipple again, making her catch her breath.

"I do need you, you know," he rasped. "If I dared, I'd strip you bare and take you right on this table. But that would ruin you." Then he straightened to gaze down at her, eyes smoldering. Slowly, he began dragging her skirts up her legs. "Still, I can give you a taste of what it would be like to experience that kind of pleasure without ruining you."

"I-I don't understand."

He flashed her a wicked smile. "You will." Then he began to kiss her again, all the while moving his hand higher and then pushing his body between her legs, parting them for him.

She tore her mouth from his. "Wait! I know how ruination works and if you put your . . . your . . . member . . . inside me . . ."

He uttered a rough laugh. "As badly as I wish to, I won't put my 'member' inside you, I swear." With that, he slid his hand between her legs, where she was so damp and eager, where it felt as if she'd been waiting her whole life for him to touch her.

But he didn't just touch her. He caressed her, fondling parts of her she'd never touched herself. And what a revelation! It felt magical and perfect and daring, all at the same time.

Then he slid his finger inside her *fountain of love*, and she let out a throttled groan. "That is . . . oh dear . . . my word . . ."

He pressed his mouth to her ear. "You're so hot and wet for me, sweetheart, it drives me to insanity."

"You're doing . . . the same to me," she rasped.

He groaned. "Good. I only wish I could . . . *we* could . . . But we can't. So this will have to be enough." He swept his thumb against a very tender spot, and she nearly jumped off the table.

"Ohhh, Jon . . . That is . . ."

He said nothing, merely filling his free hand with her naked breast, and thumbing her nipple over and over, the way he was thumbing her down below in a rhythm that made her start to pant and strain against his hand.

Meanwhile, he thrust a second finger inside her, stretching her a bit, but not unpleasantly, until his thumb and fingers were working in concert, stroking her inside and outside, until her body smoldered like coals on the edge of erupting into flame.

"Yes . . . like that . . ." she choked out, as little fires began to break out below. "More . . . please . . . Jon . . . *more.*"

"Tory . . ." he whispered against her cheek. "I wish . . . damn . . . how I wish . . . you could be . . ." Then he took her mouth again as if to blot out anything reckless he might say.

But she was beyond speech. She pressed her mons rhythmically against his thumb as more fires erupted. Then she strained against Jon's hand, her body seeming to ignite into flames, and for a moment, all was ecstasy. She could feel her *fountain of love* convulse around his fingers.

Apparently, so could he, for he whispered, "That's it, my beauty. My sweet . . . angel . . . My dearest."

She delighted in his possessive words as she clung to his body.

They added to the warm embers left behind after he'd pleasured her as he kissed her cheeks and mouth and throat. He might not want to desire her, but clearly, he did. And that gave her hope despite all her cautions.

"That was amazing," she whispered. "I . . . I had no idea."

He nuzzled her neck. "So, you enjoyed it, did you?"

"You know perfectly well that I did. But did you?"

"I enjoyed watching you enjoy it."

That's when it dawned on her—he hadn't ruined her, which meant he hadn't gained his own satisfaction from their encounter.

She drew back to stare at him. "Isn't there something I could do to give *you* pleasure without being ruined?"

He blinked, clearly surprised by the question. "Perhaps one or two things . . . But I'm afraid I must forego that particular enjoyment. Because if you did them, I'd never be able to walk out of here without someone guessing what I'd been up to, and eventually they'd figure out who I'd been up to it with."

"Even if they did," she said hotly, "I wouldn't make you marry me."

"I'd make *you* marry *me*." He kissed her with a leisurely thoroughness that left her gasping once he drew back to say fiercely, "I would never let you lose your reputation simply because I couldn't control myself."

"And I'd never make you sacrifice yourself for my reputation." She kissed his throat, then stared up at him. "Never."

"It wouldn't be a sacrifice," he rasped, his eyes gleaming in the semidarkness. "Not for me, at any rate. But it very well could be for you."

"Why?"

"Because . . ." He seemed to catch himself. "Because you've already said you don't wish to marry. I took you at your word. Should I not have done so?"

If anything could throw cold water over all their pleasures, it was the reminder that although she wished to marry, she dared not.

With a sigh, she slipped off the table to pull her skirts down. "No, you should take me at my word. Indeed, I should go. We've lingered too long in here. And though the rules of precedence may make me one of the last to go in to supper, if I know Lady Sinclair, she won't announce that supper is served until she's sure every one of us is in place."

He helped her straighten her attire, then gave her a quick kiss before she headed to the door, praying that Lord Knightdale and his friend weren't standing about in the hall.

But as she slipped into the ballroom unnoticed, she realized she'd unwittingly become Clytie, yearning for Helios the sun god, whom she could never have.

And there wasn't a single thing she could do about it.

Jon sat in the library, trying to get his arousal to subside, no small feat when he couldn't stop thinking about how it had been to kiss Tory, caress Tory . . . make Tory come. He ought to be proud of his success.

Instead, he wished he'd asked her to marry him.

Damn you, Morris, he thought, for the first time remembering his mentor with anger, not guilt. *Why couldn't you have had a stupid or cruel or ugly daughter, preferably all three? Why did it have to be the witty, kind, and sensuous Tory?*

Thinking of Morris did the trick. Now he could slip out of the Sinclairs without provoking anyone's notice. Still, it was better he walk home and leave the phaeton, if only to help his mother maintain her tale. Although if he had the choice, he'd march into the supper room, throttle Knightdale for being a randy arse, and sweep Tory from the room and off to Scotland to be married.

But he couldn't. Knightdale might call him out, and he'd have to shoot the fellow. Tory might refuse to marry him. And he didn't fancy driving the phaeton to Scotland. He suspected she wouldn't either, even if she *did* agree to marry him, which wasn't certain.

Why was she being so determined not to marry, anyway? After tonight, he would swear she liked him well enough. Yet she'd made it clear marriage *still* wasn't in her plans. Yes, she did wish to use the money for her school, but he began to think there was more to it.

Or perhaps that was just his pride talking, trying to find a reason for her not wanting him as a husband other than that she didn't like him. She'd said she found him arrogant, after all.

He scowled. He had to stop this and go home while everyone was at supper. Thank God he successfully slipped out unseen so he could walk home.

Unsurprisingly, the moment he entered Falcon House, his mother waylaid him. "I had to leave a perfectly delightful ball because *you* forgot to stay for supper and insulted our good friends the Grenwoods!"

He acted surprised. "Forgive me, Mother. I forgot I was to take the duchess in to supper. I'm not used to being around so many people, and the chatter and music was too much for me after years in near solitude." It was the only excuse that might be acceptable to his mother, although if she believed that, she was more gullible than he thought.

She sighed. "I'm sorry to hear that, Jon, but you can't just do as you please at these affairs."

"Can't I? I am the duke, after all, as you keep reminding me."

That put a steely glint in her eyes. "Yes, but you're the duke who means to take the dukedom in hand. Which means you can't be insulting half of society."

"Duly noted, Mother." He bowed. "Now if you don't mind, I—"

"Where were you, anyway? I thought I might encounter you on the ride home, but I didn't see hide nor hare of you. Not even long ears."

That flummoxed him. "My ears are . . . long these days?"

"You know what I mean. Like a *hare's* ears! *Hide nor hare!*"

"Right." He sighed. "I walked around Mayfair for a bit."

"At night? Alone? I'm surprised you weren't accosted by footpads."

Oh, for God's sake. "Yes, we know how riddled Mayfair is with footpads. Besides, after Bitche I don't go anywhere without a knife at least."

"You carry a *weapon?*" she exclaimed, eyes wide.

"Don't worry, I promise never to use it on you. Now, if you don't mind, I'm going to bed. We can discuss this further in the morning." Especially since he was planning to go riding with Grenwood quite early, at which point he would apologize profusely for the insult to Grenwood's wife.

She glared at him. "You can't go to bed yet. You have a visitor."

"*Now?*"

She sniffed. "I told your friend Heathbrook he could wait for you, since I knew you'd show up eventually. I put him in your study."

Damn. Something must be seriously wrong if Heathbrook was paying him a call this late, not to mention coming to town at all. Jon started to head that way, then paused to kiss his mother on the cheek. "Forgive me for causing you such trouble tonight. It won't happen again, I promise."

"Hmph. It had better not, young man."

He couldn't help laughing. She still saw him as eighteen. But then, she was a mother, so that was to be expected.

Moments later, he entered his study to find Heathbrook pacing, with a glass of Jon's whisky in hand.

Instantly, Jon went on the alert. "What is it? What's happened?"

"Mademoiselle Bernard and her mother are in England."

Jon stopped short. "How do you know? When did they get here? Where are they now?"

Heathbrook sipped some whisky. "Another détenu, who'd settled in the village near my estate, told me. He said when he'd first arrived back, he'd encountered them in some watering hole. Apparently, they'd acquired passports in France. But they didn't tell him when they arrived or where they were living."

"We have to find her. Them."

"I agree, if only to put to rest your suspicions about Mademoiselle Bernard." When Jon scowled at Heathbrook, he added, "I'm just not sure how to go about it."

Jon mused a moment. "Actually, Beasley will be coming here tomorrow afternoon, so I'll ask him if he knows where she went."

"Good idea." Heathbrook stared at him. "Why is Beasley coming *here?*"

Jon explained, but that didn't seem to satisfy Heathbrook.

"Scovell thinks you've invented a dowry for Miss Morris, since we both know Morris had no money at the end. None of us did."

"He had a little."

"Not five thousand pounds." Heathbrook refilled his whisky glass. "And it seems to me it would require changing the codicil to Morris's will. Beasley would certainly know how to do that."

Jon crossed his arms over his chest. "What are you accusing me of?"

"Providing Miss Morris with a dowry because you feel guilty over how our escape went."

Pouring himself a glass of whisky, Jon drank deeply of it. He should have told his friends the truth from the beginning. But he'd known they would disapprove. They had never understood the depths of his guilt. How could they? "Morris asked me on his deathbed to get her a good husband. What was I supposed to do?"

"Introduce her to eligible gentlemen."

Jon scoffed at that. "You and I both know she'd have no chance at marrying if not for that dowry."

"Morris wouldn't have expected you to go to such lengths." When Jon didn't answer, Heathbrook asked, "Can you afford it?"

"From what I've determined so far, yes."

"Does she know?"

Jon turned to fix him with a fierce look. "God, no. Neither do my mother and sister. And don't you dare tell her. She'd be mortified."

Heathbrook gazed at him coolly. "I daresay she would. She's probably holding out for true love, as most women are these days."

"If so, they're fools. If Morris taught me anything, it's that the sort of love women want doesn't exist." Even this feverish desire he felt for Tory would cool in time. At least he hoped it would. He couldn't imagine going on for years in such agony. "When even a man like Morris, who professed to love his wife dearly, can take a mistress—"

"And I'm still not sure that he did."

"Fine. Forget Morris's . . . behavior toward Mademoiselle Bernard. What about the many men in Verdun who tired of not having wives and looked elsewhere for company?"

"Those exist everywhere, Jon. That doesn't mean love isn't real." Heathbrook narrowed his gaze. "If you ask me, you seem very much like a man in love yourself. It begs the question of how you can push Miss Morris at other men."

"I'm not pushing her at anyone," Jon ground out. "I'm just giving her a chance at a decent life and future. That's all."

"If you say so. But I do hope you're prepared in case she finds out that you manufactured her dowry."

He flinched. "I've taken steps to make sure she doesn't."

"Well then." Heathbrook set down his whisky glass. "It seems you have matters in hand. I'll be going now. I'll see myself out. If you need me, I'll be in town for a week tending to business."

"Why would I need you?" Jon snapped.

Heathbrook shook his head. "In case you don't have things as well in hand as you think."

And before Jon could answer that, the earl left.

Chapter 17

Two mornings after the Sinclairs' ball, Tory had Mr. Beasley shown into the drawing room. He looked startled to see her, and even more startled when she explained who she was.

"You're Dr. Morris's daughter," he said warily.

"Yes! Did you know him?"

"I did, indeed. He was a fine man. Knew more about art than I expected." He glanced around. "When the duke sent a note setting our appointment for this morning, I thought he'd be here."

"He's been very busy." She'd barely seen him in the last two days. Jon had already been long gone when she'd stumbled out of bed at eleven yesterday morning. That was understandable since he'd retired at a decent hour, whereas she and Chloe hadn't managed to leave the ball until nearly three AM.

He'd been at dinner last night, but that wasn't an environment conducive to speaking about anything important—like how he and his friends had tried to escape Verdun. For one thing, his mother had monopolized the conversation, eager to tell them who had done what at the ball. And Chloe had peppered Jon with questions about Lord Heathbrook, which he'd answered reluctantly.

When dinner was over, he'd disappeared into his study, which he'd done often of late. This morning, he'd been gone by the time she and Chloe came down. But she did know where he was, at least—speaking to one of his estate managers.

"Today the duke has another obligation, I'm afraid," she explained, "but once I told him I could meet with you about the engravings in his stead, he was happy to have me take care of it." She smiled. "I hope you don't mind meeting with me instead of him."

"No, indeed, miss. Not to say anything bad about the duke, but I'd rather spend the afternoon with Dr. and Mrs. Morris's daughter any day." He leaned close. "I daresay you know a great deal more about engravings than His Grace."

She laughed. "Let's just say I know a bit more about art in general, although prints aren't my area. Fortunately, I have *some* knowledge of printmaking, thanks to my late mother."

"Your father boasted to me about your mother—said what a fine engraver she was."

Tory brightened. "She was, indeed. I wasn't sure if Papa appreciated how good she was, so I'm glad to hear he spoke of it. I still have some of her engravings, if you ever wish to see them."

"Oh, yes, miss, that would be an honor." He rubbed his hands together. "Now, where are these prints His Grace wanted me to examine?"

"This way," she said, leading him up the stairs and into Aubrey's old room. "His Grace left a note saying I was to tell you that they weren't originally affixed to the wall, but he thinks they can be loosened fairly easily so they can be framed."

Beasley was now examining the prints with a magnifying glass. "These are very rare and quite beautiful. The hand-painted ones are exquisite. I can't believe His Grace allowed them to be affixed to the walls."

"He didn't," she said dryly. "His half brother did it while the duke was in France."

"Ah. A common tale, I'm afraid. Détenus came home to find their wives had left them for other gentlemen, their children had tried to have them declared dead, and their property had been taken over. Some détenus never came home because they'd formed new families in France. The lack of communication for so many years . . ." He shook his head. "It tore families asunder. And many people assumed their loved ones had passed away."

"Yes. We thought the same thing, primarily because His Grace and my father were moved to Bitche prison from Verdun."

"That's right." He'd started to look a bit anxious.

She smiled at him. "Captain Scovell said it was because of their attempt to escape."

Now Mr. Beasley appeared positively uncomfortable. "I-I believe that's true."

"But my understanding is that Verdun was a decent place to live. Why risk going to a real prison just to escape France?"

He sighed. "For their families, of course. Lord Jonathan feared that his brothers might be mistreating his mother and sister in England. Lord Heathbrook knew his cousin was running things in his late father's absence, and he didn't approve. Apparently, his cousin is something of a scoundrel. Your father worried about you and your mother. And Commander . . . *Captain* Scovell wanted to get back to his ship."

She stared hard at him. "You must have known them all quite well."

He tugged at the stock he wore around his neck. "I helped them with a small matter involving their escape."

That surprised her. "Didn't you wish to leave with them?"

He shook his head. "I did, but I couldn't. My family was all with me. Escaping Verdun with three children and a wife in tow would have been impossible, and I dared not leave them behind."

"Of course not. No one would expect you to."

"Some of the gendarmes were . . . rude to the women there who had no male companions. So it was better for me to stay. I must admit that the *townspeople* of Verdun were very kind, for the most part. The détenus generally spent their funds, such as they were, in the shops, which the locals appreciated. Still, we were subject to our commandant's whims and those of his gendarmes. It was easy to cross one unwittingly, and then you found yourself marched off to another camp on foot, with or without your family, at great expense to yourself."

He sighed. "Many of us ended up having to survive on charitable accounts set up for the indigent of the camps. That's why there were plenty of escapes, especially early on, but most were of young, healthy fellows like the duke and his friends. Well, except for your father."

Her heart pounded. Until now, it hadn't occurred to her that Jon and his friends could have left her father behind—or her father could have chosen to stay behind. The fact that neither happened . . . well, she didn't know what to make of that. She would have to press Jon for more information.

"One man was taken captive with his son, who escaped seven years later without him," Mr. Beasley went on. "The father refused to go—said he would just slow his son down. He stayed behind. But his son made sure not to implicate him in the escape and ended up making his way back to England safely."

"What happened to the father?"

Mr. Beasley frowned. "Died of disease a couple of years later. His son never saw him again."

"That's so awful!"

He shrugged. "It was life at Verdun."

She digested that. "Let me ask you something. How did the duke and his friends get caught? I mean, they said that they were betrayed by someone, but they never explained exactly how their escape went wrong."

He blinked. "You'll have to ask His Grace that. They didn't tell me what their plans for the escape were, so I don't know the details."

"But you just said you helped them—"

"Yes, but . . . well . . . they only told me enough for me to provide them . . . something they needed. And once they were recaptured, we never saw them in Verdun again, although we suspected where they'd been sent. To 'the Mansion of Tears.' That's what everyone called Bitche." Now he seemed truly uncomfortable, for he pulled out a handkerchief and began mopping his brow with it.

She took pity on him. "Forgive me, Mr. Beasley, for asking so many questions. I'm just so curious about what happened with all of them, especially my father. The duke doesn't like to talk about it."

"It was a painful time for them all," he ventured. "The stories we heard of what went on at Bitche—" He halted, apparently remembering that her father had been there, too. "Anyway, it's understandable that they don't want to speak of it."

"I'm sure. And you're right, I should ask the duke." She gestured to Mr. Beasley's magnifying glass. "Now, why don't we see to those prints? I know His Grace is eager to have them appraised by someone who knows what he's doing. I'm afraid I wouldn't be much help with that. My mother was the only one aware of the value of such things, not me."

His relief was so palpable that she felt guilty for pressing him.

They spent the next two hours examining each print as he looked for evidence of artists and printmakers, then made notes in a notebook he'd brought with him.

Meanwhile, Tory took notes herself, fascinated by Mr. Beasley's breadth of knowledge. She learned more watching Mr. Beasley assess Jon's prints than she'd ever learned from her mother. Then again, Mama had known that engravings didn't interest her the way sculpting did, so her mother had been more focused on teaching Tory everything she knew about sculpting.

Mr. Beasley finished the last print, and he was writing out a bill for his work that she could give to Jon when something popped into her brain.

"Oh! I almost forgot. His Grace said you would be bringing a list of détenus who could use work. I promised to get it from you so I could give it to him."

Mr. Beasley broke into a smile as he reached into his pocket. "I have it right here."

When he handed her the list, laid out on several pieces of paper, she said, "So many?" There had to be at least a hundred names on there.

He nodded sadly. "My friends and I shouldn't complain. There are thousands of former soldiers and sailors looking for work, and they deserve it more than we do after all they've been through. But—"

"You still need to feed your families. And at least sailors and soldiers chose their banishment from home. You did not." She pulled her own list out of her apron pocket. "Speaking of your particular situation, I spent some time this week looking up Mama's old printmaking friends, and they were happy to offer me names of printmakers who could use an experienced engraver."

Mr. Beasley looked stunned as she handed him her list. He scanned the names, his face lighting up as he read them, probably realizing that they were some of the top printmakers in London. "Oh, Miss Morris! You cannot know what this means to me and my family!" Grabbing her hand, he kissed it repeatedly. "You are an angel come to Earth, I swear!"

Tory was blushing and trying to figure out how to extricate her hand when a chuckle sounded behind them.

"She is indeed," Jon said as he entered the room. "Dare I ask what exactly Miss Morris has been using her angelic skills for?"

"Oh, Your Grace," Mr. Beasley cried, "Miss Morris has given me a list of printmakers in need of experienced engravers! It is . . . so kind, so generous, so—"

"—typical of Miss Morris," Jon finished for him. Then he turned to Tory, regarding her warmly. "On behalf of both me and Beasley, thank you for doing that, madam. I know it will mean a lot to his family."

"You're both very welcome, Your Grace. Oh, and here is the list of détenus needing work." When she handed it to him, their fingers touched.

His gaze shot to her, full of heat and remembrance of the last time they were together. Her own look was bittersweet. She still didn't know how she stood with him.

Then he spoke to Mr. Beasley further about the prints.

After not having seen him for two days, Tory took her chance to drink her fill of him. My, my, but didn't he look delicious? Wind-blown hair, tan buckskin breeches, a chestnut riding coat with a striped waistcoat, kid gloves, and a pair of chestnut top boots. A sigh of pleasure escaped her. He might be thin, but he was still a fine figure of a man.

Given what they'd done the night of the ball, she was now noticing all sorts of things about him. Like how well-proportioned his body was, how muscular his thighs looked in the form-fitting buckskin, how large were his hands.

It got quiet all of a sudden, and she realized he was now scanning Mr. Beasley's list of détenus.

"By the way, Mr. Beasley," he said very casually—too casually, really. "Did you happen to encounter Giselle Bernard and her mother among the détenu community?"

Mr. Beasley looked discomfited again. Indeed, he practically squeaked the words, "Here? In England? Why should I? They're French."

"Yes, but Heathbrook tells me that a détenu encountered the Bernards at a watering hole. Somehow, they got their hands on passports to England and are living in our country. He didn't know in what town they'd settled, however." Jon lifted his head from the list to stare hard at Mr. Beasley. "You wouldn't happen to know anything about that yourself, would you?"

"No, Your Grace, certainly not." Mr. Beasley shot her a furtive glance. "You *are* speaking of Mr. Morris's friend, are you not?"

Now it was Jon's turn to look discomfited. "Were they really friends? Or just acquaintances?"

"I think friends, to be sure. Mr. Morris taught her English."

That seemed to take Jon by surprise. "I . . . I didn't know that."

"Oh, yes. Mademoiselle Bernard had regular lessons up until the time you four were sent off to Bitche. Then she left Verdun for Paris, and I never saw her again."

"Ah. I see." He tucked the list of détenus in his pocket. "Well, I do appreciate you coming to look at my prints. Follow me, and I'll get you paid for your work." He turned to her. "And thank you, Miss Morris, for all your help. I'm sure I'll see you at dinner. To my knowledge, we have no fixed engagements this evening."

She winced. "Er, tonight is my night off, Your Grace. I get one every Friday."

He blinked at her. "Right. I'm sorry, I completely forgot." He smiled thinly. "I guess we'll see you tomorrow then. Enjoy your night off."

"I will, thank you."

But not nearly as much as she'd enjoyed their night in the Sinclairs' library. Then again, she doubted she could find anything else to compare to *that*.

Jon wished he could see Tory at dinner. He wished he'd continued their lessons in sculpting. He couldn't stand that Beasley had been given more time with her than Jon had today.

And it still nagged at him that she really didn't want to marry anyone.

That was why he couldn't bear to be at dinner tonight, listening to his mother go on and on about some outrage a member of the *ton* had committed. Or his sister peppering him with questions again about Heathbrook. Instead, he was going to White's, curious to see if they would transfer Alban's membership to him, and if it would even be worth it to be a member of the gentlemen's club anyway.

But as he walked out the front door of Falcon House, he noticed that Tory was leaving by the side gate and heading in the opposite direction he was. He paused to watch her walk down the street. He'd noticed that she always walked briskly. There was no leisurely strolling for Miss Victoria Morris, oh no. She was always ready to go about her business efficiently.

Tonight she was dressed in a simple blue gown and a bonnet that sadly hid her hair from his view. It dawned on him he'd never seen her with her hair down.

Damn. Now he had one more thing he regretted—not taking her hair down when he'd had the chance two nights ago. Of course, that would have ruined her as surely as, well, ruining her would have, but still . . .

She turned down a side street and disappeared from view. He walked down the steps and was about to go the other direction when he noticed someone in a hooded cloak cross the street from the little park in the square and start walking down the same side street.

Instantly, his every instinct went on high alert. All right, the fellow might be going the same way coincidentally, but on the off chance he wasn't, Jon turned to follow the pair. When he reached the corner, he looked down the side street, and spotted the gentleman—or lady, for it was hard to tell which it was—following Tory, just far enough behind her to escape her notice.

It worried him. It was dusk now, but it would soon be dark, and if this scoundrel—whoever he was—really was following her, she might be in danger. Years of avoiding Courcelles's gendarmes had taught Jon how to walk softly and inconspicuously when need be, so he began to follow the follower.

At one point in their parade of three, he glimpsed Tory ahead of the fellow, and it was clear she had no idea she was being followed. That only spurred him to anger. Just thinking of her in peril from some footpad made him wish he had a pistol on him, but his knife would have to do.

Yet it soon became obvious that his quarry had no intention of catching up to her, even when the street they were all on passed through a desolate wooded area. What was the fellow's intent?

Tory had now entered a little neighborhood of neat cottages, and just as Jon passed one, a hound awoke and barked at him. Ahead, Jon saw the follower halt and glance back. Jon wasn't close enough to see the face beneath the hood, but the person certainly saw him, for the scoundrel took off between two houses at a run.

Jon ran ahead to where the fellow had just been, but he'd vanished. Jon considered whether to hunt farther afield for the follower, but Tory was still walking, and Jon couldn't risk the man getting ahead of her. Besides, he wouldn't know how to find Tory if he didn't locate the rogue, and the fellow might return later to catch her alone.

The very thought made Jon's stomach roil. So, he decided to follow Tory to her cottage, then stand guard to make sure the man didn't come back after dark.

She continued on a good quarter of a mile before halting at a pretty stone cottage on the edge of the neighborhood. Even as he approached, he saw an older woman walk out the cottage door and head in the opposite direction from Jon. That must be Mrs. Gully, the servant Tory had said stayed with her while she worked.

That had clearly been a lie. Mrs. Gully might have cleaned up and made dinner as Tory had said, but she clearly didn't stay around to watch it being eaten.

Tory was in there alone? That was dangerous in itself, especially with footpads roaming around. Never mind that he'd teased his mother about footpads in Mayfair. This was clearly not Mayfair. It was the more rural environs of London west of Falcon House.

There was no way in hell he'd leave Tory here by herself when some arse had been following her. Jon had at least scared the scoundrel off temporarily, but that didn't mean the fellow wouldn't return.

Unfortunately, Jon standing in the midst of a street in his finest evening attire had begun to draw attention. So, after pretending to fish a stone from his shoe, he walked on until he was out of sight of the village. Then he retraced his steps, but through the woods that ran behind the cottages.

Once he got back to Tory's cottage, which was smaller than he'd expected, he found a spot where he wouldn't be noticed by her neighbors but could still see both the front and back. Then he sat down on a log to wait.

It wasn't hard. He'd spent the past eleven years waiting for his life to begin again, so this was nothing. He liked listening to the birds calling before night crept over them, watching the sun set, feeling the hum of activity from the little neighborhood.

He tried to figure out if any of the cottages he could see were that arse Dixon's. One of these days, he meant to find the fellow and put the fear of God into him, if he could figure out how to do it without rousing gossip about Tory.

She was in there now, molding clay or chipping away at marble or perhaps even creating a mold for some bronze statuette. He liked thinking of her that way, perhaps wearing a smock to keep her clothes clean as she worked intently.

Suddenly, as if his very thoughts had conjured her up, her face appeared in the window opposite him, which had been dark until now. There must still have been enough light to see him by, for she came marching out the back door.

Damn. Well, perhaps it was for the best. Because she needed to hear exactly how dangerous it was for her to be staying here alone at night.

Chapter 18

Tory couldn't believe it. Jon was here. But how? No one in the Falconridge household knew where she lived. She'd taken great steps to make sure of that, mostly because she hadn't wanted his half brothers here.

But she didn't want *him* here for different reasons. Fortunately, she'd already put Cyril to bed. Unfortunately, she'd hurried out here so fast that she'd forgotten she was wearing only her nightgown and her wrapper. Together they covered her respectably, but if any of her neighbors saw her . . .

Well, as long as they were back here in the woods, nobody would.

Jon rose from the log to look her over in a rather thorough manner, so she did the same, only to swallow hard at the sight of him in a sinfully black tailcoat, trousers, and even waistcoat. Only the white of his cravat shone brightly in the forest.

Oh, Lord, why must he always look so delicious in evening attire? Not that it mattered, devil take it. "What are you doing here?"

"I'm watching over you."

She couldn't let herself react to the sweetness of that. Or to the thrilling way he was making her aware of her unbound hair and her state of undress. "I don't need watching over," she said firmly.

He stared at her, eyes gleaming in dusk's waning light. "I'm afraid you do. I was leaving to go to my club when I saw a man—or possibly a woman—follow you."

That sounded alarming, but still . . . "It was probably just someone from my neighborhood coming home the same way I was."

"Wearing a hooded cloak during the hottest season of the year? He'd been watching for you to come out of Falcon House."

She crossed her arms over her waist to hide the shiver that gave her. "How could you be sure?"

Jon steadied his grim gaze on her. "He followed you all the way from the park across our street, where he'd been waiting until you came along."

Good Lord. "Well . . . well, I can't imagine why." She really couldn't.

"Neither could I, so I followed him covertly. Unfortunately, he spotted me when I was a quarter mile from your cottage, and he darted off down a side street. That's when I lost him. So I followed you the rest of the way home to make sure he didn't circle back to attack you."

It finally dawned on her that she'd been home quite a while. "And you've been sitting out here all this time?"

"Long enough to see your Mrs. Gully leave, and to know you were now alone." He scowled. "You lied to me about her. You said she stayed with you all night."

"She does sometimes," she lied.

He didn't look as if he believed her, either. "The point is, I wasn't about to leave you unprotected. The scoundrel was clearly up to no good. I'm still not sure he won't return in the wee hours of the morning when you're asleep."

She swallowed her rising fear. "I-I'll lock the door as I always do."

"Yes, it's so hard for someone to punch through a window," he said sarcastically. "What about when you're not here? Someone could break in and lie in wait for you."

Then Mrs. Gully would bash the scoundrel over the head with her frying pan and set up a hue and cry. Sadly, she couldn't tell him *that*, not when she'd already said no one was here during the day. "You're being absurd." She sincerely hoped he was.

"All the same, from now on, when you come to the cottage, you must at least take a footman with you. Or, if you prefer, a groom or

I will drive you here in the phaeton. But you must be accompanied. Especially through that forested area."

Alarm made her tense up. "I *must,* Your Grace?" She strode up to him and lowered her voice. "What we did at the ball did not give you the right to dictate terms to me!"

"Damn it, Tory, I'm trying to keep you safe!"

"For pity's sake, keep your voice down," she hissed. "I don't want the neighbors to hear."

He dragged a hand through his hair. "What could it hurt for you to be accompanied home?" he asked, his voice thankfully lower.

The footman or groom might discover Cyril playing, or someone from the neighborhood who greets me might mention Cyril, or... anything could happen. And once the cat is out of the bag, so to speak, I could never put him back in.

She could say none of that, nor could she tamp down the panic rising in her chest. "There's no need for it, that's all. Besides, if you start showing that sort of interest in me, your servants will notice and so will my neighbors. It won't be long before they're assuming I'm your mistress, and my reputation will be ruined. So go home!"

Turning for the door, she hoped he'd take the hint, but of course he didn't. He marched right behind her, following her into the cottage. "I'm not leaving tonight, I tell you! You're in danger! Can't you get that through your thick head?"

"My reputation is in more danger with you being here."

"You'd rather protect your reputation than your life?"

"Of course not," she said. "But..." He was liable to wake Cyril and learn the truth. She couldn't bear to see his shocked expression— or worst, his recoiling reaction—when he met Cyril. Nor could she deal with whatever came after.

But he clearly wasn't going to leave until they settled this, preferably somewhere it wouldn't rouse Cyril.

The kitchen they stood in presently wasn't ideal for the former. She couldn't talk to him in the parlor, for it faced the street, and the curtains were paper-thin. The whole neighborhood would see she had a man in here. But her workroom was next to Cyril's bedroom, and that was too close for her comfort. Which left only one good room—her bedchamber, which faced the back of the house.

"Fine. Come with me. Since you insist on continuing this conversation, it must be somewhere it won't attract the attention of my neighbors."

When she walked into her bedroom, he followed her as far as the doorway, then gave a start. Only then did she realize what he must think of her choice of rooms. Swiftly, she lit the lamps and turned them up. She didn't want to give him any ideas.

He stood there scanning her bedroom, then glanced back at the kitchen and over to the parlor. "This seems a very comfortable abode. And where do you do your sculpting, anyway? This cottage can't have more than a few rooms at most."

"My workroom is next to this one. And before you say anything, it's too packed with materials for two people to move around in." That seemed as good an excuse as any.

"I see." He strolled in and narrowed his gaze on her. "Are you sure you're not planning to keep leasing this cottage? You seem to have it set up very cozily for somewhere you only use once a week."

"Well, when I *am* here, I do have to sleep, you know. Might as well keep the place the way it was when Mama was alive. But no, I can't continue to lease it. It costs too much."

"I can see why it would. In fact . . ." He frowned. "Your solicitor tells me that even if you could afford it, you wouldn't be allowed to lease it again. A group of investors is buying all this land for development, and the owners have already agreed to sell their leases. Which means you and your neighbors will soon have to move anyway."

Her heart sank. "We've heard the rumors, but I didn't realize it was so . . . imminent. I was hoping to get a few months' grace to get everything together."

"I'm sorry, sweetheart, but London isn't the same as when you and I grew up here. It's expanding daily. Tavistock Square, Brunswick Square, Russell Square . . . they didn't even exist when I left. Vauxhall Bridge was built while I was away. Before then, we had to take a boat across to the pleasure gardens."

"What are you saying?"

"You cannot stop time. It will march on, with or without you, and you must do your best not to be trampled in the process."

She was about to retort when a noise sounded from down the

hall. It was Cyril getting up to use the chamber pot, no doubt. She and Mrs. Gully had only recently succeeded in teaching him how to manage it on his own.

But the sound put Jon on high alert. "Someone's in the house," he whispered. "Stay here."

She grabbed his arm. "It's my cat. Pay him no mind." Walking over to her bedroom door, she closed it. When Jon arched an eyebrow, she added, "Just to keep him out of here." And make it less likely that Cyril heard them.

He gazed at her suspiciously. "You have a pet?"

"Yes. What of it?"

"Who feeds it while you're gone for six days? Who cleans up after it?"

"Mrs. Gully, of course. She lives close by and has a key. She's been with our family for years." That was mostly true, at any rate.

"What's your cat's name?" he asked, obviously still wary of her explanation.

"Fluffy."

"Odd name for a tomcat."

"He's an odd tomcat," she said.

He cocked his head. "Don't you miss your pet during the days you're not here?"

"Not really. He was Mama's cat and is getting old and blind. That's why he runs into things and makes noise. But he's still good at catching mice."

"Your blind cat is good at catching mice," he said skeptically. When she was at a loss for how to answer that, he added, "Well, if you want to bring him to Falcon House, I'm sure Mother and Chloe wouldn't mind. Chloe has always wanted a pet."

"Thank you. I'll consider it, but he's more comfortable in a place he knows." Clearly, she had to get Jon to leave, or he would keep asking questions. "Now, you must go before someone in the neighborhood figures out you're here."

"How would they? Besides, I can't leave until we settle the matter of your coming and going with an escort."

"Ah, but we have. I don't need one."

"For God's sake, Tory—"

"You worry too much, Jon." She walked up to lay her hand on

his cheek. "I don't know why that fellow was following me, but clearly he's gone now. I'm sure you scared him off for good."

"I doubt it."

Another noise sounded from Cyril's room—her brother could be very loud when using the chamber pot—and Jon gave a start. "That's the biggest cat I've ever heard." He started to leave her, and she pulled him close. "Don't go," she said in what she hoped was a seductive voice. "I've missed you."

Then she stretched up to kiss him square on the mouth.

At first, he resisted her, but when no more noises sounded from outside the bedroom, he pulled her to him and began kissing her back with great enthusiasm. And as always, the moment his lips took hers, her heart started hammering and her blood thundered in her ears. He not only looked good tonight, but he smelled of freshly starched linen and tasted of heaven.

All the foolish parts of her clamoring for him these past two days sat up and took notice. It wasn't fair.

"Jon," she whispered, "what are we doing?"

"I don't know. I don't care." He slowly backed her toward the bed, kissing her cheek and neck as he went. "I've thought of nothing but you these past two days. I need to feel you come apart in my arms again."

"Not this time," she said firmly.

"Why not?" he asked in a low rasp.

She pressed a kiss to his cheek, then whispered in his ear, "Because I want to see *you* come apart in *my* arms." Then she laid her hand on the fall of his trousers and exulted to find a prominent bulge already there.

She told herself she was only doing this to distract him, to keep his focus off of what might be happening down the hall.

But that was a lie.

There was something so . . . breathtaking about being able to do this to him, rouse this in him. And his answering groan as she rubbed him only added to her eagerness. She no longer cared that it was wicked, that she was veering dangerously close to losing her maidenhood.

He was here, he wanted her, and she, curse it all, wanted him. What could one time together hurt? Her courses were due any day, so she was unlikely to conceive, and it wasn't as if she could ever marry anyone else after Jon. She *wanted* to know what she might be missing. She didn't want to spend her life a maiden. Not when Jon was around wanting her as much as she wanted him.

She would simply have to make sure it was only the one time.

"But you'll have to show me what to do to please you," she continued, working loose the buttons of his fall with one hand while she stroked him with the other.

"What you're doing now is pleasing me," he growled, and pushed himself into her hand. "If you pleased me any more, I might die from a surfeit of pleasure."

"That pleases *me*," she whispered with a coy smile. She finally got his trousers undone enough so she could get her hand inside, only to find another set of buttons to work loose. His drawers, most likely.

That was when he got impatient and brushed her hand aside so he could undo them for her. Then he placed her hand on his . . . "stiffened penis," as Mama had referred to it, and she was taken aback.

"I see what you mean about not learning male anatomy from statues," she murmured. "This is . . . rather unexpected." It was larger, harder, thicker . . . and more responsive to touch than she'd thought it would be. Indeed, the moment she stroked it, it leapt in her hand, as if it had a life of its own.

"Oh, God," he gasped. "Please . . . Tory . . . hold it tight."

Curious, she did as he asked, and it stiffened even more.

"Yes," he whispered. "Now . . . pull on it."

Hmm. When she did so, the skin moved. She let go. "Oh! Did I hurt you?"

"Only if you count . . . making me insane with . . . pleasure." Taking her hand, he placed it on his aroused member, then closed her fingers around it. "Like . . . this."

He guided her hand in caressing him, and she found it fascinating. Nothing her mother had told her, or the statues had shown her, had prepared her for *this*. His eyes slid closed, a look of such pure enjoyment spreading over his face that she couldn't help but revel in it.

"Ah . . . Tory . . . sweetheart . . . You have . . . no idea what it's . . . like to have your hand . . . on me."

"I hope it feels the same as when you had *your* hand on *me*."

He hardened even more in response to *that*. After only a few strokes, he took her hand off. "If you keep doing that," he choked out, "you might get something else unexpected."

"I like the unexpected," she whispered.

"I know you do. But I want to be inside you when I give you that. And that's not . . . I know I can't . . ."

"You can," she said softly. "I want you to."

His eyes shot open, and he searched her face. "I don't want to take your innocence."

"You're not taking it." She untied her wrapper and dropped it on the floor. "I'm giving it."

He was staring at her breasts as if he could already see them naked through her nightdress. When she reached up to unbutton the placket until it gaped open nearly down to her waist, he sucked in a sharp breath.

That pleased her inordinately. "Didn't you say the other night that you wanted to see me displayed in all my naked glory? Now you can."

His trousers and drawers were still open, so she could tell from his thrusting member that he liked *that* quite well. With his breath quickening, he used his teeth to tug off each glove and tossed them on the floor. Then he pushed aside the placket to bare her breast. Tracing the shape of it with one finger, he paused at the nipple to tease it to a hard point.

How could such a delicate touch make her crazed for more? But it did, so she pressed his hand fully against her breast.

His eyes glinted in the lamplight. "I never guessed you were a seductress, sweetheart."

"I'm trying the role on for size."

"God help me," he rasped, pulling her to him for an all-consuming kiss as he fondled her breast a few moments, sending frissons of pleasure from her breast to her loins. Then he slowly dragged her nightgown off her, baring her completely to his gaze.

"God help us both." He swallowed hard. "*Finally*, I get to see you in all your naked glory, with your golden hair hanging down about your lush body." He took a lock of her hair in his hands, then kissed it before laying it over the front of her. "You're the loveliest woman I've ever beheld. Do you realize that?" He skimmed both hands from her shoulders to her hips. "But then I knew you would be. I imagined you like this so many times in my bed at night . . ."

"You did?" she said, taken by surprise. "Then why were you so determined to marry me to someone else?"

"Because you deserve better." He smoothed his hands over her hips. "But I'm beginning to think I don't care. That's how much I want you. And I'm tired of not having you."

"You needn't be tired of it anymore," she said, thrilled by his words. "You can have me now."

"Can I?" he choked out, then pushed her back until she fell on her bottom on the bed. "I hope you know what you're doing."

"I don't. But I can learn."

A laugh sputtered out of him. "You're nothing like any woman I've met."

"Is that good?"

"Very good," he murmured as he nudged her knees apart to stare down at her mons.

Suddenly eager to see how he compared to all those statues she'd studied, she reached up to tug at his tailcoat until he shrugged it off impatiently. Then she watched as he feverishly unbuttoned his waistcoat and shrugged that off, too.

"Now the shirt," she whispered. "Please. I've so wanted to see your bare chest."

He lifted an eyebrow. "Looking for models for your sculpting, are you?"

"Always."

With a chuckle, he undid his cravat and tossed it aside, then pulled his shirt off over his head.

My, oh my. He had a chest worthy of being sculpted by Michelangelo, all finely wrought muscle and sinew, with only a smattering of dark hair around his nipples and in a line leading down to his navel and then lower. She followed the line with her thumbs until it reached his rather impressive privates, if she were to judge from statues. Then she pushed his trousers off his hips and down.

Quickly, he kicked off his trousers and bent toward her, a sudden clear intent in his expression. She scooted back onto the bed, not sure whether she was trying to escape or to accommodate him. But when he crawled onto the bed to kneel between her legs, she knew it was the latter.

When she lay back, he reached down to cup her between her legs, where she'd felt the same warm wetness from two nights before. Then he rasped, "I see you're ready for me." He caressed her so expertly there, that he had her gasping within moments. "Are you still sure you want me to—"

"Yes, please," she whispered, and widened her legs.

"It might hurt."

"I'll manage." She stared up at him, her hands clutching his surprisingly muscled arms. "Besides, I'd rather it be you than anyone else."

His expression showed pleasure, then uncertainty. "I ought to take my time with you, arouse you more."

"If you aroused me any more, I'd die of a surfeit of pleasure," she murmured, echoing his previous sentiment.

"I'd argue with you if I didn't want to be inside you so badly," he said hoarsely.

"Take me, my darling Jon."

That was all she had to say to have him entering her.

She'd expected pain, but this was . . . more awkward than anything. When he stopped, apparently fully seated in her, she waited for him to do something else. She knew there had to be more. How could there not be more to this?

"Are you all right?" he bent to mutter in her ear.

She nodded and thought, *All right, but not exactly enjoying it.*

Then he began to move, and everything changed.

Chapter 19

Jon couldn't resist moving. God, it felt so bloody good to be inside her that he could hardly hold himself back from taking her swiftly. Her warmth . . . her responsiveness up until now . . . he'd never felt the like.

But he could tell from the uncertainty in her eyes that this hadn't yet become enjoyable for her. He wanted beyond anything to make it so. Since he'd already broken his own rule about seducing her, the least he could give her was pleasure.

Now, if only he could hold off long enough to do so.

"It's uncomfortable, isn't it?" he asked, even as he wanted to plunge into her over and over like a maddened bull.

"N-Not a bit," she said.

"Liar," he whispered, then brushed a kiss to her tangled hair. "But I'll make it better for you, I promise." He pulled her knee up on one side, then the other. That not only seated him further inside her, but made her eyes widen.

"Better?" he asked.

"Much," she whispered against his shoulder.

"Hold on," he said, and reached between them to finger her where they were joined. Only then did he thrust inside her again.

"Ah, sweetheart, you feel like . . . warm velvet. I love . . . being inside you."

Especially now that she was relaxing more by the minute. That was encouraging. He kissed or caressed everything he could reach—her amazing breasts, her swanlike neck, her slickening cleft . . .

"Jon!" she cried, grabbing his hips as if to pull him into her. "That is . . . oh, *heavens* . . ."

At *last.*

Only then did he let himself go, driving into her the way he truly wanted to, reveling in her moans and the way she shimmied beneath him and clutched him to her as if to gain every drop of the pleasure he could give her.

She was his now, damn it. *His.* The way he'd wanted her . . . from the time he'd first met her. "Tory . . ." Her name was a prayer on his lips as he thrust into her luscious body. "Tory . . . good God, Tory . . . my lovely angel . . . my sweetheart. Mine. Mine. *Mine.*"

And as he felt her cry out and convulse around his cock, milking it, making it her own, he spent himself inside her hot, tight quim and collapsed on top of her.

It was only as he lay there, replete and satisfied and feeling her shake beneath him so wonderfully . . . that he remembered he'd intended to withdraw before spending.

Not that it mattered. They'd be marrying now. It was a tribute to how far gone he was that the thought of that made him glad beyond words. He shoved any thought of Morris and how the man might feel about that to the back of his mind. It didn't matter anymore. All that mattered was Tory.

He moved off to lie on his side next to her. She cast him such a beatific smile that he was tempted to take her all over again. But it was much too soon for that. For one thing, he could see from the smear of blood on her thighs that it was her first time, not that he'd doubted it. For another, he didn't want to hurt her.

Instead, he gave her a long, warm kiss. When he drew back, he murmured, "You look like a woman well-satisfied."

She stretched her arms over her head. "I *feel* like a woman well-satisfied. I suppose you learned how to be so good at this in France?"

"Actually, I had a rather misspent youth," he said, an echo of the shame he'd felt years ago resonating deeply. "It's why my father packed me off for a grand tour in the first place." He waited for her condemnation.

"I see." She ran her hand down his chest. "Then thank heavens for a misspent youth."

Her reaction took him off guard, then made him glad that in this, as with many other things, she was so unconventional. "I had no idea, Miss Morris, that you were such a wanton in the making."

Her eyes danced as she looked up at him. "I had no idea, either. It's quite the surprise." She sobered. "But I do appreciate your patience. I had no idea what I was doing."

"I could be patient for days if that's what it took to satisfy you," he said sincerely.

"*Days*, sir?" she quipped.

"Perhaps not days, but several hours, at the very least. I was rather quicker tonight than I would have liked, but it's been a long time since I . . . did this."

She leaned over to kiss him, then caressed his cheek before slipping off the bed. "Unfortunately, right now we don't have hours," she said as she found her nightdress and put it on. "Mrs. Gully comes rather early to make my breakfast, and she mustn't find you here." She gazed sadly at the sheets, now stained with her blood. "And I'll have to get those hidden and put new ones on before she arrives. So, you'd best get dressed, sir, before I throw you out."

"We still have plenty of time, sweetheart," he grumbled, but left the bed to appease her and began to dress. "Thank God, for we have much to discuss."

She faced him warily. "I'm not letting you send a footman home with me whenever I come here," she said, "and that's final."

"That's not what we'll be discussing." He walked up to draw her into his arms. "You do realize we have to marry."

She blinked up at him. "What?"

Damn. He'd expected her to be more pleased at the prospect. "I took your innocence, dearling. We must marry."

"I'm not marrying you." Pulling away from him, she wandered to the window to gaze out into the dark forest.

Pain seared his throat. "Would it be so awful to be married to me?"

"Of course not." Yet she still kept her back to him. "But you never once mentioned marrying me before. And I don't wish you to wed me simply to assuage your guilty conscience. I seduced you. I absolve you of all responsibility for it."

He ran his fingers through his hair, frustrated and unsure of himself. "I'm not marrying you to absolve anything. It's as I told you the other night—I don't deserve you, and I know it."

"That's ridiculous. You deserve someone far better than me. A princess or a duke's daughter or someone closer to your rank."

"I don't want any of them. I want *you,* Tory."

She whirled around to scowl at him. "For *what?* For this?" She gestured to the bed they'd just been in. "You could pay any woman you like for that. Unless that's why you want me. For my dowry."

"Oh, for God's sake," he snapped, "I don't want or need your bloody dowry. I need *you.*"

Her features softened, and she looked as if she were about to say something when the door opened, startling them both.

A boy of about ten or eleven wearing a nightshirt and clutching a worn blanket stood there staring at them through sleepy eyes. "Sissy? Where's Mrs. Gully?"

Sissy?

Bloody hell. There was a child here. A *child,* for God's sake. A million questions leapt into his mind as Jon examined the boy. Morris's? It was possible. He looked eleven years old and was the spitting image of Morris.

Darting a nervous glance at Jon, Tory answered the lad. "This is Mrs. Gully's night off, Cyril, remember? That's why your Sissy is here."

He rubbed his eyes the way a smaller child might, with his fists. Then he seemed to notice Jon there. "Who are you?" he asked in a guileless voice that no eleven-year-old who'd found a strange man in his sister's bedroom would ever use.

Thank God Jon had finished dressing. "I'm—"

"This is Sissy's friend." She shot Jon a warning look. "Did you want something, my dear boy?"

He gave her a sweetly innocent smile. "I can't find my little horsey. Do you know where it is? He gets scared alone at night."

"He's in the kitchen. Come with me, and we'll fetch him. But then you have to go back to bed. Understood?"

He bobbed his head, then gave her his hand and went off with her, his blanket clutched close to his chest.

Judging from young Cyril's childish tone and the way he was acting, he was either very sleepy or his mind wasn't quite right. Emotions swamped Jon—pity and guilt and unutterable sadness. Morris couldn't have known, or he surely would have said something about it.

The moment she came back in and closed the door behind her, he said, "I take it that Cyril was born after your father left?"

"Yes. Nine months almost to the day."

"The boy is the reason you keep this cottage, isn't he? I daresay Mrs. Gully stays here to care for him."

A heavy sigh escaped her. "Yes."

"And you don't own a cat, I suppose."

She glanced away. "No."

He thought how to phrase his next question. "Is Cyril . . . all right? I mean, he behaves very . . . childishly for a boy of eleven."

She nodded, then dragged in a deep breath. "I suppose you might as well know everything. Cyril is in good physical health, if that's what you mean. But his mental state . . ."

"He was born that way?"

"Yes, but only because the umbilical cord got wrapped around his neck at birth. It took some doing for the midwife to get him loose. He seemed fine at first. But as he grew, it became evident that . . . that . . ."

"—his brain had suffered some damage."

She bobbed her head.

"Did Morris even know your mother bore him?"

"Mama couldn't bear to tell him in a letter, so she said nothing about him. And early on, when we didn't realize Cyril was injured, we kept thinking Papa would be coming home soon. Then the war started again, and we didn't know where Papa was for the longest time, and by then, Cyril was showing signs of . . . not being like other children. He was slow to crawl, slow to walk, slow to speak."

He nodded. "We had a similar situation in the camp with a little girl. Something happened at birth, and her mind never quite grew up. She was sweet, though."

Tory turned a piercing look on him. "Were people kind to her?

Or did they treat her like an imbecile, mocking her or ignoring her or calling her names? Because that's what they do here in England."

Unexpectedly, guilt swamped him. If Morris had not been in France, he could have looked after his wife and son, not to mention his daughter. But Morris had been forced to go to the aid of the foolish young duke's son whose parents had shipped him off because he'd become a reckless risk to the family name.

Jon swallowed. "France wasn't all that different from England in that respect, Tory."

"How shocking," she muttered, and crossed her arms over her chest.

He could see her withdrawing from him, and it cut him to his soul. "That's why you don't want to marry? Because of Cyril?"

Her eyes blazed into his. "Of course! No man wants a wife who comes with a child like my brother. Especially one who's getting larger by the day, yet will never be able to care for himself, will always be treated cruelly by his friends and family, and will forever be a burden on the husband."

"Tory, I can afford to take care of you both. As you may have noticed, I have a rather large house and more than enough servants to deal with him. Cyril could live with us—"

"Until you tire of dealing with him and . . . and send him off to one of those horrible places where they put people like him!" Tears trickled down her cheeks. "Even Mrs. Gully, who adores him, advises sending him to a farm in the country where he can . . . can work and live with strangers. Why wouldn't you?"

Did she really have so little faith in him? That shook Jon a bit. Why had she thought she couldn't tell him this? But, of course she thought it. He'd kept his darkest secrets from her, and she knew it, sensed it somehow in her usual perceptive Tory way. And honestly, his secrets were worse.

Still . . . "You forget, dearling, that I spent three years in a prison with your father. I would *never* put my brother-in-law—Morris's *son*—in such a place, no matter how inconvenient his care."

She swiped tears away, and he approached her to offer her his handkerchief. Taking it from him, she wiped her eyes and blew her nose.

Then she stiffened. "Your mother might have something to say about that, you realize."

"She doesn't know about him?"

"No one knows except my neighbors. Not Chloe, not the duchess, not even your servants. Why do you think I resisted having anyone from your household accompanying me home?"

"Ah. Right." He'd been wondering if they'd all known and had simply kept it secret from him. What a relief to hear that wasn't the case.

"Hence my concern about your mother," she said.

She had a point. Mother was unpredictable. "If Mother objects to Cyril living with us, then she can stay in town, and we'll decamp to one of my many estates." He dared to tug her into his arms. "We'd only see her on certain occasions."

"You don't want that," she whispered. "You just got your family back. You would never leave them."

That was the sticking point in his plan. He might have to choose her family over his. Could he do that?

Perhaps he wouldn't have to. "That's why she'll accept Cyril. Because I would order her to or else watch me go away."

"Jon . . . you wouldn't—"

"Think about it, at least, will you? Let me deal with Mother."

She gazed up at him with reddened eyes and nose, and he realized she had never looked dearer to him than at that moment.

A sigh escaped her. "Only if you think about it, too. I'm not sure you realize what you're offering to take on."

"Probably not. But it would be worth it to have you."

"Don't say that if you don't mean it."

"I do mean it." He gripped her arms. "Give me a chance, Tory. Just think about it."

She searched his face. "I will. But for now, you must go. If anyone in the neighborhood sees you leaving here in evening dress in the morning . . ."

"Of course. I don't want to make things harder on you than they already are."

"Thank you."

She walked out into the hall, and he followed her. But before they could reach the back door, he caught her around the waist and pulled her close. Then he kissed her long and thoroughly, determined to make her see that her brother's situation didn't change anything as far as he was concerned.

When he drew back, she was very nearly smiling again. "*Now*, Your Grace." She pushed him toward the back door. "You must go! Lord knows I'll have a hard enough time as it is convincing Cyril not to tell anyone he saw a man in my bedchamber in the middle of the night."

God, he hadn't even thought about that. And he was fairly certain a child like Cyril wouldn't know how to keep a secret.

"Will I see you tomorrow?" he asked.

"Of course. Unless you're planning on dismissing me."

"Don't be daft," he said as he opened the back door. "You still owe me sculpting lessons."

"And you owe me a come-out," she quipped, her eyes gleaming at him. "Who knows? I might still have a chance to find someone better than a duke to marry. I'm holding out hope for a royal duke. Or, perhaps, Lord Knightdale."

Despite everything, she made him laugh. "You can't marry him," Jon said as he sauntered out. "You're marrying *me*."

"We'll see," she said, then smiled softly before she shut the door.

Yes, they would see, indeed.

Chapter 20

Tory awakened slowly, realizing she was sore in some unusual places. Within seconds, she realized why, and then could only luxuriate in the reason. She'd lost her innocence. She should regret that, but how could she? Jon had been so considerate, yet so fierce in his desire for her. Just thinking of it now made her want to swoon. So it didn't even bother her that she was no longer chaste. No one would ever know, not even Mrs. Gully.

She had a moment's panic and glanced at the clock, then relaxed to find it still quite early, only six AM. Mrs. Gully wouldn't be here yet, and anyway, Tory had done all she could to hide the truth from her loyal servant. She'd remade the bed last night and hidden the bloody sheet in her satchel, intending to dispense with it in the garbage from Falcon House.

As for a husband finding out she wasn't chaste, the only man she would ever choose to marry, anyway, was Jon and he obviously already knew. A smile crept over her face. Jon. The sweet things he'd said after their lovemaking and his unexpected offer of marriage had quite taken her by surprise.

Granted, he'd said such things the night of the ball, but she hadn't dared to let herself believe them. Not until he'd offered marriage last night and then stood by the offer even after meeting Cyril.

Cyril! Oh, Lord, she'd forgotten about cautioning Cyril against any mention of her "friend" to Mrs. Gully! Then she heard voices in the hall—the warm tones of Mrs. Gully followed by the childish ones of Cyril.

What was the woman doing here so early? She generally didn't even appear until seven!

Tory leaped out of bed and pulled on her wrapper, then hurried into the kitchen, surprised to find Cyril already dressed and eating breakfast. "Good morning, Sissy!" he said cheerfully. "Mrs. Gully made me eggy bread and rashers!"

"What a treat!" she said, forcing gaiety into her tone. "Did you tell her 'Thank you'?"

"Thank you, Mrs. Gully!" Cyril said as he attacked the slices of fried egg-dipped bread.

"Come into the parlor with me, miss," Mrs. Gully said. "You stay right here, Master Cyril, and enjoy that eggy bread. I need to speak to your sister a bit."

That didn't sound good. Dread settling in the pit of her stomach, Tory followed her into the parlor. When Mrs. Gully shut the door, she knew for certain something was wrong.

"There's sumpthin' you should see," Mrs. Gully said grimly, and handed her one of those gossip rags that Chloe always loved to read.

This one was open to a certain page with a particular column circled. It read:

We have it on good authority that a certain former governess now appearing in Society circles as an heiress is not quite that. The dowry supposedly provided to her by her late father, a well-known bear leader who died in France, is actually being provided by his pupil and newly returned heir to a dukedom, the Duke of F———. Is this a case of the duke showing his gratitude to his former tutor by helping the man's daughter? Or could there be more between him and Miss M——- than anyone knows?

Tory's mind whirled until it landed on the one salient implication in the whole piece: that Jon had been the one to supply her dowry. Was it true? It didn't seem like the sort of thing even the gossip rags would just invent. And if it was the case, it explained why he'd become so angry when she'd teased him about wanting to marry her for her dowry.

Still, why would he provide her with one? It made no sense. And who would set out to ruin her reputation by telling the press about it and implying that it meant something salacious was going on? How would such a person even find out about it?

Mrs. Gully folded her hands over her waist. "Now, George says as I should mind my own business, but I've watched you grow up from a child to a woman, and 'twouldn't feel right not tellin' you when I see sumpthin' wrong, 'specially considerin' you ain't got a mother and all anymore."

"Mrs. Gully, I can explain—" Tory began.

"And furthermore, when I hear from the lad that you had a man visit you in the middle of the night—"

"First of all, it wasn't the middle of the night. You know Cyril. He thinks anything that happens after he goes to bed is 'the middle of the night.' It was right after sundown, truly. And yes, it was His Grace here. He stopped by to . . . to . . ."

"To what? Cyril says you were together in your bedchamber, miss. Your bedchamber!"

She stifled a groan. "We were. It was the only place I could be sure His Grace didn't hear or see Cyril or couldn't be seen by anyone in the neighborhood through the parlor curtains. He even entered through the back door to protect my reputation."

Mrs. Gully crossed her arms over her ample bosom. "And why exactly was he here and hiding the fact from folks if he weren't up to no good?"

Tory considered telling her the truth—that Jon had seen a man following her, but Mrs. Gully would just say that Jon had used that excuse to get to see her alone.

Had he?

No, that was absurd. He'd already proved it was easy enough to get her alone at his mansion. He needn't have followed her home for that.

Still, telling Mrs. Gully about the man following her might make the woman so alarmed that she'd worry about her *own* safety here alone during the day with Cyril.

Perhaps Tory should tell Mrs. Gully *part* of the truth of what happened last night. At least then she could get the woman's advice. "His Grace came to propose marriage to me." That was what had happened in the end, anyway, so it wasn't *entirely* a lie, was it?

Mrs. Gully blinked, then broke into a broad smile. "Truly? His Grace wants to *marry* you? Oh, Lordy, don't that beat all—a governess marrying a duke!" She scowled. "Wait—so, has he truly been offerin' gentlemen a dowry to marry you?"

"He has. Remember when I told you Papa left me an inheritance, and you were skeptical? You were right to be so. If I'm to believe the gossip rag, that was the money His Grace was offering for my dowry." She forced a smile. "But it appears he's decided he wants me for himself."

"He has, has he? Well, he couldn't do no better than you, and you sure couldn't do no better than *him*. I daresay you accepted his proposal."

She swallowed. "I told him I'd have to think about it."

"What?" Mrs. Gully roared. "*Why*, for pity's sake?"

"Because of Cyril, of course."

Mrs. Gully's face fell. "Oh, right. I forgot Cyril came in on the man. I suppose it was a shock for the duke, finding out about the lad all sudden-like." The woman sighed. "I take it His Grace wasn't keen on having a wife with . . . a brother like Cyril."

"Actually, the duke claimed he would bring Cyril into his home. And if his mother didn't like it, he'd take me and Cyril to the country to live."

"Then why wouldn't you accept his proposal?" A frown darkened her brow. "Though I don't know as if I like him leaving his mother behind. The duchess waited a long time for him to come home."

Tory dropped onto the sofa. "I know. I think the duke was trying to reassure me about Cyril. But I fear . . ."

Mrs. Gully sat down beside her. "What is it, dearie?" She patted Tory's knee. "You can tell me."

"I worry that once he has me, he'll . . . he'll send Cyril away. He promised he never would, but . . . well . . . He said a lot of lovely things last night. Yet he said naught about love. About being in love with me. And now that I know he offered the dowry himself, I wonder if . . . this is all just some way to repay Papa for being his tutor or to assuage his guilt that Papa didn't live and he did, or . . . I don't know what to think."

Mrs. Gully took her hand in both of her own. "What about you? Do you love *him*?"

"I don't know. I never thought I'd get the chance to love anyone, so I'm not sure what love is even like."

"Oh, dearie. That, you'll have to figure out for yourself. But ask yourself this. Does being around him make you happy? Make you want to see him even more? Is there anyone else you fancy more? Because if the answer to the first two is yes, and the answer to the last one is no, then you're halfway to figuring it out already."

Tory patted their joined hands. "After three husbands, you probably know a lot more about love than I ever could."

"I dunno about that. Never loved the first one—just wanted to get away from home by marryin' him. I fancied I loved the second one—but once he died, I didn't miss him near as much as I expected to. But George? I'd die if I couldn't have him beside me. To me, that's love."

"It does sound like it. I just don't know what to think about the duke and me."

"Well, before you start ponderin' the matter, mayhap you should ask His Grace all your questions. Because you ought to know why he wants to marry you so's you can decide if'n his reason is good enough. Don't you think?"

"I do." Tory reached over and hugged the woman who had lived with them longer than her own father had. "Thank you for the advice. I feel better just discussing it with you."

The door to the parlor opened. "Sissy, do you want any of the eggy bread?"

She knew from long experience that Cyril was hoping she'd say no so he could eat it all himself. "I don't much feel like eating right now, sweetie. Why don't you finish it off?"

"I will!" he cried, and went running back into the kitchen.

"There goes a lad who always knows exactly what *he* wants," Mrs. Gully said.

"Especially when it involves his belly."

They both laughed. But Tory sat there long after Mrs. Gully had returned to the kitchen, thinking of everything the woman had said.

She had to know more about Jon's feelings if she was to figure out what *she* wanted. And there was only one way to do that. She had to talk to him.

Jon was feeling ridiculously happy this morning, even though his valet seemed oddly subdued and quiet as he helped Jon dress. Well, even servants were entitled to their moods. It wouldn't dampen his. He *had* to marry Tory, and that was that. Even Morris would approve under the circumstances.

No, Morris would insist on thrashing him for seducing his daughter.

Jon thrust that thought from his head. Morris was dead, and Jon had kept his promise to the man. As long as Tory accepted him, that is. But she would. Jon meant to court her until she did.

Still feeling quite jovial, he entered the dining room for breakfast only to find his mother and sister awaiting him, looking as grave as his valet had. No doubt he was about to get an earful from Mother about some transgression of Society protocol he'd made.

Well, he refused to let it affect him. Once he told them about marrying Tory, they would forget all about whatever he'd done.

"What is it this time?" he asked with a smile as he set about filling his plate. "Did I neglect to address someone important at the ball? Use the wrong hand to pass the potatoes at supper the other night?" He grinned at Chloe as he sat down across the table from her. "Accidentally insult one of your suitors, Sis?"

Chloe winced. "You'd better read this, Jon." She shoved a copy of that ridiculous gossip rag she liked to read across the table.

"I'm not in the mood for—"

"Read it, son," his mother ordered. "*Now.*"

"Oh, very well." He picked the thing up, noticing that a column had been marked. As he read, his heart sank. "No," he muttered. "No, no, no . . ." He glanced up at them. "Has Tory seen this?"

His mother's eyebrows rose. "*Tory?*"

"Miss Morris," he snapped. "Has she seen this?"

"She's not here yet," Chloe said. "So, probably not."

"Don't show it to her." He rose to his feet, his breakfast forgotten.

"She'll find out eventually," Mother said, "probably sooner rather than later."

"With any luck, by then it will be dealt with," Jon said. "I know I can fix this. Somehow."

"Don't be ridiculous, son," his mother said. "Anything you did to 'fix this' would only make it worse. Unless the information about the dowry is a flat-out lie." His mother looked at him hopefully. "Is it?"

Jon tensed, realizing he'd have to tell them something. "No. It's true. But before you chastise me, I should tell you I've asked Miss Morris to marry me."

Mother gaped at him, but Chloe burst into applause. "How wonderful! I'm so happy for you both!"

"That might be premature, Sis. She hasn't yet said yes."

Chloe waved her hand dismissively. "But she will. I know she will. She'd have to be a fool not to. You're perfect for each other. And now I'll have a *sister*! I've always wanted one."

His mother, however, hadn't voiced her opinion. Nor was she smiling. "Chloe, dear," she finally said. "Would you give me and Jon a few minutes alone?"

"Very well." Chloe looked flummoxed, but had the good sense not to go against their mother.

The moment she was gone, Jon said, "Mother, I know what you're going to say, but—"

"I don't think you do know," his mother said frostily. "As it happens, I am aware of some things about Victoria's situation that I don't believe you are."

That caught him off guard. "Like what?"

"For one thing, she has a brother who is . . . not well."

Jon caught his breath, shock settling into the pit of his stomach. "You know about Cyril?"

"Oh!" she said. "So you know about him, too."

"Yes." He crossed his arms over his chest. "But I was told you did not."

"Well, your mother isn't quite the shatter-brain you seem to think. I wasn't about to hire Victoria to be Chloe's governess without having *some* knowledge of her home situation. I've had my spies in her neighborhood for some time. So, yes, I know about young Cyril, though I've never said a word to Victoria about it."

She marched over to pour herself a cup of tea. "I also know of Victoria's determination not to have her brother sent away somewhere, so I realize the unlikelihood that she will indeed marry you."

That shook his own firm feelings on the matter. "If you were certain she'd never marry, why on earth did you even agree to see that she had a Season?"

"Because I hoped to be proved wrong. You must understand— I like Victoria quite a bit. I was rather hopeful she would snag some gentleman who could convince her to marry *without* bringing her brother along. Or even that some gentleman would agree to take him in. That she'd find the sort of match she'd be a fool to turn down. But I never dreamed you would be the gentleman she snagged."

"Why? Because I'm duke? Because you figured I'd marry who you told me to?"

"Of course not . . . I just . . ."

"You might as well know—I told her that Cyril could live with us." He stared down at his mother. "And I meant that."

"I don't think you fully comprehend the ramifications of—"

"I do, actually. It will be awkward. There will be gossip. Cyril will need understanding servants to care for him." Jon leaned forward to plant his hands on the table. "I will make sure he has those. I want Tory to marry me, and I will do whatever I must to ensure that it happens."

She blinked. "I see. So you're determined to marry her."

"I am."

Going over to the sideboard, she opened one of the cupboards beneath it and took out a bottle of brandy, then poured a healthy amount into her tea before she drank deeply of it. Thus fortified, she faced him once more. "Have you considered what happens if your child—your heir—inherits Cyril's . . . problem?"

Jon sighed, tiring of this pointless argument. "That's unlikely, Mother. Cyril's 'problem' occurred while he was being born. A mishap with the umbilical cord that cut off his breathing for too long. You don't 'inherit' that sort of thing."

"How do you know? For that matter, how do you know that what Tory is telling you is the truth—"

"She wouldn't lie to me about that," he growled.

"That's not what I meant," she said hastily. "I mean, Tory is telling you what her mother or the midwife undoubtedly told *her*. That doesn't mean it's what happened."

A thought occurred to him. "Have you ever met Cyril, Mother?"

His mother blinked. "Well . . . no. How would I?"

"Why don't you reserve judgment until you do? Because I have met him. And I think you'll find him to be a sweet child."

She frowned. "All right. I suppose that's the least I can do."

"It is."

A long silence ensued, during which his mother took another generous swig of her brandy-laced tea.

"And now, if you have no more cautions for me," Jon said, "I must go."

"Where?"

"To find out who learned the truth about Tory's dowry, for one thing. Clearly someone in my employ has a loose tongue."

"It might be one of your friends," Mother said. "Did they know?"

Jon thought over the conversations he'd had with both Scovell and Heathbrook. "They figured it out, but only recently. And they would never betray me. But I must get to the bottom of this before I can fix it."

"I already told you, son, you can't—"

"Yes, yes, I heard you—I can't 'fix it.' But I have to try. For her sake."

"I am all for that," his mother said. "Victoria doesn't deserve the scandal you've brought down on her head."

"So *now* you're on her side?" he asked skeptically.

"I've always been on her side. *And* yours. I'm just not on the side of both of you as a couple."

"*Yet*," he said. "But you will be. Just give it a chance. That's all I ask."

He didn't wait for her answer. He now had two women he was

trying to coax into accepting this marriage, and the effort had become greater than he'd expected. He wasn't quite sure what to make of that, honestly.

All the same, at the very least, he had to find out who'd revealed the truth about the dowry. Tory deserved better than to have sly insinuations made about her around town. Marrying him might get rid of most of them, but there would still be whispers. It would be better to have them stamped out effectively at the outset.

First, he sent off notes to both Heathbrook and Scovell, who was supposed to be back in town from the naval review, asking them to meet him at their usual meeting place at noon. Jon needed reinforcements.

Then he went to the offices of the gossip rag to learn who had told them about the source of the dowry. When they hesitated to answer, he threatened to have them shut down for good if they didn't reveal it. Finally, they admitted they didn't actually know who'd told them. The information had come in an anonymous letter left at the offices when no one was watching. But it was supported with copies of documents from Jon's bank, which was enough for them to deem it legitimate. After threatening to sue them if they didn't print a retraction, he stormed out.

Now seething, he paid a visit to his banker, who categorically denied having given anyone papers about Jon's private affairs. But he did admit, with great embarrassment and effusive apologies, that the documents *had* come from the bank, and he would get to the bottom of it.

Jon talked to his solicitor who hadn't even read the gossip yet, so that let him out. He even went to talk to Morris's solicitor, but Mr. Trimnell had been with a client when Jon arrived, so the man couldn't see him. By then, it was time for Jon to meet with Scovell and Heathbrook.

He could tell from their grim expressions when they met him at Travelers' Inn and Tavern that they were no happier about the gossip than he was.

"I wish you'd consulted us before you decided to bestow a dowry on Miss Morris in her father's name," Scovell said. "We would both have been happy to contribute and then you wouldn't be in this mess."

"I would be in this mess regardless the minute I asked her to marry me."

"You're going to propose?" Heathbrook asked.

"I already proposed," Jon said with a sigh. "She just hasn't yet accepted my offer."

"Why not?" Scovell asked, sounding incredulous.

"She has an issue I can't disclose. I'm working around it, though, and I'm confident the matter will be resolved."

"Good God, man," Heathbrook said, "you're 'confident the matter will be resolved'? You sound like a bloody solicitor. Using that sort of language won't help you gain a woman's heart."

"Look, I don't want to talk about hearts right now," Jon snapped.

Especially since his was a bit battered after her response to his proposal.

No, not his heart, for God's sake. He wouldn't let it be engaged. Because if she refused him definitively, he didn't know how he'd recover.

"I need to find out who told the press about the dowry," Jon went on, and explained everything he'd learned. "I also need you both to hear about something that happened last night."

"Oh?" Scovell said, exchanging a glance with Heathbrook.

"Someone followed Miss Morris home. Or tried to, anyway. I followed him when I saw him go after her, but he spotted me along the way and ran off."

That put both of his friends on the alert. "Why would someone follow her?" Heathbrook asked.

"Honestly, I don't know. I've been racking my brain to figure it out."

Scovell began to pace. "It must concern Morris."

Jon stared at Heathbrook. "Does Scovell know about Mademoiselle Bernard being in England?"

"I told him when we arrived," Heathbrook said. "But I don't see how she would have anything to do with it."

"You never do," Jon shot back. "But whoever followed Miss Morris was in a hooded cloak—I couldn't be sure about the sex of the person. It could have been Mademoiselle Bernard or a man she hired. After all, if she was the one who betrayed us, she might wish to determine if Morris's wife is still alive and knows the truth about her betraying us. Or she might even want to determine if Miss Morris knows what happened. She or the man she hired might want to . . . to silence Miss Morris."

Scovell laughed. "If that's her plan, she's chosen a very convoluted way to go about it. She wouldn't have to go to Miss Morris's abode either to talk to her *or* 'silence her.' She could simply meet Miss Morris at any public affair and tell her that she knew Morris. The way we did at the theater."

Jon scowled. "Mademoiselle Bernard doesn't know what Miss Morris looks like or what places she frequents."

"Yet she managed to follow her from your house?" Scovell said.

"It wasn't her, I tell you. I can't see it."

Scovell was being logical, which was always maddening.

"It's far more likely," Scovell went on, "that the person following Miss Morris was with the press and trying to find out about the dowry. But you frightened him off."

Heathbrook, who'd been very quiet, said, "I don't think that's it, either. That night in the theater, Jon, when you and Scovell went off to fetch refreshments, I questioned Chloe about the dowry, since I knew Morris had no money at the end. She confirmed that Mrs. Morris had been in dire financial straits before she died, which was why your mother hired Morris's daughter. Then I happened to notice a fellow in the next box paying close attention to our conversation. I only glimpsed him before he left, but I thought he looked familiar. I just couldn't place him."

Jon groaned. "If it was a détenu, it wouldn't have taken much to put together from that discussion that I was funding Miss Morris's dowry, especially if the fellow was in Verdun when we were there and knew of Morris's circumstances. Although they'd have to know someone at the bank who would help them. And why punish Miss Morris by trying to ruin her reputation?"

"Why punish *us* by betraying us to Courcelles?" Scovell said. "We assumed that if it was a détenu, the person might merely have wanted the money or extra benefits that came with being Courcelles's lackey. But there might have been some other reason."

"True," Jon said, scrubbing one hand over his face.

"Didn't Morris have a solicitor?" Heathbrook asked.

"Yes," Jon answered. "He was the one who accepted the codicil to the will."

"Perhaps he got suspicious about the codicil and figured out that you'd doctored it," Heathbrook said.

"You *doctored* it?" Scovell said. "For God's sake, Jon, that's forgery!"

"They'd have to prove it, and trust me, no one could."

Heathbrook nudged Scovell with his elbow. "He got Beasley to do it."

"That's even worse," Scovell said. "You have the money to fight such a charge, but Beasley—"

"I wouldn't let Beasley hang for it, damn it," Jon said irritably. "And unless he opens his mouth, no one will think he did it."

"They might if they know about the help he gave us in escaping," Heathbrook mused aloud. "And our betrayer might know that, too."

"Is it possible *Beasley* is the one who went to the press?" Scovell asked.

"No," Jon said firmly. "Miss Morris did him an invaluable service—helping him to find a post with a London printmaker when he could find no work. He would never do anything to hurt her. And speaking of that, at my request, Beasley has given me a list of détenus who haven't been able to find work since their return. If I get you both a copy of the list, might either of you find a place for some of them at your estates or other establishments?"

"Absolutely," Heathbrook said. "I could well use several people, and at least these are probably men and women I know. Besides, if our betrayer is among them, I'll get the chance to observe them more closely."

"That's partly why I offered—so we could be closer to the détenu community in general."

"Good idea," Scovell said, "Just give me the list, and I'll see what I can do."

"Thank you. I know it will be appreciated by those who simply need the work. And it might enable us to find our betrayer, too." Jon sighed. "I've got to go. I just wanted you two to know what's going on with this business involving Miss Morris, so we can all be keeping an eye out. And since I haven't yet spoken to Morris's solicitor, I'm going to return there and try to see him."

They nodded.

"We should probably meet more frequently now that things are happening," Scovell said. "I'll be in London for a while. I . . . er . . . may be selling my commission and staying."

"Wonderful!" Heathbrook clapped him on the back. "Dare we ask why?"

"Let's discuss that another day, shall we?" Scovell said. "Jon needs to handle this muddle first."

"I do, indeed," Jon said. "But I'll let you know what I find out as soon as possible."

The three friends parted at the door to the tavern, agreeing to meet again soon. Jon climbed into his carriage only to find Tory waiting for him inside.

And she was holding a copy of that damned gossip rag.

Chapter 21

Jon appeared startled to see her when he climbed into the carriage. That rather pleased her. He was always the one surprising her— might as well be the one to surprise *him* for a change. Though she *was* relieved to discover that he'd come here to meet with his friends and not some woman.

Then he smoothed his expression to the one she'd grown used to, which never showed what he was thinking. "Where to?" he drawled.

"I don't care where," she said irritably. "Wherever *you* were going. I just needed to talk to you privately."

"So you crept into my carriage on the sly?"

"Of course not. I know your servants, remember? I merely told Will Coachman I was supposed to meet you here, and he happily allowed me to wait in the carriage."

"I see." He opened the panel to the driver's box, and said, "Home, Will."

"Yes, Your Grace."

As soon as the carriage rumbled off, Jon closed the curtains. "It wouldn't do for anyone to see us together. I know Will will keep quiet about it." He faced her. "How did you find me?"

She shrugged. "When Mr. Trimnell's clerk said you were waiting to speak to him, but would return soon, I rushed out so I could have my waiting hackney follow you. I'd already finished my business with Mr. Trimnell, for the most part."

"*You* were the client Trimnell was meeting with?"

"Of course. I was there to look over the codicil to Papa's will. I should have done it before. Then we could have avoided this messy business in the paper." She held up the gossip rag.

The color drained from Jon's face. "I see."

"I must admit—whoever forged that last bit of the codicil was very accomplished. It looked so much like Papa's handwriting in the rest of the will that I had to examine it very closely to see the differences. Then again, I'm an artist and notice such things. I can't imagine you did it yourself, though. Mr. Beasley forged that part, I suppose?"

Jon dragged in a deep breath. "I can explain—"

"Good. That's why I'm here. For your explanation." She folded her hands in her lap. "You went to great lengths to arrange this dowry business, after all."

He tensed. "Before we get into that, you didn't happen to tell Trimnell that you thought it was forged, did you?"

"Of course not." She tipped up her chin. "Forgery is against the law, after all, and I like Mr. Beasley. I wouldn't want to see him hang. Besides, he'd already told me he played a part in your escape, and it didn't take much for me to figure out how. He provided the four of you with false passports to enable you to move about France, didn't he?"

"Yes," he admitted. "For all the good they did us."

That was an interesting bit of information. Apparently, they'd never had the chance to use them. She set down the gossip rag. "So. Now you get to explain *why* you made up a dowry for me that you are providing out of your own funds."

"That should be obvious."

"You felt sorry for me?" she said, her stomach knotting up.

"No!" Jon got flustered. "Yes. Sort of."

"Which one is it?" she asked softly.

He muttered a curse under his breath. "Since your father asked me on his deathbed to help you find a good husband, this seemed the best way to do it. I owed him so much. I figured the least I could do was make sure you married well."

That hurt more than she'd expected. "So, if I'm understanding you correctly, this has all been about repaying my father? Even though I said I didn't *want* to marry?"

"You only said that because of Cyril." He leaned forward to grab her hands. "Tell me honestly—if Cyril hadn't been born, don't you think you would have married by now?"

"I-I don't know," she said honestly. "I would still have taken the position as governess to Chloe because Mama would still have died. Cyril had nothing to do with that. And when I was serving as Chloe's governess, I never met anyone who appealed to me. Nor did any man ever seem interested in me. Well, except for men who wished a more . . . illicit connection." When he groaned, she added hastily, "So, marriage would have been difficult for me even without having to consider Cyril's situation."

"That's why I stepped in. It didn't seem right you should be alone all your life. Especially since you lost your father because of me."

That statement brought her up short. "Why on earth would you think that?"

"Because it's the truth." He released her hands to throw himself back against the seat. "I haven't told you everything. I should have from the first, but I . . . I knew if I did, you would hate me." He fixed her with a tortured gaze. "And once I met you, I couldn't bear for you to hate me."

"Unless you murdered my father in cold blood," she said tenderly, "there's nothing you could tell me to make me hate you."

"Don't say that until you hear the rest." He glanced out of the window. "First of all, your father didn't want to be my tutor. He didn't want to leave you and your mother. He went because my father was concerned, even ashamed, of my behavior as a lad of seventeen. My father talked him into it."

"I know," she said.

That seemed to catch him by surprise. "You know?"

She shrugged. "I mean, you did say your misspent youth was why your family sent you on the grand tour. Besides, Papa discussed it with Mama. But he was only reluctant to take you on because he wasn't sure he was up to the task. He said it had been different when he was younger, the previous times he'd shepherded someone through their grand tour. He'd had the stamina then. But now he was in his forties, and he was worried he couldn't keep up with you."

Jon snorted. "Your father had more energy in his forties than many men have in their twenties."

"He certainly seemed energetic to me when I was a girl. Undoubtedly, that's why Mother told him she could think of no one better able to straighten out a young noble than him. It helped that Papa said he'd talked with you at length and determined you were a bright young fellow tempted into vice by the pleasures of London. He agreed with your father that a sojourn abroad might help temper your more reckless side and allow you to develop your better qualities."

Jon looked skeptical. "He really said that?"

"He did. Although, he also said you had a bit of an eye for the ladies." She fought a smile. "I assume that was really the 'misspent youth' you mentioned last night?"

"Yes," Jon said with a rueful smile. "I'm afraid it was."

"So that's it? You feel like your need for a grand tour took Papa away from me and Mama?"

"And Cyril." He sighed. "But no, that's merely a small part. I suppose I should begin at the beginning."

"That depends," she said lightly. "I'm not sure our carriage ride will be long enough for a description of your entire eleven years in France."

He lifted an eyebrow. "You're rather jocular about this whole matter."

"Forgive me. I'm just nervous about what you might say. And when I get nervous, I . . . tend to make jokes."

"Ah. I have a bit of that habit myself. Along with a tendency to behave rashly and rebel against what I'm told not to do." He smiled faintly. "Like seduce you."

"Who told you not to seduce me?" she asked.

"I told myself. Apparently, I even rebel against my own good judgment. And by the way, while I don't regret one bit seducing you, it definitely has the potential to ruin your life."

"Or enrich it. Only time will tell." She shot him a coy look. "Besides, I think the seducing was fairly mutual."

"All the same, your father worked hard to educate the recklessness out of me, and seducing you was absolutely reckless. Clearly, he only partly succeeded in his aim." Jon sighed. "As became evident the night of our attempt to escape Verdun."

She worried the strap on her reticule, suddenly nervous again. "I thought that the escape might be part of why you . . . blame yourself for his death."

"More than a small part, to be honest." He squared his shoulders. "I know our wish to escape probably seems foolish to you, having the advantage of hindsight. But you have no idea how useless we felt—unable to help our families, barely able to help ourselves, and seething with anger over the situation, which only worsened over time."

"I can well imagine." But, of course, she couldn't. How could she? The idea of thousands of people being forced to halt their lives for a decade was nothing less than appalling.

"Life in Verdun became harder once the new commandant came in," Jon continued. "Courcelles was cruel. He would send prisoners and détenus alike on forced marches to other camps, sometimes separating families. He demanded money at every turn, and if someone was five minutes late to *appel*—our daily signing of the parole record—Courcelles put him in Verdun's prison, the Citadel."

Jon shook his head. "When one fellow escaped, leaving his wife behind, Courcelles imprisoned the wife. Another time, angry at some midshipmen for rioting in the Citadel, he thrust fourteen of the worst troublemakers into one cell, where they nearly suffocated. Hell, he even sent one of our friends—who was supposed to escape with us—off to another depot for the most minor of infractions a couple of weeks before our attempt. Truth was, we all walked on pins and needles, waiting for the next outrage."

She could only nod, trying to imagine her father—and Jon—having to endure such things daily.

"At that point in the war, Napoleon seemed to be winning," Jon went on, "and having already been there for eight years, we feared we might end up spending the rest of our lives in Verdun. All we could see before us was a bleak future. Emboldened by the fact that some prisoners had recently succeeded in escaping, my friends and I agreed to escape ourselves."

"And Papa, too?"

Jon dragged in a rough breath. "At first, he refused to go. He thought it unwise. He pointed out the disadvantages to it, cautioned us we could end up like those whose escapes were unsuccessful, some of whom died in the attempt. We wouldn't hear of it. Once he realized we would do it with or without him, he said he would go with us."

The regret in his voice made her reach over to grab his hand, but he shrugged it off. He seemed bent on putting himself through this recitation alone. So, she settled back to let him say his piece, no matter how alarming it might be.

"I wanted your father to join us and so he did. I knew his reasons for wanting to stay were more . . . personal—they don't matter now—but I didn't think them strong enough for him to remain in Verdun. And I was so bloody sure of my plan—that it would succeed, that we would at last be free—that I pushed him to go. I should never have done that."

"I'm sure he wanted to leave as much as you did. He was just being cautious."

"Probably," he said in a noncommittal tone that made her wonder what he was leaving out. "In any case, we put our plan into action. Since those of us on parole were allowed to go a short distance beyond the walls of the town for the occasional excursion into the countryside, we planned a fishing party."

"And then you just didn't go back?"

"It wasn't that simple, I'm afraid. Whenever we *were* allowed out, it was only for a few hours, and we were forced to leave our passports behind. If we didn't return in time for *appel*, the alarm would be sounded and every peasant in the countryside would beat the bushes looking for us, eager for the reward they'd be given if they caught an escapee. The only way to escape successfully was at night, when we had more time to get away. And winter was best since they never expected prisoners to brave the harsh conditions."

She swallowed. "I suppose it gets very cold in Verdun in winter."

"Very. I knew of previous unsuccessful escapes where the men lost limbs to frostbite. That's why we'd chosen to go before the snows were expected to begin. Getting out of Verdun was only the first stage of any plan."

"How did you hope to escape France?" she asked.

"By crossing the Rhine and traversing the countryside there until we could reach Austria. We knew the Austrians, being enemies of Napoleon, would welcome us and help us get home."

"That sounds like a long way to go."

"It would have been. That's why all the prisoner towns were chosen from among places deep in the interior of France or on the borders with France's allies, although at that point, no one was sure which side the Germans were on."

"I see," she said, though she didn't know enough about the war to "see" any of it.

"Anyway," he went on, "before our fishing expedition, we gathered up items we'd been hoarding for weeks: provisions, small tools, coins that we sewed into our coats, and fake French passports. We'd also secured some thin, strong rope we intended to use for our escape, and we'd wrapped it around our bodies under our clothes. When we left the town for our day of fishing, the gendarmes didn't search us or our picnic basket too closely, which we probably should have wondered at, but didn't."

He drummed his fingers nervously on his thigh. "Once out of sight of the city gates, we found a copse of trees where the underbrush was overgrown, and we stashed the contents of our coats and our provisions in a burlap sack, which we hung over a branch to keep from the animals. Armed with a couple of fish we'd caught to support our story, we deliberately returned fifteen minutes late."

"Why, for pity's sake?" she asked, confused. "Didn't that draw attention to you?"

"Yes, which is what we wanted. Believe it or not, it was harder to break out of Verdun once the gates were closed at night than to break out of the Citadel if one knew how. I'd already been in the prison once for some infraction, so I knew its weaknesses, one of which was that—if we could get to it—the wall on one end was all that separated the Citadel from freedom. I had a plan for getting to it—I won't go into that. The hard part would be getting over the wall. On one side it was easy to climb, provided we could evade the sentries, but on the other, I estimated, from observing it on the out-side, there was a drop of about thirty to fifty feet or so, depending on which end of the rampart we were situated."

A sickening feeling assailed her. He'd said her father had frac-tured his leg in a fall. She began to fear she knew how. And judging from how deathly pale Jon had become, she'd guessed right.

"That night we were successful in getting free of where we were being held, and we got almost to the wall without encountering a sentry. But there was one sentry we couldn't avoid, and it was very dark. So, we had to move to another section of the rampart."

He seemed to close up into himself. "We'd brought all the rope we could scavenge—enough for fifty-five feet—and had already knotted it together. The plan was for Scovell to go first since he could navigate by the stars to get us back to our copse of woods. Heathbrook was to go second, me third, and your father last."

"Why last?"

"He had insisted upon it, so we'd all agreed to it, because if there were soldiers waiting for us at the bottom, your father could throw down the rope and return to the cell, with no one being the wiser. He was the oldest and the one least eager to escape, so we didn't mind giving him as little risk as possible."

He took a shuddering breath. "Everything went to hell from there. The drop from that part of the wall ended up being sixty-five feet, not fifty-five. Scovell leapt down the extra ten feet without in-cident, even though it took him by surprise. But he was a naval of-ficer used to jumping long distances. Still, he couldn't warn us about the extra drop without calling out and alerting the sentry to our presence. So, Heathbrook got bruised pretty badly in his fall, but at least he didn't break anything."

"And you . . . hurt your hands," she said through a thick throat.

He shrugged. "I have big hands—it was harder for me to grip the rope, especially since I was overeager to get down. Although I made it most of the way, I lost my grip a few feet from the bottom of the rope and slid down it, which sliced into my hands. Thank-fully, when I fell, I landed partly on Heathbrook, who cushioned my fall and kept me from breaking anything."

"Though it caused more of Lord Heathbrook's bruises?"

He snorted. "He still gives me grief over it sometimes."

She should laugh, but she couldn't. He hadn't mentioned her father yet. "And Papa?"

Reaching forward, he gripped her hands. "I thought he'd asked to be last because he intended not to go through with it. I wish to God I'd been right. He'd be here now with you if he hadn't joined us." He glanced down at their hands. "But he did. Except that when he dropped to the ground, he landed worse than the rest of us and hurt his leg."

He released her hands. "We couldn't tell at first that he'd fractured his femur. No bones were sticking out, and the only thing we knew was he was in a great deal of pain. We assumed he was just badly bruised, like Heathbrook. Although our original plans had been to keep going while it was dark, we laid low until the morning instead, hoping his leg would feel better then. Unfortunately, he could scarcely stand. We were resolved to stay in our copse until he could walk, but we never got the chance. The gendarmes surrounded us and ordered us out."

"Is . . . is that why you three think someone betrayed you?" she whispered. "Because they found your hiding place?"

"Actually, Scovell overheard a gendarme mention the betrayal in French. Scovell's fluent, you know. Unfortunately, the gendarme never said who it was, just that it was 'one of their own people.' Heathbrook interprets that to mean an Englishman, but Scovell and I believe it could be anyone in our circle. It's hard to know. But, yes, whoever it was did know of our hiding place, because they sent the gendarmes there. They also had to know what night we were planning to leave. We've yet to learn who it was, however."

She thought through that. "But . . . but if the gendarmes knew you were going to try to escape, why didn't they just grab you four as you came down the wall?"

"First of all, they couldn't have known precisely where we would come down, since *we* didn't know until that night. Besides, Courcelles wanted to make a spectacle of us, I suspect, which required daylight. Far more effective to clap us in irons and parade us through the streets in a bit of theater engineered to impress upon the other prisoners that no more escapes would be tolerated."

"They made Papa walk in irons, too?" she asked, her throat raw from unshed tears.

"No. He was well-liked among the French because of his tutoring, so although they hauled him about, still in irons, it was in a cart, thank God." A look of shame crossed Jon's face. "It was the only kindness they showed him, however. After days of browbeating us, trying to find out which of us had planned the escape and who'd forged our passports, they realized they'd get nothing out of us. That's when they packed all four of us off to Bitche."

He pulled aside the curtain to gaze out the window as if trying to figure out where they were and how much time they had. "We're nearly home. Hold on." Opening the panel, he told the coachman to take them to Hyde Park and just keep driving around it until he said otherwise.

"Now," he said, "where was I? Oh. Right. They made us walk to Bitche, of course, chained together like common criminals." He wouldn't look at her. "After one day of that, it became apparent your father couldn't manage it, and it would take weeks to get to Bitche if they tried to force him. So they grudgingly put him into a cart again. But in each town where we stopped for the night, all four of us were thrown into whatever jail was there."

She fought to contain her tears, but it was getting harder by the moment. Her poor father. How he had suffered! It was abominable.

"In one such town," Jon went on in a harsh tone, "they did finally get a doctor to look at him. The man did what he could, wrapping his leg up and giving him a crutch, but he said that in order to see how badly the bone was fractured he'd have to cut into the leg, and that was unwise. The risk of your father dying of infection was greater than if Morris just learned to make do with the leg as it was."

"But . . . but didn't that mean he lived in pain?" she whispered.

Jon closed his eyes and grimaced as if her every word drove daggers through his heart. "Yes. Daily pain. Toward the end of our time at Bitche, Morris had a fall, and it must have knocked a piece of bone loose, for it began working its way to the surface. It broke the skin in a . . . a sore that brought the . . . infection the French doctor had feared. Your father had gangrene. He . . . he died of it just as we were learning of Napoleon's abdication."

She could only sit and stare at him. His horrendous tale showed just how much he and his friends had endured before leaving

France. How much her father had endured at Bitche. It was monstrous. Papa had lived in constant pain his last three years, all because of a cruel commandant and the twist of fate that had him falling from a great height at his age.

The thought of it finally broke the dam of her tears. Looking alarmed by them, Jon handed her his handkerchief, and she accepted it gratefully. If she kept this up, she would end up with quite a collection of them.

But she didn't care. She wept for how her father had died. She wept for her little brother, who would never know his father. And she wept for Mama, who hadn't been able to see Papa again in this lifetime. Tory shed a veritable river of tears.

All the while, Jon sat there in an agonizing silence, as if waiting for her to finish.

Chapter 22

Jon watched as Tory cried softly, but messily, blotting her eyes, blowing her nose, and in the process, driving nails through his heart. He'd known that telling her the truth would lead to this, which is why he'd put it off for so long, but it was even worse to watch it now that he knew how much he cared for her.

She hadn't seemed too angry over the dowry business, so he'd allowed himself to think things might be all right after all. Clearly, he'd been wrong.

After a while, her tears seemed to abate enough for her to manage speech. "Forgive me," she shocked him by saying. "I feel like every time we're alone together, I . . . I turn into a babbling fountain. I'm really not the sort to cry over every little thing."

"Every little—" He choked down a manic laugh. "Good God, sweetheart, you have nothing to apologize for. This was certainly not a 'little thing.' " He swallowed his pain, knowing he'd never make it through this speech if he didn't. "I am so very sorry about what happened to your father. I've felt the guilt of it every day since the escape. Indeed, that's why I know I don't deserve you. Thanks to me, your father suffered greatly in his last three years. Thanks to me, he didn't make it home. If I knew any way to make it up to you, I would, but—"

"Wait a minute," she interrupted, her eyes widening. "You . . . you truly blame *yourself* for what happened to him?"

Her incredulous tone took him aback. How could she not see this was his fault? "Of course, I blame myself! I pushed him to escape when he didn't wish to. I misjudged the height of the wall we had to come down, and thus we lacked enough rope to tackle it. He would never have fractured his leg if not for those two things. And our unsuccessful escape meant he was dragged through France, then put into a dungeon cell with no chance of recovering the use of—"

"None of that was your fault." She laid her hand on his knee. "Did *he* blame you?"

Feeling as if he was choking on his pain, Jon hesitated before answering. "He said he didn't. But if I'd been in his place, I would have."

"I doubt that. You have too keen a sense of right and wrong to do so."

Her tone held so much sincerity that it fairly slayed him. He wasn't quite sure he could place his faith in it.

She rubbed his knee. "Do Scovell and Heathbrook blame you for what happened?"

"No. But neither of them suffered permanent injury. Whereas your father—"

"—took a risk, just as the rest of you did." She moved to his side of the carriage to seize his hand, and when he tried to pull it free, she refused to release it. "I don't blame you for what happened, my darling."

She called him "darling"? And said she didn't blame him? How could that be?

"I mourn that I lost my papa," she added, "but he could have died a thousand ways over there—from disease or injury or apoplexy or heart attack. And you know it. You told me of others who died for no more reason than they were being held in difficult circumstances. You and your friends did your best to shield him from harm. What else could you have done?"

"Not tried to escape?" he said hoarsely. That was the crux of it. If they hadn't attempted the escape, Morris might have come home.

"You may see now that your attempt was doomed to failure,

that the war was to end in three more years, but you couldn't see it then. You were young, and you couldn't wait forever. You had to try to get away. Didn't you say there were countless attempts by others to escape? Why should you have been any different? And if Papa didn't blame you, why should I . . . and why should *you* blame *yourself?*"

He gaped at her. Did she realize she spoke the unfathomable? "You . . . you really don't blame me for his death, hate me for what happened?"

"No! I'm shocked you four got as far as you did. I'm sure plenty of escapees didn't."

"You don't understand—"

"Believe me, I do. In your mind, your 'crime' lies in the fact that you convinced Papa to escape, and you misjudged the height of a wall. Regarding the former, you forget Papa had a mind of his own. He decided to go with you three because he had his reasons, missing home probably being one of them. Trust me, I remember enough about my father to know that no one ever persuaded him to do something he didn't wish to do."

She squeezed his hand. "As for the second part of your 'crime,' I'm not shocked you misjudged the height of a wall without being able to measure it; I'd have been more shocked if you *had* judged it correctly. Lord knows I never could have. So if you're seeking absolution for what happened with Papa, I give it to you freely."

She couldn't know how much that meant to him. He'd been carrying around the guilt over Morris's death the same way they'd dragged those chains through Verdun. After spending years blaming himself for Morris's torment, hearing that she, at least, didn't blame him was almost more happiness than he could stand.

Then her expression clouded over, and she stared down at his hand. "But I think it only fair I point out that if your wanting to marry me is just about making up for some perceived injury you inflicted on my family, you needn't sacrifice yourself for that. I don't want you to."

"Sacrifice!" He folded her hand in both of his, his heart thumping wildly. "Until last night, I resisted even the thought of marrying you because I knew I was unworthy of you."

"You are *not* unworthy of anyone," she said hotly. "Honestly, before you can be entirely free of the guilt that has you in its grip, you have to learn to forgive yourself for what happened with Papa."

That was easier said than done. "I'll try. But my point is, I wanted you from the moment I saw you, from the moment you informed me that I did indeed need a governess to teach me, but that you couldn't because you were busy with my sister."

"You remember that?"

"I remember every conversation you and I have ever had," he said, and kissed her hand.

"You can see how poorly my vow not to teach you turned out," she teased. "I daresay I've spent more time instructing you than Chloe in these past two weeks."

"Only because of our bargain," he pointed out. "And I've enjoyed every moment."

"To tell the truth, so have I," she said shyly.

"I tried every way I could think of to talk myself out of wanting you, needing you. Yet I never fully succeeded. So, know this, Victoria Morris," he said, fiercely eager to convince her to marry him now that he knew it was possible. "It would be no sacrifice for me to marry you. It would be the greatest privilege of my life, and one I still don't think I deserve."

"I don't deserve a duke for a husband," she shot back, "so we'll simply have to get over our mutual lack of deserving if we are to marry."

"If?" he asked, his eyes boring into hers.

"I still have questions that need answering, some of which—"

He cut her off with a long kiss, unable to bear another moment without tasting her again. He didn't want any more of her questions, because they might change the hope sparking within him. Her words said she didn't blame him, but he trusted actions more than words, and how she reacted to his touch would tell him how she truly felt.

Fortunately, she reacted by throwing her arms about his neck and returning his kiss with great enthusiasm. In that instant, his need for her roared to life again. Not that it ever had fully gone away since their private moments at the ball had stoked it to unendurable heights—it had merely been in abeyance after each new encounter.

He dropped to his knees in front of her, determined to give her more pleasure than he'd managed last night when his desire to be inside her had made him take her far too hastily.

She grabbed his shoulders. "Wh-what are you up to now?"

"Bear with me, sweetheart. I'm about to behave recklessly again." He felt positively giddy now that he knew she didn't hate him for her father's death. "I intend to remind you of the advantages you might find in sharing my marital bed."

"I am fully aware of—"

He lifted her skirts enough to spread her knees apart.

"Jon!" she cried as he shoved her skirts up to her waist and looked her over. "What the devil are you doing?"

"Surveying the ground I mean to cover for the day when I sculpt you unclothed. I'm very glad you haven't yet embraced the new fashion of wearing drawers."

She blushed deeply, and he chuckled. Beneath her skirts, she was naked as a Venus statue, and every bit as lovely. He took his time looking at her, which he hadn't had much chance to do last night, as eager as he was to take her. Her blond hair was a shade darker here than on her head, but it glistened in the dim light of the curtained carriage, making him exult in having aroused her.

"What if your coachman opens the panel?" she hissed.

"He won't. He knows better."

"Well . . . what if he hears us?"

"I don't care." Jon parted those curls to expose her sweet cleft, damp with her arousal, and his cock hardened to stone.

"But if he thinks we are . . . doing something we shouldn't . . ."

"It won't matter once we're married." He placed his mouth right there, where he wanted to swive her with his tongue.

"Good Lord," she whispered, "you're very wicked, aren't you?"

He licked her a few times before answering. "I told you I had a misspent youth." Then he sucked her pearl, and she nearly came off the seat.

After that, she said nothing more, just gripped his head in an unconscious bid for him to keep going. Which, of course, he did.

He reveled in the musky scent of her arousal, the twitching of her mons, the low moans she made as he increased his sucking. He loved the feel of her silky thighs beneath his fingers, and hoped he wasn't gripping them too hard.

Most of all, he prayed he could keep from coming off in his trousers before she came against his mouth. Because Tory in full arousal was a glorious sight. He wished he could see her bared breasts, too, and her curvy bottom, but that would have to wait until he could get her in a bedroom again, preferably his own.

Then she pushed against his mouth, and he felt her release just as she whispered, "Jon! Good Lord!"

He didn't know whether to be glad she could restrain her cries to a whisper or to wish she couldn't. Either way, he would leave "making her scream her pleasure" for a future encounter, one that really *would* have to take place in his bedchamber, after they were married.

At last, she gave a soft whimper and relaxed beneath his mouth. Only then did he pull away. He rose up on his knees, intending to sit next to her, and she murmured, "Where do you think *you* are going?"

He paused to kiss her thigh. "What do you mean?"

"You know how I feel about you giving me pleasure but taking none of your own," she whispered. "I hope you weren't meaning that to be some sort of . . . penance for the past."

"No. I merely thought that after last night . . . I mean, surely you're sore from—"

"A little. But I want to feel you inside me." She caressed his cheek. "You can do that here, too, can't you? Kneeling where you are?"

His cock sprang to full attention. "I have a better idea." He unfastened his trousers and drawers and pulled them down before pushing himself up onto the carriage seat opposite her. Then he hauled her over on top of him until she was kneeling on the seat, straddling his thighs.

"Well!" she said, looking down to where his cock was nicely cradled between her thighs. "That's certainly . . . interesting."

"It will get even more interesting in a moment. Because now it's your turn to seduce *me.*"

She grabbed his shoulders as the carriage made a turn. "I don't understand."

He caught her by the waist to urge her up. "Please, dearling. Rise up and come down on my . . . er . . ."

"Oh!" she exclaimed. "I-I think I understand now."

It took her some maneuvering to get all her skirts out of the way again, and then position herself properly, but when at last she slid down on him, it was sheer heaven.

"Ohh, *yes*," he half spoke, half groaned. "Yes, like *that*. God in heaven, you're . . . a wonder, a veritable wonder, Tory."

She squirmed a bit on top of him as if trying to get comfortable, and that made him insane. "Now what?" she whispered.

He would have laughed if he hadn't been so bloody aroused and frustrated at the same time. "Now, my sweet angel, you must *move*."

Chapter 23

Move? How exactly was she supposed to do *that*?

Tory shifted a little, but that didn't seem to be what he wanted, for he did that odd thing again where he tried to push her up off of him with his hands on her waist.

That was when it hit her. *Move.* The way he'd moved inside her last night, only upside down. Hoping she'd guessed right, she came up on her knees a bit, then lowered herself on him again.

"Ah, yes, sweetheart, *yes,*" he murmured, his gaze seeming to melt before her very eyes. "Like that. Exactly like that."

"So I'm doing it properly?"

"*Properly?*" he said with a strangled laugh. "No. What you're doing isn't remotely proper. But, damn, does it feel good."

"In that case . . ." She moved again and realized it felt rather good for her, too. Almost as good as Jon's mouth on her privates.

Almost.

But now she realized something else. She could *make* it be however she wanted. Because she controlled the motion, and she could do it as fast or slow as she pleased.

So, she did a bit of experimenting. And wasn't that just wonderful? The more she moved, the more sensations she discovered. A pleasurable heat was building down between her legs that made her wish to squirm and increase the speed of her up and down motion. Sometimes, when she came down a certain way, she felt this little zing of a thrill. So, she did *that* more.

If he minded her experimentation, he certainly didn't show it, for he was rocking with her, his eyes closing as a look of sheer bliss crept over his face.

And the carriage motion made it even more interesting. "I do think . . . I like this, Jon."

"Good," he choked out. "We'll keep a carriage . . . just for this."

He meant, *when we marry*. She dug her fingers into his shoulders. He was so sure they would. Yet she wasn't quite as sure . . .

She thrust that thought from her mind. If this ended up being their last time to enjoy each other's bodies, she meant to make the most of it. She wanted to send him to the same oblivion he'd sent her to, *was* sending her to. His hands were urging her on, so she followed his rhythm, moving faster . . . harder . . . more freely.

Heavens, but he was . . . a veritable wonder himself. The same feelings he'd provoked with his mouth he was now startling to life with his loins and other . . . parts, which had fallen into their own special pace. Soon she was climbing the sky with her private sun god on the same chariot he'd carried her up on before.

Good *Lord*.

"Tory . . . yes . . . like that . . . my sweet angel . . ." he chanted.

Meanwhile, her mind chanted, *My darling . . . yes . . . like that . . . my love . . . my dear, wonderful love . . .* as she abandoned herself to the motion.

He was *hers* now . . . her love . . . the only man she would . . . *could . . . ever love . . .* No matter what happened . . . he was hers . . . *hers . . . Hers . . .*

And with that she reached the pinnacle of her pleasure just as she felt him fill her with his essence. She clutched him to her as the delicious sensations of release held her in their grip. Then she slowly drifted back down, the two of them still joined together, and him murmuring soft, delightful words in her ears.

It took some time before her own words echoed in her consciousness. She'd called him *her love*.

Oh dear. She *loved* Jon. She truly did. She may not be able to marry him—she wasn't even sure of that yet—but she loved him all the same.

Meanwhile, all the delicious words he'd murmured hadn't included that one little word: *love.*

She wouldn't think of that right now. She would just enjoy sitting here draped over his lap, being embraced by him and kissed by him. Because she loved him. But she dared not tell him, for he might use it against her to make sure she married him. She needed more answers to her questions to know if she would.

If she would ever do these lovely things with him again.

Not wanting to think about that, either, she slipped off his lap and onto the seat next to him, though she did pause to twist and pull her skirts down. Following her cue, he wrestled his drawers and trousers back into place and refastened them before tugging her into his arms.

They sat quiet a moment, with him brushing kisses to her hair, which was probably quite undone by now. Not that she cared. Her heart was starting to pound, making her nervous about what he was going to say to her questions.

"Have you . . . talked to your mother and Chloe about marrying me?"

He nodded. "Chloe, of course, was ecstatic."

"And your mother?"

A sigh escaped him. "She's . . . cautious. It turned out she was fully aware of Cyril and his problems."

"What? How?"

When he explained that his mother had been spying on her, she wanted to be outraged, but at the same time she could understand the duchess's concern. Chloe was her daughter, after all, and she had just been trying to protect her.

But that did make Tory nervous. "So . . . how does she feel about Cyril?"

He pressed a kiss to her head. "A bit wary. But she'll come around, especially if she meets him. The lad is too sweet not to win Mother over."

Tory wasn't so sure. The duchess could be unpredictable. Still, they would cross that bridge later. Right now, she had more pressing concerns.

Like what he'd said about her father. "Jon, you told me Papa resisted escaping at first. I can understand why he would see the danger in it, but what did you mean when you said that Papa's reasons for not wanting to escape were more 'personal'?"

"It's nothing," he said, so quickly that she knew it *wasn't* nothing.

"Please tell me, Jon. I need to know."

With a groan, he threaded his fingers through his hair. "I shouldn't have said anything. He wouldn't have wanted me to."

"Did he ask you not to?"

"Well . . . no, but he kept his secret even at the end, so I assumed he did so because he feared I might tell someone and didn't want me to."

The word "secret" alarmed her. She pulled away from Jon, her breath sticking in her throat. "Mr. Beasley said that some détenus created new families in France. Is that what . . . what happened with Papa? Did he—"

"No, nothing like that." He hesitated a moment longer, then sighed. "But he did have a very close female friend—a Frenchwoman named Mademoiselle Bernard."

"Oh, yes! The one Mr. Beasley mentioned, to whom Papa taught English."

"Um, yes. I'm not sure he was teaching her English, though. She was . . . is about three years older than you. They spent hours together, and I couldn't help but suspect—"

"That he was breaking his marriage vows to Mama with her," Tory bit out. "You thought this Mademoiselle Bernard was his mistress."

"I didn't say that."

"You didn't have to." She moved to the other side of the carriage, needing more distance from him, needing space to breathe. The thought of Papa turning to another woman for solace . . .

No, he wouldn't. He just wouldn't. "Was there any proof?" she asked, her heart faltering. Now she wished she hadn't begun this discussion. But she'd needed to know why Papa wouldn't be eager to come home to them.

"No," he said with a pitying look.

At least that was something. "Was she . . . pretty?" When he hesitated, she added, "Tell the truth, Jon. You've gone this far. You might as well give me the rest."

"She was reasonably attractive, yes."

She stared at him. "Did he put her in that codicil to his will? The real part of the codicil, I mean, not the part you had Mr. Beasley forge."

At least he had the good grace to wince. "No." When she arched an eyebrow, he added, "I swear. There was no mention of Mademoiselle Bernard in the codicil or the will. Actually, that rather surprised me. I was afraid he might have left something to her. They seemed very . . . close. They were 'friends' almost from the beginning of our stay in Verdun, so if he'd wanted to, he could have sent a letter to Trimnell to revise his will. Clearly, he didn't."

That was interesting. "And what about Commander Scovell and Lord Heathbrook? Do they agree she was probably his mistress?"

He let out a frustrated breath. "Scovell is keeping an open mind about it. Heathbrook is convinced she was not."

"So, why are you so sure?" she asked, now curious.

Jon crossed his arms over his chest. "It wasn't like him to spend so much time with a young woman."

"It also wasn't like him to have an adulterous affair. Perhaps he really *was* just teaching her English," she said petulantly. "He and Mama were always so close, so happy together. I refuse to believe he would have a mistress for any reason."

Jon reached over to clasp her hands. "Sweetheart, after eight years away from home, any man starts to long for a woman's touch. Many of the men in the camp took mistresses, and as Beasley also mentioned, some—even the married ones—built families in France and stayed there after the rest of us were released. It's not impossible he yearned for some female companionship."

"And preferred this Mademoiselle Bernard to Mama, who, by the way, was quite pretty and only thirty-four herself when Papa left England?"

That seemed to shake him a little. "Yes, but your mother would have been forty-two by the time we were discussing escaping."

"I do hope you're grasping at straws to bolster your argument," she said, slipping her hands from his. "Otherwise, I'll have to start worrying how you'll feel about *me* when I reach forty-two. Assuming we do marry."

A hint of alarm showed in his eyes. "I didn't mean to imply women are ... are unattractive past a certain age. I just meant that your *father* might have preferred ... that is ..."

"You're saying that Papa would have chosen to stay with the young Frenchwoman rather than return to his slightly older wife and his child. I'm sorry, but I can't believe that. I *can* believe he might have been concerned about the feasibility of your plans. Papa was always overly cautious. But to stay for some woman—" She shook her head. "Did *you* take a mistress?"

He threw himself back against the seat, clearly frustrated. "No. The English women who were in the camp were there for their husbands, and their daughters were ... chaste. No one laid a finger on them. So, that left French women, and I just couldn't bring myself to consort with the enemy in that way. Heathbrook did, but I couldn't."

"Yet you think a man you claim to have admired, a man you thought of as a father, took one," she pointed out, "even though he was happily married."

He stiffened. "Plenty of husbands who claim to be happily married also take mistresses. Plenty of wives take lovers."

"And you would know, wouldn't you?" she said.

He cast her a wary look. "What do you mean?"

"I overheard Papa tell Mama you were sent on the grand tour to get you away from London's vices, which were tempting you to do such things as, among others, bed a married woman and nearly get shot by her husband. Is that true?"

She regretted her words the moment she saw the mortification and self-loathing in his expression. She hadn't meant to wound him so ... just to make him see how unfair he was being to Papa.

"Jon," she said softly, "we both know you had a 'misspent youth.' I don't blame you for it—you were young and young men often rebel. Yet you didn't even take a mistress as a bachelor in France, something many of your rank do routinely in London. So, surely you can see that Papa might not have chosen to do so, either."

She reached over to take his hand. "Or perhaps it's precisely *be-*

cause of your misspent youth—and what you saw in the camp—that you have such a cynical view of marriage."

"He was just so *secretive* about it, damn it!" Jon cried, snatching his hand from hers. "I was his closest companion for *years* and stood by him at every turn. But he . . . he wouldn't admit why he was close to her. That says to me he was ashamed of it."

"Yet he didn't hide it, either?" she asked, truly confused. "You knew, as did Mr. Beasley and your friends, that they were spending time together. Usually, a person hides something if they're ashamed."

That seemed to bring him up short.

"Can't you just trust me when I say I know my father's character and my parents' marriage, and it wasn't what you think?"

"Tory—"

"But you *can't* trust me, can you? The truth is you have a rather poor view of marriage in general. First, you give me a secret dowry to ensure you can fulfill your promise to my father to get me married, which implies you didn't think I could find a husband without the fortune."

"I never once thought—"

"Then," she cut in, "you offer to marry me yourself, but only because we shared a bed." A lead ball had settled in her stomach, making it hard for her to go on, even though she knew she must. "And finally, you inform me you believe my father broke his wedding vows because he had a woman friend, even though there is no evidence whatsoever of any kind of . . . lurid relationship between them."

She dragged in a heavy breath. "Yet you expect me to marry you, when it's clear you don't have much faith in the institution yourself."

"I never said that," he protested. "Besides, my feelings about marriage are immaterial. I took your innocence. We have to marry." He winced. "I mean—"

"That *is* what you mean, Jon. That's the problem. Because we don't *have* to marry. We have a choice."

He muttered an oath under his breath. "But you need to marry. At least admit that. Your dream of an art school for women aside, you need to take care of Cyril, and I can do that for you, however you wish it done."

"What about love? Does that play no part in your plans?" When he gaped at her, clearly caught off guard, she added, "I guess I know my answer. But the thing is, I love you. I shouldn't say it when it makes no difference to you, but I do."

She flashed him a sad smile. "And loving you means I don't want half a marriage. I want a real marriage, my darling, not one chosen out of your guilt or my need for Cyril to be cared for. I want a husband who's marrying me because he loves me, too. So I'm afraid this must be our last time alone together."

"You can't mean that," he said hoarsely. "I want you—"

"And that is lovely, not to mention quite enjoyable. I want you, too. But I also love you, and that beats everything else." Realizing she was on the verge of tears, she reached up to open the panel. "Will, would you please let me off here?"

"We need to talk about this more, damn it," Jon said.

The carriage shuddered to a halt. "I don't," she said. "I-I need to go figure out what I'm going to do from now on."

A bleak expression crossed his face. "At least take the dowry money . . . for your school. I've put you in your present pickle regarding your reputation, so the least I can do is fix that by giving you those funds."

Her heart melted. Somewhere in that stern, unyielding body of his, he clearly felt *something* for her. But as long as he couldn't admit it to himself, it wasn't real to him.

"I don't think it wise for me to take the money," she said. "I'll be fine. Papa left me a little money in his will, and I can always find another post as a governess or an artist or something. Now, I have to go home." *Before I make a fool of myself. Or worse, change my mind.*

"Then I'll get out. You can't be let down in the middle of Hyde Park alone. It's not safe." When she opened her mouth to protest, he growled, "This isn't negotiable, Tory. Either I get out or we both do, and I walk you back to the cottage." Without waiting for her answer, he leaned forward to say through the open panel, "Will, take Miss Morris to wherever she wishes to go. I'm walking home."

Then before she could protest, he jumped from the carriage and strode off, clearly angry and upset. She was tempted to call him back . . . or join him in walking, but that would just prolong the pain.

After giving the coachman the address to her cottage, she closed the panel and burst into tears. Anyone would tell her she was a fool. She could have a duke for a husband. It was what every woman in Society wanted.

But she'd never been part of Society, not really. She'd been raised by a professor and an artist, and she'd been skirting the edges of respectability ever since. It was time she returned to where she'd come from. Somehow, she would find her way again. Without him.

She fished out her own handkerchief to blot her eyes and blow her nose, then straightened her back. She'd be fine. Truly, she would. She had her dear Cyril who loved her and Mrs. Gully who spoiled her. She might even still have her friend Chloe to spend time with . . . assuming Chloe didn't side with her brother in this.

And if sometimes Tory couldn't help dreaming of a certain fellow with golden eyes, a teasing smile, and a hundred ways to make a woman swoon . . .

Well, a cat could look at a king, couldn't she?

Chapter 24

Jon stalked Hyde Park like a man bent on a mission. Except he had no mission anymore. He'd done his best to find out who'd told the press about the dowry yet had learned nothing of substance. He'd decided he should do his penance with Tory, but instead had discovered she loved him.

Loved him! Was the woman daft? It would have made sense if she'd wanted to marry him to save her brother or to become a duchess or even to experience more of the sensual delights they'd been so eagerly tasting. Any of those would have seemed perfectly rational to him.

But to want to marry for love? That wasn't rational in the least.

He didn't deserve her, as she would find out eventually. He'd practically killed her father, which she would finally realize one day. And he'd intended to be ready for when that happened by protecting his heart.

She didn't want him protecting his heart, apparently. She wanted him throwing it wholeheartedly into the air and hoping she caught it and didn't let it crash to the ground.

But you can't *trust me, can you?* she'd said.

No, he couldn't. How could he? He'd spent nearly half his life in a place where no one could be trusted. He'd cultivated only a few trustworthy friends, and Morris had seriously shaken that trust. Although Jon had to admit—when it came to Morris and Mademoiselle Bernard, Scovell and Heathbrook were nearly in accord with Tory.

What if he was wrong about Morris? What if Heathbrook was right that Mademoiselle had done nothing to betray them? What if he was throwing Tory away out of some fit of pique simply because she wouldn't agree with him?

No, surely he wasn't that petty. Not after everything that had happened between them. He had good reason for his suspicions. *He* was in the right, and she was expecting too much.

What about love? Does that play no part in your plans? . . . I love you . . . And loving you means . . . I want a real marriage, not one chosen out of your guilt or my need for Cyril to be cared for. I want a husband who's marrying me because he loves me, too.

She loved him. Ergo, the woman was indeed daft.

But if he believed that, then he'd have to throw away everything she'd said about absolving him of his guilt. And he didn't want to.

His eyes watered, and he gritted his teeth. He'd been living with that guilt all this time. He could continue to do so. Indeed, the fact that she only wanted him if he loved her was clear evidence that she secretly wanted him to keep living with that guilt. Right? *Right?*

He quickened his pace. This was insanity. She didn't want him because he wouldn't dance to her tune, and he was never dancing to anyone else's tune again. Not in this lifetime.

But over the next week, he found himself continuing to replay their conversation, sometimes agreeing with her, sometimes reinforcing his own feelings. At least when she'd been in the house, he'd been able to look forward to seeing her at breakfast or dinner, to perhaps passing her in the hall.

Not now. She was truly gone. Meals were . . . dull. Chloe was subdued, making him wonder if she still saw Tory and just wasn't saying anything about it. His mother tried to pretend nothing had happened, especially after the gossip rag printed the retraction he'd demanded.

He didn't get a damned thing done. He tried, but mostly he read and reread the same words and numbers over and over until he gave up on that and finally just went to bed. Alone. The state where he belonged, apparently.

The nights were pure misery.

Tonight he was suffering another one, his longing for Tory an ache in his chest that never seemed to go away. They'd never spent one minute in his bedchamber, yet he could imagine her here as clearly as if they had.

She would join him in bed, wearing only the nightdress she'd worn in her little cottage. She would make him forget Bitche prison when he roused in the night. She would banish those memories of Morris at the end, when he was suffering.

She would hold him close and soothe his sore heart . . .

God, she had him thinking of hearts again. Another week without her, and he'd be giving his heart to her freely.

Would that be so bad? She would marry him if he did. That's all he wanted, wasn't it? Tory in his bed at night? In his days of restoring the dukedom to its former glory? In his life?

Life without her had hardly been worth living so far.

He'd thought she might come to *him* after she realized what a mistake she'd made, but she would never do that, would she? Not the principled Tory he knew, who loved with her whole heart and would never take a marriage by half measures.

The same principled woman who'd gone out of her way to find work for Beasley. Who'd been willing to fight tooth and nail to protect her little brother from anyone who might not love him as fiercely as she did. Whose heart had gone out to him and his friends simply because of what they'd suffered in France.

Who'd absolved him of his guilt over her father's death with such sweetness and love.

Yes, love. *That* was love.

And he'd foolishly driven her away. Surely, he could still fix things, still get her back. Somehow.

Yes, he told himself. That was what he had to do. Get her back. Only after resolving to do that did he finally drift off to sleep.

But the next morning, he wasn't sure how to go about it. Would she even see him? She hadn't said a word to him in a week. What if she'd taken another post or . . . or had been thrown out of her cottage since she couldn't pay the lease?

It was in that moment of panic that Kershaw announced he had a visitor. The most unlikely of visitors, really. Mademoiselle Bernard herself.

After a moment's hesitation, Jon growled, "Show her in." Then he rose to pour himself a whisky, noticing that his hand shook as he did so. The woman could very well be Morris's mistress . . . or worse, their betrayer. He had to be careful with what he said. But he meant to determine the truth once and for all.

To protect Tory.

"Lord Jonathan . . . I-I mean, Your Grace," spoke a crisp voice that had less of a French accent than he remembered. "How kind of you to meet with me. I know you must be very busy these days."

He turned to see the woman he'd remembered as being extraordinarily beautiful, only to realize she couldn't hold a candle to Tory.

Oh, she was pretty enough. But she was taller and slenderer than Tory. Her hair was the color of mahogany, not the golden oak of Tory's. And her complexion was more ivory than Tory's alabaster. They did have oddly similar crystalline blue eyes, but beyond that, there was no comparison. Not for him. Tory's looks outshone hers as far as he was concerned.

Suddenly, he realized he was standing there studying her instead of asking the questions he was burning to know the answers to.

He would start with an easy one. "Although it's good to see you again, mademoiselle, I confess I'm curious to know—why are you here?"

She smiled at him. "Forgive me for any intrusion, Your Grace, but I was merely hoping to gain an address for Monsieur Morris's daughter. Mr. Beasley told me you might be able to give me one."

Jon stared at her, shaken. "Why do you wish to know her address, if I may ask?" When she blinked at that, he added, "She worked for my family until recently, so we feel a vested interest in her welfare."

She looked as if he'd taken her off guard. "You see, sir . . . That is . . ." She steadied her shoulders. "I have a journal and some letters for her from her father. The last time I saw him, shortly before your attempt to . . . um . . . leave Verdun, he entrusted them to me to pass on to his family in case he never returned."

Her chin quivered. "I only recently learned of his death from

Mr. Beasley, who also told me that Madame Morris died some years ago as well. Mr. Beasley says Mademoiselle Morris is alone in the world now. So of course I wish to give her these letters as soon as possible."

"I could pass them on to her for you," Jon said, still wary. What if the young woman meant to tell Tory of her illicit connection to Morris?

But Mademoiselle Bernard merely looked regretful, not devious. Indeed, the picture of the scheming Frenchwoman he'd built her up to be in his memory bore no resemblance to the anxious lady before him.

"Forgive me, sir," she said, "but I promised Monsieur Morris I would place them into her hands myself. I-I came a long way to do so. If you could but direct me where to go, I would be most grateful."

And just like that, Jon realized Tory had been right. He'd had no real reason to believe Mademoiselle Bernard was Morris's mistress. Jon's desire to unveil their betrayer had somehow become twisted up with the friendship between Morris and the Frenchwoman, whom the man had never spoken of with anything but the utmost respect.

Tory had been right about something else, too. He should have trusted Tory. She might not have seen her father for years, but she'd seen him with her mother, which Jon never had. And she had good instincts about people.

About *him*. She'd believed in his worth when he couldn't even believe in it himself. The least he could do was believe in her, too . . . trust her, too.

"I tell you what," Jon said, putting down his whisky glass. "It will be best if I take you there. It's not far. We can walk it easily."

"Oh, I would not wish to inconvenience you, sir," she said with consternation in her expression.

"It's no inconvenience." And he was going regardless of what she thought, partly because he still wanted to be there for Tory for whatever the letters said. And partly because he might perish if he didn't see her right now and tell her what was in his heart.

In his heart?

God, he loved her, didn't he? He'd tried so hard to protect himself from it because he'd known it could bloody well hurt when the person he loved was taken away from him. No, was *driven* away from him by his idiotic pride. Well, forget pride. He loved her. Was *in* love with her. He would get her back, regardless of what it took.

Because what good was being a duke and having all this power and property and wealth if he couldn't have the woman he loved?

Chapter 25

Tory sat in the parlor sewing a new shirt for Cyril. A week home had given her time to catch up on undone tasks. She'd kept Mrs. Gully on so the woman could still watch Cyril while Tory looked for work in an artistic field.

After having little success, Tory had been told by Mr. Beasley of a post for a colorist at the printmaker's where he now worked. She'd applied and was hired on the spot. It didn't pay all that well, but it would keep her and Cyril fed at least, and the hundred pounds Papa had left in his will for her and Mama would enable them to pay a year's rent in one of the lower-cost areas of town.

Chloe kept begging her to come back and just serve as her companion, which sorely tempted Tory. Despite the difference in their ages, Chloe had been the closest thing to a sister Tory had ever had.

But the idea of seeing Jon every day while staying resolved not to marry him was daunting. She missed him too much. If she worked at Falcon House, it wouldn't be long before she ended up in his bed, and things would just go downhill from there.

Had she made a huge mistake in turning down his offer of marriage? Some people made marriages without love work, didn't they? Of course, those people generally had a mutual lack of love for each other. When one was in love and the other wasn't, the one in love would suffer. She just couldn't bear that in the vain hope that Jon would one day wake up and decide to love her. Marriage was hard enough even *with* love. Look at Mrs. Gully, who struggled to endure Mr. Gully's mother. Jon's mother had watched her own son sent away by his father and then kept in exile for years, a situation that had strained their marriage. Even Mr. Beasley, who adored his plump little wife, fought with her over their oldest son's prospects. There were always things to test a marriage. A lack of love could only test it to its limits.

She put the last stitch in Cyril's shirt, then stood to shake it out. "Cyril!" she called, "Come try this on!"

The door to the parlor opened, and Cyril came in, tugging a man by the hand. "Sissy, look who *I* found outside! Your friend!"

Jon.

Tory's heart did a little flip, and her stomach joined it. All she could do was look at him, taking note of his serious expression, his pale complexion, and the way his clothes hung a little more loosely on him again.

"Are you . . . well?" she couldn't help asking.

"Is it that obvious that I'm not?" he said with a faint smile.

"I just . . . it merely seems as if . . ."

Unwittingly, Cyril piped up to save her. "He brought a lady, too! She's really pretty."

"Giselle Bernard," Jon explained hastily. "She wanted to talk to you, so I agreed to bring her here. She has some letters and a journal that your father gave to her for you." He nodded his head toward the door. "She's waiting out in the kitchen. But if you don't want to see her, I'll just—"

"No, I would like to meet her." She had to see this woman Jon kept painting as a Delilah who seduced Papa.

"Can I go fetch her, Sissy?" Cyril asked.

"If my 'friend' doesn't mind," she said with a glance at Jon.

"I don't mind a bit," he said in the rumbling voice that always set her blood on fire. "Cyril, why don't you go get her while I speak to your sister a moment?"

"Yay!" Cyril said merrily, and ran out the door.

"Before she comes," Jon said, "I just wanted to tell you that you were right. There was nothing between her and your father."

"She told you that?" Tory asked, her heart pounding.

"No. She has told me nothing beyond the fact that he left letters and a journal with her to give to your family." He stepped closer. "I merely realized that in my heart I *did* trust you, not only in this, but in everything."

Her own heart was soaring, though she had so many questions. "Jon—"

"Here she is, Sissy!" Cyril announced, tugging "the lady" into the room.

Cursing her little brother's tendency to rush everywhere, Tory scanned Giselle Bernard critically. Jon hadn't lied about the French-woman's looks. She was gorgeous, like a younger version of Jon's own mother, who was also tall, elegant, and had once been bru-nette.

As Jon performed the introductions, Mademoiselle Bernard kept giving Cyril furtive glances. "Little Cyril is Monsieur Morris's son, *non?*" she asked.

Tory nodded. "My mother bore him nine months after Papa left." The woman certainly had an odd interest in Cyril for some-one who was just a friend of Papa's. It made Tory a trifle nervous.

"Cyril, dear," Tory said, "I finished your new shirt. Please take it to Mrs. Gully and ask her to try it on you to make sure it fits. Then tell her I said to give you a big slice of that apple cake she made this morning. Judging from the delicious smell, it should be coming out of the oven any minute. You can have it with some milk."

Cyril looked uncertain as Tory handed him the shirt. "I can't stay here with your friend and the pretty lady?"

"You can come back as soon as you're finished eating and trying on the shirt," Tory said.

That perked him up and he went running out, trailing the shirt behind him. Jon swiftly closed the door. "Mademoiselle? You may wish to have a seat and get right to business. Knowing young lads, I suspect Cyril won't be gone all that long."

Tory walked over to the sofa and waited for her guest to sit.

The woman looked suddenly nervous as she glanced at Jon. "For-give me, Your Grace, but I should prefer to speak to Miss Morris alone."

"That's all right," Tory said. "Anything you can say to me can be said in front of His Grace."

She shot the two of them an assessing look. "I see," she said as she took a seat on the sofa not far from Tory. "Very well."

"The duke said that you brought me letters and a journal of Papa's?"

She nodded and laid them on the sofa between them. "But first I must explain. Your father asked me to do so once you and I met, but I confess it is much easier without your mother also here."

A feeling of dread sank into her stomach. She shot Jon a look, expecting to see triumph in his expression, but what she read was chagrin. Apparently, he'd told the truth about his change in feelings concerning Papa and the mademoiselle. Tory didn't know whether to be glad over that or disappointed in her own instincts.

"I suppose you know," Mademoiselle Bernard went on, "that the first time your papa came to France he was young. Twenty-eight, yes?"

Tory blinked. That wasn't the story she'd been bracing to hear. "I-I think so, oui. I know he was Lord Bragg's bear leader then." She caught Jon's frown, and added, "Yes, Jon, I realize Papa wasn't fond of the term, but that's what he was, and you know it."

Only after Jon smiled warmly at her did she realize she'd called him by his first name. Oh dear.

Noting Mademoiselle Bernard's interested look, she said hastily, "But do go on, mademoiselle."

"Monsieur Morris was a bachelor then, and Lord Bragg was rich enough to have his own rooms in Paris. So your father took a room in my grandpapa's hotel, where he met my *maman*. She was young and pretty and engaged to my grandpapa's son, but it was to be an arranged marriage, and she was unhappy about it. Thus she had—how do you say it in English? Ah yes, a love affair. An *histoire d'amour*." Mademoiselle Bernard paused and swallowed. "With your papa. Who is . . . *was* also *my* papa."

It took a moment for that to sink in. Tory couldn't have heard the woman correctly. Professor Isaac Morris, who'd never met a rule he didn't like, had sired an illegitimate child? It would have been before he'd ever met Mama, but still . . .

She didn't know how she felt about it. It just seemed so unlikely. Wait, did that mean she now had a *sister*? A half sister, but still . . . She'd always wanted a sister.

Her head was still reeling from the information when Jon groaned. "Oh, God, that makes so much more sense than my suspicions. And it explains the blue eyes."

Mademoiselle Bernard looked at him. *"Excusez-moi?"*

Gathering herself together, Tory shook her head and said dryly, "His Grace is merely realizing that the ideas he'd had in his head about Papa and you were patently false."

At first, the Frenchwoman looked confused. Then deep in thought. Then outraged. "His Grace did not think . . ." She glared at Jon. "You did not think that Monsieur Morris and I were . . . That *we* were . . ."

"He did." Tory reached over to pat her new half sister's hand. "Don't worry, mademoiselle. I told him he was wrong."

That softened the young woman. "You must call me Giselle, Miss Morris. We are sisters, after all. And may I call you . . . Victoria?"

"Tory," she answered.

"Tory," Giselle repeated. Then she laughed before gazing at Jon. "But Your Grace, I cannot believe you thought . . ." She shook her head. "Monsieur Morris was the most strict gentleman I ever met. Followed the rules always."

"He certainly did," Jon muttered. "I don't know what I was thinking."

"Clearly Papa didn't follow the rules with your mother," Tory said softly to her half sister.

Giselle nodded. "But our father did offer marriage to Maman. She refused him—a poor professor, and English at that. He and Lord Bragg moved on to the next place in the grand tour. Maman married Monsieur Bernard two months later, and that was the end. I was born 'early' and knew no better. Until Monsieur Morris came back to Paris with his new charge—Lord Jonathan—and came to visit Maman. What a shock he had!"

"And you, too," Tory said, a lump filling her throat.

"Yes. And Maman, although my stepfather was dead by then.

Maman was trying to marry me off to a rich baker I despised, so I ran away to Verdun to find Monsieur Morris. I took a post there so we could know each other better. And you can figure out the rest."

"Ran away, did you?" Jon drawled. "So you're as much of a rebel as Miss Morris here."

"Ignore him," Tory told Giselle. "He thinks any woman who takes her own fate into her hands is a rebel."

Giselle chuckled. "Monsieur Morris called him 'a rebel' a time or two in the early days at Verdun, so His Grace cannot fault us for being the same."

Jon grimaced, making the two half sisters laugh.

"Did you never call our father Papa once you knew who he was?" Tory asked.

"Oh, no. He feared I would forget and call him such while someone else was nearby. I did not dare. I knew he did not wish to embarrass your *maman.* Or you." She offered Tory a shy smile. "But he wanted to know me, too."

"Of course he did," Tory said, patting Giselle's hand. "You seem perfectly lovely."

"And you, as well. Although Monsieur Morris . . . my true papa, that is . . . said that you were." She laid her hand on the letters. "He was clearly very fond of you and your *maman.*"

"He was." Tory's eyes misted over, though she refused to cry in front of Jon yet again. Besides, this was a happy moment. She had a sister! "Is that what is in the letters? An explanation about you and your mother?"

"I have not read them, so I do not know. I did not believe it right to intrude on his and your privacy. But I do not think the letters say who I am. I imagine he speaks of life at Verdun as so many other Englishmen have."

The door to the parlor burst open, and Cyril ran in. "I'm wearing my shirt, Sissy! See? And I ate the apple cake."

"Oh, good," Tory said. "You're just in time. There is someone I would like you to meet. This is Mademoiselle Giselle Bernard. She is your . . ."

"Friend from France," Giselle said. "I hope to be your very *close* friend from France. You may call me Giselle. I knew your papa."

Tory cast her a grateful smile. Cyril wasn't ready to be told he had another sister, and he would never keep quiet about it, which would raise questions in the neighborhood.

Cyril clapped his hands. "I like friends. Now I have one of my own!"

"You do, indeed," Giselle said.

Jon rose. "Mademoiselle, do you mind if I steal Miss Morris away for a few moments? I have something of great importance to tell her. I can bring Cyril back to Mrs. Gully if you wish to sit here and wait."

Giselle looked at the two of them with clear curiosity. "No need for that. Cyril can sit here and keep me company. He can tell me all about his favorite entertainments."

"Can I show you today's butterfly?" Cyril asked. "I only keep one for a day. Then I let him go and get another one. They don't like staying in the jar too long."

"That sounds fun," Giselle said with a smile.

Jon ruffled her brother's hair. "Oh, and Cyril, feel free to call me Jon."

His face lit up. "I will! Does that mean we're friends, too, Jon?"

"Very good friends." He leveled a heated look on Tory. "But how good will be up to your sister to decide."

Hope sprouted in her heart, but she was still hesitant to embrace it. Not until she heard him out.

"Shall we take a walk, Miss Morris?" Jon asked.

"Certainly, Your Grace. Or perhaps you'd like to see my sculpture workroom."

He arched an eyebrow. "The one that's too crowded to enter?"

The reference to the night they'd shared a bed made her blush. "I-I have cleaned it up since then."

"Then I'd be honored," he said, offering her his arm.

They walked out into the hall and went past the entrance to the kitchen. Tory was relieved to see that Mrs. Gully was too busy to notice them.

Once they were in her workroom and she'd pulled the door enough to give them a modicum of privacy, she couldn't resist teasing him. "You really want Cyril to call you 'Jon,' Your Grace?"

Jon gazed seriously into her eyes. "I thought it might be easier for him, not having to navigate the various ways to address me. After all, I'm hoping he will soon be my brother-in-law."

She sucked in a harsh breath, determined to be honest with him, though she yearned to believe his words. "Only if things between us have changed."

"They have, at least for me." He took her hand in his. "I love you, Tory," he said simply. "I was just afraid to let you into my heart. I knew that loving you would mean trusting you, and it has been a long time since I trusted anyone."

Now hope was sending runners out to climb all over her. "I can understand you not trusting anyone in France," she said truthfully. "Someone betrayed you, your captors abused you—sometimes on a whim—and your own government ignored your very existence. But surely you could trust your family and friends. Surely you could trust Papa."

He snorted. "How? I was completely convinced he was engaged in an affair. If I couldn't even trust Morris to take the moral high ground, then whom could I trust? My family? The mother who'd agreed to send me away because I'd become a trial to her and my father? Or the sister who'd grown up so much while I was gone that I scarcely knew her?"

Her heart faltered to hear how he'd seen things. "You have to know they love you."

"I do. Now. But when I first got home, I barely had time to catch my bearings, let alone know whom to trust." He kissed her hand. "As for my friends, I had many chances to tell them about you, about the dowry, about how badly I wanted you in my life. But I didn't. I couldn't. I was afraid they'd urge me to take a chance on loving you, and I didn't need them to further convince me of what I already wanted."

He gazed down at her, his feelings hard to read. "Instead, I used my guilt over your father's death as my shield against you. Because I was terrified that once you knew everything, you'd hate me. So I dared not get too near, like Icarus flying too close to the sun."

A smile crossed his face. "Except I couldn't stop myself from flying too close. Every time I saw you, I wanted only one thing—to be with you, to make you mine, and not just in my bed, but in every part of my life. You enthralled me as surely as Venus enthralled Mars, and I could not resist you."

He drew her into his arms. "This past week has been a hell of my own making. You tore down my shield, sweetheart, that day in Hyde Park, leaving me naked and exposed. You were right. I was never going to have any kind of redemption until I first forgave myself."

Her blood roared through her veins, her skin, her heart. "And have you?"

"I'm beginning to. I don't really have a choice. Because if you could forgive me, it seems like the ultimate in hubris not to forgive myself. Besides, you said that day in Hyde Park that you loved me. So, I'd be a rebel indeed if I didn't at least strive to become worthy of that love."

She leaned up to kiss him on the lips. "No striving necessary. You're already more than worthy of my love, not to mention that of your family and your friends and—"

He cut her off with a long kiss of such sweetness and heat that she thought she'd melt right down like the wax in a casting. When at last he drew away, he was smiling. "Does this mean you're ready to marry me at last, my love?"

"I don't know if I should," she said coyly. "You'd be a fool to marry me without a dowry to my name, and I cannot marry a fool."

He chuckled. "I tell you what—I'll give myself your dowry, and then we'll call me a very clever man for marrying you."

"In that case," she said lightly, "I do believe I might be willing to marry you. On one condition."

"That I help you get your school started."

"Could you?" she said, surprised that he would say such a thing. "That would be lovely, but I wouldn't expect that."

"Why not? I'm the duke and you'll be the duchess. And as everyone keeps telling me, that means I can do whatever I bloody well please."

She couldn't help grinning. "Except curse."

"Fine. Was that the condition? That I stop my cursing?"

"No, although I'm sure that would make your mother happy.

I'm just hoping you'll still accept the idea of Cyril coming to live with us." She held her breath as she watched for his reaction, but when she saw no hint of consternation in his expression she relaxed.

He brushed a kiss on her forehead. "I wouldn't have it any other way, sweetheart."

Cyril's ears must have been burning, for he chose that moment to come running in. "Sissy, can I go for a walk with Giselle?"

When Tory pulled away, Jon still kept one arm about her waist. "Why don't we all go, Cyril? I have something I need to ask you."

"All right." Cyril then blithely ran ahead to where Giselle stood waiting in the hallway.

Tory called out to Mrs. Gully that they were going for a walk, and they left the house to stroll down the middle of her neighborhood. She could see the neighbors pausing to stare at the unlikely group—a duke, a maiden, a boy, and an exotic Frenchwoman. As soon as they reached the forested area, Cyril said to Jon, "What do you want to ask me?"

Jon ruffled his hair. "Do I have your permission to marry your sister?"

Giselle flashed Tory a startled smile, but Cyril eyed Jon closely. "Like Papa married Mama? Only I never met Papa because he went to France. Are you going to France, too?"

"Not if I can help it," Jon said.

Tory stifled a laugh.

"Then where will you live?" Cyril asked. "In the cottage with us?"

Jon smiled at him. "I was hoping you'd come live at Falcon House with me and your Sissy. That's where the duke and the duchess always live. I'm the duke and your sister is going to be the duchess once she marries me."

Cyril stopped on the path. "But duchesses are *old*."

"Well," Tory said hastily, "Jon's mother is an older duchess, and she'll also be living there with us, but young duchesses exist, too, and I'll be one of those."

"I don't know." Cyril frowned. "Can't we all live in the cottage? You and Jon and Giselle and me?"

Tory could see Giselle stifling a laugh. "There's really not enough room in the cottage for all of us, dear. But at Falcon House, there will be lots more room. And Giselle can come to visit whenever she likes."

"You can ride in my carriage," Jon said, "and play in the garden. You can feed the horses apples—"

"You have *horses*?" Cyril said reverently. "I like horses."

"You should have started with the horses," Tory muttered, making Jon laugh.

"Then it's settled," Jon told Cyril. "Your sister and I will get married, and you and she will come to live with me."

"And the horses," Cyril said, as if to clarify it.

"And the horses," Jon repeated, obviously fighting a laugh. "Although I'm not letting them stay in the house if that's all right with you."

"Horses live in stables," Cyril said, thrusting out his lower lip. "I know that."

"Of course, you do," Tory said hastily before Cyril could get his feelings hurt.

Jon stared down at Cyril. "That also means you'll become my brother."

Cyril's eyes went wide. "That would be *grand*. I don't have a brother."

"I don't have a wife," Jon said. "You get a brother, and I get a wife. That sounds fair, doesn't it?"

Cyril bobbed his head.

"And what do I get out of this arrangement?" Tory said archly.

"You get horses," Giselle quipped, making the adults laugh.

Then Jon gazed at her, love shining in his eyes. "You get a husband who loves and worships you. Who can't believe how lucky he was to find you."

The warmth in his expression sparked heat in her heart. "As long as I have you for the rest of my life, I have all I need."

Epilogue

September 21, 1814

Jon ushered his two friends into his study and offered them whisky or brandy. Unsurprisingly, they all chose the whisky.

"Let's get this started," Heathbrook said. "The sooner we finish, the sooner I can have some of those amazing curd puffs Elegant Occasions always provides for parties. I can't believe you're having one of our secret meetings on your wife's birthday."

Jon shrugged. "She said she didn't mind. And since both of you have been out of London except for our wedding, it's not as if I had a choice."

"True." Scovell swigged some whisky. "If I had my choice, I'd stay in here the whole time drinking. Don't like crowds much."

"None of us do," Jon said. "Had enough of that in prison. But I did want to inform you both of something beforehand. Just remember that no one is to know of this but we three and my wife, understood? And if you simply must give me grief over it, I will tolerate it only for the duration of this meeting."

"Now I'm intrigued," Heathbrook said.

Jon groaned. "I guess I'd better get this over with since Mademoiselle Bernard will be attending the party. So, as it turns out,

Mademoiselle Bernard—Giselle—is actually Morris's illegitimate daughter by a Frenchwoman. That's why they were so close. She followed him to Verdun so she could get to know her real father. By then, the man her mother married while already with child was dead."

Both men just gaped at him.

"Oh," he went on, "and she brought a sheaf of letters and a journal to Tory from Morris. He'd left them to Giselle to deliver in case he never made it home. So . . . er . . . I was very mistaken about their relationship. I admit that now."

"Well, as long as you admit it," Heathbrook said in a bad imitation of Jon's voice. "Good God, man, that is enormous news. So she's here? The mademoiselle?"

"We . . . er . . . see her quite a bit, actually," Jon said.

"How does Tory feel about it?" Scovell asked.

"Apparently, she likes having a sister. But we haven't told Cyril. She's afraid he won't keep it quiet, and it might embarrass Giselle."

His two friends had met Cyril at the wedding, where, fortunately, no one else spoke to him long enough to realize his situation. It would have ruined Tory's wedding entirely if anyone had slurred Cyril. She loved the boy dearly, as did Jon.

Heathbrook shook his head. "That old dog. I didn't know Morris had it in him."

"Neither did I," Jon said. "Tory was shocked herself. Morris was even more rule-bound with her and her mother than with us. But it was before he met her mother, so it wasn't as if he was unfaithful, which made a big difference to her."

Scovell looked as if he were contemplating something. "Has your wife read the letters and the journal yet?"

"She's working through them, but hasn't finished," Jon said. "Why?"

"Because if whoever betrayed us knew of them," Scovell said, "he or she might have been following Tory out of an assumption that she already possessed them and a fear that Morris mentioned him or her in them."

"You mean, in connection with the escape!" Heathbrook exclaimed. "Why else try to follow Tory? And no one knew where her cottage was, after all."

"Mother did," Jon said, "but perhaps the person didn't realize that. Besides, they wouldn't want to call attention to themselves by asking around."

"You might want to read those letters and the journal yourself, old chap," Scovell said.

Jon nodded. "Excellent idea. Then again, how would this person even know about them? We should question Giselle about who might have known."

"I can do that," Heathbrook said.

The other two men eyed him with surprise.

"What?" he said defensively. "I've always found her interesting."

Jon scowled. "You mean you've always found her beddable. She's my sister-in-law, for God's sake. Tread lightly."

"You're always trying to ruin my fun." Heathbrook put down his empty glass of whisky. "Now, are we done yet?"

"I suppose," Jon said. "How long will you two be in town this time?"

"Quite a while." Heathbrook turned serious. "I'll be in court for weeks with my cousin. But I have a good lawyer. We'll prevail. Still, it's a messy business."

"I remember," Scovell said. "I'll be here, too. My eldest brother is being seen by a physician for his heart and is insisting upon me preparing to become marquess. The fool thinks he's dying."

"Don't tell Mother," Jon said. "She'll try to marry you to Chloe for certain."

Scovell set down his whisky glass with a grim expression. "I doubt Lady Chloe would have me, marquess or no."

Jon was about to question that when the door swung open.

"There you are, Jon," Tory said. "The party is about to start! I've been looking all over for you. As host and hostess, we have to be in the receiving line."

"I'm coming, my love," Jon said, ignoring the way the two bachelors chuckled as he left.

He didn't care what they thought. She had enriched his life already in just the month they'd been married. He never wanted to be without her again.

An hour later, after having a rousing conversation with his good friend Grenwood about managing an estate, he wandered over to where his mother sat watching Cyril play with the wooden horse she'd just bought him.

So much for his worries on Cyril's behalf. Just as Jon had expected, once Mother had met the boy, she'd taken to him instantly.

As Jon approached, he heard her say, "Cyril, darling, come sit by your grandmama."

"Yes, Grandmama," he said happily, and perched on the settee at her side.

When his mother caught Jon frowning, she said, "What? He doesn't have one. I might as well fill the position until you and Victoria give me actual grandchildren." She turned to Cyril. "And how old is Grandmama?"

"Forty!" Cyril said cheerily.

"Very good, young man," his mother said.

"Mother!" Jon said. "I don't think you should teach him to lie."

"What lie?" she said blithely. "He really thinks I'm forty. Nothing wrong with that."

With a shake of his head, Jon went in search of his wife but got waylaid by Chloe and Giselle.

"Have you shown it to her yet?" Chloe whispered, rather loudly.

She and Giselle giggled like a pair of schoolgirls. It was unsettling, to say the least. Even though they were nine years apart in age, the pair had become as thick as thieves, or as mother would say, quick as thieves.

"No, I haven't," Jon said. "You two did not let it slip what I was giving her for her birthday, did you?"

"Certainly not," Chloe said. "We wouldn't spoil it."

"She will be *très content* when she sees it," Giselle said. "Can we be there when you show her?"

"No, indeed," he said. "It's my *private* gift to my wife."

They sighed. Then Giselle glanced across the room. "He's looking at you again, Chloe."

"Who?" Jon asked sharply.

"Your friend Scovell," Giselle said.

Chloe rolled her eyes. "You and Tory always think he fancies me, but I don't see it. He's just being annoying as usual."

"Excuse me, ladies," Jon said, "but I really must find my wife."

He finally spotted Tory, who was hard to miss in that gown of peony red. She was in a serious discussion with Beasley, who was becoming somewhat famous in their circle as an engraver of Rowlandson's drawings. Not to mention, he was one of the teachers at Tory's budding school for female artists.

"I tell you, Mr. Beasley," Tory said, "part of the school could be used as a provider of colorists for the printmaking industry. The fashion journals already use a select group of women to color their prints. Only think how many widows and daughters of détenus and women détenus themselves we could employ! You know that your ladies suffer, especially the ones who lost their husbands in Verdun. If we were to hire them out, some of the money could go to the school."

"I agree, Your Grace," Beasley said. "I'm just not sure we have the room in our present location."

"This sounds like a discussion I need to be part of," Jon put in.

"There you are, Jon," Tory said, pausing to tuck her hand in the crook of his elbow. "Could you please tell Mr. Beasley that this would be a lucrative enterprise that would also benefit hundreds of women?"

Jon chuckled. "First of all, sweetheart, my mother would say that the words 'lucrative' and 'enterprise' should never come out of the mouth of a duchess."

Tory cocked her head. "And what do *you* say?"

He smiled. "That I can see I'll have to give you my birthday present early."

"What on earth are you talking about?" she asked warily.

"Do you remember that place in Chelsea we looked at that you loved, but said was too dear for the school?"

"Ye-e-s."

He handed her a set of keys. "It belongs to you now."

"Jon!" she cried, her face awash with joy. "You didn't!"

"I did. I'm a duke. I can do as I please, remember? And it pleases me to treat my wife to a bigger building for her school. It probably cost less than that ruby necklace you're sporting, anyway, so I figure I saved money in the long run."

She clutched the necklace, her eyes going wide. "Good Lord, I must take these off and put them somewhere safe."

"Don't you dare," he said, laughing. "Those are the Falconridge rubies. Why do you think I wanted you to wear them tonight? They've been worn by the Falconridge duchesses for generations. Which you are now one of."

She stretched up to kiss his cheek, then turned to Beasley. "Did you hear that, Mr. Beasley?"

"I heard, Duchess," he said, grinning from ear to ear.

"Now we can teach women to be colorists *and* other sorts of artists," Tori said.

"Perhaps even sculptresses," Jon said, with a wink at Beasley, who looked shocked that the duke had just winked at him.

"Certainly," Tory said. "Or at the very least, relief artists for Josiah Wedgwood. We've already got one lady in his employ. Who knows how many others we might soon have?"

"I'm just glad to see you so happy." Jon turned to Beasley. "Would you mind if I steal my wife away for a few moments?"

"No, indeed, Your Grace," Beasley said. "I'll find the missus and see if she'd like a few of those cheese tarts."

Jon escorted Tory to the stairs, then led her up toward the art room.

"What are you doing, Jon?" she asked.

"Giving you my other present." When they reached the top, he made her cover her eyes with her hands, then pulled her into the art room. "All right, you can look now."

Tory opened her eyes, then gazed around at the room in wonder.

"I had everything moved over from your workroom at the cottage since the lease was about to be up anyway, and I supplemented with supplies where needed. Chloe and Giselle helped me. They knew which things you were wanting."

"This is so lovely." Her hands covered her cheeks. "I can't believe you did all this!"

"Obviously, we'll have to put the schoolroom somewhere else once we have children, but there's plenty of other rooms in the house we could use, and this was never the ideal setup for a schoolroom anyway."

She turned to kiss him full on the mouth. "I love it," she said, her eyes misting over. "It's absolutely perfect."

"And to show you my lessons weren't a total loss . . ." He tugged her over to where sat his admittedly bad clay model of an apple.

"This is for you. In case you can't tell—and you probably can't—it's an apple for my teacher, since I'm a duke and all and can afford one out of season."

She was biting her lower lip very hard.

"It's all right—you can laugh," he said.

"I'm merely trying to figure out," she said in a voice trembling with repressed amusement, "how you could make the model of a round piece of fruit lopsided."

"I have no idea." He drew her into his arms. "First, I *tried* to do a naked rendition of you, but you can only imagine how that turned out. And no, I didn't keep it. I repurposed the clay into that apple. Clearly, there will only ever be one sculptor in this marriage."

"That's all right," she said, laughing. "I don't need a sculptor for a husband."

He kissed her forehead. "I don't suppose you would sculpt a naked rendition of yourself for me, would you?"

"No need." She looped her arms about his neck and pressed her breasts suggestively against him. "I can show you the real thing whenever you please."

Taking her by surprise, he picked her up and carried her over to the table they'd used for lessons previously. Then he set her down on top of it. "Thank God," he murmured as he began kissing his way down the slope of her bosom. "I like the real thing best of all."

Author's Note

I first read about this aspect of the Napoleonic Wars in a footnote in Deirdre Le Faye's *Jane Austen's 'Outlandish Cousin': The Life and Letters of Eliza de Feuillide*. (Eliza barely escaped becoming a détenu herself by bribing someone to help her flee France.) Then I had to know everything about the détenus.

Not much has been written in our age about the mass imprisonment of English civilians in France for eleven years, but several books were written at the time by those who escaped or came home after the war. I drew on several of those books, many of which can be found online, to tell some of the stories I included that were primarily true.

The young Duke of Newcastle was indeed on his grand tour with his mother and stepfather when they were forced to spend three years as détenus before his mother arranged for his release. The Marquess and Marchioness of Tweeddale died of cholera at Verdun. One son of a duke spent ten years there. Several sons of earls, viscounts, barons, and baronets spent various amounts of time as détenus in one of the ten camps that served as the gilded (or not so gilded) cages for the English who'd ended up trapped in France. Even more English commoners visiting France for business or pleasure found themselves forced to halt their lives for eleven years in a camp. Entire families spent their time there, some of them growing impoverished since they had no way to earn money. I used the tales of several different escapes to fashion the escape of my heroes. Bitche dungeon was exactly as I described it, and you can find an image of the lower dungeon on my website. It was indeed called "the Mansion of Tears" by those who were punished by being sent there. And yes, when Napoleon finally abdicated the throne, the détenus were mostly marched to the coast so they could return to England.

For a list of books about the détenus and life in the camps (and escapes), check out my website. You might find yourself as fascinated as I was!

Visit our website at
KensingtonBooks.com
to sign up for our newsletters, read
more from your favorite authors, see
books by series, view reading group
guides, and more!

Become a Part of Our
Between the Chapters Book Club
Community and Join the Conversation

Betweenthechapters.net